DRAGON BLIND

The Lightbearer Series

Iman Christians

IMAN WILLIAMS CHRISTIANS

CONTENTS

PRONUNCIATION GUIDE

Characters

Asha Osei — *AH-sha OH-say*

Adriel — *AY-dree-el*

Kwasi — *KWAH-see*

Nayeli — *Nye-ELL-ee*

Kitchi — *KEE-chee*

Ashkii — *ASH-kee*

Enapay — *EN-ah-pay*

Ekon — *EH-kon*

Zariah — *ZAH-rye-ah*

Kaliyah — *KAH-lee-ah*

Iná — *EE-nah*

Dragons

Drakkar — *DRAH-kar*
   Morin — *MOR-in*
   Nira — *NEE-rah*
   Akimba — *Ah-KIM-bah*
   Zyphur — *ZYE-fur*

Kingdoms & Places

Ujuima — *Oo-JEE-mah*
   Wiyotak — *WHY-oh-tak*
   Firepeak — *FIRE-peek*
   Entioch — *EN-tee-ock*
   Wyrmwood — *WIRM-wood*
   Saeleria — *SAY-lair-ee-ah*

Terms

Dracite — *DRAH-site*
   Mategwes — *MAH-teg-wess*
   Tribulterres — *TRIB-ul-ter-es*
   Echinacea — *EK-ih-NAY-sha*

ACKNOWLEDGEMENTS

This book would not exist without the unwavering love and support of the people closest to me.

To my husband, thank you for being my anchor, my encourager, and the one who believes in my words even when I doubt them. Your patience and love carried me through late nights and endless rewrites.

To my parents thank you for pouring love, wisdom, and strength into me. Your encouragement has allowed me to dream this big.

To my dear mother-in-law, friends, my editor K.F. Starfell, and my amazing beta readers, your insight, honesty, and enthusiasm shaped this story into something far greater than I could have ever managed alone. Thank you for laughing with me, crying with me, and holding this dream as tenderly as if it were your own.

And to every person who reminded me that stories matter, you reminded me why I write. This book is as much yours as it is mine.

To all the little girls who have been told their dreams were too much—may your roar shake the heavens, and may your flame burn their words to ash.

PROLOGUE

If given the choice between dragons and men, I would pick a dragon every time. A dragon might burn you to ash, but at least you would see it coming, and more often than not, you probably deserved it. But men? You never knew what they might do or what lies they would tell. Their motives were hidden behind pretty words and false smiles, their true intentions cloaked in games of deceit.

Dragons didn't play games; they burned.

CHAPTER ONE

Asha

I never thought I would die over a strawberry, but here we were.

The thought came bitterly as I straightened my shoulders, mimicking the beasts I tended in the pits, though my staff trembled in my grip. Two pairs of boots echoed against the stone, rounding the landing where I stood.

I should have kept walking. Instead, on the way home with my basket of berries, I'd brushed against palace armor. A mistake. A fatal one.

The guards hadn't recognized me. Why would they? The Oseis no longer claimed me, and my frayed dress carried none of the royal finery I was born into. Even if I'd stopped to tell them I was once the daughter of Emperor Idris Osei, they would have laughed. The city had long forgotten the unseer. I did my best to forget her, too.

I reached into my pocket to grab the key to the pit. It was so early that the pit masters had not yet assembled. I was alone. The men, emboldened by this fact, quickened their pace. My breath hitched at their pursuit, but instead of panicking, I focused on getting inside. I let out a sigh of relief when the gate creaked open, and I slipped into the tunnel. Normally, it would be lined with lit torches, but it was too early for that. Now, they were in my territory because I knew these tunnels better than I did my own hand.

Silently, I moved forward until my outstretched hand met another gate. This one was heavier and older than the first. My pulse hammered in my throat as I fumbled with a second key; every scrape of metal against metal seemed deafening.

There was no keeping quiet now as the key screeched before clicking into place. A hand grabbed my shoulder and whipped me around.

"We nearly lost you in here," a man leered.

I swallowed hard against the bile rising in my throat and forced myself to stand taller despite his grip pinning me down.

"Aren't you a pretty thing?" he continued, his tone turning mockingly sweet as his rough fingers brushed against my cheek again.

"She is," another voice added in from somewhere behind him. "It's a shame she'll have to be cast out."

My stomach twisted. I should have looped through the tunnels to give myself more lead time.

"I have a vocation," I said. "You cannot cast me out."

"You are an unseer, are you not?" the second man replied. "It is a wonder you have not been cast out already."

"You can't," I said more forcefully.

"We won't right away, pretty girl," the first man purred. "We can have some fun first."

I flinched away as he brushed his rough fingers along my cheek. He stank of ale and day-old fish stew.

"We should just get on with marching her into the desert," the second man said sharply, unease settling in his voice. "I don't like this place."

"What do you mean? This is just perfect."

I pushed myself onto metal bars, pulling out a pouch from my pocket as they debated on how to proceed. I cursed at the strings as I worked it open to reveal juicy, ripe strawberries. I squeezed one to allow the juices to coat my fingers.

A small rumble sounded behind us, their argument dying on their lips.

"What is that?" the second man asked. He grabbed my wrists, which sent the pouch of berries flying. "What is this place?"

The growl was quiet for now, with an edge of menace that vibrated through the stones beneath us. I restricted my movements, not wanting to be the target of the beast behind me.

The man released my hand, both of them taking slow, deliberate steps toward the entrance. "What . . . what is that?" he whispered.

"To hell with you, girl," the first man said. Before they could get far, a stream of fiery heat soared past me in the direction of their voices. Loud screams of agony reached my ears, and the smell of burnt flesh filled my nostrils as they scrambled desperately back through the tunnels.

I turned to the dragon behind me. "Morin."

He wasted no time pushing his snout through the bars near my skirts.

"You smell them, don't you? Just a few for now." I opened my hand, and he gently lapped up the bundle I carried.

"You saved me, you know." I shivered, thinking about what might have happened had he not been there. I'd have to be more cautious next time I leave the pit.

"I'll be back with more," I promised, stepping away.

Morin was the biggest dragon in the pit. No one would go near him except for me. I happened to know berries were his weakness. My fingers deftly sorted through the sacks of meat piled around me. The metallic smell of blood and offal coated my nostrils and clung to my skin. It was not a pleasant smell, but one I had grown used to. The slick, raw meat and fish in my hands were not random scraps. Each dragon had its preferences, and ignoring that could get you killed or worse.

When I think back on my life, it can be divided into two parts: the time when I could see the world in all its vibrant, colorful detail, and the time after my sight was ripped away from me, along with my standing in my family. Now, the only parts of the world I could see were tiny bits of light from auras, the brightest of which belonged to dragons.

I was grateful to these creatures for accepting me. Not long after exile, my mother, the empress, walked into the pits to beg to be set alight. I didn't blame the dragons. I thanked them for giving her the mercy she desperately cried for. I understood that, unlike me, she did not have dragons to comfort her in her despair. There'd been no one to save her.

I shook off the depressing thoughts, preferring to focus on my duties of arranging the meat onto trays according to each dragon's tastes. Feeding the dragons was an entire event. They had voracious appetites, and keeping them fed was crucial for their health and ability to fight.

A distant rumble sounded as the dragons stirred, anticipating their next meal. Their auras shifted, some dull and muddy, others cool and unassuming.

"Good morning, Akimba," I said, tapping my walking staff in a distinct pattern, letting him know I was near before tossing his feed bag of griffin and mountain goat.

Nira's melodic growl echoed around me. Her scales held a subtle floral scent reminiscent of the wildflowers that bloom in the gardens within the palace. She was a pescatarian and preferred fish heads. I ran my fingers over her cool scales, a calming ritual we had developed over years of companionship. She was the only one who allowed me to handle her comfortably on a daily basis. She had come into the service of the kingdom when she was an adolescent and had grown accustomed to my ministrations.

Finally, there was Morin, whose feed I topped with a few extra strawberries.

"I owe you one, Morin," I said. He roared in appreciation. At least, that was what I told myself.

The dragon pits were scarce these days. I had grown accustomed to caring for half a dozen dragons at a time, at the very least, but many were off training with the Ujuima regiment. The dragons were growing agitated, sensing the change in the air as the kingdom prepared for the long-awaited Fire Festival that would bring people from the neighboring kingdoms. Wyrmwood and Firepeak were two of Ujuima's closest allies. There was also Entioch, which sat on the coast in the east, and Wiyotak, which lay south of Ujuima.

The Fire Festival was an opportunity for me to hear news from the other kingdoms, taste new and exotic foods, and leave the confines of the dragon pits for a short while. It was also a chance for all the monarchs of the neighboring kingdoms to rub elbows with the Osei's the only family allowed to have dragons.

Dragons could not fly. It was thought that dragons lost that ability when men discovered dracite and learned to tame dragons with it.

The door creaked open. A familiar cadence of footsteps reverberated through the room. I recognized the subtle nuances in the sound, the weight of each footfall, and the familiar pattern of movement. His aura burned cool like glowing coals in a fire. I had lost my sight many years ago, but could still see Ekon's presence vividly. The last time I'd seen him, he was tall and lean, still awkward as he was growing into his body.

"Are you trying to sneak up on me, Ekon?" I said.

"That is impossible around you, Asha," he quipped.

Since losing my sight, we'd become fast friends. Ekon helped me learn to navigate the world using other senses, like learning to use my walking staff to navigate the keep and how to assess the distance and depth of any room.

But something was different today in his gait.

"Are you wearing chain mail?" I asked curiously.

There was a rustling of hair. He had a habit of running his hands through his short hair when he was on edge.

"Like I said, nothing gets past you."

I reached my hand out, and he led it to his chest. I felt the dracite under my fingertips immediately. I pulled back quickly as if it burned.

Dracite was a metal mined from the northern mountains of Firepeak, used to forge swords to keep the dragons under control. It was why my father, Emperor Idris, kept such a firm relationship with its leaders. However, the rumor was that Firepeak was growing restless, causing conflict in the north. It was making the dragon warriors nervous, from what I could glean from their conversations.

"You'll agitate the dragons with that."

He sighed. "I won't stay long. I wanted to see you before tonight, when the festival begins. We need to talk," he said, attempting to guide me to the observation deck where there were chairs.

I slapped his hand away. "I can manage on my own. I did not lose my ability to walk."

I heard a slight pause and the grinding of teeth before he said, "Do you always have to be so stubborn, Asha? I am trying to tell you something, and you are making it difficult."

I threw my hands up, exasperated. "Well, I don't need you to sit me down like a child. What is it? Spit it out." My heart thumped wildly in my chest as I tried to imagine what he wanted to say and why he was dressed for war.

He inhaled deeply as if the air around him would give him courage. "I'm entering the Fire Challenge."

My heart leaped out of my chest. Each kingdom put its best warriors through a challenge that almost always involved dragons. Most did not survive, and that was the point. It was how my father reminded the other kingdoms of his power and why he was emperor. "What? Why?"

I could hear him starting to speak and then stopping. My hands dug into his, pleading for him to say more. "It's a long story," he said finally. "But the short of it is, I am ready to become a dragonlord."

I crossed my arms in frustration at that. "You'll get yourself killed. If I can take you down in a fight . . ."

"I let you!" he interrupted.

It was a familiar jab we threw at one another, a way for me to cope with what he'd just shared. He wrapped his arms around my shoulders, pulling me close. I tried not to stiffen in his arms. It was becoming alarmingly obvious that Ekon held feelings for me that I did not fully reciprocate, confused more by the few times I had allowed him to kiss me. It had felt nice, of course, but I had always imagined a kiss to feel like—more. I did not know what *more* was or if it even existed, but his feelings for me did not seem to warrant risking our friendship over.

"Don't worry about me, Asha. I am a Ujuima warrior. I do not fear death."

I rolled my eyes at the Ujuima creed. "You said it was a long story. Tell me."

Before he could speak, sharp, staccato footsteps reached my ears as they approached from beyond the corridor. I felt more relief than I should have when Ekon removed his hands from my body.

"Kwasi?" I asked. "I have not had your company in the pits for some time, brother."

Kwasi was second born, the spare, as he often referred to himself. Our relationship was complicated as he was partly responsible for my blindness, which resulted from a sparring match. Truthfully, I'd never blamed Kwasi, but that did not stop him from feeling responsible. He had taken charge of my education after that, teaching me to read books in Elliarb, text that could be read using one's fingertips. I especially loved the books concerning dragons and how to care for them. He brought a new one back after every trip he took.

I felt Ekon standing rigidly by my side, his joints popping from the tension. While I held no ill will toward Kwasi, Ekon certainly did. Still, he bowed as was customary for his rank.

"Prince Kwasi, I am honored."

That was a lie. We stood awkwardly, the silence thicker than a dragon's hide. Before I could break the silence, Ekon said, "I was just leaving."

Kwasi let out a breath of relief. "You don't have to. I had a surprise I wanted to show her from my travels."

Being the second son, Kwasi was already a dragonlord.

"I'm afraid I have to get ready for the Fire Challenge tonight."

Kwasi stilled. I could feel a silent conversation happening between them, and I did not like it.

"What is going on? What haven't you told me, Ekon?"

Ekon sighed heavily. "I will let Kwasi tell you. I am going to take my leave," he said once more before gently squeezing my hand.

I listened as he bowed, a gesture he never did when we were alone, before he turned to go.

Kwasi waited until the chamber door closed behind him before he reached out to embrace me, breaking untold counts of protocol, even if he was my brother. I had not seen Kwasi physically in many months, but I could feel how tall and muscular he had become from being a dragonlord in the Ujuima regiment. Kwasi had taken our mother's death hard, and when he was not with me, improving my reading skills or teaching me the history of all the kingdoms, he was on the battlefield or out exploring lands that were not yet on the emperor's map. I had never known him to have a lover or even friends. It was not that he was dull—quite the opposite. He commanded the eyes of everyone when he walked into the room. They weren't frightened in the presence of royalty, but rather, they were drawn to him, like sap on a tree. It was like that between us at one time. But that connection was lost the moment I'd lost my sight, replaced with a far more tenuous one.

"What was that about?" I asked.

"You know I don't care for that guy."

I shoved at his chest. "Stop stalling. Just tell me."

Kwasi hesitated, his aura flickering like a flame in the wind. "Come. I have a surprise for you before we get into all that."

"Unless it is a dragon, I am not interested."

Kwasi's aura blazed as it often did when he was up to something. "Follow me."

CHAPTER TWO

Asha

D ragons were an obsession Kwasi and I shared. Kwasi loved reading about their histories and learning how they came to be in their current form. So, I was not surprised when he led me to the quarantine section where we held newly captured dragons. It was essential to capture them because, despite countless attempts, we had yet to understand how to breed dragons in captivity. That is, many had tried, but unfortunately, all had paid with their lives.

"I wish you could see this one, Ash. She's deep blue, like Mother's eyes, and I'm telling you, she has the strength of two fully grown dragons. It took our whole regiment to bring her down. She's the biggest female we have ever captured." I couldn't help but smile at the giddiness in his voice as he continued. "I figure if anyone could calm her, you could."

My heart pounded in my chest, and soot coated my tongue as the dragon tried to let out a fiery blast. I sensed the deadly power of the creature nearby, even though I couldn't see it. Gripping my walking staff tightly, I prepared for the possibility of having to flee. Dracite could do only so much.

"Don't worry," Kwasi whispered. "She is heavily sedated now."

The auras of others shuffled into the room, no doubt adding additional dracite to the perimeter of her cage. My nose crinkled. I rarely used it myself, and even when I did with new dragons, a small handful was enough. It sounded like they were filling shovels with the black shiny metal. Too much was counterproductive and could drive the dragon mad.

A loud, thunderous roar shook the ground. I grabbed Kwasi's shoulder to stay upright on my feet as a rustle of bedding catapulted in our direction. The massive dragon that approached had an aura that shimmered like a blue veil. Heat emanated from her massive body in voluminous slate blue waves. The fury in that growl was unmistakable, causing every hair on my head to curl tighter.

I waited, giving her time to reveal what she was planning to do. I couldn't see the dragon, but I could feel her anger pulsing through the air around her. I knew I had to tread carefully.

"I mean you no harm," I said softly, my voice steady despite the fear coursing through my body.

Something that everyone who survived the dragon pits came to know is that dragons have a contempt for fear. You had to approach with deference and respect, removing all signs of unease.

"I am Asha," I said before bowing my head.

There was a moment of silence, broken only by the sound of the dragon's heavy breathing. Her aura warped, and I could almost see the skepticism and mistrust of my words within. She huffed, sending smoke throughout. Kwasi and I both leaned over, choking in the confined cavern.

"Do you think she can be tamed?" he asked. "I'd hate to have to send her to the hearth."

I shivered. The hearth was a volcanic pit used to dispose of dragons that were no longer of use or too dangerous for battle. I hated that it even existed, and I had never sent a dragon in my care there.

"You know she can hear you," I hissed. "She will be just fine. We will make a home for her here."

I wanted to reassure him more, but I stopped speaking when I heard multiple footsteps heading toward us with a heavy stride. Every step was filled with dominance, creating an air of unease. I could never mistake those footfalls or the cadence of Prince Elan. What was he doing here?

I always made a point to make myself scarce around him. Elan had developed quite a reputation for cruelty. Unfortunately, I had been a recipient of it on multiple occasions. Ever since I lost my eyesight, Father had ignored it, especially when it came to me. That meant Elan could do as he pleased. Kwasi often stepped in, but that just meant Elan would wait to implement his malevolent acts when he was gone on a raid or a diplomatic trip.

I fought the urge to shrink as he entered the room. Kwasi noted my reaction and placed a comforting hand on my back.

As Prince Elan strode into the dragon pits, he immediately remarked, "Ah, what a magnificent beast you are."

The scraping ground against my eardrums was like metal on concrete—the unmistakable sound of a dracite stick. The sound made me shudder. Poured dracite around the cage was torturous enough, but a dracite stick was forbidden with the dragons in my care. They were cruel and outdated tools that only served to destroy any trust a dragon might have with its rider.

The prince's stick clanged loudly against the metal bars, almost as if he were intentionally trying to provoke a reaction from the dragon. She emitted a low growl in response, showing her displeasure at the intrusion.

"Splendid creature," Elan murmured.

I continued to stand silently nearby with growing apprehension. Kwasi did the same, his fists clenching tightly. He had never said so out loud, but it was very evident to me that he detested our brother and yet would rarely stand up to him.

"Enough, Elan," I declared, hearing the dragon's growing frustration. "We must show respect. She is not here for your amusement."

Elan's attention shifted abruptly to me. I did not need eyes to know he wore a dark expression on his face.

"It's a pity you live in such filth," he said, words dripping with disdain. "You'd better clean up soon, Asha. After all, you wouldn't want to disappoint your future husband, would you?" he sneered gleefully.

My jaw tightened. Though I remained in place, my expression must have read as confused because his laughter grew in fervor.

"Brother, you did not tell her. Oh, this is so delicious."

I felt Kwasi straighten behind me.

"Do you want to know what our dear father has planned for you? He has decreed that whoever wins the Fire Challenge this year will marry you."

I shivered as all the warmth drained from my body. Marriage? Why?

"I, for one, hope it is the man from Firepeak. Atar, I think," Elan continued. "You know their women aren't even allowed in public after marriage. That would suit you perfectly, sister."

I felt sick. Father was marrying me off. Why now? He had not even spared a glance my way since I'd been banished to the pits several years ago. From then on, I had to source my own food, make my own cloth-ing, and generally learn to fend for myself. It had been miserable, and I likely would have died if it weren't for Ekon and, eventually, Kwasi, sneaking me food until I had the means to buy my own. Marriage seemed like another level of cruelty. Why not just take me to the burn pit? The death would be quicker, poetic even, for me to meet the same end as our mother.

Kwasi cleared his throat. "I was hoping to tell her more gently than that."

"Oh, I am sure, but what fun is that?" I could feel Elan reach for me, and I instinctively raised my staff to prevent it. He chuckled. "Is our little sister finally growing a spine? How delicious. Save that for the wedding night."

I tried to maintain a stoic facade, but I could feel the tears welling up in the corners of my eyes. It would be a big mistake to show tears to anyone in Ujuima, let alone to Elan.

Since we were four years old, all citizens took a warrior's vow to reject vulnerability and harness the power of battle magic, which we called battlemage, that every person was born with. Most anyway. Those who showed no promise were sent into the desert. If battlemage was going to manifest, it would do so under extreme circumstances, and those lucky souls would be welcomed back. Most were never seen again, at least not alive.

My brother Kwasi had a knack for manipulating shadows, while my father could conjure fire from dragons. As for Elan, his battlemage was particularly terrifying—he possessed the ability to inflict searing burns on his victims from a distance. He had used this power on me many times before. There were no memories of Elan not being cruel, and without our father's intervention, it had worsened.

I refused to give him the satisfaction of seeing me break, so I willed my composure back.

"It sounds like I need to get ready for the opening ceremonies tonight."

I bowed before walking out. After quiet words to Elan, Kwasi followed behind me.

"I was going to tell you."

"When?" I shouted. "After I was fully distracted by a new dragon?"

There was silence and shifting of feet before he said, "You are right. I should have led with this: our father, the dragon's ass, has decided to marry you off to one of his allies."

I put my hand against his mouth to silence further words. I was not sure who else was within earshot.

"Hush. You must not say anything against the crown. Even you are not safe if others overhear."

He clenched his jaw, grinding his teeth, then let out a deep, weary sigh. "Ash, I am tired of saying nothing, doing nothing. I stood by once, even participated."

I knew what he was referring to. I stopped him with a look before he could go down that line of thinking.

"I don't want to stand by anymore," he whispered. "You will not marry *anyone*. I will find a way out of this for you."

I shook my head, acceptance washing over me. "There is no way out. Nowhere for me to go."

This was true. If I tried to leave the city, even with provisions, I would probably die. I could try to hide, but I held no skills other than tending dragons. "The decision has been made, and the sooner we both accept that, the better."

Kwasi leaned his forehead against my shoulder. "I wish Mother were here," he whispered, pain etched in his voice. "She always knew what to say. I fear I always say the wrong thing."

I ran my palm against his shoulder, patting his back like our mother used to do for all of us. "She would not be able to save me. This life drove her to the burn pits."

Often, when I felt the tangle of guilt and sadness, especially when talking about our mother, I said things to soothe his aura, running a warm palm over his heart. Kwasi described it as a warm hug after a nightmare. I wanted to do that for him now, but I did not have it in me. I could not even do it for myself.

"I will fix this," he repeated.

"I know you will," I whispered. I wanted to believe he could.

CHAPTER THREE

Adriel

This land was not my own, and I loathed it. The arid desert and relentless heat were like a curse, punishing me for daring to venture through it. Who in the five kingdoms would ever call this place a paradise? Sure, there were strategic advantages to living in Ujuima—enemies wouldn't dare cross these unforgiving sands to attack it. But at what cost? There were no rivers to swim in, no mountains to climb, no trees to offer shade from the relentless sun. War and the pursuit of territory were expected. It was the way of life for all, but none were as ruthless and power-hungry as Ujuima. And then there were the dragons, a privilege reserved only for the emperor. But perhaps I could change that if my mission proved successful for Wiyotak.

My thoughts swayed to my brother, King Enapay Foxtrail, and the foolish errand he had sent me on. While I was his newly appointed war chief, it wasn't as if that meant anything. We'd grown up together, and I'd always considered him my closest friend, but that all changed when our father died and he ascended to the throne.

Since then, he had become guarded and surrounded himself with flatterers and yes-men. It was a miracle that he'd given me this mission at all, though his trust had limits. My eyes flicked over to Guardian Winnow as he dismounted from his horse, which he had driven relentlessly during our long journey. The poor animal looked half-dead. I raised my scarf to my eyes, not to keep out the sand but to hide my disdain for this man. I would never have selected him to be my second in command if I'd been given a choice. He was here purely to keep his allies in power and to maintain influence over my brother.

Though I loathed Winnow and his methods, I had to ensure the horse received proper care. I couldn't help but wonder if it would be kinder to just put the poor creature out of its misery. That was the way of Guardian Winnow. He treated his steed as roughly as he did the men he led.

"How did you talk me into making this awful trek with you?" Kitchi said with exasperation as she urged her horse to catch up with mine.

I grinned. "Because I promised you there would be swaths of women for you to conquer while you are here."

She rolled her eyes. "You are such a man. Women do not conquer. We entice. We charm and captivate," she said, shaking her head. "Honestly, Adriel, no wonder you don't have a woman." She put a hand on her hip in outrage, but I knew it was just for show.

"No one loves women as much as you. Why should I bother?"

Kitchi raised her brows at that, slapping a hand on my shoulder. "You are lucky I like you, or I would have abandoned you a long time ago. You need to expand your horizons, my friend. You clearly aren't doing it right."

She winked at a group of Ujuima women clothed in colorful chiffon gowns. They giggled at her, and one peered shyly up at me.

"That is not what I am here for. We have things to do."

Kitchi sighed. "I know, but there is not a shred of evidence that what you are looking for is here."

I smiled, flashing all my teeth. "I was going to say we are here to deliver this marriage proposal."

Kitchi scoffed. Enapay had grown bold. His aspirations were not rooted in reality anymore. There was no chance for the emperor to accept a proposal between his brother and Princess Asha. I was not even certain whether she still lived. No one had laid eyes on her in at least a decade.

"Why do you think they keep her out of Ujuiman society?" I asked. "What could be wrong with her?"

"Isn't it obvious?" she asked, her voice dripping with sarcasm. I gave her a look that signaled I had no idea. "She must be hideous!" she answered.

I shook my head. "Her mother is said to have been one of the great beauties of her time."

"Exactly my point," Kitchi offered. "Beautiful people make ugly children. That is a proven fact."

"I do not think that is how that works," I said, slowing my horse so that we drifted to the rear of our company. "I would like you to go to the castle without me."

She threw up her hands. "You want to travel around the city by yourself in enemy territory. That sounds like a terrible idea."

I looked around and signaled for her to lower her voice. "I need to move around the city discreetly, and I can't with our army behind me."

"Where exactly are you going to look? It's not like you can break into the dragon pits."

Our eyes met, and her jaw fell open. I held up my hand and looked around to make sure no one had overheard.

"Have you been inhaling the sand?"

"It is either that or the emperor's private chamber."

"So, it's the difference between being burned alive or captured and killed for treason. It doesn't sound worthwhile. Are you sure this is what you should be doing?"

"I'm doing this for Wiyotak. Nothing is more important."

Kitchi motioned to Guardian Winnow. "What would you like me to tell our friend over there?"

My hands tightened on my reins. I smiled at a woman with deep brown eyes and neatly braided hair that flowed over the back of her scalp. She fluttered her eyelashes at me shyly.

"Tell him a woman has me occupied."

She laughed a little louder than was necessary. "There isn't a woman in the five kingdoms, let alone Ujuima, who could occupy the great War Chief Adriel." She waggled her eyebrows suggestively. "And if there is, I would desperately like to meet her."

CHAPTER FOUR

Asha

The door to my chamber creaked open, and the familiar scent of vanilla and cloves filled my nostrils. I leaned into Kaliyah's warm embrace, the woman who had raised me alongside my mother, as I smiled into her wrinkled cheek. It was a bittersweet reminder of the life I'd once had.

Kaliyah had lobbied to follow me into exile, but Father had refused. Only Oseis had servants, he'd said, and he'd made it clear I was no Osei. She'd remained in my father's service, primarily in the kitchens, but for just a moment, she was all mine again. She opened her arms warmly, beckoning me closer. "Come here, child. Let's have a good cry before I run your bath."

I clung to her soft form, finally allowing myself to release the tears that I had held back just moments ago; I knew Kaliyah would never judge me. She was the one constant in my world, and being with her again reminded me of all that I had lost—my mother, my family, and my illusion of independence. For just a moment, I felt less alone.

"I suppose you know then," Kaliyah whispered, patting my head. "It is not all bad. A woman of your station would be expected to be married off at some point."

"I have not seen my father for ten years. Why would he care about my marriage prospects now, except to punish me?"

She let me sob in her arms for a time, finally coaxing me to eat some bread with the honey she had cultivated herself.

"Your father is not well, child. Everyone in the palace has tried to keep it quiet. Elan grows bolder, knowing his time to rule will soon come." She poured me tea, blowing on it like she used to when I was young. "Forgive me for saying so, but Prince Elan is not a kind man."

I scoffed at that. Kaliyah was well aware of what Elan had done to me. I had to call Kaliyah afterward to tend to the wounds on my back. He was always careful to use his power to inflict the welts on my upper back where no one would see. Kaliyah had done a masterful job healing the wounds, but the scars remained, a mosaic of pain that Elan got to admire whenever he pleased.

"It is better if you are married off," Kaliyah said. "Whoever wins your hand has to be kinder than your brother."

I shivered, thinking about what it would be like to live under Elan's rule. It would be intolerable, and yet I also hated the idea of not having any control over whom I would be wed to. What if he were cruel? What if we did not share the same interests? And the dragons. No one could care for them as well as I could. As much as I hated living away from Kwasi and Kaliyah, I loved my work rehabilitating the dragons. In some ways, they were much simpler than people, wanting to survive and find comfort and happiness. There would be none where I was going.

My ears picked up Kaliyah smoothing her hands over her thighs nervously. "I have my orders to draw you a bath and get you ready for tonight. I brought everything with me, but if you prefer, we could return to your old rooms . . ."

"No," I said. "This is my home now, at least for a little while longer. I will get ready here."

It was the truth, and I knew I'd feel out of place in my old rooms with all the expensive silks and shiny jewels. I was no Osei. I was a dragon pit master.

"Very well, Your Highness."

I winced at the title, hearing Kaliyah bow before me. "You don't need to bother with that. I have not been a princess for a very long time."

I felt the caress of Kaliyah's calloused hands across my cheek.

"You will always be my princess," she whispered.

My heart clenched, and I bowed my head to hide the emotions that must have been evident on my face.

Kaliyah said nothing further before she got to work, ordering a bath to be brought to my room and filled. She put in a few droplets of argan oil and lined the tub with floral petals. As she washed my hair, she gave it an olive oil treatment, massaging my scalp like she used to when I was a child. It was all a bit much for an exiled princess, but I appreciated it all the same. She fussed over my hair. Without servants to help, I often let my curls fall loosely, styling them with shea butter and water. Kaliyah had a gift with hair and formed several braids that came together in the back. She let the bottom half fall loosely around my shoulders and put a headpiece on to complete the look. The headpiece jingled as I walked. Kaliyah swore it looked beautiful and accented the blue tones of my hair. It felt ridiculous.

"You've gotten quiet over there. What is wrong?" I asked.

She shifted her feet and made disapproving sounds. "It is the outfit, child. I believe Prince Elan picked it for you. It is . . . not what you are accustomed to wearing."

"Bring it here." Kaliyah reluctantly held out the clothes so that I could feel them. They were gauzy and thin. "Is this it? Where is the rest of it?"

"That is all of it," she said with regret. "I can see if I can find something else."

"No, if you do that, Elan will find a way to punish you. I can't live with that." I could feel tears threatening to fall again. I closed my eyes, holding them at bay. "I cannot see them, anyway. That is a small blessing. Please just make sure all of my necessary areas are covered."

"As you will it, princess."

CHAPTER FIVE

Asha

Kaliyah allowed me a few moments alone to collect myself before I joined the opening ceremony. Acutely aware that I was wearing next to nothing, I placed my hands on my bare stomach and low neckline. If the fabric and gold disks that overlaid it were not so expensive, I would say I was dressed as one of the women in the pleasure district.

Ujuiman law decreed that women in the pleasure trade could have agency and no man could own them. It was the only good decision in memory that the emperor had made, which meant my mother likely had something to do with it. They were businesswomen and free. I was not. Right now, I envied them.

I sat in my discontent until the night's stillness was shattered by a haunting wail. The sound echoed through the darkness as if it carried the weight of centuries of sorrow. I knew the dragon's tones well, like a mother knew her children's cries. This wail was unfamiliar, which meant it belonged to the blue dragon.

I rose from my bed and grabbed my walking staff. There were many things I was not in control of, but maybe I could do a bit of good tonight. Ignoring the warnings of danger that echoed in my mind, I ventured into the deserted halls, guided only by the mournful cries growing louder with each step. My heart was heavy, feeling the dragon's growing distress.

As I approached, her fearsome presence clung to me like a second skin. Though taxing, I did my best to keep the sense of panic from creeping in. I typically spent much more time introducing myself and gaining a wild dragon's trust, but there was something about her cries that tugged on my heartstrings. When it came to the needs of my dragons, I could deny them nothing.

The dragon growled, threatening to incinerate me, and grew frustrated when she was unable to. I sang to her then. Softly at first, weaving a melody of comfort, as I moved in a soothing pattern, I had learned over the years to calm the dragons. The melody was my mother's. She used to sing to me and Kwasi. Elan was older and had long outgrown our bedtime rituals.

I could feel her eyes trained on me. Slowly, the growls began to subside, replaced by deep, sorrowful wails. I dared to draw closer, my hand outstretched in a gesture of peace.

"You are in so much pain," I whispered. "Share it with me so you do not have to bear it alone."

The dragon wailed louder, deep and visceral. It reminded me of when I used to watch my father separate his hounds' pups from their mothers. The mothers always cried in guttural anguish, as if their hearts were literally breaking before their eyes.

I swayed my hips, keeping my torso still, moving my feet in a complex pattern that caused the dragon's eyes to move from right to left.

"You are safe," I whispered. My body warmed as my aura reached out to touch hers. "Please show me what hurts you so that I can help."

Her mournful cries went on for some time. I mimicked the pitch and began to parrot them back.

"STOP!"

My walking staff fell from my hands and clattered to the ground as a gasp escaped my lips. Had this dragon just spoken to me? I had a natural affinity with animals and the ability to anticipate their needs, but never had one spoken to me.

"What . . . what did you say?"

The air around me warmed as heat emanated from her open mouth. "I said stop. Your dragontongue is atrocious."

I put my hand to my mouth, still in shock that I understood her. I swallowed before asking, "Just to be clear, you are speaking to me? I am not hallucinating this?"

"I do not have long," she said impatiently. "Do not make me repeat myself."

I shook my head, pulling myself together to respond. "Why do you not have long?"

"Because I am dying," she said without emotion.

Now, I was concerned. "Why do you think you are dying?" I asked.

She blew out a heavy breath in response. "I can feel my life force draining from my body. A mother knows," she said cautiously.

My body jerked in surprise at the words. That phrase was so familiar. My mother used to say something similar to Kwasi and me when we would sneak out of our rooms to play in the halls at night. She would always catch us. Most of the time, she would insist we return to our beds, but I had one memory of her playing in the garden fountain with us.

Whenever I was hurt or told a lie or felt sad, Mother would intuitively know without me saying.

I could still remember the feeling of my mother's hand on my forehead, her eyes searching mine, and her voice saying, "A mother knows when her children are in trouble. It is just the way it is."

"You are a mother?" I asked. "Where are your babies?"

She was quiet for a time. "Please, you must keep my secret. I am dying, and I need you to take something to my mate."

My mind scrambled to think of what in the five kingdoms she could possibly want me to take to another dragon—her mate.

"Where is he?"

"I don't know," she moaned. "We were separated. He was trying to lead the mortals away from me, but I was too slow."

Kwasi had not mentioned another dragon. He'd mentioned she had the strength of two. Maybe there were two dragons they were dealing with.

"How can I find him?"

As she sighed again heavily, I felt the pain she was in for the first time. "If you are ill, I will get you a *surjin*."

"No! Please. It can only be you. My time is coming to an end."

I knew what I should do as a dragon pit master, but something stopped me. She was just offering me a bit of trust. If I left now, it could set us back for weeks. I held out my hand tentatively. "Do you have a name?"

For a moment, I thought she would not answer. But then she spoke, "I am Seraphina."

My hands were shaking as I unlocked the gate, which I never did with new dragons. This was a reckless move, but with my own life slipping away, I was feeling bold. I needed to take control of something.

"Seraphina," I repeated. "I am Asha. May I touch you?"

She retreated into her cell. "Why?" she bellowed.

I did my best to maintain a sense of calm, even though my heart was thumping like a jackrabbit. "Sometimes, it helps to calm the aura. I have a talent for it."

Seraphina hesitated. "The others have said you are to be trusted, though they seem to be half mad by the dracite."

"I will try to have yours removed as soon as possible. They overload the dragons at first. I am sorry if it is causing discomfort."

"I will not be here long enough for it to matter. You may touch me."

Slowly, I reached out and let my fingers trail over her cheek, feeling the coolness of her scales against my skin. As I explored further, my hand came across a rough, raised patch on her side.

"I can feel where you're hurt," I murmured, my heart breaking, realizing that she was indeed badly injured. Her limbs were covered in bandages that were barely containing the blood beneath. My fingers were coated with it as my hands explored the injury.

She groaned at my touch. "My mate is Drakkar. He will help you," she whispered weakly.

"I cannot help the physical pain without a *surjin*," I said, gesturing toward her injured body.

"No *surjin*," Seraphina moaned. "It hurts." Her voice became distorted in pain as she let out a low groan.

I continued my movements. "Perhaps I can ease the pain." With a gentle touch, I pointed to where her heart might be. "Would you allow me to try?"

Seraphina groaned but did not protest further. Nervously, I began to work, tracing invisible lines with my fingers and calling forth her aura. As our energies intertwined, I felt a surge of empathy for her suffering. I shared her pain, taking it upon myself and hoping to alleviate some of her agony.

There was a moment when it almost felt like too much, when I saw a sequence of bright lights in the night sky. I pushed myself away.

Gasping for breath, I asked, "What was that?"

She groaned again before beckoning me closer. "Come child. I have something you will want to see."

I stepped tentatively forward, reaching my hand out wildly to see what she was trying to show me.

"I do not have the ability to see. Can you tell me what it is?"

Seraphina made a noise that I had learned to attribute to a laugh. "For a mortal, you see better than most."

A strange, unfamiliar sound caught my attention as something rolled toward me. I strained my ears, trying to identify the source, until an object rolled to a stop at my feet. I crouched down to inspect. It emitted an unexpected warmth.

The object was round and delicate. It felt hard, almost like a rock. I was shocked to feel two more just like the first.

"Are these . . . eggs?" I gasped. My whole body shook.

"Will you bring them to my mate, to Drakkar? He will know how to care for them."

I gently picked up the first of the eggs, marveling at its size—about three times larger than a chicken egg—and the life I could feel stirring inside. It was unbelievable. I was holding a real dragon egg, something thought to be extinct since dragons' loss of flight and reproduction. As I cradled the precious egg, thoughts raced through my mind about all the stories and books I had read describing these mythical creatures and their supposed inability to reproduce. And yet, here I held proof they still existed in some form or another. My entire body trembled with excitement and disbelief.

"I don't know how to keep them alive."

"Keep them dry and covered until he comes. The eggs will call to him. The older they get, the stronger the call. He will find you."

"And what will he do when he does? I don't want to be eaten." A sharp pain scraped across my leg. "Oh!" I cried.

"Hush. I have marked you so that he will know you are a friend. Please get something to wrap them in. We are running out of time."

I hesitated only momentarily, gripping my bleeding thigh, before gently setting the egg down to retrieve my satchel. I lined it with some hay and walked back to Seraphina. I could not sense her movements.

"Seraphina? Seraphina?"

She moaned. "It is time. Please keep them safe."

My heart clenched at her plea, the weight of her words sinking deep into my soul.

I stayed with her until she took her last breath, then placed the eggs in my satchel and wrapped them tightly. I remained by her side, offering what little comfort I could to a creature I'd barely known. I leaned against Seraphina, stroking her neck until she was gone. Tears streamed down my face, probably messing up my kohl-lined eyes that Kaliyah had so carefully applied, but I did not care. Her aura was so beautiful, and now it had dimmed into the darkness.

I cradled the eggs in my lap. What was I going to do? I was going to be married off. My soon-to-be husband was likely to find the eggs, and then what? Or worse, Elan or my father could find them.

My ears perked up at a faint rustling sound behind me. I slowly rose to my feet, clutching the weighty satchel against my chest. My hand tightened around my carved walking staff, unsure of what I would do if someone were indeed lurking behind me.

"Who's there?" I demanded, my voice echoing through the pit. Silence greeted me in response, but I remained on guard. "I said, who's there?"

Footsteps sounded.

"It's me, Kwasi. I came to escort yo— What are you doing? Get out of there, Ash," he called, alarmed.

"She's gone, Kwasi."

"What?" he said, coming to my side in disbelief. He took his time inspecting her, trying to coax her to wake. He touched my shoulder.

"I'm sorry, Ash."

I wasn't sure what I felt. Sorrow? Numb?

"Did you mean it when you said you would fix this?"

He grabbed my hands and stood back. "What do you have on?" his voice interrupted.

"Did you mean it?" I pressed.

"Of course, but Ash—"

"I need you to get me out of Ujuima tonight."

"But if we waited a few days, I could—"

"Tonight," I said.

He was silent for a moment before I heard hair rustle as he nodded in agreement. "Tonight."

CHAPTER SIX

Adriel

The dragon pit stretched ahead, darkness shrouding its every corner like a blanket of uncertainty. The only lights guiding my way were the torches placed sparingly against the walls. I resisted the urge to grab one. I'd surely be seen if anyone crossed my path. With each cautious step, I battled the unease that gnawed at my insides. My senses were alert to every sound and movement. The air was thick with the heavy scent of dragon musk, mingling with the metallic tang of fear. My fingers brushed against rough stone, guiding me forward as I navigated the labyrinthine passages of the pit. The little bit of light present in the pit danced mockingly at the edge of my vision, teasing me with its elusive form. Then, a flicker of movement caught my eye, a silhouette weaving through the darkness like a ghost in the night. With adrenaline surging, I followed, my footsteps muffled against the hard-packed earth.

As I drew closer, the figure resolved into clarity—a young woman, small and delicate, standing before the cage of the largest dragon I had ever seen. My breath caught in my throat as I watched her, mesmerized by the way she spoke to the beast as if she could understand its language of growls and grunts. She sat with the creature, stroking its scales as if it were a precious child rather than the monstrous beast that it was. I had never seen anyone get so close to one of these creatures. My body tensed, waiting for the worst to happen, but the dragon seemed at ease with her touch, at least for now.

I nearly turned to go when, all of a sudden, she held something in the light. It was oblong and delicate—an egg. I held my breath, afraid the slightest movement would banish it from existence. It was the color of the clearest sky, cradled in her palm like a precious jewel. I could not believe it. After all this time, after all my searching, what I had been desperate to find was right there, cradled in her hands. She began to inspect not one, not two, but three eggs! Maybe there were more. I had searched nearly every kingdom, crossed countless borders for a mere whisper of just one egg, and here there were at least three. If I could just get one, Wiyotak could have its very own dragon and would not have to subjugate itself to Ujuima.

The thought sent a surge of hope through me, fierce and unrelenting. For the first time in what felt like an eternity, I dared to believe that freedom was within reach. My hands trembled as I watched her, the weight of possibility surging through me. How had I gotten so lucky? After years of fruitless searching, fate had led me here, to this moment. This woman held Wiyotak's future, and I would not let it slip away.

Lost in the sight of my prayers being answered, I stepped forward without thinking, drawn inexorably toward the egg and the girl who held it. For a moment, I forgot everything else—the dangers lurking in the shadows, the risks of discovery. All that mattered were the eggs and the overwhelming desire to claim them as my own.

As I stepped into view, a jolt of fear shot through me as the girl whipped around, her eyes wide with alarm. For a heart-stopping moment, I believed my fate was sealed, and I was going to have to fight her for them.

"Who's there?" she called mere steps from me. She looked past me, her eyes blinking but without recognition.

The tension in my muscles eased as my breathing relaxed, and her gaze seemed to look past me. She was blind. She could not see me. I struggled with the waves of relief and conflict that seemed caught in my chest. It was rare for anyone with visual limitations to survive childhood. How had she survived for so long in Ujuima, of all places?

I watched her for a moment longer, torn between the temptation to seize the eggs and the knowledge that it would be an act of unspeakable cruelty. Even in the dim lighting, I could see she was beautiful, with her braided hair that matched the color of the dragon's scales, her sweet oval face, and her toned body, barely concealed in her attire. This couldn't be typical attire for those who worked in the dragon pits.

And then, as if by some silent cue, I heard the approach of footsteps echoing through the cavern, signaling the imminent arrival of another. With a sinking heart, I retreated, my mind racing with indecision. Should I go for the eggs and most certainly reveal myself? That would put all the Wiyotakins at risk. Or should I remain hidden, biding my time until the opportunity presented itself to claim the eggs for myself?

In the end, I chose the latter. I'd waited this long; I could wait a little longer. As I melted into the darkness, I vowed to seize the opportunity as soon as I could, no matter the cost.

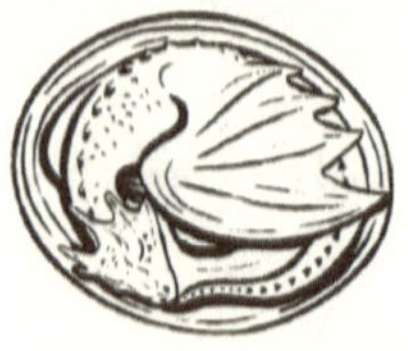

I quietly snuck out the way I came and finally made my way to the castle. The outer walls, built from sturdy stone and clay, shone brightly in the setting sun. Torches were placed strategically to highlight the intricate carvings of Ujuiman warriors along the surfaces softened by the gentle touch of time. Each stone seemed to tell a story, each curve and contour an example of the skill of the craftsmen who had labored to bring this fortress to life.

As I passed through the arched entrance, I found myself standing in the center of the courtyard, with a sparkling fountain gurgling. It was a welcome respite for my skin as I plunged my head underneath. Several men approached dressed in gold mail armor, denoting their status as castle guards. They took one look at my appearance and pulled out their swords.

"Halt! Only honored guests of the five kingdoms are allowed to enter. Identify yourself."

I held up my hands in supplication. "No reason to get so worked up. I am Adriel Foxtrail, War Chief of Wiyotak, Brother of War King Enapay Foxtrail."

Unfazed, the two guards maintained their defensive stance. They were not buying any of it.

"The Wiyotak party has already arrived," one of them said. "Try again. Who are you?"

I sighed in exasperation. I had left my papers with my things. If I were caught in the dragon pit, it would be better if people did not know immediately who I was. Now, that was working against me.

"What is going on here?" a voice called from behind. I looked over to see the questioning eyes of Guardian Winnow. He gave me a look that signaled he was contemplating telling them he had no idea who I was. It would be to his advantage to have me gone. Though I was no longer in Enapay's inner circle, I still had a bit of influence. He still listened to me at times.

"We caught him wandering around without papers," a guard answered. "Do you know him?"

Winnow raised an eyebrow. "Without papers? That is curious."

The two guards turned their eyes on me, raising their swords higher when he said, "He may not look like much, but he is our fearless leader, the king's brother. I do not think he would appreciate you killing him."

The guards lowered their swords. "Make sure you carry your identification with you. The emperor has ordered tight security for this event. You may not be so lucky next time."

I nodded in thanks before they turned to leave.

Of all the people I could run into, Winnow was the last I wanted to see, especially fresh off a dangerous mission. Winnow took in my disheveled attire.

"And where have you been?" he asked as we walked through the courtyard. "Don't tell me you left your papers in Wiyotak?"

I plastered a jovial, self-satisfied expression on my face. "I left them with Kitchi. I wanted to be inconspicuous in the pleasure district. Didn't Kitchi tell you?"

He tightened his posture. "Kitchi is not in the habit of telling me anything."

He straightened his tunic, looking me over. He leaned over to wipe a finger on my sleeve. His finger was stained black.

"You are covered in soot. Where have you really been?" he asked with suspicion.

"Come now, Winnow. Don't tell me you've never had a rough and tumble with a fire mage. Loosen up. Have a little fun while you are here. I saved some women for you." I slapped his back and winked for good measure.

Better he think I was a young, reckless fool than to guess that I was doing something my brother would disapprove of. He would understand once I brought him the eggs, but likely not before.

"I need to get washed up. I will see you in there."

I found our quarters and quickly closed the door behind me with a deep exhale. I still could not believe what I'd seen, and I had a whole night to get through before I could sneak back to steal the eggs. Why did royal festivities have to be so tedious? Perhaps this one could provide the perfect distraction.

Kitchi rounded the corner in question. She paused mid-step. "Let me guess. You found a pretty girl, after all?"

I grinned. "Yes."

She eyed me curiously. "Well, share whatever you have with me quickly. There has been a change in our plans."

CHAPTER SEVEN

Asha

My brother, ever the resourceful one, found me a matching cloak to put over my ridiculous outfit. Kwasi would not take no for an answer. I unhooked the satchel with the eggs, hoping he would not take the time to look inside.

"Give this to Kaliyah, will you? Tell her to add some supplies to it."

He put the satchel over his shoulder. If he questioned the weight of it, he did not say anything.

"I will return. Be ready," he said before turning to leave.

I stood at the double doors that would lead into the ballroom where the opening ceremony would be held. The doors opened, and I stepped onto a balcony. To my left was a staircase with very long and steep steps. If I had not gone down them a million times as a child, grabbing cushions to slide down with Kwasi, I would be nervous. There were twenty-eight steps. The fifteenth would begin the curve, and there was a crack on the seventh step I needed to avoid.

"Allow me to escort you, sister." I bristled at Elan's voice, like nails grating against steel.

He was the last person I wanted to share company with. It was as if he'd been waiting for me to show. Surely, he would not taunt me in front of so many onlookers, especially with Father in attendance. Elan preferred to serve out his torture in private.

He grabbed my arm, disposing of my walking staff before I could respond, and slowly guided my descent down the stairwell. I did not have much choice. I could either follow his lead or make a scene, which would likely end with me being pushed down a flight of stairs, knowing my brother.

"Did Father ask you to escort me?" Twelve more steps.

He laughed. "Father did not want you to be in attendance at all. He feels your . . . condition might put off the suitors and make them feel like their prize is unworthy."

The words stung, but I made sure to steel my expression so Elan would not get the satisfaction.

Seven more steps.

"I thought differently. What man wouldn't want a woman who depends solely on his goodwill? But we did come to a compromise. You could attend as long as we were discreet about your blindness."

Three more steps.

"Too bad I am not very discreet."

I inhaled deeply as we descended the final step.

"You look flushed, baby sister. Let me help you with your coat."

I felt a violent tug at the clasp around my neck, and then I was spinning, then falling. Not sure where the floor was, I placed my hands in front of me. Despite my attempts, I still landed face-first on the stone floor. Pain coursed through my hands and face.

By the quieting of the room, I could tell all eyes were on me.

"Princess, you are so clumsy. Let me help you."

Elan grasped my arm, but I pushed him away. He had made his point. I slowly stood, feeling my bare midriff exposed to the cool evening air.

A man to my right cleared his throat.

"Prince Elan Osei, Heir Apparent, Dragonlord and Protector of the Realms, Conjurer of Fire and Ash, escorting Princess Asha Osei."

I heard gasps and indistinct murmurs around me, undoubtedly curious as to why the princess had just stumbled to the floor dressed as a trussed pig for sale. Their whispered questions and judgments swirled around the room, so thick I could feel them pressing down on me.

Is there something wrong with her? Is she daft? She must be if she wore that.

I needed to get away—away from the cruel whispers, away from my tormentor. But without my walking staff, I could not get a feel for the room. I'd recounted the exact number of steps to get there, but with Elan pushing me from my path, there was no easy way to find it again. I decided to move toward where the voices were, hoping they would guide me to the Osei table. At first, it worked. I had not run into any columns, and I was making progress in the room. Then the music began to play, and my body was shuffled forward into the quick footsteps and the ruffle of long gowns.

Someone collided with me, their size so large that the force of the impact sent me stumbling backward. Before I could register what was happening, a pair of strong hands encircled my waist, steadying me with a firm grip. I instinctively grasped onto the stranger's arms for support, feeling the warmth of his touch seeping through the gauzy fabric of my gown.

"Has anyone ever told you how reckless you are?" His voice was low, threaded with amusement. "Refusing the help of the heir apparent—that was bold."

Too stunned to answer, I simply took in the smooth cadence of his voice.

"Are you alright?" His tone was softer now and laced with concern.

Finally, after the initial shock began to dissipate, I could speak. "Yes, thank you."

As I tilted my head upward, my heightened senses took in the subtle scent of his cologne, sandalwood mixed with a hint of sweat from the humid evening. His presence loomed over me, exuding a quiet, undeniable strength. A silk cloth dragged against the corner of my mouth. "It's not a party unless a little blood is spilled." I flinched at the touch, and he dabbed more gently this time. "You certainly know how to make an entrance."

What was happening? I forced myself to speak. "Thank you for your kindness."

Before I could excuse myself, he asked, "Would you do me the honor of allowing me a dance?"

His request caught me off guard. I was not sure how to refuse him without further humiliation.

"Dance?"

"Yes," he said apologetically. "You see, as much as I enjoy catching you, there are some very unfriendly eyes on me right now. And if we were to dance, I'd have an excuse for why my hands are holding onto an Osei. Without the excuse, I may not leave here with said hands, and I've grown very attached to them."

"I do not dance well," I said weakly.

This did not seem to faze him at all as he placed a hand around my waist. "A princess with two left feet? How amusing. Don't worry, I've got you."

With slight trepidation, I held out my free hand, and he grasped it. I felt the warmth of his fingers enveloping mine as he guided me onto the dance floor. He moved with confidence as he led me through a series of steps and turns.

Though I'd been exiled long before I could get proper instruction in dance, Ekon had seen to it that I kept up with the latest trends. In normal circumstances, I could hold my own, but right now, the presence of this man had a dizzying effect on me. I did my best to allow my body to follow his, but his hands were not Ekon's.

"Slow down," the man whispered, putting his hand on my chest.

I flinched.

"My apologies," he said, removing his hand as if it had touched a burning hearth. "May I show you?"

I swallowed before nodding. He placed a hand lightly on my chest again, slightly above my racing heart. Could he tell?

"Feel it in here. Get out of your head. Trust your body."

After some time, I began to relax, finally finding a rhythm.

He chuckled. "And you said you could not dance."

Finally, he stopped moving as the song changed. I did the same.

"I have something for you. Hold still."

I did not know what choice I had. I felt him walk in front of me as he draped something around my shoulders. A cloak? He drew closer to fasten it. It smelled of the desert, but it also had a faint woodsy smell, like cedar. "Is this yours?"

He finished buttoning it around my neck, but did not step away. "You looked . . . cold."

My cheeks flamed. All I could manage to say was, "Others might gossip if they see me wearing a man's cloak."

He chuckled, leaning closer. "Good. Better they speak of scandal rather than your propensity for falling."

I touched my swollen lip at the reminder. He grazed his thumb over my bruised face. I wondered what he was thinking. He definitely should not be touching me like this. "Your hands," I said. "I thought you were fond of them."

"I am," he said, his voice soft and feather-light.

"Then you'd better go," I said, pulling away slightly. "I thank you for the dance."

He allowed me the distance but did not let go. "I'm sorry," he said.

"Sorry? For what?" I knew I needed to walk away, to put more distance between us, yet my feet refused to move.

"I am sorry that everyone looked away as if nothing had happened."

My mouth fell open in shock. I couldn't help it. He couldn't have surprised me more if he'd suddenly sprouted wings.

He traced my bruised cheek once more. "I do not like bullies." Then, taking my hand, he guided me to sit down. "I must take my leave now. Stay away from that brother of yours."

I almost rolled my eyes, but instead, I asked, "Wait. What is your name?"

"I am certain you will learn it soon enough. We will see each other again, princess."

And then he was gone.

CHAPTER EIGHT

Adriel

As I stood in a corner near a table laden with gifts and tributes to the emperor, I watched the dancing couples as they gossiped and whispered behind gloved hands. I loathed seeing all the simpering nobles and hated even more that I was here to do the same thing. My eyes roamed over the table, searching for the golden dragon we'd painstakingly carried from Wiyotak. It was lost among similar jeweled items and statues. How many monstrous statues did one need? It was a distasteful display, especially considering most of the kingdoms were struggling to keep their people fed and money in the royal vaults.

My thoughts spiraled as I caught the faint scent of jasmine still lingering on my clothes. I was still reeling from the fact that the woman I'd observed earlier from the dragon pits had been Princess Asha. I had so many questions. Why was she there in the first place? Didn't her family care about her safety? I ground my teeth, realizing the answer was plain to see in the display Elan had put on. Why I intervened on behalf of the woman I was supposed to be securing in marriage to my brother, I could not tell you. Was it because her delicate frame trembled in fear at the slightest touch from her brother? It was dizzying to see her like that when I'd witnessed her walk into a cage with the biggest dragon I'd ever seen. Or maybe I'd inserted myself because she was clearly trying to hide her blindness from others?

I'd approached her, intending to extract information about the egg's whereabouts, but once I looked into her golden-brown eyes and long lashes that fluttered like the delicate wings of a butterfly, I found myself inexplicably drawn to her. The quiet strength she exuded, trying to make her way through the dance floor without her sight, was undoubtedly brave. She might have made it had a drunk guest not bumped into her.

I braved another glance in her direction. She was still sitting at the Osei table. Her chestnut skin glowed beneath the soft candlelight, and her indigo braided hair formed a crown for her head before cascading in waves around her shoulders like a waterfall. I recalled how my fingers had reached for her instinctively. It was a fleeting touch, yet it sent a jolt of electricity coursing through my veins, igniting a spark of something unfamiliar.

Though I'd allowed myself the indulgence of distraction, I needed to stay focused on my original goal: finding the eggs. I needed to formulate a plan to retrieve them. I imagined she'd stash such a valuable commodity in her room in the palace. I just needed to find it.

From all corners of the kingdom, all gathered to witness the grand spectacle that was the opening ceremony of the Fire Festival—a time-honored tradition marking the beginning of a deadly competition between the five kingdoms.

At the heart of the arena, a magnificent stage had been erected, trussed with the vibrant banners of the sigils of the five kingdoms fluttering in the breeze. I turned to catch the cadence of the drums that reverberated through the air. With a deafening roar, the Ujuima representatives burst onto the floor, their swords gleaming in the spotlight as they clashed and parried with lightning-fast reflexes. The champions of Wyrmwood followed suit, weaving intricate patterns with deadly precision, paying tribute to their ancient traditions and fierce land. As flames erupted from behind them, the Firepeak champions strode forward with primal ferocity, their movements embodying the very essence of fire itself. The Entioch dancers appeared as if from another world, their fluid motions invoking the spirit of the ocean and leaving the audience transfixed. And finally, the drummers and warriors of Wiyotak unleashed a raw and untamed energy radiating from the Wiyotakin forests I called home.

Each group left nothing on the stage as they poured their hearts and souls into their performances. I loathed such displays, preferring to settle matters by battle, but I understood their importance. The reputation of their kingdoms as powerful warriors hung in the balance, and any sign of weakness could lead to an all-out war at our doorstep. Enapay would love that, as would Guardian Winnow, but going up against Ujuima or Firepeak would be foolish. It was difficult to clamp down on my brother's worst urges. He was not cruel like the emperor. His affliction was even worse. Enapay was a fool.

My mind raced as I thought about the dragon eggs hidden away somewhere beyond my reach. I chastised myself, wishing I had snatched them when I had the chance. I grimaced, thinking about how close I'd been. I silently prayed that Kitchi and Ashkii could shuffle them away without being seen. And then what? Would the princess demand a thorough search of everyone in the palace? She did not seem to have the power to command such a thing, nor did she have a close relationship with the Heir Apparent in which to confide. She had hidden them away from her other brother and did not appear to be afraid of him. Then there was the emperor. Once he got involved, there would be no chance of ever finding those eggs again. I clenched my fists in anxious frustration and paced back and forth. Failure was not an option.

CHAPTER NINE

Asha

I tapped my foot anxiously as the emperor approached my table. I always knew it was him because of the golden scepter he carriedF. I noted the sound had grown heavier, as if it were no longer a mere display of power but an instrument to hold him up. I sensed his piercing gaze bearing into me, weighing me down with unspoken words. I could imagine the thoughts going through his head: *There you are, the disgrace, the one without a battlemage. How dare you sit at my table eating my food as if you mean anything?*

"What do you think, Daughter? Who will win your hand?"

My head whipped in his direction from shock. I had not heard my father's voice since my exile, and now he was speaking to me as if those years were merely hours. In fact, the last time I recalled being in his presence was the same day fire had claimed my mother.

His voice was frailer than I remembered, his movements slow and fragile. And now, here he was, speaking to me as if nothing had changed, as if the scars he'd inflicted upon our family had not left us broken and bleeding.

"Who do you think will emerge victorious in the Fire Challenge, Asha?" he asked once more. His voice was calm, almost indifferent, as if he were asking about the weather, not the utter upheaval of my life.

This was merely a game to him.

I swallowed hard, struggling to mask the turmoil churning within me. How could he stand there, so composed, so detached, when our family lay in ruins at his feet? But I dared not voice the bitterness seething beneath the surface.

"I . . . I do not know, Your Eminence," I stammered, my voice barely above a whisper. "The champions of each kingdom are all formidable in their own right. It is difficult to say who will prevail."

He went silent. I could not tell if he was considering my words or reading through them.

"And as suitors, Asha?" he inquired, his tone casual. "Do any of them capture your interest?"

My heart clenched at his words, the pain of his betrayal stabbing at me like a dagger to the chest. How could he ask such a question, knowing full well I had no choice in the matter? Like I was some piece of chattel he could sell off when convenient?

But I forced a smile, masking my anguish behind a facade of indifference. "I have not given it much thought. I do not know them," I replied, my voice steady despite the storm raging within me. "My focus has been solely on the dragons in your care."

"I thought maybe the one you danced with? I cannot recall his name. Only that he is from Wiyotak," he grunted. "He would not be my choice for you. Heathens, all of them."

Wiyotak? My mind scrambled to remember all I knew of the kingdom to the south. They were not closely aligned with Ujuima. Still, the attempts to overthrow their monarchy had failed, mostly because their soldiers had the advantage in their densely packed forests.

"Did you know your mother and I met at the Fire Festival?" the emperor asked, pulling me out of my thoughts.

I nodded. "Yes, she told me she had to compete with other women to win your hand."

I remembered Mother telling me the story with a smile, but that smile never met her eyes. There was a darkness that she hid from us.

"She was a country peasant, nothing special." My body tensed upon hearing him describe her. "There were much prettier girls, but she had a fighting spirit and a way with dragons. You two have that in common." He paused as if recalling a favorite memory. "That is how she won, by the way. The dragon killed the others until only she remained. She did not even look frightened."

This time, he barked with laughter. "No, she wasn't the prettiest, but still, I knew she would give me sons. I asked for three, but the third was you. If only she'd stayed alive long enough to bear me another son." He sighed. "But I have to believe the warrior gods made the right choice. I pray you should be so worthy of your husband."

I imagine my father believed he was granting me a kindness by reminiscing, but his words left a bitter taste in my mouth. I remained silent, as I always did—quiet and obedient. That was how he demanded the women in his life to behave. Seemingly pleased by my lack of response, he turned to leave.

"I must mingle with the guests," he said. As he turned, his joints creaked, like the old rocking horse Kwasi and I had played with as children. His footsteps echoed across the marble floors, slow and deliberate, impossible to ignore. Only when he was gone did I finally unclench my jaw. A thought struck me with startling clarity: I wanted him dead. I wanted him dead, and I wanted to be the one to do it.

I continued sitting alone at the grand table, listening as the guests' murmurs swirled around me like a tempestuous wind. Their hushed voices carried morsels of gossip and speculation, their words slicing through the air like shards of glass. The questions surrounding my presence were endless. Why did I not engage with anyone? Why had I secluded myself from their prying eyes? I listened to their whispered suspicions and accusations of supposed monstrosities. While the talk was vile, none of it centered around my lack of sight. They had not caught on yet.

It was all nonsense. Their gossip, their slanderous words—they meant nothing to me. All I could think about was the eggs I had given to Kaliyah without explanation. Had she opened the satchel? What would she do with them?

I caught a glimpse of Ekon's aura coming to my side. I turned to face his direction. "I'm still not speaking to you," I said, surprised at how much I wanted him to leave.

"You can't still be mad? If I'd told you what I was doing, you would have tried to stop me," he said, his voice tinged with a hint of apprehension.

I glared upon hearing his words. "Apparently, I should congratulate you for being my potential betrothed," I retorted, my tone laced with anger.

His response was sheepish, his hand grazing mine in a feeble attempt at comfort. But I recoiled from his touch, my skin prickling. "I know you are worried, but I also hoped you might be pleased," he offered weakly, his words falling flat on my ears.

Pleased? How could I be pleased when my fate lay in the hands of men? The one I had come to trust had lied to me. No, there was no pleasure to be found in this twisted game; only the bitter taste of resentment lingered on my tongue. It was a harsh reminder of the chains that bound me to a life I did not choose.

He touched his hand to the cloak around my shoulders. "Who gave you this?" he asked.

I shrugged, annoyed at the tinge of jealousy I detected in his voice. "No one of importance."

He grunted disapprovingly. "It becomes of great importance when you wear the colors of Wiyotak. You should remove it before someone notices."

"Father seemed not to care," I said defiantly.

Realizing he was not going to get the response he wanted, he said, "The reason I entered the Fire Challenge is because of you. I heard whispers of the emperor's plans, and I thought, since we are friends, it would be the best possible outcome."

He was speaking logically, but I just was not ready to hear it. "You should have told me," I insisted.

He sighed. "Maybe, but it would not have changed anything." He leaned in closer. "You have to know, Asha, that if you were my wife, I would not expect— That is, we could take our time."

Heat rose in my face and ears at the turn in conversation. He reached for my hand under the table once more. This time, I did not pull away, but I wanted to. "You must have guessed how I feel about you." My head rose, my expression blank. He cleared his throat nervously. "That is to say, I would not be opposed to a match between us. In fact, I think I would like it very much. You could move out of the dragon pits, live in the palace, live the life you deserve."

"I like the dragon pits," I interrupted.

"Perhaps you could continue your work," he said quickly. "Until the children come, of course, and then . . ."

I stood abruptly. A familiar, wrinkled hand touched my arm from behind. "Forgive me, Master Ekon," Kaliyah said apologetically. "I must powder Princess Asha's face. We will return shortly."

I had never been so relieved to leave a conversation in my life. I took Kaliyah's hand and began to walk away.

"Wait, Asha."

I turned reluctantly. "Yes, Ekon?"

"In case I don't make it through the Fire Challenge," he began.

Now, I felt sheepish. He was risking his life by entering. He was a fool to enter, but he was also my friend. He had been my only constant throughout all these years. I loved him for it. Truly, I did.

"Don't say that," I murmured.

He halted my words with a hand on mine. "If I do not make it, I want you to know that I love you. I always have, since the moment we met in that ring. Maybe even before that. I just wanted you to know."

My mind flashed back to the memory I'd spent many years trying to bury—the day I'd lost everything. I wanted to be excited by his words. I should have been, but I felt nothing—nothing but friendship. I could hear him holding his breath, so I leaned in and kissed him on the cheek.

"Do me a favor. Come back to me," was all I could manage, and it was sincere. I wanted him to win. I wanted him to live, but I did not want to be his wife.

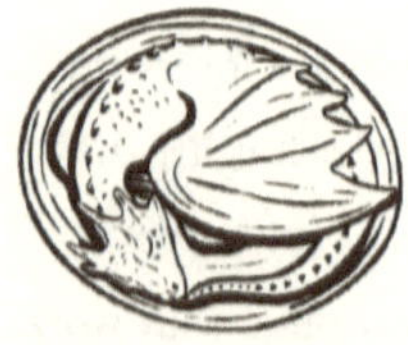

As I was pulled from the ballroom, Kaliyah's urgency was palpable as her hand firmly clasped around mine, guiding me through the maze of corridors. The clatter of our footsteps echoed off the stone walls as we passed through the bustling kitchens, the scent of spices and baked goods greeting us.

"Where are we going? Won't we be seen?" I asked.

"Kwasi ordered a shift change. That is why we have to hurry. Our window is short."

I pulled her back, putting my hand to my mouth and pointing. I watched as two auras turned a corner into our hallway. We pressed ourselves back into the alcove. I held my breath, hoping they would not look in our direction. They were engrossed in making bets on who would perish first in the Fire Challenge. The conversation got so heated that another guard called to them. They turned back to greet him before doubling back the way they had come. I exhaled the breath I was holding, but Kaliyah did not allow me a moment longer before she pulled me forward again.

We emerged into the cool night air, and there, waiting for us, was Kwasi. Kaliyah enveloped me in a tight embrace, her tears mingling with mine.

"I packed food for your journey and some supplies," she murmured, her voice choked with emotion.

I blinked back my own tears, sadness gnawing at me.

"What about my satchel?" I asked, my voice trembling.

Kaliyah's voice was stiff. I felt her gaze on mine. "Your satchel is safe and tucked away with your other supplies," she said.

I sighed with relief, and she gripped me tighter.

"Be cautious, Asha."

So, she had peeked inside. "They are why I have to leave. Please tell no one."

"I hope you know what you are doing, child. Be careful."

"I will."

Kaliyah pulled me in one final embrace. "Oh, child, I should have helped you leave years ago. But I am glad I can help you now." She rubbed my chin affectionately. "Your mother would be so proud. You have her spirit."

Kwasi stepped forward, clearing his throat. "We have to go. The guard is changing now. We have only a few more minutes."

"Thank you for everything," I said before pulling away.

As Kwasi led me to the waiting horse and cart, I couldn't help but scrunch my nose at the acrid smell that permeated from within. It was durian. The smell was unmistakable. Durian was a popular fruit among the nobility. There had to be bags of the stuff if the smell was that strong.

"In there?" I asked, raising an eyebrow.

Kwasi chuckled softly. "Actually, I need you to lie beneath them. No one would dare look closer. Come on, you've been sleeping in the dragon pits for a decade. A few durians won't hurt you."

Feeling eyes boring into me, I turned to see if I could catch a glimpse of an aura, but there was only darkness. I waited a breath before Kwasi tapped his foot impatiently. "We have to move. What are you looking at?"

"We are alone, right? You don't see anyone?"

The heel of his boot turned as he scanned the distance. He turned back toward me, placing a hand on my shoulder. "I know you are scared. I was too the first time I left. You will be fine. I will make sure of it."

Perhaps he was right. Maybe I was experiencing a bundle of nerves. This was the only home I knew. With a resigned shrug, I crouched down beneath the blankets as Kwasi motioned for the horse to start moving. The rhythmic clip-clop of hooves filled the air as we traveled in tense silence. I was really leaving. Fear gripped me before I could hastily shake it away. I'd always wanted to get out of my father's kingdom and explore the world. It was terrifying to leave everything I knew, but even more so to think about what lay waiting for me if I stayed.

"Thank you, Kwasi, for doing this," I said at last, my voice barely above a whisper.

His response was heavy, like a boulder lay on his chest. "Don't thank me, Asha. I failed you all those years ago, and then I failed our mother." I opened my mouth to protest, but he cut me off. "I did fail you both, but maybe this could begin to make up for it."

As we approached the city gate, I heard money exchanging hands. Kwasi spoke to a guard, and more money was poured into the guard's pouch.

"Greedy bastards," Kwasi mumbled as he stepped onto the cart once more.

The gates barely closed behind us when screams and shouts pierced the night air from the direction of the palace. Without hesitation, Kwasi kicked the horse forward, and we hurried away into the darkness.

"What's going on?" I cried.

"My diversion. I had to make sure they would not come after us."

"Do you think they recognized you?" I asked.

"Let's pray not, but we will make haste."

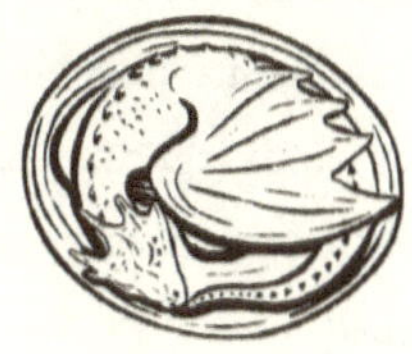

The night was heavy with the scent of wet earth, and the distant rumble of thunder echoed through the trees. Kwasi spoke to me in a short, clipped cadence, as if he were busy scanning the distance.

"We'd better go on horseback to make better ground," he whispered, his voice barely audible over the sound of the wind. "The cart just slows us down."

I nodded. Anything to get me out of the foul-smelling cart. With his guidance, I climbed onto the horse, feeling the strength of the animal beneath me. Kwasi settled in behind, his presence a reassuring weight against my back. With a gentle nudge, Kwasi urged the horse forward, and we set off into the night at a brisk pace. The rhythmic pounding of the horse's hooves matched the pounding of my heart as we raced through the darkness.

The rain began to fall, soft at first, then steadily growing in intensity until it pounded against us like a relentless drumbeat. I pulled my cloak tighter around me, seeking shelter from the downpour.

Finally, we reached the outskirts of a small town. It was the last stop before we'd have to cross the Ujuiman desert. Kwasi brought the horse to a halt, and we dismounted, seeking refuge from the storm. Kwasi's words were brief but urgent as he spoke to Lettie, the innkeeper, explaining the need for discretion. He exchanged a handful of coins with he before walking my belongings to a room.

"I will not be gone long, but I need to go back to the castle and throw them off your scent. They may be searching for you now, so lie low. The innkeeper has been paid to keep an eye on you, but do not trust anyone. Stay inside as much as possible."

I nodded, warming my hands at the fire nearby.

"You'll want to get out of those clothes and into something less conspicuous," he continued.

"I'll be fine, brother. I know how to take care of myself."

That seemed to disarm him because he said, "I suppose you've been on your own for some time."

I did not know how to respond to that. It was true, but I was uninterested in undergoing another one of his waves of guilt.

"There is one more thing I can give you," he said, putting a small piece of metal in my hand. A dagger. "I know you are not built like the rest of us, and the battlemage within you is—dormant."

I rolled my eyes. Never had I ever shown even a hint of battlemage. It was the very reason our father had hidden me away.

"But I beg of you. If you are in danger, please use this. I pray you will not have to."

"Don't worry, brother," I said in what I hoped was a comforting tone. "I will stay out of sight."

CHAPTER TEN

Adriel

Outside the grand chamber, my mind was in turmoil. I felt torn between meeting the emperor and looking for the dragon eggs. The interaction with Princess Asha lingered like a forgotten song. It was an infuriating distraction. Though I had Chato, one of my Guardians, watching her movements, that provided me little comfort. I needed to focus, to steel my resolve for what needed to be done to secure Wiyotak's future.

At last, the summons came. A guard escorted us to the twelve-foot double doors that required four men to pull open. I took in the marble floors and the onyx steps that ascended to the throne where Emperor Idris sat. I kneeled before him, feeling the weight of his piercing gaze as it bore into me. Drawing myself upright, I squared my broad shoulders and stood tall.

"Your Eminence," I began, my voice surprisingly steady. "I am Adriel, brother to the King of Wiyotak, and I am deeply honored to stand in your presence."

The monarch's once-powerful frame was now hunched with age, his long white beard reaching down to his chest, and wrinkles etched deep into his face. The emperor's response was indifferent, casting a cloud over my hopes to impress him. I pressed on nonetheless, my words measured.

Elan moved from behind a curtain to stand next to his father. He leaned to whisper in the emperor's ear before sending a cruel smirk my way.

"The emperor wishes to know why you are here and not with your king. Does he not think our emperor deserves our respect?"

I sucked in a breath, pressing my lips tightly together. The truth was, Enapay had wanted to come himself, but I had persuaded him otherwise. Diplomacy was not his strength, and his presence here would likely have ended in disaster, possibly with his head parted from his shoulders.

"Wiyotak has long been an ally to Ujuima. My king means no disrespect. On the contrary, he would like to strengthen our alliance."

Elan scoffed in disbelief. "And what could you offer us in the form of an alliance?"

I'd kept my eyes on the emperor, who had leaned in with interest. There couldn't be a better time.

I pulled a scroll out of my pocket and unfurled it. "King Enapay Foxtrail of Wiyotak, first of his name, proposes an engagement between himself and Princess Asha Osei. As a gesture of goodwill, we offer a dowry of one thousand tons of dracite."

"A marriage proposal?" the emperor rasped before doubling over in a violent coughing fit. His personal attendants rushed to his side, offering a silk handkerchief and a golden bowl to catch the blood splattering from his lips. Tinges of red speckled the crisp handkerchief.

"Unless you plan to marry one of my sons, I suggest you prove yourself in the Fire Challenge like everyone else."

That is what I'd expected after hearing her hand was to be the prize of this year's challenge. "If I were to emerge victorious in the Fire Challenge," I ventured cautiously, "I would wish my brother to wed her."

Prince Elan's laughter cut through the chatter like a knife, his mocking tone the opposite of the coolness from the emperor. "King Enapay and Princess Asha? What a laughable notion!" he sneered, his words dripping with disdain. "As if a king would *want* to marry damaged goods."

I felt a surge of anger at his callous words, my fists clenching involuntarily at my sides. My jaw set in a tense line as I struggled to maintain my composure.

"Surely being an unseer does not make her damaged goods," I asserted. I was taking a chance; I knew it. It was one thing for Elan to say it, but for me to say out loud that an Osei was less than warrior-ready could end badly.

The widening of their eyes told me I had made a grave misstep. "In Wiyotak," I explained carefully, "those with such conditions are revered and cared for, not cast aside."

A heavy silence fell over the hall as my words sank in. Prince Elan's expression shifted rapidly, first a sneer of disdainful laughter, then disbelief, and finally, unbridled rage.

"The blind cannot fight," he spat, his tone dripping with contempt. "And if you cannot fight, you serve no purpose in our society. It appears your people have lost their way," he taunted, his words laced with open disdain. "A man does not want a wife who cannot even see his cock."

I bristled at his dismissal, my temper flaring at the memory of him pushing the princess down the stairwell like a coward. My mind screamed to stop speaking, but my mouth could not stay silent.

"It depends on the cock. I could imagine a man with . . . considerably less to offer, for example," I said, holding his gaze, "might find it quite advantageous."

Elan stepped forward, unbridled rage seething from his pores. Now I had done it. I had lost my goodwill, playing right into Elan's hands. I forced myself to remain outwardly calm despite the anger boiling beneath the surface.

Guardian Winnow stepped forward and cleared his throat. "Our apologies, Prince Elan. We meant no offense to you. We are just so *eager* to strengthen our ties to Ujuima. Under King Enapay's rule, we have successfully increased crop production, and we are eager to share that with you by establishing trade in the Ujuima markets."

The emperor held up a hand to Winnow, signaling him to stop speaking. "This conversation bores me."

He turned his attention back to me. His expression remained impassive, his silence stretching between us like an unbridgeable chasm. And then, with a suddenness that caught me off guard, he offered a proposition of his own.

"Or perhaps," he suggested, his voice resonating with a quiet authority, "there is another path you could consider. Should you emerge triumphant in the Fire Challenge, *you* could replace your brother as King of Wiyotak and marry the princess."

His words hung heavy in the air, their implications echoing through the chamber with a gravity that left me reeling. I felt Winnow's stare bearing into my back as he no doubt contemplated how he would wield the emperor's words against me to my brother. I decided to tread more carefully.

"Thank you for seeing me as worthy, Your Eminence, but I am eternally loyal to my brother. He is the true King of Wiyotak, and I have no desire to rule . . . or wed."

Emperor Idris carried a whisper of a smile on his lips, very aware of the upheaval he had caused and was clearly enjoying it. It was short-lived because he doubled over to cough again, and this time, Prince Elan came to his side.

"You must rest, Father," he said with thinly veiled disgust.

Weakness, even if it came from the age of a family member, was not accepted in Ujuima and the five kingdoms. I would expect nothing less from any prince watching his father's health deteriorate. If he were not the emperor, but someone's father, I might have felt sorry for him. But remembering what Idris had cost the people of Wiyotak, I felt nothing.

Without warning, the emperor fell over in his seat, a strangled gasp escaping his lips as he clutched at his chest. My heart leaped into my throat as I watched in horror as blood began to seep from his eyes and mouth, staining his once-proud visage with a sickly crimson hue.

Elan held his father upright. "Help him!" he yelled to the servants nearby.

The servants scurried to the emperor's aid. I watched, uncertain of what to do, and decided to do nothing. The prince examined the handkerchief the emperor held, splotched with blood. He sniffed it and grimaced.

"Poison!" Prince Elan's voice cut through the chaos like a thunderclap, his words ringing out with a chilling clarity that sent shivers down my spine. "Someone has poisoned the emperor!"

I looked around the room, taking stock of our exits. This was not good.

"Shut the gates to the city!" Elan commanded, his voice ringing out with authority. His eyes leveled menacingly at me. "*You* did this; I know it."

The weight of his words hit us, filling the throne room with a chilling uncertainty. In that moment, I felt that the delicate balance of power had shifted, and we were witnessing the precipice of change. As I looked into the eyes of my Guardians, I saw the same realization mirrored back at me—a silent acknowledgment of the uncertain path that awaited us all. I pulled my sword out and indicated for the other Guardians to do the same. We needed to survive this moment. Answers to what had just happened would have to wait. I cursed as I realized the dragon eggs might be lost to me forever.

"Arrest them!" Elan cried.

As the guards moved to carry out Prince Elan's orders, I felt a surge of defiance rising within me. I could not stand idly while I was accused of this crime without Elan's word. I stepped forward, my voice ringing out clear and commanding.

"Stand down," I said, my words cutting through the melee. "We will not be arrested like common criminals. We will find the truth behind the emperor's death, and those responsible will answer for their crimes."

My heart pounded in my chest as I locked eyes with Prince Elan, his expression a mask of fury and suspicion. But I did not waver. I would protect those under my charge, whatever the cost.

As the standoff unfolded, I braced myself for the inevitable confrontation, knowing the fate of the kingdom hung in the balance, when suddenly a deafening roar echoed through the castle walls. My stomach roiled at the sound, every instinct screaming at me to take cover, to flee from whatever unseen threat lurked beyond.

Without hesitation, I motioned for my men to move out of the throne room and back into the main hall crowded with guests peering out the nearest windows into the darkness.

I searched the ballroom frantically for Asha. She was no longer sitting at her table. A hand fell on my back, and I whirled around. It was Kitchi.

"Where is she?" I demanded.

Kitchi pulled me away from the swarm of people. "Chato just returned. One of her servants took her away. They were in a hurry. I watched her get in a cart headed to the gates of the castle. He would have followed, but shouts from in here made the guards push everyone inside. She's gone."

"What is going on in there?" she asked, pulling me out of my thoughts.

"The emperor is dead," I said, my voice barely above a whisper. "And Prince Elan has accused us. We need to get out of here." Even as the words left my lips, they felt surreal, as if I were speaking of events from a distant dream rather than the stark reality that now confronted us.

I glanced out of the window, and there, looming against the castle, was a sight that froze me in place—a massive silhouette, its form obscured by shadows yet unmistakably monstrous in its proportions. A chill swept through me as I realized several dragons were roaming free outside the castle, one of which I recognized from within the dragon pits. These did not appear to be well-trained dragons for battle, nor did they seem to be checked by anyone. Their growls swept through the air.

"Fire and Ash," Kitchi breathed beside me, her voice filled with a mixture of awe and terror. "How did they get out?"

I had no answer to give her. I just knew we needed to move quickly if we were going to find Princess Asha.

CHAPTER ELEVEN

Asha

I sat by the window, listening to the sounds of horses and the heavy footsteps of warriors from Ujuima. The past three days had been torturous as I awaited Kwasi's return. I felt the weight of uncertainty pressing down on me like a heavy stone as I thought about my next move. I could not stay here forever. It was a wonder I hadn't been caught. I had done my best to tend the dragon eggs on my own, keeping them close to the warmth of the fire. I cradled them in my lap as I sang softly to them, hoping to offer some measure of comfort. But as the hours stretched on and Kwasi remained absent, I couldn't shake the growing sense of unease. I knew I couldn't stay here much longer—not with the ever-present threat of discovery looming over me like a dark cloud. My father would not rest until he found me; of that I was certain. As much as he detested me, he hated being defied even more.

As I contemplated my next steps, a wave of apprehension washed over me. How would I make it out of here without someone to guide me? How would I navigate the world beyond these walls, fraught with danger and uncertainty? I took a deep breath, trying to push aside the doubts that threatened to overwhelm me. I couldn't afford to dwell on my fears, not now. I needed to focus on finding a way out, on escaping this tinderbox of a hiding place before it went up in flames.

And what of this dragon, the father of the eggs? Where was he, and how was I to find him, or him find me? I packed up my things and resolved to leave today. I left behind most of what Kaliyah had sent with me, wearing only the clothes on my back and a pack that concealed the eggs, a money pouch, and a few essential items. I grabbed my walking staff and made my way down to the dining hall.

As I approached, the sounds of laughter and chatter filled the air. The annual Fire Challenge would have already begun, and the inn was bursting with patrons. My heart raced as I thought about Ekon competing. I prayed he would survive. I could not face the alternative.

I holed up in a corner of the inn, attempting to shrink into the shadows to evade prying eyes. Still, the inn offered a temporary reprieve from the events of the past couple of days. I heard the innkeeper's light feet approach my table with a steaming bowl of beef stew. Her name was Lettie, and she had a kind voice. She set the bowl beside me but did not leave right away.

"I was wondering if you were coming down today. I saved some stew for you, but I had to guard it with my life from all of these travelers."

I bit into the soft potatoes, savoring the buttery texture.

"Is there any word about the festival?" I asked, hoping I didn't sound too interested. "Has the Fire Challenge started?"

"That's the thing. The rumor is they haven't started."

I choked on the piece of beef. Lettie gave me a towel and patted my back.

"Sorry," I rasped.

"I knew I'd put a bit too many chilies in there. I don't like them myself, but they are popular around here."

My coughing had nothing to do with her chilies, but I was glad they gave me cover. "Why haven't they started?" I asked.

Lettie sighed. "No one knows. That is why everyone is here. They are waiting for the gates to open."

Kwasi must not be able to leave. I racked my brain, trying to think of what could be important enough to delay the festival. Surely it wasn't me. Prize or not, I was not important enough to sideline a well-timed event that should be concluding in two more days. Something must have happened—an attack, perhaps.

"Are you leaving then?" Lettie inquired gently, pulling me from my thoughts.

I had to leave now. If, for some reason, my absence was part of the delay, I had already wasted so much time.

I nodded. "My brother has not returned," I admitted, my voice tinged with worry. "I am concerned about him, but I know I need to continue on my journey."

"And where is that?" she asked, her voice laced with disappointment.

I had no idea, I thought as I clung to my satchel.

"North," I managed to say. "But truthfully, I am wary of traveling alone. Do you happen to know of anyone traveling in that direction?"

"Let me ask around," she offered, her voice filled with reassurance. "With so many travelers today, I am sure there is someone."

Gratitude flooded through me at her offer of assistance. "I would be so grateful." I smiled as she bustled away. Perhaps there was hope after all.

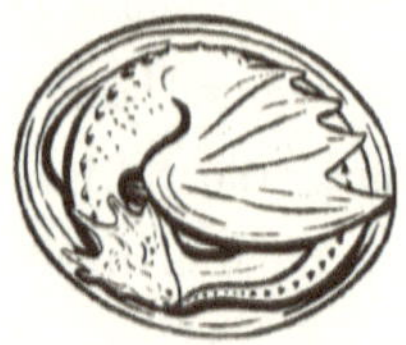

It was nearly midday when she returned to introduce me to a married couple. "This is Jandrey and his wife, Teena. They are newlyweds and on their way to make a new start in Firepeak. They would love to give you a ride."

"My name is Ana," I said smoothly, remembering the name Kwasi had introduced me under. "Are you sure I would not be too much trouble? It sounds like I would be interrupting your honeymoon."

Teena giggled and said, "No trouble at all. I've never been out this way, so we plan to make many stops and enjoy the sights."

My smile faltered slightly. "I don't know if you can tell, but my sight is challenged. I can manage my own affairs, but I thought you should know. Is that okay?"

Jandrey spoke up then. "I have known Lettie for a long time, and she has always been good to us. Any friend of hers is a friend to us."

My chest eased a bit as a wave of relief washed over me. "When are you leaving?" I asked.

"In a few minutes, actually. Do you think you can be ready?"

I patted my satchel. "I am ready." As I stood by the side of the dusty road, clutching my satchel tightly to my chest, a sense of apprehension mingled with hope fluttered in my chest. Jandrey and Teena graciously offered to let me sit inside their stagecoach.

As I approached the coach, Jandrey extended a hand to assist me, his touch gentle and reassuring. "Allow me to take your satchel, miss," he offered politely.

I hesitated for a moment, my fingers tightening around the worn leather strap of my bag. Though Jandrey seemed trustworthy, I felt surprisingly territorial over the eggs.

"Thank you, but I'll hold on to it," I replied softly.

Teena climbed into the stagecoach beside me, her voice filled with excitement for the journey ahead. I could hear Jandrey closing the door and the unmistakable sound of a lock clicking. A pang of unease prickled at the edges of my mind as the click of the lock echoed in the confined space.

I forced a smile, pushing aside my doubts as I settled into the cramped carriage. This was the smart move, I reassured myself. There was no way I could make my way around by myself.

The rhythmic clop of hooves against the sand road echoed in my ears as we set off. As we sat in the carriage, Teena asked, "So, where are you from originally?"

"Entioch," I responded.

"Entioch?" she said with a pause. "I've heard of their lanterns. Isn't Entioch famous for the lanterns that glow at night?"

"That is us," I said smoothly. "You must make it there if you haven't been.

"What brings you to Ujuima?"

"I have always wanted to attend the Fire Festival. I have heard such wonderful things."

"Why aren't you there?"

"I could not get in," I lied. "They turned me away at the gates. I decided I'd experienced enough. Plus, I heard it would be overly crowded."

The sound of a paper fan opening greeted my ears as cool air wafted my way periodically. "Yes, the crowds there are unbearable. You are not missing anything."

My hand tightened slightly on my walking staff. I hoped they had not noticed. Hadn't she said she had never been out this way before?

To fill the silence and buy myself time to think, I turned the conversation back to her. "You must be from Wiyotak?"

"Hmm, oh yes."

"I have never been there," I said, placing my hand on the dagger underneath my cloak, unsure what I was going to do with it. "What is it like?"

"Oh, you know, hot and so, so boring. I'm sure Entioch is much prettier."

"Nothing beats our sandy beaches. What part of Wiyotak? The north or the south province? I heard both are great."

"Oh, um, the south. A bunch of country folk. Nothing fancy."

My heart raced, beating so loudly it nearly drowned out the sound of hooves hitting the road.

The stagecoach came to an abrupt halt. My chest tightened as I tried to gauge why.

"Oh, hell, Teena. Give it up!" Jandrey called. "She knows. Grab her bag."

"Gladly. I loathe small talk." Teena's voice, which was once bubbly and fun, was now husky.

My heart pounded as she reached for me. I lifted my walking staff and tripped her before launching myself against the carriage door. It was locked.

"The sooner you give in, the easier this will be," Jandrey said as he rounded toward us.

I pulled on the coach desperately, which gave Teena time to jump on my back. My immediate worry was for the dragon eggs. They had layers of protection, but a hard fall could crush them. Teena pulled at the satchel, and I whipped around with my dagger pulled out.

"Get back!" I called.

Teena paused. "Give it over. The satchel alone will get us a good price. Is that real leather? Between that and your staff, I can tell you come from a good family. What are you hiding in the satchel, girl?"

I felt the door shift behind me, and I fell back, arms around my shoulders. I kicked my legs, arching my back.

"Let me go!" I yelled.

"Calm down, Ana, or whatever your name is," Jandrey said as he held onto me. "You are going to fetch us a good price on the black market. There are plenty of men who would pay handsomely for a woman of wealth. We just can't mark you up too badly."

"I thought you were friends of Lettie's!"

Teena chuckled. "We are. She reached out to us as soon as you arrived unchaperoned. Easy money. Now let's see what's in that bag."

She unbuckled it from my side and kicked. I lashed out to no avail. Jandrey had me pinned against him. I heard the top flap being pulled open and her hands rustling through it. I yelled helplessly.

Teena was silent for a second and then gasped, "Jandrey! You have to see this."

"Hold on!" he said as he struggled to secure me. As I fought against the ropes that bound my wrists, panic clawed at the edges of my mind, threatening to overwhelm me.

Teena and Jandrey, the couple I had foolishly trusted, stood before me, their auras bearing down. His hands moved swiftly, securing the knots with practiced precision as I writhed against my restraints, the coarse fibers biting into my skin.

"No! We don't need her. She has . . ."

I did not hear the rest of it because a sudden commotion shattered the silence hanging in the air. The sound of approaching footsteps echoed along the road, accompanied by the unmistakable clash of weapons and urgent voices raised in alarm.

I redoubled my efforts to break free from the bonds holding me captive, my muscles straining against the unforgiving restraints.

"Who are you?" Jandrey asked. "We are just a newlywed couple traveling north."

A familiar voice answered. "And you happen to have a girl tied up alongside the road. I've never been married, so you'll have to let me know how a third figures in."

The clash of swords continued until I heard a cry, then a gurgle.

"No!" Teena yelled.

Feet pounded the ground, and once again, I heard steel meet flesh and then silence.

A pair of delicate hands reached for me, their touch surprisingly gentle.

Before I could let out a scream, a soft voice whispered, "You're okay." The reassurance was enough to make me pause, though my heart still raced.

She began to cut through the thick rope around me. I arched in pain, realizing the restraints had cut off blood flow. I managed to lift my head. My fingers trembled as I brushed away strands of hair that clung to my sweaty forehead.

"That's what they told me," I replied, my voice tinged with both anger and relief. I rubbed at the angry indentations on my wrists, wincing as the skin burned under my touch.

As my legs gave out, I felt large hands catch me and hold me steady. "I see you have not lost your recklessness," the familiar voice said. "I don't mind catching you, but there has to be a better way for us to meet." Gone was the humor we'd shared a few nights ago, replaced with a clipped and almost annoyed voice as he helped me stand.

"So, you've come to take me back?" I said, dusting off my skirts. "I won't go."

That made him chuckle. "And you believe you are in a position to be demanding anything?"

"I am your princess," I said with more conviction than I felt.

"Well, as much goodwill as we would earn turning you over to your brother, I don't think I will."

That surprised me. So, he wasn't here to bring me back. Why, then, had he intervened?

"Could you please retrieve my satchel?" I asked, holding out my hand. My fingers grasped the familiar smooth oak of my walking staff being placed there.

"I'm afraid I cannot," he said.

"I command you to hand it over," I demanded.

He stepped forward and gently pushed the hair from my face. "I'm afraid I cannot," he repeated. "I will not return you to Ujuima just yet, but you are coming with us to Wiyotak."

My mouth widened in surprise. "So, am I to replace one captor with another?"

He was silent for a moment before replying, "If you choose to see it that way. I'd prefer not to tie you up, but that is entirely up to you. What will it be?"

My foot was wild and restless, tapping with frustration and, if I was being honest, fear. "You know this is treason. You know what my father will do to you." Actually, I was not sure my father would care. Likely, his pride would be more wounded than his concern for his daughter.

Silence fell around us. It was as if everyone held their breath. "You have not heard then?" he said, clearing his throat. "I am sorry to be the one to tell you this, but the emperor has died."

The air seemed to leave my body as I stumbled back in shock. Dead. The man who had ordered me beaten and exiled from the palace was now gone. He'd mistreated my mother, ignored his sons, and refrained from showing me even an ounce of affection, and yet, sadness clung to me like I was drowning, dragged down with every excruciating breath. I'd wished him dead, at my own hands even, and now he was. The elation I'd always imagined did not appear.

Both of my parents were dead. No wonder Kwasi had not returned. He must have been caught up in it all. "How did he die?" I croaked.

There was silence, and feet shuffling around me. "It is believed that he was poisoned," he finally said.

"By whom?"

"There are many suspects. Even you, with your absence."

"Me?" I asked incredulously.

"Elan has pointed the finger at everyone."

A chill ran through me as I realized that Elan would be emperor. Now there was nothing to hold him back from his violent proclivities.

"We must go," the man said.

"And my satchel?"

"I will keep the contents safe. Come," he said.

He placed his hands around my waist and settled me on a horse. To my horror, I felt him climb up behind me. I had ridden with others before, most recently my brother. But his hard body behind me did not feel like my brother's. Suddenly, every move we made against each other felt intimate.

"Why are we going to Wiyotak?"

His grip around my waist tightened slightly.

"My brother, King Enapay, plans to marry you."

My eyebrow arched. "Brother?" It was clicking into place now, even Ekon's anger at the cloak I wore at the ball. "You are War Chief Adriel Foxtrail then?" I asked, though I knew I was right.

"You know of me, then. That is surprising."

"Surprising that I would know all the royal families in the five kingdoms?" I asked. When he did not answer, I sighed heavily. I had exchanged one shackle for another.

CHAPTER TWELVE

Asha

"I don't need your help," I snapped, shoving his hands away as he reached to assist me off the horse.

"As you wish," Adriel said, stepping back. "Kitchi will take you from here. Do not leave her sight."

I seethed. After learning he was stealing the eggs and forcing me into an arranged marriage, my mood had soured considerably. Who did he think he was, and why did he think Elan would stand for this? A thread of doubt crept in. Would Elan stand for this?

I attempted to dismount the horse on my own, but it bucked, and I went flying into the mud. Kitchi's warm hands circled my torso, and I instinctively pushed them away. I moved in the direction of the horse.

"I wouldn't," Kitchi said. "That horse has a wild streak. She likes only Adriel. I've told him many times to get rid of the beast."

I shushed her. "She can hear you, you know," I said as I continued my approach. "What is her name?"

"Beast," she said as if it were obvious.

I shook my head. "Well, that won't do."

I hummed to the horse as it whinnied and bucked. Finally, she took notice of me and bumped her head angrily into my chest. I held my hands out patiently. Beast was stubborn, but after some time, I was rewarded with her prickly-whiskered nose nudging at my palms.

"I am so sorry, I don't have any treats, girl. I will find you some. Do you like apples?"

She snorted at that, seeming to shake her head against my hands. "What about carrots?"

Again, she shook her head and seemed agitated.

"Chocolate?" I asked, trying to be funny. But Beast settled down and gently nudged her nose into my palm. "Ah. Is that it, girl? Do you like sweets?"

She nodded in appreciation.

"Me too. Perhaps we could find some sugar cubes," I whispered. "What is your name, sweet girl?"

I stood listening and waiting for her aura to speak to me.

"Willow?" The horse shook her mane. "Beauty?" She snorted.

She allowed me to rub her neck, whinnying affectionately. Finally, the name came to me, and I laughed.

"Is it Candy?" I whispered. She nudged her nose against my forehead and licked my cheek with approval.

Kitchi snorted with laughter. "Candy? Oh, wait until our war chief hears this." I heard the loud crack of her hand against her body as she laughed. "Come on. I have my orders to get you settled."

I felt the coolness as the sun dipped low in the sky. It had been relentlessly hot all day, and the temperature would be below freezing tonight. My feet sank into the sand as Kitchi led me through the camp, where weary Guardians began nailing stakes into the ground to erect makeshift tents.

My muscles ached from hours of riding, and it felt like my skin was caked with a thin layer of sand that felt as if it would never wash away. I had learned to ride as a child along with my brothers, but found little use for it once I worked in the dragon pits. I'd never left Ujuima until now. Kwasi was the one who went on long, elaborate missions.

I trailed behind Kitchi into our tent. She guided me through the different areas to help me get my bearings. I could tell the blankets and other essential items were weathered from countless journeys, but they would serve us well tonight.

"Here we are," she said. "Make yourself comfortable."

Kitchi busied herself with tending to the needs of the camp. She worked nearby, never going more than a few feet away. That was going to make escaping very difficult, especially if I was going to have to find Adriel's tent to steal back the dragon eggs.

"So, Kitchi," I began, attempting to break the silence between us. "How long have you been a Guardian?"

"I've wanted to be a Guardian all my life. I entered the same year as our war chief did. Although he was not much when I met him," she laughed, but there was a note of respect and admiration in her voice.

"Tell me about him."

She groaned. "I don't know if you've noticed, but Adriel is easily pissed off, and I much prefer that be directed at you than me. You can ask him yourself if you are curious."

I nodded. "Fair enough."

I listened to Kitchi very efficiently unrolling her pack to begin setting up sleeping pallets for both of us. Her pack exuded an earthy scent of dried herbs and cured meat.

"I know this is probably not what you are used to, but this is as good as it gets until we get to Wiyotak."

"This is better than what I am used to."

Kitchi paused, then said, "You do not have to pretend on my account. You princesses get the finest things. It is nothing to be ashamed of. I saw your castle."

"I did not live in the castle," I whispered.

"Of course you did. Where else would a princess live?" she said. I heard a piece of wood being lifted to make a base for our fire.

I grabbed small sticks and dry grass around me and offered them to her. She paused as I handed over my bundle.

"I lived in the dragon pits," I explained. "It is much like camping, as my quarters were minimal. Living in the desert means winters are mild, but the drop in temperature at night made it necessary for me to learn how to build my own fires, especially if the dragons did not want to share space." Admittedly, I usually was able to find one who did, but I kept that to myself.

Kitchi dropped the kindling in her hand and sat down. "I am sorry. You are going to have to explain this. Come again? Explain to me how an Osei is living in the dragon pits?"

"I was not favored," I said simply. I did not have the emotional capacity to say more. No need to get into the full truth of it. "I just bring it up so you don't worry about my comfort."

"Right. Well, I know a thing or two about having shitty parents. Mine kicked me out at fifteen. That is why I joined the Guardians."

I noted the tension in her voice. "I am sorry. No one should be treated that way because of who they love." Kitchi was silent for a beat. It was so long that I finally said, "I'm sorry. Did I offend you?"

"No," she said quickly. "I am just wondering who told you that. One of the other Guardians?"

I shook my head. "No. Sometimes I can just sense these things. It is hard to control at times." I reached out to her, and she allowed me to take her hand. "I can see people's auras, and yours shines brightly; only you try to dull it to please others."

She snatched her hand from my grip. "That's enough of reading my . . . aura. I revoke my permission." I released her hand and waited for the questions that were sure to come next. "Can you do that with anyone?"

"Nearly. Some are more defined than others."

"Wait until Adriel hears about this. I bet his is all dark and moody."

I said nothing. Adriel's aura was one I had not unraveled yet. In truth, I could not see it clearly.

"Let's go over some rules," Kitchi said after getting the fire going. "I am in charge of you, and I take that role very seriously. If you don't attempt to run away, you can remain unbound. However, if you cross me and even think about running away, things will get very unpleasant for you. Is that understood?"

I nodded in affirmation. "I understand."

"Good!" she clapped her hands. "What do you like to eat? I have rabbit or rabbit."

I chuckled. "Rabbit will be fine."

She got to work. I flinched as I heard her separating the skin from the meat. That was always my least favorite part. I warmed my hands by the fire, continuing to listen as her hands shuffled pots and other utensils.

"Can I help?"

"Can you chop vegetables? I have a couple of yams I've been meaning to roast."

"You're in luck. I am a master of yams."

She shuffled some things and handed me two large tuberous vegetables. She hesitated a beat before handing me her knife. "You're not going to cut yourself, right? That knife is sharp."

"I can manage," I said before throwing myself into finely chopping the vegetables. "Your king," I said, "my soon-to-be husband, what is he like?"

"Enapay?" I noticed a slight inflection in her voice. "He's Adriel's brother."

"I gathered that. Do you think he will be a kind husband?"

She paused long enough for me to understand the answer was no. "He's like most rulers, I would guess. You won't have long to wait to form your own opinion."

I nodded at her non-answer. "Have you ever spoken to her again?" I asked.

I felt her sharp gaze shift to me. "Who?"

"The woman with the pink hair. The one your parents forbade you to see."

"How are you doing that? You can see all that from my aura?"

"I just see glimpses, but yes," I said.

Her voice changed as if she were hunched over. "She has chosen another. I suppose I cannot blame her. We have not talked since I joined the Guardians. I wasn't allowed to at first per the covenants, but when I got out to look for her, she had already moved on. I cannot blame her. It's not meant to be, I suppose. Right?"

I heard the faintest glimmer of hope in her voice. I shrugged. "I cannot tell the future, I'm afraid. If I could, you would never have found me," I said with a wry smile.

"Right. Can you see if this rabbit will ever get done?" she asked, turning back to the fire nonchalantly. I heard the faint rustle of her sleeve brushing against her cheek, and a hitching breath she tried to stifle. She was crying, though she didn't want me to know.

Chapter Thirteen

Adriel

I awoke with a start, my breath coming in ragged gasps as remnants of dreams lingered like a sticky web. I shook desert sand out of my hair, and it tumbled down in waves, coating every surface. Fire and ash. I could not wait until the desert released its hold and forus to make it to the crystal blue shores of Wiyotak. I never wanted to see the desert again. I dragged a hand across my sand-caked face, willing the remnants of sleep to fade away as I rose from my makeshift bed.

Outside, the world was still painted in twilight, but dawn was not far away. I walked around the perimeter of the camp, ensuring those on watch were still alert, before making my way to the edge of the camp, seeking the quiet of the morning. We'd need to keep our pace. There was no water this far south of the desert, which meant we would need to be careful with our water reserves.

In my hands rested one of the dragon eggs, its shell smooth and cool to the touch, and the same blue as the kailay seashells that dotted the Wiyotakin shore. As soon as they came into my care, I realized I had no earthly idea how to keep them alive. What was I supposed to do with them? I desperately wished I were back home where I could raid the library. There had to be an old text somewhere detailing how to care for and successfully hatch them.

Lost in thought, I decided to check on Kitchi and our captive. For such a pretty thing, she'd turned out to be a thorn in my side. My mind drifted to how the men laughed at learning how she had managed to turn my horse against me with nothing but a whispered command. Kitchi had spun tales about auras and energy. I'd loudly dismissed them as nonsense, but the men continued to talk. It was a wonder how hardened Guardians could fall for such parlor tricks. I was not so easily fooled.

I debated going to the mess tent, but decided I'd better check on the princess before I did. I nestled the eggs inside my traveling chest for safekeeping and clicked the lock closed before I made my way to their tent. Peering inside, I found Kitchi passed out in front of the tent door. Peering in further, Asha's bed was rumpled but empty.

"Kitchi!" I yelled, stirring her awake. I looked around the tent furiously. "Kitchi! I gave you one job."

She stood alert, her sword in hand, as all Guardians were trained to do when awoken from sleep.

Adrenaline coursed through my body, jolting me awake far better than any cup of coffee could. I hurried through the camp, my steps quickening with each passing moment. Asha was nowhere to be found. Panic clawed at me as I searched frantically, calling out her name into the darkness. It was bad enough that she was in our company without her brother's blessing; it was quite another to have her lost or worse under my watch.

Kitchi was by my side, her expression mirroring my own sense of urgency. Together, we combed through the camp, our eyes scanning the shadows for any sign of her. Where could she have gone?

It was only when we reached the very center of the camp that we found her, surrounded by a group of Guardians. Relief flooded me at the sight of her, quickly followed by frustration. What was she doing out here in the open so early in the morning?

As we approached, one of my Guardians stepped forward, a sheepish expression on his face. "I'm sorry, war chief," he began, his voice tinged with embarrassment. "We heard that the girl could see auras, and, well, we all wanted to have ours read."

"Read?" I blinked in disbelief, my mind struggling to process the absurdity of the situation. "She is not a fucking fortune teller. Get back to your posts!"

I turned to glare at her and frowned when I was met with a small smile playing at the corners of her lips. That glint of amusement quickly left her eyes at the sound of my voice. To my surprise, she did not flinch as so many did when I had lost my temper.

She nodded to the Guardian beside her and said, "I'm sorry, Kanen. I will finish telling you about your future bride another time. Please congratulate her for me."

"Princess," I said with exasperation. "What are you doing? What is the meaning of this?"

She shrugged nonchalantly."I couldn't sleep," she admitted, her tone light.

Kitchi stared down at her feet, looking guilty as sin. "I might have told some of the Guardians what she can do. How was I to know word would spread so fast?"

"Kitchi,"I began rounding on her, "if you were not you, I'd have you on latrine duty."

Her lips tensed as if she held something back, but she wisely kept whatever sharp words she had for me at bay.

"My apologies, war chief." She bowed before strutting off, leaving me and the princess alone. I inwardly sighed, knowing she would give me a piece of her mind when there were no onlookers.

Asha leaned back to stretch. "Well, you sure know how to clear a room."

"You do not go without your chaperone," I gritted out. "Do I make myself clear?"

She wiped the sand off her tunic and stood. "How are the dragon eggs doing?"

I leaped to her side, throwing my hand over her mouth. I looked around and sighed in relief that we appeared to be truly alone.

"Do not speak of them out loud, ever. It could be the end of both our lives," I whispered furiously.

"You still haven't answered my question."

I rolled my eyes to the heavens at that. "They aren't scrambled as of yet."

"That isn't funny," she scowled.

My eyebrows rose. "Neither are you running off without Kitchi."

"I demand to see them."

"Well, unfortunately for you, I am not keen to grant favors to women who do not obey my authority."

Her body recoiled as if I had slapped her. The movement was subtle, but I was well-trained in tracking body language. She was afraid.

I softened my tone slightly as I cleared my throat. "Come on then. Since most of the Guardians are up, we should be on our way before the heat of the day is upon us."

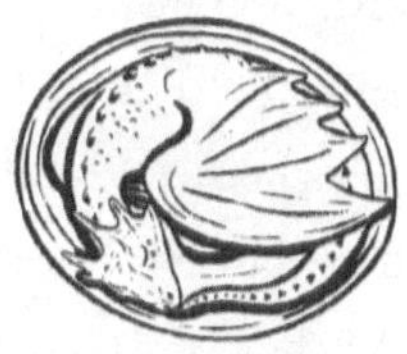

"What have you done to my horse?" I grumbled.

I had made every attempt to put a saddle on Beast, and every time she walked backward and whinnied. She was a stubborn creature for sure, but she tended to tolerate me well, until today.

The princess sat on a rock, with a wistful smile playing on her face. "Do you happen to have any Suklaat cubes?"

"How far do you think Suklaat would have lasted in the desert?" I asked incredulously, pulling on Beast once more.

"Anything sweet, then?"

"No. I can't have Beast getting fat on me. She has to be lean for battle."

Beast huffed, yanking the reins out of my hands before walking toward Asha. I stood baffled as my horse nudged Asha's hand with her nose. The princess bent her head down, speaking so quietly that I could not make out the words.

She looked up suddenly and said, "Her name is Candy, and she does not appreciate your comments about her weight."

"She's a damned horse!" I yelled, throwing down the saddle.

The princess held out her hands. "Let me."

I watched her skeptically as she shouldered the heavy saddle and placed it on top of Beast, and to my amazement, she allowed her to. Once the saddle was secure, she pulled herself up top without assistance, and the horse allowed her without a fuss.

I shook my head at Beast. "You are supposed to be loyal to me, you know," I said as I approached. Beast snorted before side-stepping me.

"Am I not to ride my own horse?" I demanded.

Asha leaned down as if to whisper in Beast's ear. I vaguely wondered if there was any truth to Kitchi's words about auras or a prank put on by the other Guardians. I'd make them all pay if it were the latter. If it were the former, I was not sure what that would mean.

Asha reached into her pocket and pulled out some sugar-coated dates. She placed them in her palm and held them out to me.

"What am I to do with this?" I demanded.

She sighed in exasperation. "Feed them to her and then apologize."

I almost lost my temper again at the thought, but I noted the tension that had crept into Princess Asha's shoulders. I wondered about the treatment she'd gotten at the palace. Was it just Elan who was cruel, or were there others?

I looked around and noted that the eyes of my men were upon us. I could not let this girl steal my horse from me while they watched. I'd never hear the end of it.

"Fine," I said through clenched teeth.

I opened my palm, and Beast just stared at the dates. I moved closer, but again, the horse made no move to consume them. Asha cleared her throat. I sighed.

"Beast—I mean Candy. Candy, I am very sorry I called you fat. You are a very trim horse. Will you please eat these damned dates?"

Candy did not respond immediately, but after a few moments, she relented and consumed the dates in one lick. I curled my hands in disgust, hearing barely contained laughter from behind me. I groaned. Too late. Somehow, this woman had managed to get the upper hand with both my horse and my men.

Satisfied, Beast—I mean, Candy—allowed me to get in the saddle. I settled one hand on Asha's hip and another on the reins.

"Let's go. We have already wasted enough time."

CHAPTER FOURTEEN

Asha

I had to admit that I was highly entertained by Candy and her antics. I'd taken pity on him and promised Candy that if she behaved for him, I would sneak her an extra treat. She complied, though she made him sweat for it.

As nice as that distraction was, now we were back on our journey toward an unsanctioned marriage between me and the King of Wiyotak. Dread filled my heart thinking about Kitchi's words. She had said just enough for me to know that being married to Enapay would not improve my situation. I needed to escape, but I could not without the eggs. I was not sure where to take them, but I knew Seraphina wanted me to keep them safe. I wasn't even sure where Adriel had stashed them. He clearly did not carry the eggs with him.

The crew had grown quiet. All of us had donned *helos*, light fabric worn around our foreheads to reflect the scorching sun.

Unable to bear the silence any longer, I asked, "Who do you think killed my father?"

Adriel shrugged behind me. "I am not sure. Unfortunately, being the most powerful ruler of the strongest kingdom makes you a target. And the emperor was better at making enemies than he was friends."

This was true. My father was highly intelligent. Not only had he secured sole control of the seven rivers that fed fresh water to four of the five kingdoms, but he'd also ensured his army was the only one allowed to possess dragons. Other kingdoms had tried, but it takes time to build an army of dragons, and Father was brilliant at snuffing out any signs of rebellion. No one had been able to stand successfully against him. Not only was he a brilliant strategist, but he was also ruthless, especially when he felt slighted by another kingdom. Elan had inherited many of those traits. It was odd that I felt a tinge of sadness thinking of my father, especially after the last decade of being neglected by him. I was convinced he was responsible for my mother's melancholy and her eventual death, and yet he was the only father I'd ever known.

"Kitchi mentioned the king is a kind man," I said, switching topics, hoping he did not catch the glint of wetness in my eye.

Adriel growled. "Kitchi should keep her mouth shut about such things."

"I think if I am going to be forced into a marriage, I should know a bit about him. I understand your goal was to marry me off to your brother, but surely things have changed now that my father has died. My brother will never support it. You'd be wise not to make him an enemy."

He did not answer right away. Just when I thought he wouldn't, he said, "Because it is what my brother asked of me. He may very well look at you and decide not to go through with it, but my mission is to get you there."

I rubbed Candy's mane. "Well, you have settled it for me," I said.

"Settled what?" he asked.

"That your brother is the opposite of kind. A kind man doesn't steal women from their homes."

I listened as he ground his teeth behind me. "Kindness is not an attribute my brother is known for, but if you are lucky, you may receive indifference."

"Let's hope I am lucky," I murmured.

Kitchi chatted happily on our journey, which seemed to annoy Adriel, so I encouraged it all the more. Kitchi described Wiyotak, as well as the culture and people. While the people of Ujuima lived in large structures of sand and rock to avoid the blazing sun, the Wiyotakins lived in smaller structures of bamboo and red clay. They apparently lived among heavy vegetation and happily shared the land with animals. After a full day of riding, we finally stopped for the evening. We were just a few days away from Wiyotak. I had not thought of anyone but Kwasi all day. I hoped he was safe and not too worried when he came back to find me gone.

I was giving Candy the rest of the dates I had hidden away when Adriel called for Kitchi and me to follow him to his tent. My lips turned upward in amusement. I guess he did not trust us after I was absent from my tent this morning.

After the tents were erected and the three of them were securely inside, he unbuckled the satchel. Kitchi inhaled deeply. "Wow, those are huge. How do we know the little guys are okay in there?"

"We need to talk," he said, interrupting my thoughts.

"About?" I asked.

"I want to know more about them. How should they be cared for? What to do once they are hatched?"

"Why would I know those things?"

"Because I saw you talking to their mother, the blue dragon, just like you did Beast."

"Candy," I corrected.

He'd been watching me, I realized. For how long? I'd been able to speak to a number of creatures over the years. Mostly, I read their auras, but there had been a few I could actually converse with. Seraphina had been my first dragon.

I learned to hide this ability. I once confided in Kwasi about it, but he had warned me never to speak of it again. There was no telling what Father would do with this knowledge. Most likely, it would be another disappointment and lead to my permanent dismissal from the castle grounds.

"How long have you been watching me, then?" I breathed.

"Just that once. I have been searching for dragon eggs for some time. I knew if anyone had them, it would be the Oseis." He breathed deeply before admitting, "It was lucky I was there."

Or unlucky, I thought.

There was something amiss, because I could not see it clearly. It was rare for me to see nothing. Was this how he had spied on me without my knowing?

"I'd hoped you could use your ability to . . . sense their auras." The request fell off his tongue like a large boulder. It was clear he held doubts about my abilities.

"Do animals have auras?" Kitchi interjected.

"Of course, they do. May I?" I asked, holding out my hands.

He pushed the satchel in front of me. I gently leaned down and cradled the first egg in my hands. The egg was cool to the touch, but its aura shone a vibrant purple. It seemed to hum, as if it felt content when held. All three eggs hummed when cradled in my arms.

"I think they like being held. That was what Seraphina was doing when I found her."

"What did she tell you about these eggs?" he pressed.

I did not want to reveal everything. He might become even more protective of the eggs, and then I would never be able to escape with them.

"She begged me to keep them safe, is all," I said smoothly. "She knew her time was short."

"Did she say anything about the father?"

I tried not to give away that he'd asked the right question. Did I dare lie? I just shook my head. I did not trust myself to speak. He was silent for a time, likely trying to discern whether I was telling the truth or not.

He gently took an egg from my arms. "Does it hum when I touch it?"

Yes, I realized, but I could not tell him that. I needed the eggs near me. "Not as loudly," I said.

He grunted and replaced the egg in my arms. "Very well. We need to continue to keep this quiet. My Guardians are loyal, but dragon eggs have not been seen for centuries. It is better not to chance it. You will sleep in my tent tonight."

I flinched. "That is hardly proper," I protested.

Kitchi shuffled uncomfortably beside me. "I know I failed you this morning, war chief, but I will not again."

"You cannot be expected to stay awake days on end. You will be of no use to me. And I will not let those eggs out of my sight."

"If you share a tent, the men will talk," Kitchi said simply. "People could get the wrong idea. The king and others would be displeased."

He grunted as if he really did not care for the opinions of his men or his king. "These tents are too crowded for all of us. What do you suggest?"

"Wait until the changing of the guard tonight," she said. "We will switch tents."

"Fine. But the eggs do not leave my sight. They will sit in my satchel until then."

I nodded, realizing this could be my best chance. I would escape with the eggs tonight.

After days of clipped commands and hostile tones, the voice outside my tent startled me. It was warm. Gentle. Almost melodic. "Hello, Princess."

"Hello," I said tentatively.

His bright yellow aura peeked within the tent. "Forgive the intrusion. I am Ashkii,"—he lowered his voice nervously, the pitch wavering slightly, betraying his youth—"I'd hoped you could read my aura, that is, if you are not too busy."

I smiled at him evenly. "Won't your war chief disapprove?"

He shuffled on his feet. "Ah, yes. I was hoping you would not tell him. I would not have come to you unless it were important."

A grin tugged at my lips despite myself. I wasn't about to pass up a chance to defy my captor. "I won't tell him if you won't."

Taking that as an invitation, he stepped inside and settled down in front of me. The tent filled with the fresh scent of wildflowers and sunshine.

"How does this work?"

"Do you want to tell me a little bit about what you want help with?"

"Ah, yes. You see . . . I love being a Guardian, I do!" he said too quickly. "My father was a Guardian, and my brother before he died in the last war." His voice shifted with sadness. "I am the next oldest, and I have six younger brothers who look up to me."

"And?" I queried.

"And"—he swallowed—"I wonder if there is more . . . for me, I mean. Is there more to me than preparing for the next battle?"

I lowered my hands. "I do not know if you need your aura read for this. The answer is, of course, there is more."

He inhaled sharply. "How do you know?"

I thought about his question. "Let's start off with what you hope to do with yourself instead."

He sucked in a breath. "I don't know if I can say it out loud."

I reached for his hand. "Allow me, then." I circled his hand with my fingers, searching. "You're a writer," I said.

He gasped. "Yes, I mean"—he bent down to whisper—"I hope to be a poet."

"Hope to be? Have you written anything?"

"Yes! Loads of things in my notebooks. I can't seem to help it, even though I know I should stop," he said.

I traced his hand again. "Let me ask you this: can one be a father and a Guardian? Can one be a great forager and a Guardian?"

"Well, yes, of course."

"Why can't you be both? It sounds like you already are. Your real question is, will it ever be acceptable?"

He let out a breath. "You are reading me well, Your Highness. I worry I am setting a bad example for my younger brothers, that I am disappointing my family."

"That is a lot of responsibility you carry," I said. "What if your brothers also have interests outside of war? What would you say to them?"

I noted he scratched at something, probably the back of his head. "Well, I'd support them, of course."

"And what if they were only brave enough to explore that other interest because you were brave enough to explore your own?" I said, pointing a finger at his chest.

He was silent, thinking over what I'd said. Suddenly, he reached out to embrace me.

"Thank you," he said, his body shaking.

I awkwardly hugged him, sensing that he needed the contact, but wary because the only person I'd ever hugged outside of my family had been Ekon.

A throat cleared sharply behind us. Ashkii stood quickly. "Forgive me, war chief. I will leave immediately."

"See that you do," Adriel barked, his voice cold and cutting. "And keep everyone away. If I see anyone else even talking to the princess, tell them they will be dealing with me. Understood?"

"Yes," he said, voice shaking, before he scurried out of the tent.

I sighed before standing. "I really don't mind, you know."

"Tell me, princess. Do you often allow men to touch you so freely?"

That was not a question at all. "It is none of your business who I allow to touch me. Burn it all, I can hug every man in this camp if I want to."

"I need hardened men of war, not the sniveling children you have reduced them to with your . . . affections. No more!" Adriel barked.

"Last I checked, I outrank you," I challenged, allowing my anger to simmer to the surface. "I do not have to listen to a word you say. In fact, I demand you give me my eggs and release me now."

"Or what?"

"I'll find a way out myself," I said through clenched teeth. My face flamed at the words that had inadvertently escapedmy lips. Dammit to hell.

He was still for an agonizing moment before he said, "Is this how you want it to be then?"

"Free of you? Absolutely."

"Very well." He turned and left the tent abruptly. I briefly wondered if I had won when he returned with several other Guardians. They reached for me, and I screamed.

"What are you doing?" I shouted.

"Giving you some space." Adriel's voice was sharp and commanding, like the crack of a whip. The Guardians hauled me into another tent and began binding me to a pole with rope that bit into my skin.

"No one will bother you here," he continued. "You are free to walk around as much as you like, or as much as you are able."

"I loathe you," I hissed before launching spit in his direction. The only sound that followed was the rustling of clothes as he raised his sleeve, likely to wipe away the saliva.

"You are not the first and will not be the last. Sleep well, princess." The sound of footsteps faded away as he left the tent.

I refused to cry, refused to show any emotion. But I was scared. What would he do to me?

The ropes binding my hands were rough and abrasive against my skin, leaving behind small cuts and scrapes. The wooden pole I leaned against provided no comfort or relief. I crouched, holding my knees to my chest. Kitchi came by a couple of times, trying to coax me to eat, but I refused. After some time had passed, she said, "While I don't approve of his methods, things will be easier if you don't fight him at every opportunity. He is royalty, same as you, and not used to being challenged. Once you get past his hard exterior, I promise—"

"He is like every man in my life, Kitchi," I interrupted. "You don't have to endear him to me. I know exactly who Adriel Foxtrail is."

She sighed heavily, putting a hard piece of food in my mouth before silently leaving the tent.

The next day, Adriel once again demanded my obedience. Before I could spit another curse at him, he dragged me toward the horses and lashed me to Candy, intent on forcing me to walk at his command. But Candy, ever loyal, planted her hooves and refused to move, the earth groaning beneath her defiance. His patience frayed quickly, and when it became clear he could not bend her will, he turned to another horse for the task. As I was being pulled along, Ashkii walked past and whispered a quiet apology. Of course, it wasn't his fault; I held nothing against him. My anger remained focused on War Chief Foxtrail.

The hours dragged on, and I spent the entire day plotting ways to make him suffer. But by midday, exhaustion took over. Even my thirst for revenge couldn't keep me on my feet. My legs burned, and my breath came in ragged gasps, each one scraping my throat raw. The ground beneath me was uneven, littered with sharp rocks and jagged roots that bit into my bare feet. Every step was painful, but I refused to cry out. The sun bore down mercilessly, baking the sand and filling my nose with the dry, earthy scent of the trail.

"War Chief, perhaps we should . . ." Kitchi began.

"Stay out of it," Adriel growled. I heard a slap, and the horse I was tethered to cried out in distress before it bolted. I screamed, feeling the pull of the horse as it dragged me behind. "Heel!" Adriel yelled over and over again, his voice distant and frantic. Others ran after me, their shouts blending into a blur. It took several of them to calm the horse and bring it to a stop. I lay on the ground, my body trembling, every inch of me screaming in pain. My arms felt like they were on fire, the skin raw and torn where the rope had bitten into them. My face and legs were caked with sand and blood. The cuts and bruises were already beginning to throb. I tried to catch my breath as the metallic taste of blood mixed with the grit of sand coated my tongue.

Kitchi and Ashkii were by my side. Kitchi did not even bother asking Adriel's permission before she cut my ropes.

"Are you alright?" Ashkii asked.

I nodded. "Water, please," I breathed out. A flask was pressed against my lips as Kitchi and Ashkii sat me up to drink.

"What was that, Adriel?" Kitchi shouted, foregoing his title. "Ash and bone, what has gotten into you? All over a reading, that one of *your* men asked for. What is this really about?"

"Is she okay?" he asked quietly.

"You don't get to ask that right now! This is not you. You don't treat people like this, much less someone who is not a Guardian. She is an innocent." The tension between Kitchi and Adriel crackled like electricity in the air.

"Are you going to let her talk to you that way?" a gruff voice said in the distance.

"Stay out of this, Winnow," Adriel growled. "We make camp here!" he yelled.

"But it hasn't even been a full day of riding," Winnow protested. "And we've had to slow down for your little stunt."

A sword was being removed from its scabbard. "Are you having a problem following orders, Guardian?" Adriel asked.

Winnow quieted. "You have lost control of this unit. Don't think I won't report this."

A sword fell to the ground. "Do it. It's been your plan all along, hasn't it?" Adriel said. Winnow did not respond.

"Break for camp," Adriel barked again before storming off.

CHAPTER FIFTEEN

Asha

I insisted on making our dinner that evening, pushing away Kitchi's protests. "I'm fine. I need to keep my hands busy." She relented, and only because she felt guilty about the war chief's behavior, even allowing me to forage.

Very little grew in the desert, but I was familiar with all that was edible, and the few things that weren't. I let my hands drift through the underbrush, feeling the dried leaves of trees until I was rewarded with the lush foliage inside. My fingertips landed on a small cluster of broad, velvety leaves. I paused, breathing in deeply as I crushed a leaf between my fingers. The sharp, citrusy scent of lemon balm filled my senses as I pulled the root, a smile tugging at my lips.

My hands were constantly in motion, chopping, stirring, and ladling stew. The Guardians had caught several foul-smelling creatures. Ashkii explained that the creatures tasted gamey, and the smell would dissipate once it hit the fire. My stomach roiled at the thought of eating meat that reeked of decay. In its place, I offered a vegetable stew, carefully cutting the vegetables we had on hand. As I worked, I could feel Adriel's suspicious gaze upon me. I didn't blame him; I had snuck in totum root, along with the garlic and ginger. Used in Ujuima for troubled sleep, the root had mild effects for most, but for those unfamiliar with it, the impact could be powerful. I needed to put in enough to bring down the war chief, who easily had eighty pounds on Kitchi, but not enough to irreparably harm.

I was unsure of how much to put in a whole pot of stew, so I settled on putting half in, and I prayed it would not be too strong. The stew simmered in a savory broth, the aroma of herbs and spices filling the air with warmth and, most importantly, masking the subtle scent of totum root. Kitchi, Adriel, and I sat around the campfire sipping our stew. In my lap rested the eggs, safely covered by a blanket. Kitchi made loud slurping sounds as she happily devoured her third bowl, undoubtedly trying to make up for this morning's events. A pang of guilt hit me. But I needed to get out of this situation. It was the only way.

Kitchi patted her stomach appreciatively. "I've got to give it to the Ujuimans. You really know how to cook. That was delicious."

"Thank you," I said, pushing away the twinge of guilt that plagued my thoughts. "It is my mother's recipe."

Kitchi sounded mournful. "All were devastated to hear what happened to her. She seemed to be the opposite of your father, no offense."

"She was the opposite of him in every way," I agreed. "She was soft where he was fierce. She was kind, where he was . . . not. She was the best you could ever ask for." I closed off the sadness.

"Has he always been this dark and brooding, or is this a new development?" I asked, desperately needing to change the subject.

Kitchi chuckled. "I think she means you."

Adriel only grunted in response.

"Yes, for as long as I have known, Adriel, he has been this way," she confirmed. "Though he was in rare form today."

I sensed there was a silent fight occurring, but neither of them said a word.

"So always then," I said.

"The rumor is that he came out of the womb as a moody and contemplative babe," she confirmed. "He was already set on joining the Guardians at age four. It is a wonder that Odina was so different from Adriel and Enapay."

The mood shifted suddenly as Adriel stood abruptly.

"I . . . I'm sorry, war chief," Kitchi said. "I should not have brought her up. I don't know what came over me."

I did. The totum root had taken effect and was loosening her tongue. I could only hope that Adriel was not far behind.

"I think that is enough chatter for one evening," Adriel said, shifting the satchel with the eggs. "I will come by in a few hours."

He kneeled in front of me. "I am sorry for how I behaved," he began. "That is not how I want to lead, nor the person I endeavor to be. I won't behave like that toward you again."

I nodded, nearly breathless at his nearness. What else could I say?

When he saw that I wasn't going to speak, he walked away.

I was not sure what to make of it. Neither Elan nor my father ever apologized after they treated me badly, so this was a new development. Still, he was a man and had already proven what he was capable of. I'd made up my mind. Once the root took effect, I would leave tonight.

Kitchi threw water onto the fire, yawning forcefully. As we made our way into the tent, I worked up the nerve to ask, "Who is Odina?"

Kitchi was already spread out on her pallet. "Hmm? Oh, that is Adriel's little sister. She died a few years ago. Please forget I mentioned her. Adriel has forbidden any talk of her."

I certainly knew grief, but if I were never able to talk about my mother again, I don't know if I could bear it.

"Why can't you talk about her?" I asked.

But Kitchi was already snoring. I quietly listened as her breathing slowed to a steady rhythm of sleep. The effects of the totum root had finally taken hold, easing her into a peaceful slumber. With a soft sigh of relief, I waited for what felt like an eternity, ensuring that her sleep remained undisturbed before daring to make my move.

Carefully, I slipped out of our shared tent, the night air cool against my skin as I ventured into the darkness. At least Adriel felt guilty enough not to have restrained me tonight. I would get my eggs quickly and take off with Candy. Where? I had no idea. I just knew I could not stay.

My heart pounded in my chest with each cautious step. I quietly entered Adriel's tent, and for the first time, I saw it clearly—his aura. It shone brighter than any I had ever seen, a deep blue, but tangled like a web. It was a wonder I had never seen it before. It was unmistakable now. It was soothing, like the hum of a distant melody you couldn't quite place but that stayed with you even when you were out of earshot. Why had I not seen it like this before?

Adriel snored softly on his pallet. I caught the eggs' aura by his side. He had to be cradling them to his chest, I realized. I had to get them, had to ensure their safety, but I was painfully aware of my own unfamiliarity with the layout of Adriel's tent.

I picked up my walking staff to prevent noise as I crept closer. Without my staff to guide me, my foot caught on something solid, and I stumbled forward. I stifled a gasp as I collided with a chair. The sound echoed in the silence, ringing in my ears as I frantically tried to regain my balance.

But my efforts were in vain, and before I knew it, a sharp pain shot through my knee as it collided with the edge of Adriel's pallet. I bit back a curse, my hands reaching out blindly to steady myself as I struggled to remain silent.

For a moment, I froze, my heart pounding in my ears as I waited for any sign that I had been discovered. But as the seconds ticked by, Adriel's steady breathing remained uninterrupted. I did not dare breathe even a sigh of relief as I contemplated how to get the eggs from him. Suddenly, he sat up, and my heart leaped into my throat, but he did not speak. The web of his aura that, moments ago, had been still, began to vibrate.

"I must get to her," he said in a strained breath. "Let me get her."

He was still asleep. I kept my breath steady, worried I might wake him. I was able to pull the satchel from his pallet and sling it across my body. My fingers trembled slightly as I pulled the straps of the satchel tight against my chest. The cool fabric rubbed against my skin. I needed to go now. But I turned back to Adriel. I listened to his haunting words as he said them over and over: *I must get to her. Let me get to her.*

His aura, a puzzle before, seemed to have a pattern. It could be untangled. I couldn't help myself. I reached out and touched it lightly, and it pushed me back. Suddenly, his arms were upon me. Heat seared through my gown as his body pressed to mine, his breath warm at my ear. His strength surprised me as his arms snaked around my waist.

"Get down!"

Adriel's voice shattered the stillness, sharp and urgent. "Get down," he commanded again, his tone brooking no argument.

My heart skipped a beat as I obeyed, my hands tightening around my walking staff as a sense of unease settled over me. His arms pushed me to the pallet, and I was getting ready to tell him he was having a nightmare when I heard a second voice.

I listened intently, every rustle of fabric, every whispered breath, painting a picture of the scene unfolding around me. I strained my ears, the distinct sounds of a struggle reaching me from the other side of the tent. Two men grappling for control. My pulse quickened, realization dawning upon me. Someone else was in the tent—an intruder. Panic clawed at the edges of my mind. This was the perfect opportunity to get out with the eggs, but I couldn't leave him, not when I had been the one to slip him the totum root.

I wrapped my hands tightly around my walking staff. I swung it wildly, hoping to catch the attacker off guard.

"Oh!" Adriel's voice grunted.

I adjusted my aim higher and felt a satisfying crack, adrenaline pumping through my veins, drowning out the chaos around me. The intruder's voice, harsh and menacing, cut through the air like a knife.

"Come here!" he spat, his words dripping with malice.

I heard the sharp whistle of a sword slicing through the air, and searing pain tore across my shoulder and cheek. But still, I didn't falter, didn't retreat. I couldn't afford to. Amid the chaos, a new sound echoed through the darkness. The clash of steel meeting flesh, the sharp cry of surprise as Adriel fought back against our attacker.

The tent was filled with more Guardians, their footsteps and swords thundering as they rushed to join the fray. Adriel's voice rang out, a beacon of strength in the midst of the night. "We are under attack!" he bellowed, his words a rallying cry.

As chaos engulfed us, I grabbed my shoulder, slick with blood, and pushed myself off the ground. I grasped the eggs tightly before barreling my way out of the flimsy tent and into the chaos of the night.

"Kitchi!" I shouted. "We are under attack! Wake up!" I would never forgive myself if something happened to her because of me. "Kitchi!" I called, running toward our tent. I tripped over our pallets to shake her sleeping figure. "Kitchi!" I called again.

I reached out to help her stand. "We need to move."

She stirred, her movements sluggish as she attempted to stand alert and take stock of the situation. "What is going on?" she mumbled sleepily. "I don't feel quite like myself."

"We're under attack," I said, forcing calm into my tone. "Get your sword, Kitchi."

I grabbed her blade and pressed it into her hand, but her grip was weak, her fingers barely closing around the hilt. The sedative, I realized. My stomach churned. This was bad.

The air shifted, and a sense of fear took hold. I tensed as my senses went on high alert, as the sound of footsteps echoed through the tent. Someone was here with us.

"Did I catch you two doing something naughty?" our attacker taunted. "Such pretty ladies. I would love to take my time with you, but I have my orders."

My blood turned to ice at his words. I turned to Kitchi, desperation rising in my chest as I pleaded for her assistance. But she remained listless, her strength depleted by the effects of the totum root.

With no other options available, I made a split-second decision, wrapping myself around Kitchi as a shield against the impending assault. The attacker's sword sliced through the air, the force of the blow sending shockwaves through my body. A burst of energy erupted from the satchel at my side, a blinding flash of light that sent us all flying to the ground with a deafening roar. I was so used to my world being dark that, even though the light was painfully bright, I could not turn away. I reached for my satchel, but once my fingers touched the clasp, the eggs immediately dimmed. I collapsed to the ground as if the light had been the life force pushing me forward. But we were alive.

CHAPTER SIXTEEN

Adriel

A thunderous pop sounded from Kitchi's tent. By the time the other Guardians had heard my shouts and had come to assist, I had already made quick work of the men in front of me. Racing toward the sound, I found a man on the ground outside of Kitchi and Asha's tent.

Fear gripped me as I spared a glimpse of the man who writhed in pain as if he were on fire. He was still alive. When I was certain he was not a threat, I turned my attention to the two women on the ground. I put my hand to my throat as I relived a memory that I only allowed myself to revisit in my sleep. I dropped to my knees. I was too late. Again.

"You look like death," a voice rasped. My heart fluttered as my eyes found Kitchi's.

"Kitchi," I exhaled with relief. I did not dare to hope as I leaned my ear close to the princess's lips. Her breathing was shallow, but it was there. She was alive. They both were. Thank the gods.

"What happened?" I asked.

"She saved me," Kitchi murmured. Her eyes were still clouded with grogginess. "She could have run, but she came back. She stayed and tried to help me."

Kitchi looked around the charred contents of the tent. It was as if a fire had exploded within the canvas walls.

"There was an explosion," Kitchi continued, her voice trembling. "And then . . . the assassin was on fire."

"Was it her battlemage?" I asked.

Kitchi shook her head weakly. "No . . . I don't think so. I think . . . I think the eggs had something to do with it."

My hands moved instinctively to check Asha for injuries, and that was when I felt something wet coating my fingers. Blood. My heart lurched as I saw the deep gash on her right shoulder and the jagged cut across her cheek.

"I need to get her to the healing tent."

I wrapped my arms around her petite frame. She looked like a sleeping doll in my hands, save for the injuries. My throat tightened as I saw the blood that had pooled beneath where her body had lain. I carried her out of the tent, briefly surveying the aftermath of the attack.

The attacker lay still on the ground. He'd succumbed to his injuries. His wounds were strange and grotesque, with blistered skin and charred flesh. My mind barely registered the curious marks, nor could I worry about the fires that had been set to our supply wagons, or the horses that had been cut loose. All I could focus on was making sure Asha was looked after.

Setting Asha down outside the shaman's tent, I allowed the healer to take charge. He turned her to lie on her side so that he could inspect her shoulder better. I couldn't help but notice the healed-over lash marks on her back. There were so many of them. Some fresher than others. She'd endured lashes recently.

A wave of fury rose within me. I could feel the strain of the muscles in my neck as I tried to temper it. How could a princess bear such scars? She was not just a princess but an Osei. There was no question she was born into the most powerful family in the five kingdoms, and yet someone in her household had allowed this to happen. What could she possibly have done to deserve them?

There would be time later to ask these questions. The healer was focused on her care. The Guardians needed me to lead. I left the tent to check on the wounded and to make damn sure the threat was neutralized.

Guardian Winnow lectured and lamented my failure to anticipate the attack, and as much as I wanted to take my anger out on him, he was right. I needed to be better prepared in the future. Never had this many Guardians under my command ever been wounded in a single attack. I had failed them.

I was grateful to see Kitchi walking about. She had taken charge, speaking to every Guardian who had witnessed the night's events, piecing together what had happened. Her efforts revealed that the remaining assassins had taken a deadly toxin to avoid capture and interrogation. Their attire, plain and unmarked, told me they were paid mercenaries, not the personal guard of any kingdom. This reeked of Prince Elan. Would he really order his sister's death? We needed to get to Wiyotak quickly.

"We can't do this alone," Kitchi said. "We need to call reinforcements."

I looked back at the shaman's tent. I'd willed myself to stay back because I feared that if I didn't, I would not be able to leave. The image of Asha, wounded and defenseless, clawed at my mind, igniting fierce protectiveness. The shame and guilt felt like a burn in my chest for failing to shield her when she needed it most.

"Not yet," I answered. "But soon."

Chapter Seventeen

Asha

I awoke with a start, unsure of where I was or why I'd been wrapped in bandages. Strong arms grabbed my waist and left arm, gently tugging me back down.

"Easy. You are okay," Adriel said, his voice low and calm. "I've got you."

For a moment, I allowed myself to relax, leaning back into the solid warmth of his thighs. His presence was a comfort, but it didn't last long. Memories of the night came rushing back: the satchel, his bed, the moment I'd been caught. My stomach twisted. He knew. He had to know I'd been trying to escape. How could I possibly explain it away? But what excuse could I give to justify standing over his bed, with the satchel in my grasp?

"Are you in pain?" he asked with an edge of concern. "I can get the shaman. We've been dosing you with devil's claw, but I can get some more."

That was why my mouth felt chalky and dry. "I am okay. How long have I been out?"

"A full day."

Fire and bone, I lamented, touching the bandages gingerly. They ran up my arm and back and along my face. I realized my state of undress and pulled away from the warmth of his chest, covering my body. Had he seen the scars on my back? Heat rushed to my cheeks at the thought that he had seen a part of me I'd fought like hell to keep hidden from all but Kaliyah.

I felt him stand from the pallet and move to another area of the tent. "We are in Kitchi's tent. I can go get her if you would like some privacy."

"Is she okay?" I asked.

He did not answer right away, which made me even more anxious. "Yes, she does not have a scratch on her. But had I not arrived, she could be dead because of you."

There it was—the anger I had been waiting for. There would be no explaining away what I had done.

"I am sorry. I meant no harm. I just wanted to leave."

"Leave?" he asked as his voice grew more intense. "So, you thought to dose us with totum root?"

When my eyes widened, he said, "Yes, that is right. I know what it looks like. I saw you put it in the stew, and the fact that I only pretended to eat it is the only reason any of us are alive."

He had pretended to be affected by its contents, I realized, to see what I would do. He'd set up a trap, and I'd walked right into it.

"And how far do you think you could have made it? Hardened soldiers can't make it through these lands. How is a blind princess meant to survive it?" he demanded.

Now my anger was rising. "It is none of your concern. I am not yours. I am not your property."

I could hear him practically leap in my direction. His voice was a low whisper, laced with fury barely held in check. "You are what *I* say you are, and right now, you are mine."

Breath left my lungs as I braced myself for something. His rage. His fist. A whip. But instead, he pulled back abruptly, the warm breath on my neck now cool from the night air.

"So, are you going to tie me up again? Maybe tether me to a cart next time so it will crush me with its weight," I seethed.

He sighed, his footsteps sounding toward the front of the tent as if in retreat.

"Wait! The eggs!" I called after him.

Just when I thought he would speak, he stalked away instead.

Kitchi walked into the tent moments later. I steeled myself for her fury, but instead, her aura sang as she embraced me tightly. "You gave me such a scare. Are you alright?"

I began to tell her I was, but a sob ripped through me instead. Tears were not an asset in a warrior society, so it made sense why Kitchi was caught off guard by my reaction.

She patted my back awkwardly. "You're okay," she murmured, smoothing my hair. "You survived. You are okay."

"Kitchi, I am so sorry for slipping you the totum root. I would have never forgiven myself if something had happened to you."

Kitchi held me as my tears soaked through her leather tunic. "Is that what the tears are about? I thought it was Adriel who had made you cry. I was about to lose it on him, war chief or not."

I smiled bitterly at that. "He's right. I could have gotten you killed."

"Hey, hey. I am here. I am whole. The only one banged up is you, and that is because you put yourself between me and that assassin twice, I'm told. If anything, I should be thanking you for saving my life."

I opened my mouth to protest, but she stopped me. "No, stop," she said. "You don't even know me. If that is not badass, I don't know what is."

I was getting ready to say her life would not have needed saving if it weren't for me, but she interrupted. "Honestly, I don't even blame you. It took guts to pull off what you did, and to be fair, we are kidnapping you, so I'd say we are even."

A smile escaped my lips. "No, not even close," I whispered, brushing away the last of my tears.

Kitchi moved to stand in front of me as familiar footsteps approached.

"Fire and ash, Kitchi," Adriel said. "You were supposed to look after her, not make her cry."

Kitchi lifted her hands from me, and to my surprise, she confronted him. "What did you say to her, Adriel?"

He paused mid-sentence, clearly not expecting this turn of events.

"Do you think it is okay to throw last night in her face after what she did for us?" Kitchi demanded.

"Don't you mean what she did *to* us?" he seethed.

Kitchi let out a frustrated laugh. "Maybe she did dose me, but you watched her do it and then allowed me to consume it. If anything had happened to me, that would have been on you. She did what any captive would do, and when things got tough, she stayed to help us when she could have run. What is your excuse?"

I wasn't sure what to think. No one had ever stood up for me except for my mother. Even Kwasi was afraid to stand up to our father. He would have been cut down like anyone else. I reached my hand out and clasped Kitchi's, our fingers intertwining. She smoothed out my hair and kissed my forehead.

"Don't let him kick you around," she whispered before turning to go. "I will see you both in the morning." She said it as if she were giving a warning to Adriel.

I watched Adriel's aura at the entrance of the tent. "We are bunking together, I take it?" I asked, deciding to break the silence.

"She is the only person who scares me," he said in a pensive tone.

I was taken aback, wondering if I had hit my head in the attack.

"What?" I asked.

"Kitchi is right. I am sorry," he said, as if he were trying to find the words. "I did not mean to scare you. The way you flinch around me—it . . . it is my fault. I hope you can forgive me."

I was stunned that he had watched my reactions so closely. "It is already forgiven," I said.

He let out the breath he had been holding. "No," he said firmly. "You shouldn't forgive me that easily."

I raised an eyebrow. "Are you going to dictate my forgiveness now, like you do everything else?"

"Yes," he said quickly. "I mean no. I just—" He paused as if trying to find the words. "It is okay to be angry with me. It's okay for you to demand better; that's all."

I turned away again, not wanting him to see the fresh tears that had surfaced at the corners of my eyes. Did he know these were the words I'd craved as a child from my father? Did he know that was all the little girl inside of me ever wanted?

"I will," I murmured. "I will expect more from you moving forward."

"Good," he said. "And yes, we will be sharing sleeping quarters until we arrive at Wiyotak. I am convinced those assassins were looking for you, and I do not think they had any intention of bringing you back alive."

"My brother, Elan," I said. "That is something he would do. Break his toy so no one else can play with it."

"It could be anybody," he said.

"You should let me go. Surely, I am of no use to you now."

"Our king will decide that. Also"—he began removing a strap from his shoulder and placing the dragon eggs in my lap—"they need you."

I eagerly opened the satchel and was relieved to hear their glorious hum of approval. I picked up each one, inspecting them with my fingers and holding them to my body.

I winced. The wounds under the bandage were painful.

"Here, take this," he said, pouring me a cup of something. "It is for the pain."

I downed it quickly. "I need some help," I said, motioning to the pallet.

He came to my side and gingerly helped me lie down. I quickly covered my body with the blanket, very aware of how exposed I was with little more than bandages and a robe covering my body. Living without my sight for most of my life, I could not say that I missed it per se, but in this moment, I so wished I had it, if only to gauge the expression on his face. I lay down awkwardly, unsure of what to say or do. He put down a blanket and swaddled the eggs in a breathable cotton fabric before laying all three of them beside me.

I listened as he removed his boots before sitting on his pallet a few feet away. I hummed along with the eggs, wondering what the dragons would look like once they hatched. Would they be large like their mother? Would they even hatch?

"Who did that to your back?" he whispered.

I flinched, his words pulling me sharply from my thoughts. I caressed the eggs by my side as if to draw strength from them. I'd never told anyone about the lashes. Not Ekon. Not even Kwasi knew. I feared what Elan would do if I did. "This is a dark conversation to have before bed."

"Tell me, who did that to you?"

My mind raced, thinking about the time my father ordered it and all the times since, because Elan enjoyed hurting me.

"Your father?" he asked. There was a hint of something in his tone, as if he were personally offended by what had happened.

I sighed. "There have been many men in my life who had a duty to protect me, but chose not to."

"So, it was your father . . . and your brothers," he pressed.

I turned sharply in his direction. "Kwasi is the only one who has ever tried to help me." Ekon, as well, though in a way that I did not ask for. "I am a woman of royal blood. My body is not my own, even now."

Adriel shuffled on his pallet as if he were trying to find a comfortable spot. "You would never be treated like that. In Wiyotak, women are celebrated."

My mouth turned up bitterly. "And apparently forced into marriage. Sounds to me like I've traded one pair of shackles for another."

"You will be cared for. My brother is not a monster," he said, but the waver in his voice betrayed the truth.

"Maybe not a monster," I began, "but he is a man I will have to pretend with. A man that I will have to hide myself from."

He had nothing to add to that. There was nothing to say.

Awakened by a jarring noise that pierced the still of night, I lay frozen in bed, ears straining to catch the faintest sound. Faint whispers and murmurs reached me. My heart raced with apprehension, every nerve on edge as I strained to make out the source of the sound.

It was Adriel's voice that broke through the whispers, his tone urgent, tinged with a desperation that gripped me.

"Odina! Where is Odina?" he cried out, his voice heavy with emotion. "Oh, no!"

Worried, I called out to him through the darkness. "Adriel?" There was no response, no sign that he had heard me.

With effort, I swung my legs over to push myself up from the pallet, careful not to disturb the eggs. Every movement sent sharp pains shooting through my body, but I gritted my teeth and forced myself to move.

As I approached his pallet, I could make out his aura, tangled and writhing in the darkness. His breathing was distressed as he tossed and turned in his sleep, trapped in a nightmare that seemed all too real. My hand found his chest and retreated at the unexpected sensation beneath my fingertips—jagged ridges and lumps of scar tissue.

"Where is Odina?" he cried out once more, his voice raw with pain. "I must go back."

I shook him gently, my voice pleading as I tried to rouse him from his troubled sleep.

"Adriel, wake up!" I urged, my words echoing in the stillness of the night.

But he remained trapped in the grip of his dreams, his cries growing more frantic with each passing moment. And as I stood helplessly, my heart ached for him, for the pain that haunted his every breath and the images that tormented his restless mind.

His sudden movement sent a surge of adrenaline coursing through me, and I remained still, a small blade pressed against my throat. The sound of my own heartbeat thumped in my ears, the rustling of Adriel's movements echoing through the tent. His voice was deep and rough, laced with anger and confusion.

"Burn it to hell! What are you doing?" he exclaimed, as his body moved frantically, trying to make sense of his surroundings. "Are you running away again?"

I swallowed hard, the sharp edge of the blade biting into my skin as I spoke. My mouth was dry, and I could taste the metallic tang of fear on my tongue.

"You were having a nightmare," I said tightly.

His hands softened slightly, the tension in his body easing as he realized his mistake.

"That's no reason to sneak up on someone," he muttered, pulling the blade away and releasing the pressure on my throat.

I let out a shaky breath, relief flooding through me. But as I looked into his aura, I saw a depth of pain and sorrow that I recognized because it resembled my own. It shimmered with a strange intensity, a puzzle that I couldn't quite decipher.

Unable to help myself, I reached out tentatively, my fingers brushing against his long hair, half-braided at his back. The rest of the strands hung loose.

He allowed me to touch him. His breath halted as I traced the contours of his aura with trembling hands. But when my fingers brushed against his chest, he reacted swiftly, gripping my wrist before slowly loosening his grip.

"Did I hurt you?" he whispered, placing a hand on my neck.

"It's nothing," I said, but I heard him rustling through a pack of supplies and the sound of tape ripping in his teeth.

He brushed some foul-smelling ointment onto the wound and put a small bandage over it.

"I must look a sight," I said, trying to break the tension in the air.

"Even beaten and bruised, you are still a marvel."

I inhaled sharply. Had he just said that? The callous and controlled Guardian had just paid me a compliment.

"For a princess," he added.

I snorted and decided to change the subject. "How often do you have nightmares?"

He began packing away his supplies so nonchalantly that I thought he would not answer.

"Nearly every night."

My jaw dropped. "Doesn't that keep you from sleeping?"

He shrugged. "Most Guardians don't sleep well. It is part of the trade."

"You called out for Odina?"

His fists clenched. I had hit a nerve.

"Do you need help getting back to your pallet?" he asked, ignoring my question.

I shook my head, and he stalked out of the tent. He did not return until it was time to pack our belongings.

As I sat up, wiping my sleep-filled eyes, he said, "Today we go home."

We had to cross over to Wiyotak by boat, as it was a peninsula. The salty spray from the water occasionally landed on my lips, leaving behind a hint of brininess. As the boat glided smoothly across the shimmering waters, anticipation and fear built within me. This was my first time experiencing Wiyotak, and though I couldn't see it with my eyes, the air was alive with the whispers of its beauty.

The rhythmic swaying of the waves against the sides of the boat did little to calm my racing thoughts as we approached the shore. The forest surrounding us was filled with the chatter of birds and insects. The air was thick with the scent of rich soil and blooming flowers, mingled with the tang of salt from the water.

As we drew closer, the sounds of bustling activity filled my ears, echoing through the trees. The voices of Wiyotakins carried on the breeze, their native tongue full of life and energy.

Stepping onto the soft sand, I reached out and touched a nearby structure made of rough bamboo walls. Kitchi excitedly described her homeland to me in great detail, pointing out how some homes were built into the trees themselves, with branches intertwining with the structures. She explained that these structures were designed primarily from natural materials so that they blended in and became a part of their environment and disturbed it as little as possible.

We eventually came across a lake. Kitchi described that the lake was filled with stunning pink birds called flavins wading in the water on one foot, their long necks gracefully arched, apparently a common sight in this area. Monkeys ran overhead through the trees. Many of them were domesticated by the villagers, much like fennec foxes were for the Ujuimans. One curious creature even jumped into my hair and snatched up a dragon fruit offered to me by a passing villager.

"They are quick little things," Kitchi chuckled.

We continued our journey through several villages, occasionally stopping to browse at the various merchants selling handmade soaps, fresh fruit and fish, and crafted jewelry. Adriel greeted them kindly and examined their wares. I soaked in all the sounds and smells around me.

One particularly enthusiastic female merchant beckoned me over to her stall, eager for me to try on her handmade scarves. I hesitated at first, concerned about potential scratchiness.

But she insisted with a gentle tone. "You must try it for yourself, ma'am," she said. I dismounted my horse, and she wrapped one such scarf around me. It did indeed feel incredible against my skin.

Kitchi gushed, "Oh, it is in Wiyotakin blue! It looks like it was made for you." She called Adriel over. "Don't you think this was made for her?"

There was a brief pause before he grunted in response. Kitchi pursed her lips in exasperation. I could just picture her rolling her eyes at his male nonchalance.

"What is the thread?" I asked. I could feel it throughout the garment, twisting and turning effortlessly.

"A blue dragon," the merchant answered. "They used to roam this land, you know, before people pushed them out. Some say the dragons will return one day."

I admired it a bit longer before giving it back to her. "You are so kind, but I cannot take this. Please give it to someone else."

"I will hold it. It was made for you, I am certain," the woman said. I just shook my head. "You are too kind."

We journeyed into the evening before finally arriving at Empira Palace. I placed my hand upon the wall of the structure, surprised to feel the hard, cool stone.

"Limestone," Kitchi explained. "Our lands are full of the stuff. It's heavy and much more durable than bamboo."

She took my hand as we walked through. She described the walls as made of red limestone, and the halls held corbel archways, vaulted ceilings, and a stepped pyramidal design. We walked through a series of rooms. I could hear people shuffling about. I had forgotten what it was like to live in a place with so many people, having lived in a single-room dwelling attached to the pits.

Adriel opened the door and gestured inside. "This will be your room. Enjoy the comforts that we have provided. We will come back soon to check on you."

He didn't need to tell me twice. I was relieved at the thought of having some peace and perhaps time to think about a route of escape. But as I stepped through the doorway into my room, I was greeted by a flurry of movement. My attendants. They all kneeled on the floor to touch my feet before introducing themselves.

"May I have a bath?" I asked, my voice unfamiliar and exhausted after being on the road.

Without hesitation, they sprang into action, drawing hot water and adding fragrant oils and herbs to create a soothing soak for my aching limbs. As they worked, I gingerly removed the bandages covering my wounds, revealing tender skin beneath. When the bath was ready, I dismissed the attendants with a grateful smile and slipped into the warm water, feeling the tension and pain melt away with each passing minute. The scent of lavender and rosemary filled the air, lulling me into sleep. I was finally alone.

I wasn't sure how much time had passed when a voice broke through the haze of my sleep. "Excuse me, princess." A gentle tap on my shoulder jolted me awake. "I apologize for waking you," the elderly voice continued. "I am the royal shaman. War Chief Adriel sent me to tend to your wounds. May I assist you out of the bath?"

The water had run cool to the touch. How long had I slept? She led me out of the water and helped me slip on a robe. She then placed her worn and calloused hands gently along my wounds.

"Whoever stitched you up did so poorly. I will need to open these up and restitch them," she said in a disapproving tone.

I nodded, remembering all the times I had let down my guard with one of the dragons in my care. I was no stranger to stitches and pain. Injuries were just a part of life in the pits. Once she finished, she ran her hands along my back. I could feel the questions burning on her tongue. I wrapped my robe tighter around me.

"We have remedies to soften the tissue around these scars. I can bring a bottle if you'd like."

Though tempting, I couldn't bring myself to do so. I couldn't tell you why other than they were the reminder I needed that people were not kind, no matter how they presented themselves, and that only I could keep myself safe.

"No, thank you," I said, torn between wanting and never wanting to forget.

She hummed curiously. "I know someone else here who feels as you do, but I urge you to reconsider. If I may say so, you have such a beautiful back. It is a shame to cover it up."

I cleared my throat. "When am I expected to meet the king?"

She clicked her tongue. "There is no hurry to meet him. I am afraid you will be sorely disappointed."

I leaned back, shocked that a royal shaman would speak of him in that manner. Did she expect me to as well? Was this a test? She gave a husky laugh and clasped her hands along my thigh as she gathered her supplies.

"I have been instructed to tell you that there are guards stationed outside your doors and windows, should you try to escape again. I am really intrigued by how you managed to do that the first time. Perhaps you will tell me sometime?"

"Clearly, I did not get far," I said dryly.

She laughed again. "Well, you'll just have to try again, won't you? Keep our war chief on his toes. Call me if the wound begins to fester and stop scratching at it."

I stilled my fingernails, pulling them back from the itchy stitches.

"Thank you, shaman," I said with a bow as she closed the door to leave.

I was alone, enveloped in the stillness of a room fit for royalty. The scent of a lavish dinner lingered in the air, but my stomach turned at the thought of eating. Exhaustion weighed on me like a heavy blanket, and I moved toward the bed, each step achingly slow, as if my body were reminding me how long it had been since I'd last rested. I sank onto the edge of the mattress, under the soft silk comforter. For a moment, I just sat there, letting the stillness settle over me, before finally lying back. The sheets were cool against my skin, with a faint scent of lavender weaving through the ironed sheets. I released the tension in my muscles, grounding myself in the rare moment of quiet.

My mind, however, refused to rest. It raced, circling back to my current predicament, unable to focus on anything else. This room was far more opulent than my usual accommodations. My room in the dragon pits was small and modest, but it was mine. I longed for it now—for the familiar creak of the wooden floor, the rough texture of the wool blanket, the faint smell of smoke and ash that always lingered in the air. It may not have been a luxurious life, but it was mine. In that little room, I had some semblance of control over my fate, even if it was just an illusion.

I hoped Adriel would bring the eggs to me soon, but until then, I would wait. And I would plot my next move.

CHAPTER EIGHTEEN

Adriel

The once-red rug in the room was worn down to a dull burgundy from my furious pacing. The handwritten note was crumpled in my hand, its words scrawled in angry black ink.

My brother would not meet with me, the man who ruined his marriage prospects and made him a traitor to Ujuima. I knew I should have ridden ahead to get to him before Guardian Winnow did. Now I was shut out, and I would not be able to set Enapay on the right course.

"You are going to tunnel under the palace if you don't stop pacing," Kitchi said, cutting a slice of apple with a blade before popping it into her mouth.

The room filled with the smell of burning paper as I tossed the note into the fire. "All of that work to get her here, to get the dragon eggs here, and he won't even see me."

"Maybe it is good that he does not want Asha. She can go home to her people." She took another slice of apple and chewed it with enthusiasm. "Besides, I'm starting to like her. I'd hate for her to have to endure Enapay."

I seethed. "That's not the point. My brother is being foolish. If we do not salvage this mess, Elan will be on our doorstep in a matter of weeks."

"Why do you care so much, Adriel? I have long told you that you would make a better ruler than Enapay. Everyone says so. Even the . . ."

I held up my hand to stop her from speaking further. "We agreed never to speak of that here, Kitchi. There are ears everywhere. It's treason," I whispered furiously.

"Well, maybe we need a little treason around here," she said, throwing her knife into the wood of my armchair. "The way I see it, whatever bonehead move your brother makes is going to get a lot of people killed. Let him—we will be waiting on the sidelines to pick up the pieces."

I clenched my eyes shut. Ruling did not come naturally to Enapay, but with the right guidance, maybe he could learn.

"You know I cannot just let people die," I said. "We have to find a way to reach him."

She sighed heavily. "I know you feel that way. But do we have to do this to Asha?"

"Since when are we so familiar? She is a princess and an Osei. She was born to be wed to some foreign dignitary and an important piece to our survival," I said, cradling the eggs to my side.

"When are you going to tell him about the dragon eggs?" she asked, eyebrows raised.

I smiled bitterly. "When he is in his right mind and allows me back into the inner circle."

A knock sounded on the door. I returned the eggs to the satchel before the door clicked open. It was Tribal Leader Chaska, head of the castle guard. I had trained him myself. He looked more than a little uncomfortable.

"What is it?" I barked.

He handed me a rolled-up piece of parchment. "The Tribal Council calls for your presence at the round table. You are to come with me at once."

I read the parchment. This was not good.

I casually lifted the satchel off my body and set it beside me. I communicated with Kitchi with a silent glance before leaving. The meaning was clear: Get the eggs. Tell no one.

"You went too far," the king said coolly, leaning over the council table.

The dim light of the council chamber flickered against the stone walls, casting long shadows over the faces of the elders gathered around the massive table. All eyes were on me as my brother stood at the head, leaning forward. They were cowards, all of them eager to lick the boots of the king rather than tell him the truth.

"I had no choice," I said.

"By fire and bone, you didn't. How is kidnapping the beloved daughter of the late Emperor Idris going to win me any favor at court?" he seethed.

"I think I can salvage this if you just—"

Enapay's eyes narrowed as his neat braid swiveled down his back. "How dare you think anything on my behalf? I am the king!" he roared, pounding his fist upon his warrior leathers.

The elders of the Tribal Council all nodded their heads in assent. Guardian Winnow smirked from the shadows in the corner of the room.

I clenched my fists tightly, pushing down my rage. "So, you will not marry her?"

"Marry her? Right now, I am contemplating trying you for treason, and you speak of marriage?" he laughed. "No. What we will do is strike Elan before he can strike us. Guardian Winnow is certain that he can lead our men to victory."

A muscle in my throat throbbed. "If you strike Elan, we will lose."

Enapay struck his hand on the table. "You doubt the army that you have built?"

I shook my head. "Not at all. They are the toughest, most loyal men you will ever come across," I said with a pause. "But Elan has dragons."

"Dragons that cannot fly," an elder interjected.

I frowned. "Even so, they can destroy whole armies with one breath. Do not forget, we have seen it with our own eyes," I said, parting my vest to reveal the scars left by those flames. The elders in the room inhaled sharply.

Enapay sent me a disgusted look. "And you believe the marriage to Elan's estranged sister will save us?"

"I do not think Elan will want to look weak. That is why he sent assassins. He does not want the world to know that we have her, that we stole her right from under his nose."

The smirk fell from Guardian Winnow's face as he watched Enapay contemplate my words. "Your Highness, you are not considering—"

"Is she at least pretty?" Enapay asked, admiring the jewels that encircled the chalice in his hand.

Yes. Much more beautiful than Enapay deserved. I shrugged. "I am not worthy of judging such things. You should meet her."

He lowered the chalice and leveled a stare at me as if to call me on my shit. "Very well. Bring her to me now."

I cleared my throat. "If I may, she has had a long journey. She was injured in the attack . . ."

"I am told she was injured because of your incompetence," he said, pointing a finger at my chest. "Bring her to me now."

CHAPTER NINETEEN

Asha

A knock at the door pulled me from my thoughts. I did not rise, surprised anyone would be so courteous as to do so. At this point, the whole palace had been in and out of my room. Why knock now?

"Come in," I called.

Broody footsteps trudged into the room. I clasped my robe around my body, realizing who it was.

"I was not expecting you. What do you want?"

Adriel did not answer right away. I was growing used to these silences and decided to wait rather than ask again.

"You did not touch your dinner. Are you unwell?"

I folded my arms across my chest. "Is this why you are in my room, to inquire about my eating habits?"

There was a faint inhale—so soft I almost missed it. I felt a flash of coolness, and my movement had revealed my full thigh. He cleared his throat loudly to alert me, as if I would miss the open air on my exposed leg. "My brother would like to meet you now. He is a bit impatient.

You must dress quickly and"—he swallowed—"you might want to wear something more appropriate."

My temper flared. *Appropriate?* As if I were some prized possession to be summoned and dressed to his liking. The audacity to dictate what I wore opened a wound, but I refused to let it show. Instead, I loosened my grip on the robe, letting the fabric slip just enough to expose the curve of my other thigh. I reclined further onto the bed, my movements deliberate, languid, as if his words had barely registered.

My jaw tightened. *Let him see*, I thought. *Let him see I won't be commanded, won't be molded into whatever Adriel deemed "appropriate."* My fingers traced the edge of the robe, lingering there—a silent challenge. The air in the room grew heavier, my defiance on full display as I dared him to say more.

He didn't. But the hitch in his breath told me he'd noticed. And that was enough.

"That will displease him greatly," he said in a muffled voice, as if he'd turned around. "I'm afraid this meeting is not up for debate. He has commanded your presence."

I stood, allowing my robe to hang unhindered, not caring how much or little it revealed.

"I command that he meet with me when *I* am ready," I said stubbornly.

"You can either get dressed and come to him, or he will have you dragged to the council room full of the elders of the Tribal Council in what you are wearing. It is your choice."

Some choice. But I would not give in without getting something in return.

"I will go," I said, tying the robe closed. "I will go only if the eggs are placed in my care full time."

He whirled on me. "You are not in a position to be making demands."

I smiled. "You need this to go well, don't you? You need me to play the part of the dutiful princess." I stalked closer. "Admit it. I can hear it in your voice, Adriel. You need me, so give me what I want." I said the last between clenched teeth.

I could feel his gaze upon me, searching, contemplating. Finally, he broke.

"Get dressed. I will be back with the eggs shortly."

At the sound of the door closing, I collapsed to the floor. I had been acting far braver than I had felt, but he'd bought it.

In a flurry, attendants stalked into my room with purpose. The sound of their footsteps echoed off the walls as they moved to dress me. Surrounded by the gentle rustle of fabric and the hushed whispers of my attendants adding jewelry and ribbons. My hands reached out to touch the Wiyotakin dress they had carefully selected. The delicate fabric felt supple against my skin, with a softness that enveloped me. I suppose it was similar to being dressed for war; instead of mowing down my enemy, I needed to win him with my femininity and charm. I was being dressed not to conquer, but to captivate.

I traced my fingertips along the lines and curves of the dress, marveling at the intricate patterns and designs adorning it. My attendants whispered descriptions of the earthy hues, each one reminiscent of different aspects of the land. As they guided my hands to the collar, I could feel the weight of stunning beadwork.

They were just putting the final touches on my hair, sweeping it on the crown of my head in some intricate design, when Adriel returned. It was the latest fashion they'd claimed, but it just felt ridiculous. I stood to face him, holding out my hand expectantly. He quickly dismissed the servants before placing the satchel in my hands. He clenched my wrists.

"If you try to escape with these eggs, burn it to hell, I will make it my mission that you never hold them again. Do you understand?" His voice was authoritative and meant to scare me into obedience. It was a tone I had grown used to as an Osei.

I nodded. I understood, but understanding only meant I couldn't afford to get caught. Carefully, my fingers lifted the satchel, brushing against the eggs nestled inside. They hummed softly, a contented vibration through my fingertips.

"Put them away. We cannot have anyone see them."

I went to place them on my bed, but he grabbed my hand and led me to a corner of the room. I heard him tap and lift a piece of wood.

"Here. This is where you put them when you have to leave them in the room. You cover it with the rug when you are done."

I reached down to the hole in the floorboard. It felt dry and safe. I slowly lowered the satchel underneath.

"I will be back," I whispered before rising. "Okay, I am ready."

He led me out into the hallway. Once we were in the main part of the palace with onlookers, Adriel was quiet. The whole place was. It made me wonder if people were stopping in their tracks to stare at me. The silence made my palms sweat. I stopped, realizing the gaze I felt was Adriel's.

"What?" I asked, tapping my feet. "What is wrong?"

"Nothing," he said with an exhale. "It's just not quite right. Allow me to . . ." and before I could protest, he began undoing the elaborate braids in my hair.

I opened my mouth to object, but the words caught in my throat.

"You wanted your precious eggs back," he whispered to me. "This is part of our deal."

My hair felt weightless and foreign as Adriel undid the braids, his fingers deftly working through the strands. My hair fell loose around my face, and his fingers brushed against my skin as he finished.

"Perfect," he murmured.

My heart thudded loudly. We stood so close together. Taking a deep breath only made things worse as I inhaled his scent—sandalwood and ash. It overwhelmed my senses.

"Let's meet your king."

My mouth felt dry as I nervously licked my lips, anticipating what was to come. I could almost taste the bitterness on my tongue.

We were to meet King Enapay in the Sacred Fire Room. The air was thick with the scent of burning wood and the smoky flames in the hearth. As I entered, my senses were on high alert, absorbing the warmth of the fire and the weight of the king's presence. Enapay stood from his throne to approach me. I felt his piercing gaze and straightened my posture. It was one that demanded acknowledgment.

Beside me, Adriel paced. I resisted the urge to reach out a hand to steady him.

"King Enapay," I greeted with a demure bow, my voice steady despite the nerves threatening to betray me. "I am honored to be in your presence."

Enapay's voice, like the crackling of flames, filled the room as he acknowledged my greeting. His words carried a weight that settled into my bones.

"I am told that you cannot see, Princess Asha?" he asked, his tone as sharp as the crackle of the fire. "How did that come to be?"

"I lost my eyesight at eight years old," I replied, my voice unwavering. "But I assure you, I am quite capable without sight."

Enapay nodded slowly, seemingly satisfied with my response.

"Very well," he said, his voice softer now, tinged with approval. "You are quite beautiful, even if you are . . . not whole."

I did my best not to wince at his words, plastering on a fake smile.

"Your hair reminds me of a blue flame. I've never seen anything like it."

"Thank you, Your Majesty." I smiled at him. "I have been told you are as kind as you are handsome. I am lucky indeed."

Enapay chuckled softly, his amusement evident. He placed his hands on my hips, and I felt sick. His touch was nothing like Ekon's—gentle, sweet, nor like Adriel's as if I were something precious. No, Enapay's grip was rough, his fingers pressing through the fabric of my dress with a possessiveness that made me want to recoil.

"You have comely hips, adequate for birthing," he conceded, letting his fingers linger a bit too long.

Adriel's aura shifted, and everyone in the room seemed to hold their breath.

"Perhaps we should let the princess rest," he said. "She hasn't been feeling well."

I interrupted by taking Enapay's hands in mine and twirling in an exaggerated circle, the beads on my dress shaking rhythmically before releasing his hands.

"Brother, you were coy about her beauty and charm. Even so, I do not wish to marry her without the blessing of the soon-to-be Emperor Elan."

I stilled. *Of course, he was getting ready to be emperor after Father's funeral.*

"If I may, King Enapay," Adriel began. "My thought is that you attend the emperor's coronation next spring with your new wife beside you."

"That seems like a good way to get my head severed from my neck."

"Elan needs allies. More than that, he needs to show strength." Adriel pushed. "How would it look to his rivals if he cannot protect his own sister? We will have to take precautions, of course, but he will consent to this alliance. I am sure of it."

"Why should I have to marry her? Why not one of the elders? Why not you?"

I heard Adriel suck in his breath at the suggestion. "With respect, if anyone besides yourself weds her, he might take offense. There is no advantage to her marrying me or anyone else."

I frowned at his response. Was I that distasteful to him? It was as if I were cattle, and they were haggling over the price.

"Perhaps," I interjected, "I could write to my brother. Let him know that I am well and happily engaged to you, my king."

Enapay seemed to consider this as he paced in front of us. Others in the room whispered in his ear. At last, he said, "I see you are as wise as you are beautiful, princess. Craft your letter, and we will await his response. In the meantime, we will begin wedding preparations. You may go."

The abruptness of his dismissal startled me, but I took my leave, grateful to be away from him. I'd bought myself some time, but it was clear I would need to find a way to escape, and soon.

CHAPTER TWENTY

Asha

Adriel's firm grasp on my arm guided me back to my room. The quiet tension between us hung heavy in the air.

"Will I be allowed to leave my room, or am I to be a prisoner?" I asked, breaking the silence.

"You may walk around with an escort. I could see if Kitchi would like to accompany you," Adriel replied, his voice low and serious.

"I would like to learn the layout of the palace so that I can get around without assistance. Are there any rooms I should stay away from?"

"If there are, the guards will turn you around."

Damn. He would reveal nothing. "And what of the grounds? Will I have access to the gardens and the town?" I pressed further.

Adriel paused before responding, "Let's stick within the immediate vicinity where there is more protection. We do not know if there will be more attempts on your life."

"What makes you so confident that your plan will work?" I couldn't help but ask, knowing that our lives were now intertwined, and I was reliant on his knowledge and skills to keep the eggs safe.

He ran his hands through his braid. "It has to." His determination was evident in his voice.

"You are banking on the eg—cargo," I amended quickly.

He hummed noncommittally. "I will see you very soon, princess. Goodnight."

His lips brushed across my knuckles, and then he disappeared into the silence of the hallway. Uncertainty pressed upon my shoulders as I closed the door behind me.

I used my walking staff to map every inch of the room. I stopped where we had hidden the eggs. It was not lost on me that Adriel did not mention them in my meeting with Enapay. Did he even know about them? Or was the topic so secret it could not be discussed in such a meeting? It seemed to me Enapay's leverage would be those eggs, especially if he could get them to hatch.

The eggs felt heavier than they used to. Were they growing? I tucked them against my pillows and lay beside them, wondering if what I was doing was even working. I had no idea how long dragon eggs needed to incubate before hatching. It had only been a week since they'd landed in my care.

Tomorrow, I'd make my plan for escape. There had to be a way out.

The sound of wood sliding across stone set my heart racing. Panic gripped me as I instinctively clutched the eggs behind my back and sat up in bed. Adriel's aura filled the room, and I couldn't help but feel a mix of annoyance at his presence.

"What are you doing here?" I asked, trying to keep my voice steady. "Did you forget something?"

I could hear the smirk sliding over his face. "You didn't think I would leave these eggs with you after what you did," he replied.

I groaned, knowing that my plans for escape had just become even more difficult.

"You can't sleep in here! How did you even get in?"

"I have a bedroom adjoining this one. There's a hidden panel I've known about since I was a child," he said.

I was more interested in what he didn't say. There was a familiar shift in his voice, just like every time he had mentioned his sister.

"Was this Odina's room?" I asked, already knowing the answer.

He sighed. "Who told you about Odina?"

"I . . . overheard some things while you slept," I admitted cautiously, not wanting to reveal too much about what Kitchi had shared with me.

Adriel took a deep breath. "Yes, this was her room."

The weight in his voice made it clear: just saying her name reopened something raw.

I heard the soft thud of heavy fabric falling to the floor as he stepped closer.

"What are you doing?" I asked, feeling a surge of uneasiness.

"I'm sleeping here to make sure you don't run off in the middle of the night and ruin everything I've worked for," he replied matter-of-factly.

I couldn't help but feel indignant at his assumption, though he was right. "And how do you think your brother would feel, knowing his bride is sharing a bedroom with his brother?"

"He won't find out," Adriel stated confidently.

"And if I tell him?" I challenged, wanting to test his confidence.

"Then he'll ask me why, and I'll have to tell him about the dragons before he's ready to hear it. And then he'll most likely kill you," Adriel said without hesitation. "So, it is not in your best interest, princess."

I scowled at his assessment. "You've thought this through."

"Thoroughly. I'll spend my days studying in the library, learning about dragon eggs and how to hatch them. And in the meantime, I'll be here every night," he replied, a hint of annoyance creeping into his voice.

He stood and walked in the direction of the fireplace.

"Fine," I grumbled, turning my back to him on the bed. "But you better be gone by morning."

He chuckled as he extinguished the flames. "Of course, princess."

Chapter Twenty-One

Asha

Kitchi was a welcome presence after being smothered needlessly all morning by my attendants. They insisted I wear Wiyotakin's latest fashion, which was a lot less formal and corseted than Ujuima, but it still was a far cry from my typical tunic and trousers. I had just finished writing a letter to Elan, and a separate one that I hoped could be sent to Kwasi when she arrived.

"Good morning, friend," Kitchi said. "I heard you are hoping to get a feel for the palace. I suppose if this is going to be your home, that makes sense. Where should we start? Personally, I always like the kitchen, but—"

"Can we go to the library?" I asked.

Kitchi seemed surprised. "Of course, but I would be shocked if very many of the texts are in Elliarb."

I grabbed my walking staff and hooked my hand in hers. "That is okay. After I am wed, we can conscript more."

Kitchi tensed beside me, suddenly alert. She quickly unhooked her arm from mine and bowed. I followed her lead as footsteps grew closer. I knew of only one person who would require me to bow.

"Good morning, King Enapay," I greeted with a polite nod and a small curtsy.

"Good morning, Princess Asha," he replied. "What is on your docket this morning?"

I smiled sweetly, trying to appear at ease in his presence. "I am taking a tour of the palace. Your home is truly impressive."

"I am glad you think so," he said. I felt his lingering gaze and tried but failed not to feel uncomfortable. "Soon, it will all belong to you as well. I must say, it is refreshing to see you out and about."

I resisted the urge to fidget under his gaze and kept my tone polite. "Thank you, Your Majesty. Our next stop is the library. I've heard it rivals even the grandest libraries in Ujuima."

He chuckled, dismissing it with a wave of his hand. "Oh, why would you want to go there? It's just old books and dusty shelves."

I smiled patiently, slightly disappointed that this was how he viewed libraries. "For someone like me without the luxury of sight, books are a window into a world I cannot see."

He scoffed, clearly unimpressed. "Well then, perhaps you should enjoy them on your own. I wouldn't want to distract you." This was exactly what I had been hoping for.

"But maybe we could have dinner together tonight?" he purred, running a finger along my bare shoulder as if to disarm me.

My stomach churned at his touch, but I forced a smile, playing along with his game. I needed to tread carefully. Something told me I did not want to dine alone with this man.

Kitchi, who had remained bowed at my side, said, "Your Majesty, I believe Princess Asha is due to dine with Iná Nayeli tonight."

Enapay ran a finger along my arm. I remained as still as possible, not wanting him to let on to the disgust I felt at his touch. I suspected he wanted me to feel uncomfortable.

"Tomorrow then," he purred.

"Your Majesty, I believe Princess Asha is due to attend the Unity Ball as your betrothed tomorrow night," she said apologetically.

Enapay let out a frustrated sigh, tapping his foot impatiently just as Adriel liked to do. "Very well, we will have to find another time, hopefully before the wedding."

"I look forward to it, Your Majesty," I replied diplomatically, though inside I was dreading the thought of being alone with this man.

Kitchi and I finally navigated our way through the palace and arrived at the entrance of the Empiria library. A warm, melodic female voice greeted us.

"This is a great honor. Welcome, Princess Asha, to the prestigious Empiria Library." Her voice caught in her throat. "And it is good to see you again, Guardian Kitchi."

To my surprise, Kitchi stumbled slightly beside me. After an awkward moment of silence, I cleared my throat and spoke. "I am grateful to be here. And may I ask your name?"

"Oh, I apologize," she said with a laugh. "I am Junior Elder Tazbah. It would be my pleasure to assist you with anything you need."

"I would like to peruse your collection of texts in Elliarb," I requested.

"Of course! What genre do you prefer? Romance, adventure, mystery?" Tazbah replied eagerly.

"I am interested in non-fiction," I replied. "Specifically, I would love to read about the first Wiyotakins in any biographies or historical texts."

"What a wonderful idea to learn more about our people," Tazbah exclaimed with genuine enthusiasm. "I will gather those texts for you while you take some time to explore."

"That would be greatly appreciated," I said as she scurried away. From the sound of it, she practically ran in excitement.

Turning to Kitchi, I couldn't help but burst into a giggle.

"Shhh!" Kitchi scolded seriously, pulling me aside. "She might hear you."

But I couldn't contain my amusement. This was better than anything I'd discovered in days.

"Is that her?" I asked, still chuckling.

Kitchi shuffled but could not disguise the smile in her voice. "Yes," she admitted.

I broke into giggles. Try as I might, I could not contain myself for a moment longer. I held a hand to my lips, trying to get a hold of myself.

"I'm sorry. I have just never experienced you like this."

"I never should have told you," she grumbled.

I held my breath trying to stop whatever had taken hold of me. I could not remember the last time I had genuinely laughed. "Technically, your aura told me," I said. "And hers is lovely, by the way. It is sunny and warm."

"It is?" Kitchi asked, her excitement barely contained.

"Yes," I said, strolling through the towering stacks of books. "What happened between the two of you?"

She sighed heavily. "Oh, it is not very interesting, really. I was a terrible student, and my parents wanted me to go to university, but my grades needed some help. She was hired to tutor me. With all the late-night study sessions and time spent together, well, it did not take long for us to realize we could have something deeper."

She flipped through a book. The pages turned so fast that she was clearly just flipping through them before she continued. "My parents came home early from a dignitary trip and found us together. Their finding out that way was unfortunate," she whispered. "My parents threatened to disown me. I did not care much about that, but when they threatened Tazbah's career, I decided to break it off."

I tightened my hand on her arm. "Did you explain to her why? Does she know?"

"No. I know her. She would have insisted on staying together. I could not do that to her."

"That's why you joined the Guardians? So, you could have something of your own. Something they could not take."

She breathed in deeply. "Yes. Of course, by the time I made it through my training as a Guardian, so much time had passed, and I heard she was courting someone else. I just did not have it in me to be rejected, I suppose."

"Will you try again?"

"I do not know," she whispered.

"But you want to. What's stopping you now?"

"I was brutal when I broke it off. I had to be, or she would not have accepted it, and I might have been tempted to have her stay. What if she does not want me anymore?"

I shrugged. "I can see your auras are complementary, but I cannot say with certainty that things will work out. I just know if I had the chance to make it with the love of my life, I would take it."

She did not have a chance to respond because Tazbah returned with stacks and stacks of books.

Kitchi and I had taken one more turn around the castle before she left me in my room to explore the texts Tazbah had pulled for me whilst cradling the eggs in my lap. None of the books explicitly talked about dragons, but there was one text that mentioned Atim Wiyotak, the first of the Wiyotakins.

Born into humble beginnings, Atim Wiyotak possessed a spirit of adventure and a thirst for conquest from a young age. As he grew, he honed his skills as a warrior, mastering the art of combat and strategy. With unmatched courage and determination, he embarked on a quest to conquer the untamed wilderness and carve out a domain of his own.

Legend has it that Atim Wiyotak faced countless trials and challenges during his quest for dominion. He battled fearsome beasts that roamed the land, vanquishing them with his strength and cunning. With each victory, his legend grew, and his name became synonymous with bravery and heroism.

Driven by ambition, Atim Wiyotak expanded his realm, conquering neighboring tribes and bringing them under his rule. His prowess in battle was unmatched, and his kingdom soon spanned vast swaths of territory, from the mountains to the plains, from the forests to the rivers.

Yet, despite his conquests and the vastness of his achievements, Atim yearned for something more profound. He longed for a companion, a bride who would stand beside him in his triumphs. His sights fell upon a maiden from a prominent family, known far and wide for their wealth and influence.

In a bold and daring act that would become the stuff of legend, Atim Wiyotak kidnapped the bride and claimed her as his own. Though his actions were met with controversy, they solidified his power and etched his legacy into the annals of history as a formidable and fearless ruler.

I winced at the last bit of history. It hit a little too close to my current predicament. I heard a knock on my door and quickly replaced the eggs in their hiding spot before allowing the attendants to dress me for my dinner with Iná Nayeli. I knew nothing about her except that she was Enapay and Adriel's grandmother. I was not sure what to wear to this kind of engagement. I should want to impress, but truthfully, I was being married off against my will. Being impressive was last on my list of things to do.

Not wanting to bother Kitchi, I allowed an attendant to walk me to Iná Nayeli's apartments. They were quite far away. I noted the number of stairwells we took, which had to be hard on an old woman's knees.

After hearing heavy doors open, I strode into a hallway and bowed before Nayeli in respect.

A familiar voice greeted my ears. "Get off the floor, girl. There is no need for that."

My head snapped up in surprise. "You are the royal shaman."

A laugh trickled from her lips. "Yes. I have assistants who have much more energy than I do, I'm afraid. I only make myself available for special cases, and since you are joining the family soon, I thought I would come down and meet you," she said warmly.

I was not sure how to feel about this. It occurred to me that how I felt did not particularly matter.

"Oh, don't be sore with me. I prefer to meet people who don't think of me as the grandmother of the king. Especially this one," she said with slight irritation.

"I see." I didn't, not fully.

"Come join me for dinner. Perhaps I can make it up to you by exposing you to the best food Wiyotak has to offer. Did you know we are known for our gooseberries?"

I shook my head. "I do not think I have ever had a gooseberry."

She laughed heartily. "Well, do not eat them; they are dreadful. But in a sauce, jam, or tart"—she smacked her lips—"you can hardly taste them."

I chuckled, feeling more at ease. She led me to the cushions set on the floor. An array of foods was laid on a floor dinner table in front of us, as was typical in Wiyotak. Nayeli took my hands and guided them to the different dishes. She seemed to relish explaining what they were and how to eat them. She explained they would eat a small dessert first to stimulate the palate, followed by the main course, then a smaller one, only to finish with a lush dessert at the end. Most of the dishes were made to be eaten by hand—even the soup, I was instructed to drink from the bowl.

"I spoke to the elders in our library. I hear that you checked out some of our founding texts," she said.

"Yes, I am finding them to be very interesting. I have learned so much."

She seemed to mull over my words. "I have always wished to learn Elliarb. Did you know that Atim Wiyotak was blind?"

My mouth fell open. That seemed to be a very crucial piece missing from the texts I'd just read.

"I had no idea. I was always taught that afflictions like mine were signs of weakness. In fact, it was ingrained in me that anyone considered weak was either ostracized or killed."

She let out a low hum of anger. "Absurd. Atim was not born blind; it came later in his life, but he still accomplished so much. No one made a fuss about it. That's why some of our original texts are transcribed into Elliarb."

"It all makes sense now. But I wonder why this is not commonly spoken of."

"There is much in our history that certain forces would like to see erased," she said in a hushed tone. "But I suggest looking into Atim's own texts for more information on his blindness. You may have to dig deep, as he was never one to get straight to the point."

"I will definitely do that. His life was truly fascinating. As is yours. I read that you became the youngest shaman of your generation. I'd love to hear more about your journey."

"Oh, people say flattering things when you are queen. It's a wonder I was even able to study as a shaman at all. My late husband, Ahigo, doted on me and supported my aspirations. He was a wonderful leader and father, despite what you see in my grandson."

I gaped at her openness. I was speechless, trying to think of a response.

"While you are picking your jaw off the cushions, I wonder if you would indulge an old woman like me. I would be honored to show you the shaman tent," she said.

With great effort, she stood up slowly from her seat, her joints popping with the movement. I instinctively reached out to grab her hand and offer support, although I played it off as her assisting me instead. A gentle pat on my hand revealed that she saw through my efforts. As I stepped into the tent, a wave of rich, earthy scents filled my senses, instantly grounding me in the realm of healing and magic. The warm scent of damp soil mingled with sweet floral notes and hints of spicy herbs.

With each step I took, I could feel the rough texture of the woven mats beneath my feet, almost like a gentle massage for my soles. As my guide led me further inside, I extended my hands to trace the intricate patterns of the tapestries adorning the walls, feeling the softness of fabric under my fingertips.

As she described the treasures within the tent, her voice low and esteemed, I eagerly listened and absorbed every word. My hands reached out to explore the array of jars and pouches lining the shelves.

"Here," she said, pointing to a jar that she described as holding vibrant purple flowers, "is my personal collection of echinacea. It supports the immune system and reduces inflammation."

Moving on to a small pouch filled with pulverized leaves, she continued, "This is tribulterres, known for its ability to increase a man's libido." She chuckled. "A lot of women use it in love potions, but it only amplifies the feelings that are already there," she said, patting my hand.

"What is this?" I asked.

"Nightshade. You don't want to be fooling with that one," she explained. "It is used to induce temporary paralysis."

Her voice grew reverent as she showed me a bottle of calea root potion. Made from the roots of an ancient tree in their forest, it was said to unlock secrets and bestow visions from the spirit world. My heart raced with excitement at the thought of such a powerful weapon.

Our conversation shifted to other things, such as her time as a shaman, the places she'd traveled, and then her family, especially her grandchildren. I could feel the warmth radiating from her aura as she spoke of Adriel with love and admiration. It dulled slightly when mentioning Odina's tragic death, and I could feel the grief still fresh in her voice.

Curiosity got the best of me, so I asked if she would share more about Odina with me. She spoke of her fondly, reminiscing about her kind nature and sense of humor. As she described Odina's loss and Adriel's subsequent change in demeanor, my heart ached.

"Adriel had always doted on his little sister, her bright eyes and curious nature a mirror of his own. She showed a natural inclination toward the shamanic arts, much to my delight. But perhaps it was this encouragement that led to her untimely death," she said sadly. "She died trying to save a mother who had just given birth from a house fire. Her selflessness cost her everything."

I held Nayeli's hand, gently stroking her arm as she recounted the painful memory.

Suddenly, she pulled back in surprise. "I thought I sensed something . . . I did not know you were ngangkari."

My eyes widened at the title, unfamiliar with the term.

"A seer," she clarified. "Shamans from long ago possessed such abilities. I have never met one."

My curiosity piqued, and I implored for more information about these abilities that I had had to keep quiet for so long. But before Nayeli could answer, we were interrupted by a loud knock on the door.

"Iná? May I come in?" Adriel's voice called out.

Nayeli explained that she had invited him to join us for dessert and tea. She left the tent to greet him in the common room. Once she was gone, I rushed to the shelves of herbs and grabbed the nightshade and calea, hoping to conceal them in my pockets. With quick hands, I replaced them with other bottles and tried to be as quiet as possible.

"Where is she?" he asked with suspicion.

Needing a distraction, I knocked over a few random bottles and let liquid spill onto the floor. I kneeled down to make a show of cleaning up the mess.

"Are you alright?" Adriel asked.

His muscled arms lifted me from the spilled bottles. His touch sent a shock through my body as he checked me over for injuries. I couldn't help but step away.

Nayeli chuckled from behind us. "Adriel, she is fine. If she wasn't, she wouldn't have that look on her face."

Embarrassed, I quickly apologized for the mess before we all settled down to enjoy our tea and dessert.

CHAPTER TWENTY-TWO

Adriel

I winced as Iná insisted on sharing every embarrassing story about my childhood with Asha. Iná had been such a force of good in my life that I could deny her nothing. So, when she invited me to have a second dessert with them, I quickly acquiesced, even though a part of me wanted to create some distance between the princess and me.

Iná clapped her hands. "And what, my dear, will you be wearing to the Unity Ball tomorrow? This is your reveal into Wiyotakin society, so it must be a showstopper."

Asha shook her head. "I do not know. I am not used to attending such things," she admitted.

"And why is that? Idris Osei was a man who loved to showcase his power through balls and luxurious banquets. Surely you attended a few."

"I lived in the dragon pits," she said.

I leaned in closer, unsure if I had heard her correctly. "So, the night I saw you there, the night we met, that was where you lived?" I asked, my voice tinged with disbelief. "Why would you choose to live there?"

Asha smoothed her dress nervously. Iná sent a glare in my direction, clearly displeased with my reaction.

"I rather enjoyed it," she said, turning to me. "Believe it or not, dragons are less complicated than people."

"I suppose it kept you out of sight from your father," Iná said cryptically.

"And Elan," I added. Asha lifted her head, red coloring creeping up her neck. Her reaction confirmed something I'd suspected. Elan was responsible for those lashes, and her father had allowed it.

"Well, let's not speak of such things," Iná said. "I have the perfect thing for you, Asha. It is what I wore when I met Adriel's grandfather for the first time. Let's just say I was blessed with many children, so it is quite the gown."

I knew exactly what gown she meant. She brought it up at every family gathering to embarrass us all.

I cleared my throat. "Perhaps Princess Asha would want to wear something more in line with tradition."

I watched Iná put her hands on her hips with an air of defiance. "What could be more traditional than what your grandmother wore to her first Unity Ball?"

I looked down at my shoes like I used to when she scolded me as a boy. "I just meant to say . . ."

"I would be honored to wear it," Asha interrupted. "I appreciate your kindness."

Iná beamed. I had not seen such light in her eyes in so long. It made me happy to see it again.

I brushed a kiss on Iná's wrinkled cheek, and she squeezed my hand before she turned to Asha and gave her a hug, before she bade us good night. We walked silently in the direction of her room. I watched her expertly use her walking staff to navigate the winding halls. She stumbled some, but overall, I was surprised at how quickly she had adjusted to Empira.

"Would you like to grab onto my arm? It might make it easier."

She shook her head. "No. Despite what your brother says, I am not an invalid."

"I never said that you were."

She interrupted. "I am perfectly capable of figuring out how to get to *my* room, even if you have temporarily claimed it."

"Right," I snapped back. "Well, if that is the case, I shall leave you to it. I have a lot of things to do. I will see you tonight."

Without hesitation, I took a sharp right turn. A twinge of guilt gnawed at my conscience, wondering if leaving her behind was a mistake, but I pushed the thought away and continued on. I was a different person when she was near. She could make me laugh just as quickly as she could annoy the piss out of me.

My steps brought me to the armory, an imposing building that housed our weapons and training grounds. It was where Kitchi and the rest of my inner circle could usually be found. As expected, Kitchi was hunched over a blade, vigorously sharpening it with a stone until it gleamed in the light.

The ground vibrated with the impact of swords clashing and boots pounding the concrete floor of the sparring ring. Chato, my trusted junior lieutenant, was locked in a sparring match with Ashkii, a newer recruit who had already proven himself on several high-stakes missions. Despite his small stature, Ashkii's agility and intelligence made him a valuable asset, especially when gathering intel on our enemies.

And there was Moki, our master trainer, offering guidance to Ashkii as he practiced his sword work. The air smelled of metal and sweat, and the sound of clashing swords filled the room. This was where we honed our skills and prepared for battle, a crucial part of our way of life as Guardians.

When they saw me, everyone stopped and dutifully bowed.

Only Kitchi approached me with a grin to ask, "How was dessert?"

I growled at the question. Her smile brightened further as she ran her hand along her jaw.

"That great, huh? You are usually in a better mood when you've visited your Iná. Could it be Princess Asha's presence that has you riled up?"

"We could work it out in the ring," Ashkii called before Chato knocked him from his feet. I laughed. "Careful what you ask for. One beatdown is enough, don't you think?"

Ashkii did not spare a response before he rammed his body into Chato. If Ashkii hadn't been so small, it might have worked, but Chato was tall and had one hundred pounds on him, at least. He dropped an elbow on his gut, and Ashkii groaned.

"Less talk, more skill," Moki barked. He looked over at me with a wry expression and said, "You do look more agitated than usual. Is there something you need us to know?"

I shrugged. "We sent the letter to the Oseis. I am concerned that my brother will do something to fuck it up. Ever since the Fire Festival, things have gone to shit."

"We've had to change course before," Kitchi noted. "We always come out on top. Maybe having Asha works out better for us."

"Only if Enapay sticks to the plan," I grumbled.

She sighed. "All we can do is wait. On a different topic, have you noticed Asha has not shown any signs of battlemage since she has been in our company?"

I tensed. "I have, but I wondered if her battlemage was altered because she is blind."

Kitchi shook her head. "Even infants show signs of battlemage. I've known very few not to have it. I've wondered if she was never taught to harness it."

That thought had crossed my mind as well. "Perhaps it is a good thing. It makes it much easier to keep her under control."

Kitchi frowned. "It also makes her a huge target. We don't know whether there will be more attempts on her life. She needs to have some basic defense under her belt. Let us train her."

I ran my hand through my hair, stopping at the knot of my braid. "I will think about it."

She nodded, satisfied with my response. "How is the mining going?"

"Right on schedule. Our friends are happy, but it won't be long now before Enapay hears about it. I'd hoped to keep it under wraps for longer, but maybe the timing is to our advantage. Regardless, we should ready everyone in case there is an attack."

Everyone in the room nodded. If the whole of Enapay and his allies came to our door, we had no chance. The only chance we had was those eggs, and I had yet to figure out how to hatch them.

"I'm going to the library. I will see you tomorrow."

Chapter Twenty-Three

Asha

When I woke, there was no pallet beside my bed. Adriel must not have come back last night, and honestly, that was fine with me. I rubbed my tired eyes and began the ritual of replacing the eggs when I heard a firm knock on the door.

"Just a minute," I said, racing to return the eggs to their hiding spot. I'd barely set the rug over the loose floor plank when the door creaked open. "Excuse me. I said, 'Wait a minute.'"

The footsteps did not hesitate as the figure stalked wordlessly toward me. I quickly backed away, realizing it may not be one of my attendants. I stumbled back until the wall pressed against my spine, my fingers grasping for something—anything—to defend myself with. There was nothing.

"Get away from me!" My scream tore through the air.

The sharp hiss of steel being drawn sent ice down my spine. Panic surged, my body flattening against the wall. And then—the floor shifted. My stomach dropped. I was falling.

Before I could cry out again, familiar footsteps thundered towards me along with the unmistakable sound of a sword being drawn. A strong arm snaked around my waist, yanking me against him and pulling me clear. Adriel.

Only then did I realize what had happened: I'd slipped through the hidden panel between our rooms.

"Someone is in my room!" I panted.

"Stay here," he whispered calmly. My brain tried to process how he could be so calm, like this was a typical morning for him.

Adriel left the room, presumably to catch the intruder from behind. I waited a beat, then another, worried that the intruder would come through the wall, but I heard nothing.

I was not sure how long he had been gone. It felt like hours, but it could have been seconds. When Adriel returned, his breathing was tightly controlled.

"You did not find him?" I asked.

"No, although the rug by the door is askew. I am thankful he did not stick around to look further. The eggs are secure."

I put my arms around my body to try to slow the panic I was feeling.

"Hey, he's gone," he reassured me. "You're okay."

No matter what he said, my breathing only continued to spiral out of control.

"Let me help you," he said.

I nodded, because I could do nothing else.

"Squat down," he instructed. "Tuck your head between your knees."

With trembling legs and great effort, I followed his instructions.

"Now, exhale as long as you can before taking a breath. One . . . two . . . three . . . four . . ." He rubbed my back while he counted. "Good. Just like that."

I continued that way for a while. Eventually, I laid my face on the floor to feel its coolness.

"It is alright," Adriel soothed. "You are alright."

We went on this way until my breathing slowed.

"Are you ready to stand?" Adriel asked.

I nodded, and he took my hands, his grip steady as he guided me to my feet. His touch was methodical, his hands moving over my face, shoulders, and arms, checking for injuries. When he found none, he pulled me into an embrace, his arms wrapping around me tightly.

The feel of his arms around me made the terror I'd almost freed myself from threaten to resurface. I stiffened, my body instinctively recoiling from the closeness. I should have felt comforted by the action, but instead, I felt nothing—or perhaps too much. A storm of emotions swirled within me, emotions I was not ready to feel. I wanted him to let me go, to give me space to breathe, to rebuild the walls that were falling away at his touch. But I said nothing, standing rigid in his hold, waiting for the moment I could step back and reclaim myself.

"I thought he was an attendant. He came toward me," I whispered breathlessly, "and I had nowhere to go. I felt so helpless. I don't want to feel that way anymore."

Tears escaped my eyes, and decorum be damned, it felt good. I held years of neglect and grief within my body, and it was slowly releasing itself like a pressure valve on a kettle. The loss of my mother, the loss of my family, and my freedom. I couldn't help but feel anger toward myself for being so vulnerable. I let this happen again. I allowed myself to be helpless.

Adriel held me close, allowing my tears to soak into his tunic. Unlike everyone else in my life, he did not pull away, did not even seem the least bit uncomfortable. It was a wonder he had not run. Tears were unacceptable in our world.

I vaguely registered a door opening when I heard Kitchi's voice.

"Oh! I didn't mean to interrupt. Wait, what's wrong?" she asked.

I must have looked a sight. I pushed away from Adriel, and although I'd die before I'd admit it, I immediately missed the comfort of his arms.

Before I could fully steady myself, Kitchi was there, kneeling in front of me. Her hands reached out and took hold of my arms just above the elbows, her grip grounding me. She positioned them carefully, as if I might break.

"Another assassin," Adriel informed her. "In her room this time."

"How did they get past the Guardians? We have them posted at every entrance and exit."

"That is what I need to find out," he answered grimly. "Do not leave her side until I return. I intend to get answers."

Kitchi nodded. "Of course."

Adriel was absent for the rest of the day. Kitchi tried her best to keep my spirits up, but I was in no mood to pretend. I stayed in Adriel's room as long as I could, but all too quickly, day turned to evening, and I had to get ready for the Unity Ball. I had tried to distract myself by listening to the distant hum of activity beyond the door, the occasional birds that perched on the windows, but my thoughts kept circling back to Adriel. Where was he? Why hadn't he come?

The dress from Nayeli had arrived an hour ago, and I had yet to put it on. I refused to go unless Kitchi agreed to attend the ball with me. After this morning, I needed someone I trusted to be near while I was surrounded by the elders and nobles of the court. I did not know any of them. For all I knew, one of them was my attacker. I shivered at the thought.

"Your Highness," the lead attendant called, "if we are going to get you to the ball tonight, we must get you in the bath now. It is ready for you."

"Go," Kitchi said. "I need to get dressed. Adriel's most trusted men are posted outside. I will be right back."

If I were thinking rationally, all the attendants and the guards in and out of my room would make me feel a modicum of safety. However, I was not thinking rationally, and I didn't want her to leave. I nodded, and she promised to come back as quickly as she could.

She held to her word because by the time she returned, I was in Nayeli's dress. It had layers of silk fabric and rows of delicate jewels that cascaded down my gown, reminding me of Elliarb. I ran my fingers over them, feeling each tiny stone under my fingertips.

"That cape! It shimmers like stars in the night sky! You look stunning," Kitchi gushed.

She described that the dress was made of gold silk, but the bottom looked like it was dipped in a pool of blue ink.

"I'm actually a little worried," Kitchi continued. "Is that what you want King Enapay to see you in?"

If it was as beautiful as Kitchi described, not at all.

"I do not want to offend Nayeli," I said. "Let's get on with it."

CHAPTER TWENTY-FOUR

Asha

The chatter from the crowd reached my ears and continued to rise in volume as I approached. That is why my heart raced as the room fell silent, other than a few gasps and low murmurs. I had practiced my descent many times with Kitchi, and I knew exactly where to step and where to pause so that the guests could get a look at me. I heard the crowd drop to their knees. The king must have been approaching. *I can do this*, I told myself. I bowed before him as he approached.

"Princess Asha," he said as he grasped my hand, guiding me to rise. His touch was firm, almost possessive, as he began to lead me in a slow circle, as if presenting me like livestock ready to be purchased. "You look radiant tonight," he murmured, his words dripping with honeyed charm.

I forced a smile, though it felt brittle on my lips, as his hand slid to my waist, steering me with an ease that made my skin crawl. He paused mid-turn.

"It's a shame, though," he said, his tone taking on a mocking lilt, "that such beauty is lost on one who cannot see."

I fought to keep my expression neutral, though his words stung like tiny cuts along my skin. I had grown accustomed to such backhanded comments, as they never failed to remind me of my place in the world.

My chest tightened, but I refused to let my expression falter. Inside, though, I was seething. The day's tension, the waiting, the longing for Adriel's return, all blended into a quiet fury. I wanted to lash out, to tell him where he could shove his comments. But I held my tongue, my smile unwavering, even as my nails dug into my palms.

As he completed the turn, bringing me back to face him, I tilted my head slightly, as if considering his words.

"Beauty, Your Majesty," I said, my voice steady, "is not something one needs sight to appreciate. It's in the way the air shifts when someone enters a room, the warmth of a voice, the kindness of a touch. But perhaps that's something only those who truly see can understand."

The room seemed to hold its breath, the weight of my words hanging in the air. I didn't need to see his face to know I'd struck a nerve. And for the first time that day, I felt a flicker of something other than despair. I felt powerful.

His hands tightened on my waist. I had to shift the conversation back somehow.

"You obviously have that sight. I wish I could see Your Majesty. I imagine you are quite striking."

He seemed pleased with that response because he said, "Let's give these poor bastards what they came to see. Would you join me for a dance, Asha?"

I double-checked that my smile was still in place before I allowed him to take my hand in his. As we moved together in the gentle sway of the music, I tried to steer the conversation towards safe topics.

"Your kingdom is breathtaking. I've been enjoying my time here immensely."

King Enapay acknowledged my words, his grip tightening slightly around my waist. "I'm glad to hear that," he replied, his tone smooth but unreadable. "We pride ourselves on our hospitality, and it's always a pleasure to welcome guests to our kingdom."

As we continued to dance, the music gradually softened, its tempo slowing just enough for him to draw me closer. The whole charade cast a ray of civility over us and our impending union. I focused on maintaining a pleasant facade, though beneath the surface, my mind raced with unanswered questions and lingering doubts.

"I must say, Asha," King Enapay spoke again, his voice smooth as silk, "you've made quite an impression since your arrival. Many have spoken of your beauty."

His words only deepened my sense of unease. "Thank you, Your Majesty," I replied, choosing my words carefully. "You've been so generous, and I am grateful for the warm welcome I have received."

He nodded in acknowledgment, his hands lingering on my body for a moment longer than necessary. "I heard about this morning. Are you alright?" His tone was polite but not overly concerned. He might as well have been asking how I took my tea.

I hesitated, weighing my response. "Indeed," I replied, careful not to reveal too much. "I was glad that the Guardians could scare him away. I am lucky to have such protection from Your Majesty."

"I'm pleased to hear that," he said, his voice tinged with satisfaction. "I hope we catch the bastard. I will string him up for you myself."

As the music swelled around us, I felt a sudden urge to escape this and the unsettling warmth of his breath so close to my skin. But with his grip firm upon my waist, I knew I was trapped in his company until the final notes of the dance faded away.

"As much as I would enjoy being in your company for the duration of the night, I must make my rounds. There are many important people here for you to meet, but I hope to find you after so that we can have a more private conversation." He whispered the last in my ear before planting a kiss against my lips.

I fought every cell in my body to remain still and not peel away from him. When he released me, I was unable to form a coherent sentence, and I simply nodded. That seemed enough for him, and he pulled away, leaving me stranded somewhere in the room. I could sense eyes on me, so I fought the urge to wipe him from my lips.

"May I have this dance?" Adriel's voice caused me to tingle all over as my shoulders relaxed. "Of course, but please don't leave me stranded on the dance floor afterward."

"That depends on your dancing skills," he teased, taking my hand and placing his other hand on the small of my back. His touch felt electric compared to his brother's.

"The room is so quiet," I murmured.

"They're watching you. You look . . . stunning tonight. After a lengthy pause, his tone shifted, with a hint of something sharp creeping in. "It seems you and the king are getting on."

My lips tightened, a flush of mortification heating my cheeks. I didn't need him to remind me of the spectacle I'd just endured.

"It is your Iná's dress. She had eight children after wearing it."

He cursed. "Please don't remind me. I don't want to imagine my Iná wearing this dress."

I felt he wanted to say more, though I wasn't sure I wanted to hear it. My mind grasped desperately for a change of subject.

"Where are your aunts and uncles?" I asked. "I never hear any mention of them."

"My father was paranoid and sent our family to other kingdoms. I haven't seen them in years. It hurt Iná deeply to see her children leave."

"I'm sorry to hear that. It must be difficult not being able to see your own family."

He shrugged. "Enapay has kept the same policy. Honestly, I've been waiting for him to banish me. If I weren't war chief, it probably would have happened by now."

My heart skipped a beat at the thought of Adriel being forced to leave Wiyotak, leaving me behind.

"So, you truly haven't found any trace of the man who was in my room this morning?" I asked.

He shook his head regretfully. "No, but we have put contingency plans in place in case he returns."

The music slowed, and Adriel led me off the dance floor before placing a handkerchief in my hand.

"I saw you looking for one," he murmured.

I held it between my fingers, trying to grasp what he meant. Did he see that I was repulsed by his brother, that I desired an accelerant to burn off any remnants of Enapay's kiss?

"Thank you," I said, patting my lips.

"Where is Kitchi?" he asked. "She was supposed to be shadowing you tonight."

I smiled. "Look for the junior elder from the library."

"Tazbah? Why?" he asked. "Wait, I see them."

"What is Kitchi doing?" I asked.

"I'm not quite sure. It looks like she's falling over herself." He was quiet for a moment, probably studying her. "Wait, is she flirting?" he asked with a hint of dismay.

"I hope so," I replied, very pleased at his description.

"I'm going to go get her. She should be here with you."

I grabbed his arm, stopping him. "No need. I'm sure she wouldn't have left if she hadn't seen you with me. Let them have their moment." I could tell he didn't want to leave it alone, but he stayed by me.

"Princess Asha," a voice called in greeting. I didn't need to see Adriel's face to feel the way his body stiffened at the sound.

"Yes," I replied. "Do I know you?"

"I am Guardian Winnow, first lieutenant to the war chief. I thought I'd ask you to dance if you are free to do so."

I searched my brain looking for an excuse to decline his request. When I found none, I said, "I'd be honored. Just a quick dance." I handed Adriel back his handkerchief, but he took my hand instead. He held me possessively. It could not have gone unnoticed by Guardian Winnow. I cleared my throat and removed his hand.

"He's still jumpy from this morning," I explained.

Winnow said nothing as he guided me to the floor. Every move he made was deliberate and precise, his body moving with the rigidity of someone who had years of practice. His deep, gravelly voice cut through the sound of the music, drawing my attention.

"You did have quite a scare this morning, Princess Asha," Guardian Winnow remarked. "I trust you're feeling better now?"

I resisted the urge to flinch, forcing a polite smile. "I am well, thank you for your concern," I replied, keeping my tone neutral. "The incident was unfortunate, but I am grateful for the swift response."

His grip on me intensified as his voice grew tenser. "Perhaps," he said slowly, with a subtle implication laced in his words, "it's time to reassess your security arrangements. If you believe the war chief is not adequately protecting you, you need only say the word. His Majesty and I would be more than willing to make a change."

A surge of fear rose within me at his thinly veiled insinuation, but I refused to show it and held my ground.

"I assure you," I stated firmly, lifting my chin, "I am perfectly content with War Chief Adriel's protection. He has proven himself to be a capable Guardian, and I see no need for change."

For a moment, Guardian Winnow's aura remained inscrutable, as if he were trying to read my thoughts. I could tell he wanted to say more, but our dance was abruptly halted with the entrance of a messenger into the hall.

Chapter Twenty-Five

Adriel

As I watched Asha dance with Guardian Winnow, a surge of unfamiliar emotion washed over me. It was a sensation akin to chest pain. I dared not explore it deeply.

But it was not just Winnow who elicited this reaction. When Enapay had touched her, the same feeling was there, amplified tenfold when he'd kissed her. I'd been suddenly grateful for the absence of my sword.

Then again, what right did I have to feel possessive over her? She was not mine. She was engaged to my brother, a union I had arranged. I had no claim over her, no right to feel possessive, and yet the sight of her sharing a smile with someone else filled me with primal rage.

Something fierce and all-consuming awakened in me. But I was not ready to acknowledge it, to confront it, so I pushed it down as far as it would go.

I turned to the commotion happening behind me. I watched as a man argued with two of the guards stationed at the entrance. He was dressed in the Ujuima colors of red and gold. A messenger. I signaled to let him pass, and the man moved quickly through the crowd, catching the attention of everyone present.

I stopped him. "Why are you here?"

He nodded his head nervously. "I am here to deliver a message to the king," he said.

I held out my hand. "You may deliver it to me."

His eyes widened in distress. "No. I was given very specific instructions to give it only to King Enapay."

"Come here, boy," Enapay called.

The messenger darted around me and kneeled before handing him a sealed letter.

I made my way over to where King Enapay stood, eager to learn the contents of the letter. As I approached, I caught a glimpse of the anger etched upon his face.

"What news from Ujuima?" I asked, my voice betraying a hint of concern.

My brother glanced at me, his expression grave. "Troubling news, war chief," he replied, his voice tense. "Read it."

He handed the note to me, and I frowned at its contents. My eyes focused on one specific part of it:

As you are aware, Princess Asha was promised to whoever emerged victorious in the Fire Festival. However, due to the unforeseen events surrounding my father's death, the Fire Challenge did not reach its conclusion as anticipated.

Your proposal is rejected. Return her to me, and I will consider not slaughtering every Wiyotakin we come across. I trust you understand the gravity of this situation and the implications if my orders are not followed. Consider your options and prepare yourself accordingly.

The threat was clear. If we did not return Asha, we would be at war with Ujuima and likely all the surrounding kingdoms. We would be challenged. I bristled at the idea of giving Asha back to the man who had brutalized her, permanently scarred her. And yet, I knew if we gave her back, we were likely dead anyway. We failed. I'd failed.

I glanced up at my brother. "We must convene in the war council room and devise a plan."

Enapay's gaze remained cold and distant as he interrupted me. "I am no longer interested in your counsel, little brother. You have failed to protect me and our kingdom. Your reign as war chief is over. You may remain with the Guardians, but you now report to Guardian Winnow."

With a wave of his hand, Enapay signaled for everyone to leave.

"The festivities are over. The royal wedding between me and Princess Asha will commence in a week's time."

CHAPTER TWENTY-SIX

Asha

Kitchi followed as I returned to my room. She pulled her sword free before moving through the corners of the room to check for safety. I was not sure what had happened at the Unity Ball, but I could tell it was not good by the way Enapay dismissed Adriel.

"Do you really think he meant it? That Adriel is no longer the War Chief?"

"Yes," she groaned. "He has been wanting to do that for a very long time. We have discussed what to do if it happened, but—that was before you. We should sit tight until he tells us to move."

I twirled my hair nervously between my fingers. "What do you think was in that letter from my brother?"

"Nothing good, I can tell you that. Adriel's reaction made that apparent."

I pulled at my corset in irritation. "We should go find him. Make him tell us."

Kitchi stilled my hands and released my corset for me. I immediately sucked in some deep breaths, grateful for the air filling my lungs again.

"Is that better?" she asked. I leaned over on the pole of my bed, heaving a sigh.

"Yes."

She laughed softly. "I cannot understand why women want to torture themselves with corsets. They serve no purpose but to draw male eyes. Bleh!"

I laughed with her. "I'm sure Tazbah looked very pretty in hers. What were you two talking about?"

Kitchi fell backwards on the bed and let out a contented sigh. "Nothing and everything. It was like no time had passed. We picked up right where we left off five years ago. She told me about her position at the library and all the books she was reading—speaking of which," Kitchi paused, and I heard the rustle of fabric as she shifted, followed by something small being placed in my hand. "Tazbah wanted me to give you this!"

I brushed my fingers against the objects, feeling soft leather. They were small books, no larger than the palm of my hand.

"What is it?" I asked, my curiosity piqued.

"They are personal journals from Atim Wiyotak in Elliarb, if you can believe them. Oh, she went on and on about wanting to have someone decipher it for her."

I held the journals limply in my hand. I wanted to be interested, but with all that was happening, I couldn't.

"I'll read it later," I said, pulling the remainder of my dress free. "If I'm not going to get any answers tonight, I could at least get ready for bed."

"Well," Kitchi began with great hesitation. "About that, Adriel wants me to sleep in your bed instead of you tonight. He thought it might give us a better chance apprehending the person who was in your room this morning."

"Kitchi, no. I can't have you risk yourself like that."

"I do it every day for Wiyotak," she shrugged. "Why not for you? Besides, whoever they are is expecting someone who cannot defend themself."

I frowned at that. "I suppose so."

She ran her hand supportively along my arm. "Hey, if you want to learn how to defend yourself, I can teach you. We can work on your battlemage."

"I am not sure I have one," I admitted.

"That is bullshit. There is something there. I saw it that day you risked your life for me."

"The day I drugged you."

Kitchi grabbed my shoulders. "The day you *saved* me. You did not give up on me, so I will not give up on you."

"No one has wanted to try with me in a very long time. Thank you."

"Don't get sappy on me, Princess," she said, walking away, ever the warrior. "Your first lesson with me starts now. Let's see you block."

Kitchi ran me through a series of drills, patiently explaining where I needed to bend and duck to evade a direct hit. I was terrible at all of it. Hopeless, just like when I was a child, but I tried. Kitchi seemed absolutely thrown by my lack of basic skills.

We heard a knock before the door slid open. I turned my head to the sound, leaving me exposed to Kitchi's expert strike. I was thrown backwards, the wind knocked out of me.

"Never allow anything to distract you from your opponent," she breathed, pulling me up to stand.

Adriel did not say a word, but he paced like a large cat trying to escape its cage. "Are you going to tell us what is going on?" I asked impatiently.

He stopped, or at least his aura did, and took a deep breath. "Elan will declare war on Wiyotak, unless we agree to return you to him."

My breath caught in my throat. "Why...why haven't you yet?"

"Giving you over is not an option. We will be at war no matter what. I need to find allies in other kingdoms. Entioch or maybe Wyrmwood. I've dispatched riders to see what men we can gather."

"I would rather die than go back," I said firmly.

"It will not come to that. We will keep you safe, although with Guardian Winnow as our new War Chief, it complicates things. I spent much of tonight ensuring that the Guardians remain loyal to me."

Kitchi gasped, but there was an unmistakable wave of excitement in her voice. "Are you saying what I think you are saying? You would go against your brother?"

"No. I have no interest in ruling. I wish to send my brother a message that I will not be so easily cast out."

"You are dancing on a tight rope, Adriel. He could have you executed for even a whisper of this," Kitchi said.

He put his palms on my shoulders. "Which is why we need those dragons. With dragons, we would be unstoppable."

I pulled away and walked to the window. "Kitchi is right. You need to stand against your brother. This half-measure could get everyone killed."

"I can't."

I turned then and watched his aura flare before coiling around him tightly. It was tempting to unfurl in my hands, but I resisted the impulse.

"Then what is the plan?" I asked.

"We lay low, out of sight of Enapay and Winnow. You will have to learn how to fight better than what I just saw."

I paced. "I won't be able to sleep tonight."

Kitchi cleared her throat. "Could it have something to do with your impending wedding. You haven't mentioned that at all."

I frowned, continuing to pace inside the room. I would have to accelerate my plans to leave. There was no way I would allow that man to touch me. But Kitchi had given me an idea.

"I think it's the thought that these could be my last days of freedom. I've never known anything beyond the pits and palace walls," laying it on as thick as I could. "I want to go to a tavern."

"Yes!" Kitchi exclaimed.

"No!" Adriel's sharp objection cut through the air at the same time.

I ignored his protest. "Just for one night, I want to be a regular person. No titles, no guards, no fear. Just... freedom."

"Have you forgotten there are people out there trying to kill you? It's too dangerous," Adriel objected.

I stopped pacing and moved toward him. "I have the rest of my life to fear my brother. It is all I have known. For a few hours, I would like to know something different." For good measure, I fluttered my lashes and parted my lips. "If you want me to behave, do this one thing for me."

Adriel was silent for what felt like an eternity. Just when I thought I'd lost, he said, "One hour, and we take my men," he conceded. "Don't make me regret this."

"Tonight?" I asked.

"Do you want to go or not?" he asked as if he was ready to take back everything he had just said.

I did not have time to reassure him because Kitchi's excitement filled the space. "Burn it all! We are having a hen night!"

Kitchi laced me back into Nayeli's dress. Attendants would notice if I tried to find something else to put on but I was able to find sensible boots since we'd be walking.

"Kitchi?" I asked.

"Yes?"

I wasn't quite sure what I really wanted to ask. "How do I look?" I asked finally.

"Like a princess."

I frowned, smoothing down the dress. "What if I don't want to look like a princess?"

She chuckled. "And what do you want to look like?"

I shook my head as words failed me. "I don't know," I admitted.

Kitchi circled me and inhaled deeply. "Do you trust me?"

"With my life," I said without hesitation.

Kitchi kneeled down, and I heard the unmistakable sound of steel being drawn.

"What are you—" I did not get a chance to finish as fabric ripped at my sides, and a breeze wafting through my legs.

"Kitchi!" I cried, reaching down to assess the damage. To my surprise, the cuts were neat. There were no bare threads along the seams, but the slit went halfway up my thighs. "This is Nayeli's!"

"She'll approve, I promise."

I had to admit, the slits made walking easier, but it was difficult for me not to want to close the sides with my hands.

"Leave it be. You look great," she said, loosening the top of the corset over my bosom.

"This can't be what women wear to taverns?"

"How would you know, Princess?" she said, undoing the belt that held her sword and placing it along my hips. "One more thing," she said. She put her hands through my hair and gave it a good shake.

"Now I know you've lost your mind," I said.

"Your hair was too neat, too tightly curled. Now you look like you just came from your bed."

My eyebrows rose. "And that is a good thing, why?"

Kitchi clicked her tongue before she let out the most delighted laugh. I crossed my arms, waiting for her to explain. "Sorry," she managed between chuckles. "It's not about looking as though you just got out of bed—it's about who you *might* have gotten out of bed with."

My jaw dropped as I threaded my fingers through my mussed hair. "So, you want others to envision who I might have been... intimate with?"

"It will drive men wild. Women, too," she quipped. "Come on! He is waiting." She approached the window, and a soft creak as she pushed the panes open.

"What are you doing?" I asked, slightly alarmed.

"We have to go out the window," she explained. "Hurry, the men are waiting for us below."

My heart raced as she led me to the window sill. As I climbed up, the rush of cool wind against my bare legs, caused me to shiver. I had no way of knowing how far up I was. My imagination conjured images of the distance, the height, the danger, but there was no turning back now.

"We have to go," Kitchi repeated urgently, guiding me to the edge. My fingers gripped tightly onto the frame as I tried to steady my breathing and ignore the vertigo threatening to overwhelm me.

"Jump!" a voice called from below.

"Are you sure?" I hesitated, turning back to Kitchi.

"Just jump. They'll catch you," she reassured me with unwavering confidence.

With a deep breath, I leaped into the void. For a split second, I felt weightless as the wind rushed past me. Then suddenly, several pairs of strong arms caught me, their grip firm yet gentle. Among them, a familiar set of arms, which could only be Adriel, helped me stand upright.

Kitchi followed behind, leaping effortlessly with no assistance.

"This is going to be so fun!" Ashkii exclaimed. He wasted no time introducing me to Moki and Chato as we began to walk, leaving the courtyard behind. At first, I regarded them with hesitation, but it didn't take long for them to win me over. Chato made playful jabs at Ashkii, like an older brother would. He bragged of his adventures and the battles he had won. Moki scoffed at Chato's antics. Moki, the head trainer, questioned me about my battlemage, or lack thereof. He appeared very interested in my time working closely with dragons and how they are used in war. I enjoyed the company, as I was not used to people speaking so freely around me.

As we approached the tavern, I could already hear the lively music and laughter that greeted my ears. The sound was joyous, a vibrant chorus that beckoned us inside. The rhythmic pattern of boots hitting the wooden floor, the clinking of glasses, and the unmistakable sound of beer being poured into large jugs all blended together in a symphony of merriment. Amidst the lively noise, I caught the low, rumbling growl of some kind of animal.

"It's a panther," Moki explained beside me as we entered. "This tavern is called Panther's Pants."

I raised an eyebrow in his direction. "Panther's Pants?"

He laughed heartily. "I didn't name it. Don't blame me for that one."

Before I could respond, Kitchi grabbed my arm and began pulling me towards other dancers. I felt the vibrations of the dancers' movements through the solid oak floorboards.

"Come on," she urged.

I hesitated, feeling a wave of nervousness wash over me. "What's wrong?" she asked, sensing my reluctance.

"I don't know the steps to this music," I admitted, feeling a bit embarrassed.

"Don't worry," she said reassuringly while squeezing my hand. "Ashkii and I will teach you."

They guided me into the throng of dancers, where Ashkii took one of my hands and Kitchi held the other. Together, they started to move, their bodies swaying gracefully as they guided mine in what they called the round dance.

"Just feel the music," Ashkii said. "Let it move through you."

I concentrated on the sounds around me, the lively tunes, and joyful laughter. Slowly, I began to relax and let the music take over. Kitchi and Ashkii's laughter mingled with my own as I started to enjoy myself, feeling the freedom and exhilaration of the moment.

Eventually, Chato came over with a tray of drinks. "It is not a hen party until we drink," he said, placing drinks in all of our hands.

It burned as it went down my throat. I seldom drank alcohol, but after the fire left my throat, I rather enjoyed it.

"Another," I exclaimed eagerly. Chato obliged enthusiastically.

Kitchi's hand grasped my arm tightly. "Asha. She's here."

"Who?" I asked, turning to follow her movements.

"It's Tazbah," Ashkii mused. "She is looking our way."

"Invite her over!" Chato yelled excitedly.

Tazbah joined us in seconds. "Princess, when you said you wanted to meet, I did not think it would be here."

I winced, realizing that my hand had been given away. "Yes, well, I wanted to thank you personally for the journals you lent me. And we are having a sort of hen party before I am married, only we were short on hens. Will you join us tonight?"

"It would be my honor, Princess."

"Please. I am just Ash tonight. I want to blend in. In fact, I could use another drink. Perhaps you and Kitchi could get us some."

"We already have a tray..." Ashkii began.

"I would like something different," I interrupted. "Something sweet, I think. Wasn't that what we were saying, Kitchi?"

"Uh, yes. Let me show you," Kitchi said.

Kitchi and Tazbah walked away, and I strained my ears to be able to hear their conversation.

"Princ—I mean Ash. Why didn't you just ask us?" Ashkii questioned.

"She's trying to play matchmaker for the two of them, you simpleton," Chato scoffed.

Ashkii inhaled sharply. "Oh."

"Speaking of which, I see a pretty girl by the bar who can't keep her eyes off me," Chato announced. "I will return shortly."

Ashkii stayed behind to continue our dance lessons. As the music slowed to a gentle cadence, Ashkii showed me a new dance he called the coven step. Our bodies moved in sync, swaying and gliding across the floor. We were lost in the music and each other's company.

"I'm not as simple as everyone thinks, you know."

"I've never thought that," I reassured him.

"You would be the only one," he replied with a hint of sadness in his voice.

A thought crossed my mind. "When are you going to share your poetry with me?" I said into his ear.

"If you are speaking in my left ear, I cannot make it out. My hearing is not so good," he admitted sheepishly.

I inhaled sharply. Being a Guardian meant you were in perfect form. An injury during battle could easily end a career.

"What do you mean? How are you a Guardian then?"

He shrugged. "Like I said, it was a family expectation. If I didn't go in, I'd be disowned."

My heart sank at his words, but I understood all too well the pressure of family expectations.

"But does Adriel know?" I asked.

"He figured it out."

"He figured it out and still allowed you to remain with the Guardians?" I questioned. "I mean, I'm glad he did. It's just in Ujuima that would never have happened. Even my family name did not spare me. I was sent to the dragon pits, but some families have unseers like me killed."

"It is the same here," Ashkii explained. "That's why my family kept it quiet, as did the War Chief. I am grateful to him; he saved my life."

I wasn't sure how to feel about this. It was like a puzzle piece I couldn't quite place. "That explains your hand movements. You are signing."

His breath caught. "You never cease to amaze me. How did you figure that out? I've tried to be so careful."

"When you can't rely on sight, other senses are heightened. I heard you. I wonder if you could teach me somehow." His hands moved to my forearm, and I felt a series of movements. Signing. "What did you say?"

"I said I'd be honored to teach you."

"You're hogging her," Chato interjected jovially, his deep voice cutting through the lively chatter. He took my arm and spun me around in a playful twirl.

"Not so fast, Chato," I laughed, struggling to keep up with his energetic movements. "How many of those tiny glasses have you had?"

"Oh, come on, we are celebrating your engagement!" Chato exclaimed enthusiastically, ignoring my protest.

"It's hardly a celebration when you are being forced into marriage against your will," I retorted bitterly, unable to hide the resentment in my voice.

Chato's voice turned serious as he took hold of my hand. "No, we are celebrating your freedom. You're not the dragon girl curled up in your little room anymore, Ash."

I couldn't help but laugh at his words. "Aren't I?"

"No, they tried to hide you away like you were some hideous thing. But look at you now, Ash. Your legs are—"

Before he could finish his sentence, I playfully socked him in the arm. "Watch it. I am almost a married woman," I teased.

Chato chuckled darkly in response. He leaned in closer and whispered into my ear with admiration in his voice, "That laugh. Now I know why the War Chief can't keep his eyes off you."

My lips tightened. "It's all to marry me off to his brother," I said, with a hint of anger.

"If you say so," Chato replied. "But those are not the eyes of a man who views you as his brother's future wife."

His voice held a note of knowing that gave me pause. Before he could speak further, he was pulled away.

"Chato?"

A familiar hand clasped mine, the other encircling me as his aura flickered into view.

"Two dances in one night? What have I done to earn such attention?" I asked. Adriel grunted before guiding me away from Chato, talking me through the movements of the next dance. His hand on my back was steady, but there was tension in his grip that hadn't been there before.

"Your dance steps are almost as bad as your warrior skills," he mused.

I tilted my head, feigning indifference, though his closeness was unnerving. The heat of his body, the faint scent of him made it hard to focus. "Did you come over here to ruin my night, Adriel? If so, Chato and I were having a fine time."

"I saw," he grumbled. Why was his mood so sour?

"Did you have to wear that dress?" he asked.

"It is Nayeli's dress, the same one I had on earlier," I reminded him,

He quieted, and for a moment, I was self-conscious as I felt his gaze.

He leaned in. "Whatever you did to it is drawing the eyes of every man in this place."

I sighed. "What does it matter? I'm practically married now."

His grip tightened around my waist. "Not yet," he whispered.

Feeling a bit awkward as silence fell between us, I asked, "Where is Kitchi?"

"Over in the corner with Tazbah on her lap?"

"Really?" I grinned.

"Don't look so smug. It's strange seeing her like that?"

"In love?"

"Maybe," he mused, deep in thought. "You really know how to meddle, you know. First my horse and now my best lieutenant." He spun me around and lifted me into the air, perfectly in sync with the music. "You are determined to make me regret this night."

I wished I could see his face. Something was happening, but I couldn't quite decipher it. "I... I think I need some fresh air," I said, feeling suddenly off balance.

He took my hand in his, which did nothing to soothe my racing heart, before guiding me outside. I drank in several deep breaths of the cool night air. We were greeted with the chirping of insects in the trees and the padding of animals roaming through the undergrowth. I buried my face into my hands, trying to regain control of my senses.

"Too much of that piss they call mead, I suspect," Adriel scolded. "You really shouldn't be drinking, Princess."

The sound of my title on his lips was oddly intimate, like a caress. Shivers ran down my arms. "I could use one of your cloaks right about now," I admitted, wrapping my arms around myself for warmth.

"I'm afraid I am all out of those. Maybe if you hadn't destroyed my Iná's dress."

I turned away, feeling self-conscious. "I must look like I did when you first met me," I muttered, hugging myself tighter.

For a moment, there was nothing but stillness. I heard the soft scuff of his boots against the ground as he closed the distance between us. My breath hitched as I watched his aura approach. The air shifted around me, warmer now, carrying the faint scent of him—sandalwood and something uniquely his. My heart thudded in my chest, echoing in my ears.

His hands found mine, unwrapping them from where they clung to my arms. His touch sent a shiver through me, and I froze, acutely aware of how intimate this was. His calloused fingers brushed against my skin as he lifted my chin. The gesture was tender, and it made my breath catch again.

The world seemed to narrow to the sound of his quiet exhale, to the way his thumb lingered against my jaw. I could hear the faintest shift of his weight, the rustle of his clothes as he moved, and I realized I was holding my breath, waiting for him to speak, to do something, anything.

But he didn't. Not right away. Instead, he stood there, his presence grounding me in a way I hadn't realized I needed. And in that silence, I felt seen, truly seen, in away that had nothing to do with sight.

"You looked like a scared little rabbit when I first met you," he said at last. "A beautiful one, but also very afraid. Tonight, you look... different. Trust me, my men have noticed," he said with an air of possessiveness.

I swallowed, inhaling his scent. "And you? What do you think... is different, I mean?"

He rubbed his hands along my arms, warming them. The shivers down my body did not cease.

"Maybe it is the outdoors, but you look content," he said finally.

"My father wanted me hidden away. Being confined to the pits as a child meant I did not feel sunshine or fresh air for months. I do not take being outside for granted."

"I will never understand how a man could be so cruel to his own flesh and blood."

He felt sorry for me. Good. This seemed like as good of time as any. "We are just minutes from the castle," I observed. "Does that mean we are close to town?"

His hands stiffened but he did not stop his ministrations. "Why do you want to know?"

I kept my breath even. I needed to tread carefully. "This is to be my kingdom. Shouldn't I know?"

He stopped his movements, and to my surprise pulled me closer until his chest was pressed to mine. "You think I don't know why you wanted to really come here? You really think I believed you wanted a hen night?"

My eyes widened. "Of course, I..."

"Whatever plans you have of escape," he interrupted. "Put them out of your head now. Enapay will kill you if you try."

My lips tightened. "I will not go back to Elan," I said between clenched teeth.

He stood there silently for a time before taking deep, measured step back, creating distance between us. "I think we should get you home now."

Chapter Twenty-Seven

Asha

I was covered head to toe in my sleeping robes, but I hesitated before crossing the barrier between my room and his. Tonight was the first night of our new sleeping arrangements. Kitchi had fallen asleep several minutes before. I listened as she breathed peacefully. I hoped it was because of Tazbah.

Don't be a coward, I told myself. At this point, we had already slept in the same room. This wasn't any different. But it was. I was entering his space. I tapped on the door before pushing my way through, the satchel of eggs on my hip. I had been in this room earlier, briefly, but I was not yet familiar with the layout.

"Adriel," I called. "Could you—"

"Yes," he said, placing his hand on the back of my shoulder. His voice was low and rough, like he was sleep-deprived, as he guided me to the edge of the bed and paused.

"Do you need my assistance with the sheets?" he asked.

A smile escaped my lips. "Are you asking me if I need to be tucked in?"

"I . . . I just need to know if I can go lie down now."

"I think I can manage from here."

He left my side, and I removed the eggs and tucked them around me as I had grown used to doing.

"We should name them?" I said.

"Name what?" Adriel said sleepily.

"The dragon eggs."

"Let me guess, you can see their auras, and they all have personalities."

My mouth twitched. "No. I can't see their auras yet, but when I put my ear to them, I can hear them hum. Their pitches are all different."

"What's wrong with egg one, two, and three?"

I scoffed. "Come on, we can do better than that," I said. "What about Aurora, Solara, and Zion after the elemental Guardians?"

"Aurora?" he asked.

"At least one is a girl."

He flipped over on his pallet. "I prefer the Salerian gods. How about Igbo, Mwana, and Ala?"

I played with the names in my head, trying out the sounds on my tongue. "Yeah. That sounds nice." I turned around and cradled them in my arms. And so, they were named.

Kitchi and Adriel were not kidding about training. As the first rays of sun warmed my skin through the parted curtains, Kitchi was in Adriel's room, shaking me awake and dragging me onto the sparring mat. Moki proved to be a formidable opponent, showing little patience for my title or blindness.

"You have to anticipate where I'll be," he barked.

"I can't see you to anticipate anything." I'd tried to follow his aura all morning, but auras were deceptive. They grew larger under physical exertion, making it impossible for me to find where he would strike next.

We continued in this manner for days on end. Each day, my body was left bruised and battered from our rigorous training sessions, followed by sleepless nights in Adriel's room. My dreams were fevered, tangled with images I dared not name. They burned with a kind of intimacy I told myself was nothing more than the byproduct of proximity—inevitable, with Adriel so near. And yet, even with all my careful reasoning, shame curled in my chest. I would sooner die than speak of them aloud, even to Kitchi.

From his restlessness and tense demeanor, it was clear that Adriel was not sleeping well either. I couldn't help but wonder if it was to ward off his own nightmares, or because he was worried about the plan he had put into motion. I certainly wasn't sleeping with my impending nuptials upon us.

"Be alert!" Chato's voice cut through the air just before he landed a blow on my shoulder.

"I think I'm done," I panted.

Heavy footsteps sounded on the mat. "You are not even trying," Adriel growled in frustration. "You have to anticipate and block."

"Thanks for the tip," I retorted, with sarcasm dripping from my words. "I've only been hearing that for the past couple of days."

"You heard it from me two seconds ago," Moki grumbled.

I'd tried to picture Moki from his voice many times, but all I managed was an image of a grumpy gargoyle.

Adriel approached slowly until we were nose to nose. "I am going to touch you, and I want you to anticipate where my hand is going."

My neck felt hot, and my breath quickened. My lips parted as he erased the distance between our bodies.

"Wh . . . what?"

Before I could question further, his hand was on my arm. I pulled away instantly, and then it was on my waist.

"Come on," he ground out. "Feel where I am going to touch you next."

His hand leaped to my shoulder, and what was that? I could feel the energy of his battlemage coursing between us. He was going to my left cheek next. I lifted my forearm, and it met his hand. My breath left me, realizing I had managed to block him for once.

"Again," he said.

He was going for my neck. I turned right, out of his way, and ducked. He was reaching for my knee. Block. My thigh. Block. Then my . . . I slipped, realizing he was going for my ass. I fell, but not before reaching for his aura. I grasped at the edges until it overtook me.

I gasped as I felt rage and fear and something else.

As soon as I tapped in, he shoved me out. Both of us lay on the mat panting, neither of us daring to say a word. Finally, he stood and held his hand toward mine. I allowed him to pull me up.

What was that? Before I could ask, he turned away.

"Good work," he mumbled. "Work on tapping into auras. It might just be your greatest weapon in a fight."

I was taken aback. Weapon? Yes, reading auras was a neat parlor trick that allowed me to handle dragons, but a battlemage?

Still trying to catch my breath, I asked, "What do you mean? A battlemage is a weapon. Reading auras is just for fun."

Adriel halted. "If you hadn't reached for my aura, you wouldn't have stood a chance against me. It's true that battlemages tend to be more aggressive, but let me tell you, when you grabbed hold of mine . . . it was intense. Like you could crush me in your hands if you wanted to."

I stumbled back, realization hitting me like a punch to the gut. "Wait . . . you're saying this is my battlemage? How do we know for sure?"

Adriel scoffed with barely leashed anger. "I'm sure the emperor knew. He tended to snuff out things that did not fit his agenda, and a battlemage that is deadlier than his own, more powerful than anything his sons could wield would fall into that category."

I chewed my lip, realizing that my whole life had been a lie. I'd always believed the reason I lost my sight was because I lacked battlemage, but maybe, just maybe, Father had known all along. Maybe he'd needed an excuse to get rid of me.

"What is your battlemage?" I asked.

"What?" he asked in surprise.

"You've never told me," I pressed. "Kitchi can make precision strikes, Chato can master any weapon given to him, and Moki can target pressure points. What is yours?"

Instead of answering, he said, "I came to tell you our new war chief has asked that you accompany the king for dinner tonight."

My face fell. I'd just unlocked a piece of myself that had always been a mystery, and Adriel had found a way to ruin it.

"I suggest you find something to wear other than my Iná's dress," he said.

I listened as his heavy boots stalked away. No one spoke until the door shuddered behind him. I stood, deciding to break the silence.

"I'm ready for you, Chato. Give me your best shot."

Once we arrived back at my room, I impatiently knocked on Adriel's side of the door, but his room was eerily silent. My heart sank as panic began to creep in. What if I had to face Enapay alone?

"What am I going to do?" I asked desperately, turning to Kitchi for guidance.

She placed a comforting hand on my shoulder. "You are going to have a bath and get dressed for tonight," she said calmly. "Adriel is on top of this, that I can promise. Enapay can't do anything to you without starting a war with Ujuima."

I nodded, grateful for her reassurance. But even with her reasoning, nausea washed over me at the thought of sharing a meal with this man.

The attendants helped me prepare for the evening, brushing out my hair and adorning it with simple jewels. Enapay had been "kind" enough to send up an outfit for me to wear. My attendants described it as a simple white dress made of soft silk. It hugged my curves and flared out at my ankles. The neckline was lower than I liked, but I was able to button the dress just above my collarbone.

Kitchi accompanied me through the castle halls toward Enapay's wing. She made a sharp turn.

"This isn't the way. What are you up to, Kitchi?"

"I just thought you'd appreciate a stroll through the garden first," she said.

I sighed. Normally, I would never turn down an opportunity to enjoy the outdoors. Wiyotak had a far better climate than Ujuima, but honestly, I just wanted to get the evening over with.

"Maybe we shouldn't keep the king waiting . . ."

I stopped speaking mid-sentence as we stepped through the double doors leading to the garden. The air shifted, cooler now, carrying the faint scent of blooming flowers and damp earth. But it wasn't the change in temperature or the fragrance that made me stop; it was the sudden, overwhelming sensation of light.

My breath caught in my throat, and for a moment, I couldn't move. It wasn't the kind of light I remembered from before, not the sharp clarity of sight, but something different—something alive. The world around me seemed to pulse with it, a soft, shimmering glow that I could feel more than see. My heart raced, and I instinctively reached out, my fingers brushing against the cool metal of the doorframe as if to steady myself.

A path wound through the space ahead of me, and crystals illuminated the walkway, so I could see it clearly. It felt as if every color and hue were spread out before me. Some crystals held intricate patterns. I reached out and touched one of them, marveling at its beauty.

"How can I see this?" I asked incredulously.

"They are aura crystals. We thought they might help you appreciate the gardens even more. If you like them, we can hang them throughout Empira for you. It is very inconspicuous."

"We?"

"Well, it was our war chief's idea. The real one, not Winnow. Adriel asked Chato and the others to help him. He'd read about them in one of his books. We've spent the last few days putting this together to cheer you up. Do you love it?"

I was breathless as I gazed at the spectrum of colors. It was like nothing I had ever seen, and more beautiful than anything I could remember before I'd lost my sight. I closed my eyes to hold back tears.

"Are you okay?" Kitchi asked worriedly.

I turned and reached for her hands. "It is breathtaking. The nicest thing anyone has ever done for me, truly," I breathed. "He did this at night? Is this where he's been going?"

The heavy chain mail of the royal guard caught my attention, causing the moment to shatter. I flinched, my grip on Kitchi's hands tightening instinctively. The colors around me seemed to dim, the magic of the garden retreating as the intrusion pulled me back to reality. I felt a flicker of frustration spark in my chest. I pushed it down, forcing myself to breathe. The loss of that perfect, fleeting moment stung more than I wanted to admit.

"Princess Asha, King Enapay awaits. We will escort her from here," one of the attendants said.

Kitchi bristled beside me. "I am part of Princess Asha's personal guard," she said stiffly.

The guard laughed dismissively. "What could be safer than the Guardians of the king?"

I sensed Kitchi's worry as she squeezed my palms to reassure me. "I will have to leave you now, but I will await your return in your room. Send for me if you need anything."

I nodded before a guard took my arm to guide me into Enapay's wing. This was a part of the Empira Palace I had not been allowed to venture into. This part of the palace felt cooler, like it was made of stone more than any other material. The sound of my walking staff echoed through the corridors. The attendant led me through a series of doors until I could hear Enapay's laughter.

"You will kneel upon entering His Majesty's residence," the guard instructed.

As the doors opened, I stepped forward and tried to give a presentable curtsy, although my legs protested from all the drills Chato had put me through.

As I entered King Enapay's private dining hall, I couldn't shake the feeling of unease settling over me like a stain that would not lift no matter how long it soaked.

The aroma of expensive meats filled the air, clashing with the smell of freshly polished gold.

"Princess Asha," King Enapay's smooth voice cut through the silence. "You look radiant this evening."

Forcing a polite smile onto my lips, I couldn't ignore the way his fingers lingered on my body as he embraced me. I felt exposed and vulnerable.

"Thank you, Your Majesty," I replied, my voice steady despite the turmoil churning within me. "Your generosity knows no bounds."

There was smugness in the air as he smoothed his hands over my gown. "I'm glad you appreciate my taste," he said, his tone oozing with thinly veiled lust.

The scrape of his jeweled ring against the rim of his goblet grated in my ears, sharper than the wine he swallowed. His aura pulsed with satisfaction—too steady, too smug. He was toying with me.

"So, princess," he began casually but with a calculating tone, "tell me, how have you been spending your time in my kingdom? I trust you've been keeping interesting company."

My stomach churned at his implication, and I fought to keep my composure. "The Guardians have been very kind to me," I replied, my voice betraying none of the unease bubbling beneath the surface.

"Ah, yes," he mused, his tone deceptively casual. "An . . . eclectic group, to say the least. I trust they've been treating you well?"

I nodded, though a small part of me bristled at his thinly veiled insinuation. "They have been most gracious," I replied, my voice tinged with a hint of defiance.

As the meal progressed, I couldn't shake the feeling that King Enapay's questions were anything but innocent. His desire for information left me feeling exposed and vulnerable in his presence.

"Do you know much about the history of our country?"

"Yes, I've spent a lot of time reading about Atim Wiyotak, your great-great-grandfather."

Enapay sipped his cup of wine loudly before saying, "Yes, dear old great-great-grandad Atim. I love to read about him, or rather, read what others say about him."

He'd finally caught my attention. "I'd be interested to know. I have not come across those readings yet."

He laughed loudly. "Yes, you wouldn't have heard of his brother Melo Wiyotak. He was a very interesting man. He was delighted to live a simple life with his soon-to-be-bride, Onida."

"Onida. Why does that name sound familiar?"

"Onida was the first queen of Wiyotak."

My chest tightened. Enapay's tone changed to something predatory. He was enjoying telling me this story.

"You see, Atim could not stand for his brother to have something he couldn't, so he implemented a bridegroom ceremony. Do you know what that is, princess?"

My face twisted. What I knew about these ceremonies was that women were taken against their will and often forced to lie with their captors.

Enapay laughed. "I can see on your face that you do. Yes, Atim was powerful, but only he ever referred to himself as good. Atim took Onida, and Melo left Wiyotak. He was never seen again."

The scrape of his jeweled ring against the rim of his goblet grated in my ears, sharper than the wine he swallowed. His aura pulsed with satisfaction—too steady, too smug. He was toying with me. I put my fork down. There was no need to pretend I was eating. "I'm sorry. I did not mean to spoil dinner. Time for another story, and perhaps this will whet your appetite for dessert," he purred. "Do you know why relations are so tense between Ujuima and Wiyotak?"

The hair rose on the back of my neck. Something had changed in Enapay's aura. "Ujuima has poor relations with a number of kingdoms," I said noncommittally.

"But you've had to ask yourself why hold such malice for a small, weak kingdom from the south."

"I guess I do not see Wiyotak as weak. You pose a formidable threat to my brother's forces."

"How charming you are," he chuckled. "For far too long, Firepeak has held the world's largest dracite mine, but no more," he boasted. "Wiyotak has more dracite resources than all the kingdoms combined."

"Why not offer Ujuima to mine it?"

He swirled his wine in his hand, sounding much too pleased with himself. "My brother never wanted that. He had ambitions of cultivating dragons in Wiyotak. Can you imagine?"

I thought of the eggs tucked back safely in my room. If only he knew. Too bad I was going to be taking them with me once I escaped.

"I did briefly," he continued, "but all his attempts have failed. My brother said we could not trust the Ujuimans not to take our land and sent my Guardians on foolish missions in search of dragon eggs. Do you see any dragons?" he asked before I heard the crackle of a wine glass against the floor between us.

I startled, wondering where he was going with this. I didn't have to wait long.

"So, when you arrived at my door, I realized I had quite the opportunity. I could give you back to Elan, with the promise that he could have sole access to our mines."

My body froze at his words as I tried to understand his meaning.

"It appears your brother would rather see you dead than worry about having you back. But don't worry, I worked out a half measure for you."

His words chilled my blood as I slowly stood from the table. I now understood the danger I was in, but I was unsure how to escape the room fast enough.

"What did you do?" I demanded as hands grabbed my arms to immobilize me. "No!" I yelled.

"Don't worry, princess," he crooned. "Your brother has a flair for the theatrics but I will become a very wealthy man."

"He will go back on his word!" I yelled, fighting against the hands that held me. "He will kill you!"

"Goodbye, princess. It pains me we could not make a marriage between us work, but you understand."

Hands fell onto my body as I fought and screamed, but there was nowhere to go. Panic flooded my chest, ice-cold and suffocating, as I slowly came to the realization that this time, no one was coming to save me.

Chapter Twenty-Eight

Adriel

As I paced back and forth in the dimly lit corridor, my mind raced with questions, each one more pressing than the last. What was my brother planning? Why had he insisted on dining with Asha? And why tonight of all nights, when tensions were already running high? I had instructed my men to be on high alert, sensing that something was amiss, but even their vigilant presence did little to ease my worry. I'd been sloppy today with Asha, allowing her behind the defenses I had so carefully constructed over the years. Her metaphysical touch had practically undone me. I curled my fists, realizing how close she was to learning the truth.

With a frustrated sigh, I made my way outside to the garden, hoping the cool night air would clear my mind and soothe my frayed nerves. The scent of honeybloom hung heavy on the wind as I strode along the winding paths. The soft crunch of gravel beneath my boots was the only sound to break the silence of the night.

Lost in thought, I barely noticed the shadow flitting across the moonlit lawn. Instinct kicked in, and my hand went to the hilt of my blade. My senses were on high alert as I scanned the darkness for any sign of danger.

"Who's there?" I called out. "Show yourself!"

My battlemage screamed at me to strike, to defend myself, but I patiently held my ground. My fingers tightened around the hilt of my blade, the smooth leather grip cool against my skin. I took comfort in the weight of the sword in my hand. I needed to break something.

Kitchi emerged silhouetted in darkness with a man bound with rope at her side. She pushed him to his knees with her boot. He nearly collapsed to the ground, unable to steady himself with his wrists bound behind him.

"I found him trying to break into Asha's room," she said.

"Identify yourself," I demanded, my voice low and dangerous, every muscle in my body coiled and ready to spring into action at a moment's notice. "And make it quick."

The figure with chestnut skin and a thin frame emerged as he released his battlemage. The shroud that concealed his features loosened until I could see him clearly. I tensed, my hand still hovering near the hilt of my blade. Recognition washed over me.

"I've seen you before," I said, studying his face. "You are Asha's brother."

Surprise flickered in his eyes soon kindling into recognition. "I am Kwasi Osei, Second Prince of Ujuima."

Before I could even begin to process this information, Kwasi's urgent voice cut through the air. "Listen to me, Adriel," he said, his intense gaze locking onto mine. "I risked everything to come here and warn you. I tried to warn Asha a few days ago, but she was frightened, and you got to her before I could."

The pieces clicked into place. "You were the one in her room before."

Kwasi nodded. "I'd hoped to warn her of Elan and your brother's plans. I saw you with her. You seemed . . . committed to protecting her. I hope you will heed my warning."

I had no time to dwell on the implications of Kwasi's words. "What warning do you bring?" I demanded, my voice steady despite the worry brewing within me.

Kwasi's expression darkened, his eyes flashing with anger and fear. "Enapay intends to put Asha through the bridegroom ceremony," he explained, his words heavy with dread. "It's at Elan's request. She will belong to whomever finds her first."

"What do you mean, she will belong to them?" I demanded, pressing my blade into his neck.

"I mean the champions of other kingdoms are here. They intend to hunt her and... force her into a marital union. We may already be too late. We need to take her away from here."

My blood ran cold at the mention of that barbaric tradition.

Kitchi and I locked eyes. Without hesitation, I made my decision.

"We need to find her. She is with Enapay now."

With a silent nod of agreement, the three of us set off into the darkness.

Chapter Twenty-Nine

Asha

As my eyes fluttered open, a cold fear gripped my heart. I was lying on the damp forest floor. The sharp scent of fallen leaves filled my nostrils, and the crunch of foliage beneath me sent shivers through my body. Enapay's warning echoed in my head, the memory of his words chilling me to the bone. I was being hunted. The realization washed over me like a wave of icy water.

Panic rose within me as I sat up, trying to make sense of my surroundings. The tree trunk against which I leaned felt like a barrier between me and the unknown danger lurking. But as I reached out for support, I realized my walking staff was nowhere to be found. I knew that without my sight and without a guide by my side, I was hopelessly lost. Every rustle and snap sounded like the approach of my pursuers. There was no time for fear or hesitation. The fate of the dragon eggs depended on me, and I refused to let anything stand in the way of protecting them. Relief fluttered through me as I found the steel in my boot as well as the vials of herbs I'd tucked away from Iná's tent. Thankfully, they had not searched me, probably assuming I was too weak to carry weapons. Their underestimation of me would cost them.

The forest seemed to close in around me, its branches reaching out like gnarled fingers ready to snatch me away. I grabbed the branches, trying to find just the right one. I used my blade to separate one from its tree and the lingering arms. It was not perfect, but it would do as a staff for now.

Every step forward was a struggle. My senses strained as I navigated through the tangled maze of trees and undergrowth. It was difficult to navigate, but I pressed on, determined to find a way back. Halting my progress, I strained my ears, listening intently to the night around me. The chorus of frogs and the haunting hoot of an owl filled the air, but beneath the sounds was something else—a soft, barely perceptible rustle, the snap of a twig beneath a boot. Fear clenched my heart as I heard voices nearby. Someone was out there.

I knew I couldn't keep running forever. My pursuer was gaining on me with each frantic step, and I could feel my strength waning with every labored breath. I would never outrun them. I needed to hide. I tripped on another root and went down, rolling underneath some foliage. I lay as low as I could, trying to calm my ragged breaths. The footsteps halted. I listened as he pulled out his blade.

"Princess," the man called. "I know you're in here. Come on out, and I'll play nice. If I have to drag you out, I cannot promise any-thing."

I shivered, recognizing the voice. "Come now, princess, I come in peace from Firepeak. You will like it there."

It was Prince Atar. The man Elan was particularly interested in having me meet. That could only mean bad things.

"I'm growing impatient," he continued as he walked in a different direction.

I waited, praying he would not circle back. It grew quiet, and for a moment, I wondered if he had left until an object struck the ground a few feet in front of me. An arrow?

"I know you're in there," Prince Atar called again. "Come out, and I'll stop sending arrows through."

Another sounded less than a foot from my thigh. I fought the urge to curl up in a ball to make myself smaller, trying frantically to squelch my rasping breaths.

"We could make this nice and easy," he said. Another arrow hit the tree right above my head. "Or we could make this difficult. Which do you choose?"

Silence again.

He laughed.

"I'm glad you want this to be difficult. It makes it more fun." He shot another arrow, and this one grazed my cheek before embedding in the tree behind me. I sucked in my breath.

"There you are," he said.

I leaped and ran in the opposite direction, unsure of where I was going or whether I was heading toward more danger. I hadn't made it far when my face came into contact with a tree trunk, and I fell. My head pulsed, and blood trickled from a cut under my eyebrow. I moaned as I tried to get up, but a hand roughly grabbed my leg and pulled me toward him. I winced at the searing pain as he stood me up and breathed down my neck. I fought weakly against him, trying every move that Moki had shown me, but it was no use.

"Let me go!" I screamed.

I struggled against Atar's grasp, my heart thrashing in my ears as I screamed into the void of the forest, my voice swallowed by the oppressive silence. But then, from the depths of the woods, a sound pierced the stillness—an angry roar that echoed through the trees. A chill swept through me.

Prince Atar all but jumped at the sound, his grip loosening on me as we turned to face the source of the disturbance. Another growl followed, low and menacing, like the rumble of thunder on a rain cloud.

My ears perked at the sound of leaves parting, and a form emerged from the shadows of the forest. The form was unmistakable. It was a dragon, massive with scales gleaming in the dappled light filtering through the canopy above. He was like a midnight blue piece of metal that gleamed in the darkness, honed to maim, to kill. How I could clearly see the dragon confused me greatly. He was not an aura or a source of light, but an adult dragon.

Atar released me, stepping back in awe as he seemed to gaze at the creature. "You are the biggest dragon I've ever seen," he muttered, his voice tinged with wonder. "Where did you come from? Did Elan send you?"

But the dragon paid no heed to Atar's questions. Its golden eyes remained fixed on me. With each step it took, I could feel the heat of its flames licking at the air, its powerful presence filling the clearing with a sense of raw power and untamed fury.

As the dragon drew closer, my fear melted away, replaced by a strange sense of calm. It was as if the creature recognized me, as if we shared some unspoken bond that transcended words or reason.

As it loomed over me, its eyes ablaze with intensity, I knew that somehow it was here to protect me.

With a final roar that shook the very earth beneath our feet, the dragon spoke. "Get back, mortal," he said, fixing his gaze beyond me to Atar. "You are not welcome."

My mouth gaped open upon hearing the dragon speak. Could Atar hear the words? Flames sprouted from the dragon's tongue, a searing heat emanating from him.

"Dragon, get back. She is mine," Atar said, standing firm.

The dragon regarded Atar and tilted his head, his jaws shaking. Was this dragon laughing? Then he opened his mouth wide before a stream of fire flew from his throat. I ducked my head, prepared to meet my end, but all I felt was heat along my back. When the fire ceased, warm dust scattered around me. Ash and bone. I pushed back against the tree, wiping the hot substance off my hands.

"Are you going to hurt me?" I asked. "Because if you are, I need you to be done with it."

The dragon dipped his massive head, closing the distance between us. My chest tightened, each breath sharp and shallow. Two hot gusts from his nostrils swept over me, ruffling my hair like the whisper of a storm.

"You smell good, mortal."

This was it. I would die right here. The dragon moved even closer until a warm, sticky drool trailed along my arm. I held it up, disgusted.

"What is this? Are you tasting me?"

He puffed out his nostrils again. "I am Drakkar. You are mine."

My heart lurched. "Drakkar? You are Seraphina's mate!"

He closed his eyes and whined so loudly that it pierced the night sky. The sound was filled with so much anguish.

"Seraphina," he breathed. "She's gone. Our babies are gone."

He didn't know.

"They're not!" I cried. "Your eggs—I know where they are. I have tried to keep them safe, although I am not certain how to get them back. But I will."

His eyes shot back open. He released a growl that reverberated through me, and the rocks along the ground began to clatter.

"Where are they? Take me to them!"

Before I could explain, I heard a whisper. "Asha." I turned in the direction of the voice and saw an aura the color of sunset. "It's Ekon. Asha, get back," he said. "I'll draw the dragon away."

Drakkar noticed the sound and growled. He opened his jaws, but I held out my hand, touching his indigo scales. "No! He is a friend."

He pulled his lips back against his teeth. "He does not smell like a friend. Hurry up and rid yourself of him. We have unfinished business."

"He is. Trust me."

"It is not *you* I distrust." But he lowered his gaze and took a step back. I pulled myself up gingerly before walking over to Ekon.

"Ekon!" I cried, falling into his arms.

"Asha," he said, holding me close, his large, muscular arms enveloping me. "The dragon? You are not afraid of it. Is he dangerous?"

"He's definitely dangerous, but I don't think he will hurt me. He has had a couple of chances to kill me, and he hasn't. I need your help," I said, pulling back from him. "We need to get back to the castle. I need to get the eggs."

His hands fell onto my face. "Asha, slow down. What eggs?"

"His eggs. The dragon eggs."

Drakkar growled. "We cannot trust him," he said.

Ekon wrapped his arm around me protectively. I pulled away.

"We don't have time for this," I said, shooting Drakkar a glare. "We need to get them before someone else does."

"Asha," Ekon began. "Whatever you are going on about can wait. We need to get you out of here."

"I'm not leaving without them."

Ekon inhaled deeply before cupping my face. "Then let's end the bridegroom ceremony. We can come back together and present ourselves to Elan."

I opened my mouth to speak, but I couldn't. I did not know what to say. Suddenly, his lips were upon me, wet and determined. I jerked away, my mouth still tingling from yet another unwanted kiss—the second in just a matter of days. Instantly, there was a low, rumbling growl that came from behind me, and the unmistakable blue aura confirmed my suspicion.

It was Adriel, and—

"Kwasi?" I asked, my voice trembling with confusion.

I heard a voice, clear and loud, behind us. I pulled back abruptly, very familiar with the growl and the midnight blue aura that now emanated from the man behind us. How had Adriel's aura grown so bright?

I looked back at Drakkar, ready to tell him to stand down, but surprisingly, he stood there unmoving, his eyes roving the scene with curiosity.

"I am here, Ash," Kwasi said quietly. I held out my hand, and he pulled me into a hug. "I should never have left you," he murmured against my shoulder.

"I'm alright," I said.

Kwasi paused, seeming to peer over my shoulder. "I see he has not cut us down yet. Truly, it is not going to hurt us?" he asked warily.

"I never said that," Drakkar barked. Kwasi didn't flinch, holding me tighter. Clearly, I was the only one who could hear him.

"I don't think so," I said.

"You've managed to find a dragon," Kwasi said breathlessly. "I knew you were gifted with them, but Asha—this one is the biggest I have ever seen. Maybe we should run."

Drakkar let out another guttural bark, making everyone jump.

"He's teasing you," I assured them, darting a glare at him. "Stop it!"

"I just wanted to let the mortals know that they should most definitely be running."

I sighed, stepping back. "Adriel, he was Seraphina's mate."

For a moment, there was silence. Presumably, Adriel was digesting this information. Then, tentatively, he asked, "How do you know this?"

Deciding it was a step too far to let on that I could, in fact, understand this dragon, I said, "Seraphina. She said he would come looking for them."

"And you didn't think to warn me of this?"

"I'd hoped to escape before I had to," I admitted.

"Kitchi has the eggs," he said, but there was a sharp, almost wounded edge to his tone. "I can have her bring them to us."

"She is coming with me," Ekon said, pulling his sword free.

Adriel gently pushed me behind him. "And why would I allow that?" he said with a tinge of violence.

"I found her. She has already agreed to come with me. We were just getting ready to go to Elan," Ekon said.

"Elan!" Adriel snapped. "You really are as foolish as you look. Do you really think Elan is going to let his sister live after all of this? Are you that thick?"

Tension coated the air as Ekon ground his teeth, and I heard the subtle sound of his hand falling onto the hilt of his sword. Adriel was quiet and collected, but his aura told me otherwise.

Kwasi's voice broke through the tension. "Ekon, brother. There is no need for this. We are all on the same side and want the best for Asha."

"Step aside, Kwasi," Ekon warned. "Just because you've always failed to protect your sister doesn't mean I will."

I could hear the breath leave Kwasi's body as Ekon's words struck home. There was nothing more hurtful.

I could not stand this anymore. "Hey! Is anybody interested in what I want?"

Drakkar chose this moment to interject. "I knew I liked you."

I shot him another look before turning back to the men in front of me.

"Asha," Ekon said with a tinge of desperation, "come with me. I can make Elan see reason."

"I don't wish to see Elan ever again," I said firmly. "The dragon will escort me. You all may come if you wish, but I will be getting his eggs."

"What eggs?" Kwasi asked.

"His," I said, pointing to Drakkar.

"Impossible," Kwasi said in disbelief. "No one has seen dragon eggs in at least a century."

"We don't have time for this," Adriel interrupted. "I will be going with you."

Kwasi sighed. "I suppose I have broken a few rules already. What's a few more?"

Ekon tugged on my arm. "Asha, don't be ridiculous," he said. "You will get yourself killed. Come with me—"

"Get your hands off me," I said calmly, though I felt the opposite.

I was done being dragged around by men and blindly putting my fate in their hands. I did not care if this was Ekon, my longest-held friend.

Instead of letting me go, he held me tighter. I heard Adriel approach with his blade, but Drakkar moved first. He reached with a claw, and the hand that held mine was snatched away. "Leave mortal. You are lucky that she likes you, or you would already be ash," Drakkar sneered.

Let him go. Don't hurt him.

"He needs a little pain to know that you are mine," Drakkar said. "I will not have anyone who is mine mistreated."

Let him go.

I watched Ekon's aura shift.

"Go, Ekon, please," I said.

"You are making a mistake, Asha," he panted, catching his breath. But he heeded my words and jogged away.

Maybe he was right, but I'd rather put my fate in the claws of dragons than in the hands of men.

CHAPTER THIRTY

Asha

Adriel growled as Ekon retreated into the woods. "If that is the love of your life, you sure know how to pick them."

Why did he care? I owed him no explanation.

"What was he supposed to do, Adriel?" I asked.

"Stay!" he said. "Fight for you. Do something! Do you not think you deserve that? Is that what the men in your life have led you to believe?"

Kwasi shuffled his feet but did not offer any assistance. I sighed deeply, disliking where this was going. It was bad enough that my best friend had betrayed me; now, he was just rubbing salt in the wound.

"Drakkar was growing impatient."

"Drakkar?" Adriel said. "He has a name already?"

Drakkar growled in the distance.

"Hmm . . . we'd better not keep him waiting," Adriel conceded. "I've seen what he does to men who cross you."

A smile escaped my lips, and I felt no shame. I was glad Prince Atar was dead. I had known Drakkar for minutes, and already I felt a kinship to the dragon. I'd never had anyone rush to my defense in such a protective manner. Well, no one except Adriel, I admitted to myself.

"Elan's men and the other contenders are crawling through these forests looking for you. We need to go through the mines and come up from the back."

"No mines!" Drakkar snarled.

"The dracite," I said. "It's too dangerous for Drakkar."

"The only other way is through the palace forces, and while I'm up for a fight, I do not know that we can beat an entire army."

Drakkar spread his wings. His wingspan was impressive. One wing was easily the length of thirty men. Why could I see him? Did it have something to do with my being able to speak to him mind-to-mind? I'd kept that little nugget of information to myself as well. There would be time enough to ask questions once we were gone.

"Can you fly?" I asked.

"Yes."

"Why did you not say before?"

"You did not ask," he said simply.

"But no other dragon can fly?" I challenged.

"I am not like other dragons."

I did not have a chance to respond because Kwasi put a hand on my shoulder. "Are you okay? You seem . . . perplexed."

"I . . . I think he can fly," I said, looking at Drakkar.

"How do you know this?" Kwasi asked. "Dragons have not flown for a millennium. It is not possible."

"It is also not possible for a female dragon to bear eggs," I offered, "and yet I have seen them with my own eyes."

"Can he show us?" Adriel asked.

"Can you?" I asked.

Drakkar grunted. "I won't dignify that with a response."

I cleared my throat. "We have one shot. If others see him, it will give us away."

"Will he allow one of us to ride him?" Adriel asked.

"Only *you* will ride me, Asha."

I heard the finality of that in his voice. "He will only allow me to ride."

"You can't!" Kwasi interjected.

"It's dangerous," Adriel agreed. "But there might be another way."

"And that is?" I asked.

"Your brother's battlemage. You can hide within his shadows."

"It might work," Kwasi began. "Unless another shadow warrior is in our ranks. They will see her immediately."

"You'll have to follow a few paces behind me. Even if I am spotted, it will give you a chance to get away."

"It sounds dangerous," I said.

He smirked. "Less dangerous than riding a dragon."

As we stalked through the dense foliage, my heart raced, every move putting us in even more danger. I clung to Kwasi's shadow as if it were a shield. The leaves rustled softly underfoot, a chorus of whispers that threatened to betray us to prying ears.

We followed Adriel with cautious steps, his figure cutting through the gloom of the forest. Drakkar's absence weighed heavily on my mind, yet I could feel his presence lingering nearby, a silent Guardian watching over us in the night.

Ujuima soldiers patrolled the forest, but we evaded notice, quietly slipping through the trees like ghosts in the night. Each passing moment felt like an eternity, every heartbeat a drum urging us forward. When we finally reached the gates of the Empira, Adriel ushered us inside. We entered the armory, and I could see Kitchi's aura pacing like a caged animal. Chato, Moki, and Ashkii's voices huddled together in a corner like conspirators.

"Asha!" Kitchi cried, engulfing me in a hug. "I was so worried. You did not come back to your room, and they would not tell me where you were."

I sighed against her.

"It's okay, Kitchi. I'm okay," I said.

"Who is this war chief?" Chato asked, moving closer.

"This is my brother Kwasi," I answered. "He and Adriel found me in the forest."

"Kitchi!" Adriel called as she snapped out of her conversation with me to stand alert. "Do you have them?"

"Yes."

In a matter of moments, I could feel their presence. Learning that the eggs were safe flooded me with relief. I reached out for them, but Adriel's hand shot forward, intercepting mine with a firm grip.

"I'll carry them for you." It was not a request. I frowned, realizing the modicum of trust that we'd built had dissipated. He didn't trust me.

"What's happening, war chief? What is our next move?" Moki asked.

"We need to get Princess Asha out of here without being seen. She is currently being hunted in a bridegroom ceremony by the champions from the Fire Challenge. We must not let any of them get her, especially Elan."

I turned to Adriel. "Your brother betrayed you. He made a deal with Elan so that he could trade your mines."

He placed a hand on my shoulder. "I know. Kwasi has filled me in."

"The grounds are crawling with guards," Moki informed us. "Should we use the tunnels?"

"That was my plan," Adriel confirmed.

Chato unsheathed his weapon. "I will lead the way then. I was hoping to wet my blade with some Ujuiman blood."

The air in the tunnel was thick with anticipation, worsening with each step as we moved deeper into the darkness. The rhythmic echoes of our progress bounced off the cavernous walls, guiding us forward through the depths beneath Empira.

Moki held my arm with a firm grip, his silent strength guiding me through the darkness. Chato was out front. His confidence was reassuring as we wound through the darkness. Ashkii and Kwasi followed, their hushed murmurs barely audible over the sounds in the chamber. Adriel was close behind.

As we rounded a bend in the tunnel, the laughter of approaching guards shattered the silence. They spoke of their recent winnings, their carefree chatter at odds with the tension coiled in my chest. Chato's sharp intake of breath was all the warning we needed. There was nowhere to hide, no escape from the imminent confrontation. Moki released my arm to pull out his sword. The only choice was to stand and fight.

As we stepped forward, their laughter faded into shouts of alarm. The guards wasted no time in launching their attack, their shouts echoing through the cavern as they lunged forward with weapons raised. We met their onslaught head-on, but judging by the flurry of auras piling in, the odds were against us. The narrow confines of the tunnel left little room for maneuver. As the clash of steel rang out around us, Adriel gripped my hand.

"Come!" he said.

"Kwasi!" I called.

"Right behind you," Kwasi assured.

Adriel led us through a series of narrow tunnels. The jagged stone walls pressed in around us, as if the earth itself were against us. At one point, the passage narrowed so drastically that we were forced to drop to our hands and knees, crawling through the tight space. The sound of our breaths mingled with the distant drip of water somewhere nearby. I prayed that there was an opening on the other side because there was no room in the confined space to turn around.

"It's here," Adriel called. I wasn't the only one sighing in relief that we could finally climb out. We continued moving through several turns. I could not have found my way back if I'd tried.

"Stop," I whispered just loud enough for them to hear.

"We have to keep going," Adriel insisted.

"Look!" I said, pointing to two bright auras coming toward us. "They are coming straight at us."

"I don't see anything. How can you tell?" he asked.

"I can see their auras. Trust me, they are coming."

"Burn it!" Adriel cursed. "Okay, new plan. I will go out and distract them while you all get out. It's a straight shot from here."

"What are you going to do?" I asked, tamping down the fear that I felt.

"You'll find out soon enough," he said grimly.

As the dozen or so guards rounded the corner, Adriel stepped out.

"Alright, you found me. You wouldn't by chance be willing to let me go, would you?"

The guards brandished their weapons in response.

"I didn't think so."

Metal crashed against metal, then in an instant, his aura grew several times its normal size. It practically filled the room. Was this his battlemage?

"Now!" Adriel called.

Kwasi pulled me under his cloak. Together, we slipped through the crowd of guards still attempting to take down Adriel. The moment we cleared the guards, we broke into a sprint, our footsteps pounding against the ground in unison. We didn't stop until we'd put at least half a mile between us and the chaos, finally bursting into the open air. I doubled over, hands on my knees, gasping for breath as my lungs burned.

"Where is Drakkar?" I gasped.

"You don't need a dragon when you have that guy protecting you," he said. "He is fierce, Ash."

"We cannot just leave him," I said.

Kwasi held me back. "He wanted us to keep moving forward. We have to trust that he'll make it out."

"No!" I shouted. When Kwasi and the others flinched, I said, "He has the eggs. I won't leave without them."

"Right, the eggs," Kitchi said, placing a hand on my shoulders. "We have our orders, Asha. He has to come out in the next few seconds, or we have to go. War chief's orders."

Time went by agonizingly slow, with not a whisper of him. My heart raced as I strained my ears, listening for a sign of him—a footstep, a breath, anything. But there was nothing. Just the stillness of the forest.

Just when we had turned to go, Adriel's aura moved into the clearing, unsteady, but gloriously alive. Relief crashed over me so hard my knees nearly gave way. My lungs filled as if I'd been drowning and only now remembered how to breathe. My throat burned from holding in a sob I refused to release.

"They're coming," his voice rasped with urgency. "We have to run."

There was no sign of Drakkar. My heart plummeted as a chilling fear snaked its way through my veins. Where was he? Had something terrible happened to him?

"Drakkar isn't here," I choked out.

Kwasi's grip tightened on my arm, his worry mirroring my own. "We have to run," he said again.

But I couldn't abandon Drakkar, not when we had just found each other.

"We can't leave him behind," I declared firmly, trying to keep my voice steady even as terror threatened to consume me.

"We will all die if we stay here," Adriel countered.

"We have to go," Adriel said. There was urgency in his voice and fear of the danger closing in around us.

"Maybe he's right," Kwasi murmured, his voice heavy with uncertainty.

I shut my eyes, reaching out with senses deeper than sight, searching for any hint of Drakkar. The thought of leaving him behind filled me with dread. I could never explain the immediate kinship I felt with him if I tried. It was unlike anything I had ever experienced. He felt like home. I tilted my head back, letting the wind brush against my skin, hoping it might carry some sign of him. And then, faint but unmistakable, I felt it, a whisper on the breeze. Drakkar was coming.

CHAPTER THIRTY-ONE

Asha

Drakkar was in the air. We all watched, awestruck, as his wings expanded and he soared through the sky.

"Magnificent," Kwasi said behind me. "A dragon that can fly. I never thought I would live to see such a thing."

"Hurry!" I called to him.

"It's been a while," Drakkar said. "Give me a moment to figure out how to land."

"You don't know how?"

He growled in response.

"We can't wait!" Adriel said. "Let's move. Hopefully, he will follow us on the other side of this hill." Adriel pulled me forward as I relayed the message. We ran, with Adriel practically carrying me.

"I need to stop!" I cried.

"Almost there."

Chato reached over to lift my other side, and, between the two of them, I was carried. We'd come to the edge of the hill. A perfect landing spot for Drakkar. We could hear soldiers giving chase in the distance.

"Hurry!" I called out through the strange connection between us.

A crash sounded nearby, ringing through the air like a war cry. My heart raced as adrenaline soared through my veins like liquid fire.

He's here. Drakkar had landed. I sprinted, my hands outstretched, reaching for him in the darkness.

"Are you okay?" I ask, fear clutching my throat.

"Yes," he grunted, his response clipped and tense. But there was no time for further inquiry. We had to leave before it's too late.

"Climb on," Drakkar barks hurriedly, his urgency palpable in the air.

"What about the others?" I asked, desperation coloring my words. The Ujuiman soldiers were close. We needed to leave now.

"Only you."

"I'm not leaving them behind. I'd rather stay."

Drakkar growled in exasperation. "I could take one more. My wings are not strong enough for more than two of you," he replied.

I turned to the group, realizing that they were more than people helping me escape my brother Elan; they were my friends. They'd helped me get this far. My heart was heavy with indecision.

"I don't think he can take all of us. Maybe two."

"How do we know we can trust this dragon?" Chato asked. "He could eat us as soon as we get near."

"He struck down a champion in defense of the princess. He won't harm her," Adriel said.

"And the rest of us?" Chato asked.

"The Guardians will stay behind," Adriel said ignoring the question. "My brother will be angry, but he will not kill me. Take Kwasi."

"If your brother does not kill you, Elan will," Kwasi said grimly. "And the others will die, too, if they are found with you. I can at least use my battlemage to hide them in the shadows. I will stay behind," Kwasi insisted.

Adriel's aura flashed with defiance. "You think I'm just going to leave my Guardians behind?" he demanded in challenge. "My Guardians, my responsibility. I'm not leaving them behind to face this alone."

"And I'm not letting you throw your life away out of some misplaced sense of duty!" Kwasi shot back, his voice rising. "She needs you—more than she needs me. If you stay, you're signing your own death warrant, and theirs."

The tension between them crackled like dry leaves in a fire, the weight of their silent conversation bearing down on all of us. Though every instinct screamed for us to stay together, I knew this was the best choice. I was the one they were after. We couldn't hide forever, and every moment we delayed put us all in greater danger.

"Will you be okay?" I asked, reaching for Kitchi's hand.

She clasped them between her own. "Of course. We are Guardians. We will find you soon. Go!"

I turned to Chato, who gave me a bear hug. Ashkii clung to my shoulder.

"Stay safe!"

Moki would not say goodbye, but his voice was thick with emotion. "Remember, stay alert."

Tears streamed down my face as I turned to Kwasi. He was the only family I had left. He brushed my tears away.

"Go," he whispered, his voice barely audible. "Let me do something good for once."

More tears came as he swept my damp hair away from my face.

"Take care, baby sister. I will see you soon."

Before I could protest, he disappeared with the Guardians under the veil of his shadow into the night.

With a trembling hand, I reached out to Drakkar, awkwardly climbing up his leg until I was seated on his back, nestled between the sharp ridges of his spine. Adriel followed suit, his steps awkward and uncertain, sitting behind me. Before he could get seated, Drakkar took flight, his powerful wings beating against the air as we soared into the blackness of the night, leaving everything.

The wind rushed past us, whipping my hair around me. Flying should have been an exhilarating experience, but I knew immediately something was very wrong. Flashes of color ignited in my mind, casting vibrant hues against the darkness of my vision. I blinked violently, as a panorama of color and light filtered through. It was overwhelming. I saw clouds billowing around me, their cottony forms stretching endlessly in all directions. In the distance, the lights of Empira Castle twinkled like stars against the night sky. It wasn't just distant landscapes that came into focus. I could see the trees of the forest below, and rivers weaving through the land like silver threads under the moon's glow. With a sudden realization, I understood I was seeing it all through Drakkar's eyes.

The sensation was all-consuming, a torrent of sight, sound, and feeling threatening to overtake me. I tried to absorb it all, to revel in the miracle of sight bestowed upon me, but it was too much, too soon.

Panic seized me as I felt myself begin to plummet. I thought I heard my name being called in the distance. I struggled to remain upright, to orient myself, but my attempts were futile. The sensation overwhelmed me, and I felt myself slipping away into the familiar embrace of darkness.

CHAPTER THIRTY-TWO

Adriel

I'd never been so high up. There was no experience in my life that I could compare to it. It was like experiencing life and death all in one moment. That feeling ended when I looked at Asha.

A wave of panic washed over me as she began to waver in her seat.

"Asha!" I called, but she did not respond. She continued to sway, trying, but failing, to keep her balance. "We need to land!" I called to Drakkar as if he could understand me.

"Asha!" I yelled again right before as she lost balance.

I threw myself forward, grasping for her arm and body. I squeezed my thighs, desperately trying to keep my seat and failing.

"Asha! Grab onto me."

It was as if she had woken up from a deep sleep. She turned up and faced me in a panic. I barely had time to register that her honey-colored eyes had taken on a strikingly golden hue, like a gold medallion. I recognized them. They were the same eyes of the dragon we rode, but what shocked me to my core was that they appeared to be able to see me.

That line of thinking was interrupted by the strain I felt, holding onto Asha midair. She dug into my forearms, trying to pull herself up. I barely had time to register that Drakkar was descending. Asha finally got her arms around my neck, and I pulled her against me as tight as I could, bracing for impact. The next moment, a deafening crash erupted beneath us, and the force of it sent us both flying from our seats.

Minutes went by as I lay dazed on the ground. My body ached from the pain of being flung from a dragon. I ran my hands over my legs. Nothing was broken, thankfully. I slowly pulled myself up, holding my stomach to try not to lose its contents. I gripped my head, feeling flashes of light pierce my eyes as I tried to stand. Asha was crumpled on the ground a few feet from me. Drakkar loomed over her protectively, growling as I approached. My heart sank at the sight of her. She looked so pale. I held my hands upward to signal I meant no harm.

I pointed to Asha. "Me help? Me help?"

Did he understand me?

The dragon just stared but did not make any move to attack me, so I slowly walked closer until I could pull Asha onto my lap. She moaned. There were cuts and bruises on her arms and neck, but otherwise, she seemed to be fine. What was that in the air, I wondered. Did she experience vertigo? Was it worse when you were blind?

She was quite beautiful, I once again conceded. Her hair was wild, lying in thick indigo coils. She had worn it loose, I realized, to hide her back. I could not imagine she'd choose a dress that put her scars on display. That had to be Elan's doing somehow. I traced the scars with my hands as if that would erase the pain that she had endured. As I did, her eyes fluttered open. The golden hue consuming them faded, replaced by her usual honey color. Relief washed over me as I watched her stir, my worry easing slightly.

"Are you okay?" I asked, my voice laced with concern.

She pushed herself up from my lap, wincing in pain. She was visibly struggling to collect herself, her body tensed with discomfort. But then, her movements sharpened, and I could sense the urgency in her as she placed her hands on my chest and then shoulders, searching frantically for something. The satchel that held the dragon eggs—she was looking for them.

"It's here," I said, reaching for the bag by my side. "Look."

Relief flooded her features as I handed her the satchel, her fingers closing around it tightly. Despite the injuries she had sustained and the pain that surely coursed through her, she flipped it open to examine the eggs. My heart sank as I saw that the one in the middle had a small crack on one end.

"No!" she cried.

Drakkar also let out a howl of anguish. He stood and turned away, breathing a stream of fire, setting trees in the distance ablaze.

"Drakkar!" she wailed. "Stop! She lives! Drakkar, she lives!"

Drakkar turned, and I watched a silent conversation unravel before me. I cleared my throat to get her attention. She turned back to me, startled. She seemed to realize how close we were sitting and rolled off my lap before she stood, still cradling the eggs.

"What is he saying?" I asked.

She looked down at her feet.

"Are you really going to pretend that you were not having a whole conversation with him a second ago?" I pressed.

She sighed, looking back at Drakkar. He lowered his head.

"I can hear him speaking to me . . . in my head," she admitted. Just when I thought I could not be surprised any further, she added, "I can also see him."

The first I had deduced; the second I was stunned by. "You . . . you can see him? How?"

She shrugged her shoulders. "I don't know how. I only met him last night, but it feels like—like we've known each other our whole lives."

I regarded her carefully. "Can you see me?" I asked.

She shook her head. "No, I can only see him, but before I thought I saw . . . something."

"Is that what happened to you when we were flying? You lost your balance because you could . . . see?" I wasn't certain what I was trying to say, but the memory of her glowing eyes was seared in my brain.

She seemed to think about what I was asking. "I am not sure. I saw a lot of light and color. I think I saw trees. It was all so overwhelming."

We stood in silence for a few moments, as I watched her chew her lip. I mulled over her words, trying to make sense of this new information.

"How is the egg? You said it is alive?"

She nodded. "Feel it," she said, motioning for my hand.

I tentatively placed it over the egg, and she placed her hand on top. I felt a quiet but strong pulse of energy flow through me. I could feel the life within. I pulled back quickly, and a spark shot from my fingertips.

"Yes. I felt that," I said, breathing heavily.

She looked at it sadly. "It is a hairline fracture, but I am worried about infection setting in. I wish I could ask Nayeli. I imagine she has medicine that can help. Perhaps arnica."

"You said she. How do you know it is female?"

She shook her head. "The same way I can speak to Drakkar and see him. I just know. I do not know how to explain it. She is Mwana," she said, referencing the names we had given them days ago.

All of this was incredibly difficult to take in. I was looking at dragon eggs, which were sired by a dragon that could fly, and I was standing next to someone who could communicate with them.

Drakkar emitted a low growl. She turned to him and returned his smile. "He said not now, but the day is young."

I watched the dragon warily. "Right. Well, I am not certain where we are, but by the climate, I suspect we are near Entioch." The palm trees were a clue. It was incredible that Drakkar had taken us this far east in such a short time. "If we fly, we could make it to Tideport by midafternoon and get some of this arnica."

Asha looked at Drakkar and shook her head. "He says that flying is taxing. He has not flown in nearly a hundred years and will need to regain his strength."

Interesting. "Why hasn't he flown for so long if he is able to?"

She looked at Drakkar. "He won't say," she said curiously.

"Well, on foot, we will be lucky to make it by nightfall if we get going now. Are you ready?"

Asha paused. "We both want to know. Why are you helping us?"

"Well, I can't very well go back to Wiyotak, can I? I'm invested in this journey now, and I'd like to see it through."

That was a horrible lie, I realized. I'd need to come up with a better one. Truthfully, Drakkar presented a problem for me. I wanted the dragons to use against Ujuima, but I suspected Drakkar would have very little interest in that. I would have to win Drakkar and Asha over, or I would have to steal the dragons once they were hatched. Drakkar would definitely hunt me down, but I would figure that out down the road. I was still working on the details, but for now, I'd have to play this carefully.

Enapay would welcome me back with open arms with three drag-ons. A nagging question floated into my mind as we began walking.

Could I forgive Enapay for what he had tried to do to Asha? Why did his actions bother me so much? He had certainly betrayed me to Elan. He'd soon learn that was a mistake.

Chapter Thirty-Three

Asha

We walked in silence most of the day. Adriel seemed lost in thought, and I was anxious about the eggs. I checked on them every few minutes.

"You will worry yourself to death if you do not stop lifting that satchel," Drakkar said.

I did not have my walking staff, but I found I did not need it as long as I stayed close to Drakkar. He trampled the vegetation immediately around us and avoided trees and other barriers.

"She's getting weaker. I can feel it," I said nervously.

"As can I. But there is nothing we can do about it but keep moving ahead," I grumbled at him. "You have a temper," he remarked, seemingly unfazed by my mood.

"Most people don't notice," I admitted with a shrug.

"I find that many are dimwitted when it comes to emotions," the dragon spoke casually. "You seem to be very in touch with yours. Perhaps that is why you can hear me."

I felt a sense of pride at hearing that. Being in tune with my emotions and the emotions of others would be frowned upon in Ujuima. I'd managed to hide it until I began living in the dragon pits, where the skill had been necessary for my survival.

"Have you ever met another mortal who could talk to you?" I asked.

"Not for a very long time," he replied. "Then again, I tend to stay away from mortals."

"Where is your home?" I ventured.

"In the north, beyond the mountains," he answered cryptically.

"Firepeak?"

"Dragons do not have the same names as you do, but further north," he confirmed. "We call our home Saeleria."

"What is it like there?"

"I cannot speak of it to a mortal. It is... forbidden."

"Forbidden?" I echoed, intrigued by his words.

"Yes. Dragons are held to a certain code. There are things we do not speak of, especially to mortals. You have to face a trial before you even get into Saeleria. Most do not make it past the Shadow Basin."

"Why do most not make it through?"

"All I can say is only the worthy prevail."

"Can't you share anything about it?" I pressed.

"Are you sure we can trust him?" he asks, looking ahead to where Adriel walked.

"Changing the subject, are we?" Drakkar just looked at me expectantly. *"No, we cannot trust him. I do not think he would harm us, but he wants to control dragons like Ujuima does. We will have to leave him at some point."*

Drakkar snorted in agreement. "That is as I thought. Although I sense he helps us for other reasons."

Before I could ask what those reasons were, Adriel stopped walking. "We will need to make camp here. Night will befall us soon. We will make it to Tideport tomorrow."

"Why don't we just keep going? We can make it before nightfall," I suggested, eager to get my hands on some arnica.

"I'm afraid not. The sun has been guiding us, and without it, I am not confident that we won't get turned around somewhere."

I open the satchel and touch the female egg. "I'm worried she won't make it until then."

"We will make haste tomorrow. It is better to be cautious and avoid going in the wrong direction. That would cost us even more time. I am going to go hunt us some dinner."

I nodded. "I'll work on a broth."

"No," he said sternly. "I will cook for us. I don't trust you not to poison me."

"Technically, I never did if you did not eat it."

"Not something to boast about," he said, shaking his head.

Drakkar watched the two of us closely. "You are growing fond of him," he observed.

"I've known you for a day, and I like you."

"That's different. You are mine."

"He's been my captor for weeks. How can you say that?"

Drakkar flexed his wings out in a stretch. "It is simply an observation, Asha. No need to get defensive."

"I'm not," I shot back, but turned away, realizing how defensive that sounded.

I collected sticks and branches to put together for a fire before Drakkar obliged me with a spark to get it going.

"How did you know where to find me?" I ask him.

A wave of sadness seemed to flow through him, his scales shifting like rivers of tears. "Seraphina, she marked you."

"Marked?" I asked as if trying out the word. *"What does being marked mean?"*

"It signals to all the other dragons that you have been claimed, and to harm you would be a direct challenge. Essentially, she bound you to our family. It is likely why you have such a connection to our brood."

"Brood? Your eggs? Is that what you call them?"

"Mortals don't use this terminology?" he snorted.

"No. We call them children."

I was glad to see him lighten at the change of subject. Seraphina's death was clearly weighing heavily on him.

"So, where do we go after Tideport?"

"We must go to my home to hatch the eggs."

"Am I allowed to go there?" I asked skeptically.

"I hope an exception can be made, since you have been marked. But Adriel definitely cannot. He would not be welcome."

A hollow ache spread through me at the words: Adriel definitely cannot. I tried to school my face into indifference, but inside, the protest burned. *"He's been trying to find out how to hatch your eggs. He's practically read every book he can find, but there are no records of how the process works."*

"There wouldn't be. Certain things are only spoken of between dragons. We consider hatching our young to be one of them."

"So even I cannot know."

"You cannot." He said it with such finality that I moved on.

"When we were flying, I thought for a second that I could... see through your eyes."

Drakkar eyed me cryptically. "What are you trying to ask me, Little One?"

"Was I seeing through your eyes?"

"Yes," he said.

"How can that be?"

He closed his eyes and lowered his head to the ground.

"Let me guess? You cannot tell me."

"I cannot," he confirmed.

I threw my hands up, and it was at that moment Adriel returned. "You two fighting already? I have a couple of rabbits," he said.

A thunderous rumble tore from Drakkar's wings, shaking the ground beneath me. He growled. "I must go hunt. I will be back before dawn." He walked away without another word.

"Where is he going?" Adriel asked.

"He said to hunt. He will be back before dawn. What do you think he eats?"

"Someone's livestock probably," he said, handing me a stick to roast the newly skinned rabbit over the fire. I really was not hungry, though I should have been after all of the walking. The events over the past few days had robbed me of my appetite.

"All of this is quite incredible, isn't it?" he murmured. "A dragon that can fly," he marveled.

"It is," I agreed.

"He seems quite attached to you. Any idea why?"

I shook my head. "Maybe I'm better looking than you."

He laughed. "Well, that is a given, but still, it is interesting. How did you find him?"

"I didn't. He found me," I said honestly.

"A pregnant dragon found you, then her mate. It is all very curious," he marveled.

I handed him the rabbit. "Technically, she found me. I'm going to lie down. I'm not very hungry," I said.

"Are you sure? You should eat something."

"Save some for me," I said, knowing very well that it would be unlikely for me to eat any of it. I yawned before saying, "Goodnight."

"Goodnight, Princess."

I jolted awake at the sound of Adriel's anguished cries.

"Odina!" he yelled, his voice strained with fear.

I sat up, my heart pounding in my chest, as he continued to call out for someone who was not there. This time, though, he was moving around frantically, his distress palpable in the air.

"Odina, where are you?" he pleaded, his voice breaking as he searched the darkness.

I looked around. Drakkar had not yet returned. I needed to do something. I stood and stumbled my way over to him, reaching out a hand to touch his shoulder. But before I could even speak, he lashed out, knocking me to the ground with a force that sent shockwaves through my body.

He froze, his breath catching in horror as he realized what he'd done.

"Princess, I . . ." he stammered, his voice cracked.

I pushed myself up, ignoring the pain that shot through me. "It's okay," I said, my voice steady despite the ache in my chest. "I just wanted to help."

"I'm sorry," he whispered, barely audible in the darkness.

I reached my hand out, meaning to offer him gentle assurance, but it strayed to his aura. There was something so fascinating about the tangled web it formed. It seemed chaotic at first glance, but there was a symmetry to it, like certain pieces that were out of place.

"May I?" I asked.

I didn't know if he knew exactly what I was asking, but he bent down until our foreheads touched, and our breaths mingled. This might have been intimate if I had not been so enraptured with the puzzle before me and my plan to fix it.

Slowly, methodically, I began untangling the web in my hands, careful not to make any hasty movements that could jeopardize my strategy. With each move, I saw glimpses of his life, moments shared with Odina, her tawny hair cascading as she playfully raced against Adriel. I watched him let her win and then cheat as they raced back up the hill. More memories followed, just as vivid: Adriel pacing outside a modest cottage while Odina distributed handmade remedies, his brow furrowed with concern. Her climbing a tree without hesitation to reach a stubborn branch bearing a rare herb. The admiration in his heart was undeniable. She was gifted—especially with children, who clung to her like sunshine. I felt pride, his pride, and the bitter taste of fear for her safety.

As I neared the core of the web, a sudden burst of blue flames engulfed us, scorching my skin. I'd never experienced such heat.

"GET OUT!" he screamed. In a panicked frenzy, Adriel shoved me away and delved into my deepest memories.

"Asha Osei! Mind your skirts, dear!" Mother's warning chased after me as I dashed through the garden with bare feet.

The wet soil oozed between my toes, while the sun embraced my dark brown skin with its unrelenting kiss. A hint of honey lingered on my tongue as I searched for the pale yellow flowers that sprouted from the stream. I leaned over to soak in the scent, cupping my hands into the water to drink my fill before lying on my back to stare up at the lush trees above. They were fat with golden-brown dates that cascaded down like jewels from their branches. This patch of the garden was my home. It was preferable to lose myself in this paradise than to be trapped in the dim reality of the castle and all the burdens of titles and nobility.

A shadow appeared from the corner of my eye, and I rolled onto my belly, feeling the thick grass tickling my arms and legs. My brow furrowed as I strained to see through the darkness that separated the trees.

"What are you doing, Ash?" Kwasi called, pushing his curls from his eyes.

Raising a finger, I signaled for him to quiet and pointed. A feathered, four-legged creature with lazy ears emerged from the foliage, twitching its nose to sense any danger. At first, I thought it was a rabbit, but then I saw the antlers gracefully crowning its head above its ears. Tiny, delicate, like they belonged to a mule deer. The creature was a jackalope, and quite a beautiful one.

It caught my attention as it happily nibbled on white-cap mushrooms dotted with dark purple spores. My eyes sparkled with excitement as I stealthily approached, relishing the thrill of the chase, savoring each silent movement.

When I was merely a handsbreadth behind it, the jackalope turned around in alarm. I patiently mirrored its sounds and movements with quiet practice. To my delight, the jackalope rewarded my efforts by hopping toward me, cautious but seemingly curious. I reached out to gently graze the back of its ears. They were so soft. They reminded me of the velvet of the sandy brown curtains in my bedroom window.

My hands stilled, and my muscles drew tight as a branch crunched behind us. The animal perked up its ears in alarm and quickly hopped away into the underbelly of the trees. I reached out after it, but the creature was lost behind the wall of greenery. I could not tell where the moss ended and the grass began. I tried not to let my eyes linger in the empty pockets of black between the trees.

"Kwasi," I groaned. "Why did you have to go and scare him off?"

Kwasi's crisp steps continued toward me without regard as he smoothed down his starched tunic. "How did you do that, Ash? Make it come to you?"

"Well, he wasn't there very long with you stomping around!" I snapped.

Kwasi just grinned. I hated when he looked at me like that, as if I were a silly little child. He was only three years older. That was nothing at all. He loved to tease me about being the baby sister, but I had one thing over him: he could never win against me in a game of chiyato, a classic ball toss game, much to his embarrassment. Oh, how I loved to rub it in his face.

Before I could remind him of this fact, a gong sounded in the distance. Both of us flinched, and I groaned, knowing it was a summons for everyone in the palace to convene in the courtyard to spar. The kingdom of Ujuima was just like all the others, cultivating strength and battle readiness above all else. This was the price of living in the emperor's city. In exchange for water and protection, Ujuimans were expected to take up battle training at a young age, some as early as the age of four. The earlier a person's battlemage was discovered, the better. Everyone in Ujuima was born with a battlemage, magic which could be honed and sharpened into a deadly weapon. Those who refused to take up the sword or could not keep up were cast out. Some left on their own, and none were heard from again. Their bones and the circling hawks above were the only testament to their misfortune. I was no exception to the battle training mandate, although I was terrible at it.

Before I could wallow in my dread, Kwasi put a hand on my forehead, pushing it back. "Last one to the courtyard is a rotten dragon egg!"

I ran after him, my skirts billowing behind me as I frantically tried to catch up. The fabric snagged on the thorny bushes, poking and scraping as I passed, leaving a trail of ripped threads in my wake.

"No fair!" I cried out, but Kwasi only laughed louder. His laughter was infectious—it filled the air and made the whole world seem brighter. Even though I was out of breath and struggling to keep up, I couldn't help but laugh along with him.

For a moment, all worries faded away as we raced through the courtyard, playfully pushing one another, enjoying a moment of joy that only children could conjure. As I ran, I failed to notice the crimson-hued robe lying in my path until it tangled around my ankles, causing me to stumble and fall onto scorching concrete. Wrestling to get my hands under me, I looked up and met the piercing mahogany eyes, those of Emperor Idris Osei, my father. The emperor glowered at me in disapproval, shaking me off, holding onto my eldest brother, Elan, for balance.

"Get up, girl!" he scolded.

When I fumbled trying to disentangle myself, he grabbed my arm.

"Majesty, please!" It was my mother pleading. "She is just a silly child. She meant no harm."

The emperor studied me for a moment. "All I asked for was to have three healthy sons. Instead, I have you. Your mother has always had a way of disappointing me," he said, glowering at her. "Perhaps it is time for you to show your worth. It is time to put you in the sparring ring."

While I'd had private lessons, I had not yet been required to enter the public sparring ring. That privilege was reserved for those who had come into their battlemage, which I had not. Entering the ring without your battlemage was foolish at best and deadly at worst. My mother's arms wrapped around my waist, her blue strands casting a curtain around me as if to shield me from him.

"No, please, Majesty. She is too young."

"Move, woman!" he said, raising an open hand to her cheek. He struck her so hard her neck snapped back before she released me.

My voice rang out in a desperate cry. "Mother!"

In an instant, Kwasi was by her side, his strong arms lifting her up and cradling our mother against his chest. I disentangled from her protective arms. My fists shook as I clenched my jaw, grinding my teeth. I knew I needed to appease my father. I understood what dire repercussions a wrong move from me could incur, and he would take his fury out on Mother. I steeled my expression, but internally, all I could do was fantasize about the day that I would make this man pay for the atrocities he had inflicted.

Elan's sinister smirk lingered on his face as he watched the scene unfold with morbid interest. My father lunged to my side, his hand gripping my collar to the point of bruising as he dragged me toward the ring. He scanned the rack of weapons before finally settling on a wooden practice saber, which he thrust into my hands with a stern expression. The weight of the weapon felt foreign and cumbersome in my grip as I stepped into the ring, my heart pounding with fear and uncertainty.

"Get in there. Make something of yourself," he said gruffly.

Those currently in the sparring room scattered quickly to the outside of the ring, their expressions filled with grim anticipation. I held the weapon awkwardly in my hands, feeling physically ill thinking about what I was expected to do with it. I edged into the ring, my eyes falling on Ekon. I did not know him well, but he attended some of my lessons. He was a natural in his studies, unlike me. I much preferred being outdoors, reading about animals, or experiencing the world firsthand.

The steady beat of the djembe drums echoed through the arena, signaling the start of our sparring session. Ekon and I circled each other, mirroring the movements we had been taught since childhood. My feet found their balance on the loose sand below. I tightened my reluctant grip on the sword as my body tensed with anticipation.

"Initiate!" my father's voice boomed, allowing one of us to strike.

"Asha, move!" Kwasi's urgent command rang out, but I ignored it.

The king gave his son a stern look, and Ekon took advantage of the distraction to lunge at me. I barely dodged in time, feeling the searing hot sand graze my bare arms as I rolled away.

We traded blows. I studied Ekon's movements. At just seven years old, he was tall and lean, but clumsy as he struggled to control his growing limbs. However, with his battlemage providing him incredible strength, there was no way for me to defend myself. There was no way for me to best him in this fight. Then again, winning was not my goal—only self-preservation. Ekon struck again, slamming his weapon down with force. I reluctantly lifted my sword, and our weapons collided with a thwack.

Ekon made eye contact with me, his eyes a deep brown. "Make it convincing," he whispered.

I startled at his words but nodded in understanding, realizing he was not pushing down with his saber with the full force of his weight. He gestured pleadingly with his eyes, and I realized this was my moment. I swept my foot, and he tumbled to the floor, holding his leg in pain.

"What is this?" Elan called. "Father, they make a mockery of you and our traditions. They are not even trying."

We were not convincing enough. The king gestured, and the beating of the djembe ceased. "Ekon, get out. You disgrace us all with that display. Elan, get a sword."

"No!" Kwasi called from the sidelines.

Our father looked at him incredulously. He was a man unaccustomed to being told no. "What is the meaning of this, son?"

Kwasi stepped into the ring, grabbing a sword without missing a beat. "I will teach her," he said.

"Father! Are you going to let him talk to you that way?" Elan demanded, teeth bared.

Emperor Idris ran a hand along his graying beard as if considering Kwasi's offer. Then he smiled. "Very well. But if I am not satisfied, I will have her thrown into the dragon pit."

My heart lurched. Enemies and traitors were thrown into the dragon pit, where they were quickly devoured. I knew my father disliked me, but never had I imagined his hatred went as far as to wish me dead. Fear was etched on Kwasi's expression, though he attempted to conceal it.

The djembes once again began their cadence. This time, I circled my brother, my eyes meeting his determined ones.

"Initiate!"

Kwasi wasted no time raising his sword and bringing it down on my right leg. I fell into the sand, and he kicked his knee into my stomach.

"Get up!" he yelled.

I rolled away from him, holding my stomach but raising my blade. The sweet boy I played with moments ago was nowhere to be found. He glared with an unwavering, serious resolve.

He struck again, this time landing a blow on my left shoulder. I lifted my sword arm pitifully to attack, but he shook it off and used his right arm to strike me in the face. There was a crack, and red filled my eyes.

I dropped my sword, holding my nose as blood began to fill my hands. I was certain my nose was broken, feeling the cartilage move under my tender fingers.

Kwasi paused, assessing the damage that he had done. He stood, taking a breath before glancing back at our father.

"Satisfied?"

Emperor Idris looked down at his eleven-year-old son, arms crossed. He simply shook his head to the left.

Kwasi's eyes widened. He turned those horrified eyes on me, his face ashen.

"It's okay," I whispered. "Do what you have to do."

Our mother sobbed behind us. "Idris, no."

"Someone, get her!" the king yelled as she tried to rush the arena. I watched as Mother tried to storm the pit, completely beside herself. Her sobs shook me to my core. As she struggled against the men restraining her, my heart ached for her and the agony she had to be feeling. And for what? Because I had been born a girl and worse, one who could not manage to dredge up the tiniest bit of battlemage.

Turning to Kwasi, I saw the same distress mirrored in his expression, and it only fueled my overwhelming guilt at the chaos unfolding.

I picked up my blade, letting blood trickle down my shirt, my hands slick with it.

"Come on, Kwasi!"

I raised it as if to strike him. He met the blow. I lowered it and raised it again with more force.

"Hit me!" I screamed. "Hit me!"

Tears began to trickle down his dark features. My heart hurt for him, too. This was necessary. Father would accept no less. He met my blows with twice the force, knocking me down. He grabbed my hair and began to punch me in the face, over and over, until the world went dark.

I was conscious, barely.

But that was the last day I could see the world through my own eyes. The last thing I saw was Elan's contorted face in laughter, and Kwasi holding me close, tears falling on my cheeks.

"I am so sorry, Ash."

There were flashes of images of my father, who stood by and did nothing while Elan used his battlemage to inflict excruciating pain on me with his lightning-infused touch. After each brutal encounter, it was Kwasi who tended to my wounds, overcome with guilt that he could do nothing to stop it from happening again.

Oh, how I loathed it when Elan would trap me like a cornered animal. And then came the fire and fury, as Elan inflicted more wounds upon my already scarred body. Every strike felt like a deep cut into my soul, ripping me apart from within.

Adriel screamed behind me, and with every ounce of my strength, I pushed him out of my mind, shutting him out completely. He fell back in shock and confusion, gasping for breath.

"What was that?" he whispered hoarsely.

I sat up, covering my face with my hands. He'd seen everything, the worst of me. "I could ask you the same," I said weakly.

He fell back, breathing heavily. "Is that what it feels like for you every time?" he whispered. "Princess, I—"

"I know I shouldn't have woken you."

"No," he paused. "I meant I'm sorry for what Elan did to you. What your father did. Even Kwasi . . ."

I stopped him, swallowing the bile that formed in my throat. "Please do not speak of it. I did not ask for, nor do I desire your pity."

"So, you can see my deepest, darkest memories, but I can't see yours?"

"I did not see yours. You pushed me out!" I said, beginning to shake uncontrollably.

He was silent for a moment, then said, "I killed her. The night my sister died. I was a new Guardian, eager to impress my father, and I . . . lost control. I was responsible for the fire that ran through the city," his voice caught. "Odina died because of me."

His aura, which I'd worked hard to unwind, began to twist upon itself again, thicker and heavier than ever. It had not worked. What I'd done had not worked.

We did not speak for the rest of the evening. Our silence continued even after Drakkar returned.

If he sensed something was amiss he wisely chose to stay out of it.

Chapter
Thirty-Four

Asha

We reached Tideport by mid-morning. We were greeted by the saltiness of the sea and the scent of fish and wet logs. My worry had grown with every passing hour, my focus consumed by the cracked egg cradled carefully in my arms. I could feel her life force flickering, faint and unsteady, like a candle struggling to stay lit. I insisted we find an apothecary immediately. In this part of the world, that meant finding an obeah, a practitioner of the old arts, someone who might understand the delicate magic needed to save her.

Drakkar stayed behind, his presence too conspicuous for the crowded streets of Tideport. We needed to remain anonymous for as long as possible, and a towering, battle-scarred dragon would draw far too much attention.

Adriel had tried many times to bring up what had occurred the night before, but I shut him down every time. He was never supposed to see that. No one was. I pushed away the memory. Mwana's survival was all that mattered now.

The chatter of vendors mingled throughout the square as street musicians played lively tunes. The cobblestones beneath my feet were multi-shaped and uneven as I wandered through the crowded streets. Vendors described their wares, shouting over the melee. They invited us to sample fresh fish and crab, handwoven baskets, and intricately crafted jewelry.

Adriel asked various people where the obeah was. They continued to point us forward until we found an apothecary tucked away in a corner. He described that there were strange symbols adorning the door. He did not need to say it out loud. I could feel the hairs on the back of my neck stand on end as I approached, a sense of unease creeping over me. Adriel hesitated beside me.

"Perhaps I should go in alone," he said.

I shook my head. "Not a chance."

He sighed heavily. "Okay. Stay alert."

When we walked in, we were immediately greeted with the heavy scent of incense and herbs. The chimes jingled overhead.

"Welcome to The Bush. I'm Marlon," a man announced, greeting us with a sharp clap of his hands. The sudden noise startled a creature, sending it soaring overhead with a flurry of flapping wings and a sharp, echoing cry. Instinctively, Adriel drew me closer, crouching slightly to shield me.

"Apologies for my owl's dramatic entrance. Whisk has a flair for the theatrical, but he means no harm," Marlon said with a chuckle as he ushered us further into his apothecary.

If a frown could be heard, it was screaming from Adriel's lips.

"I haven't seen you around before. Where are you from?" Marlon asked.

"We are in search of a specific herb, arnica," Adriel said smoothly dodging his question. "Do you happen to carry it?"

"Arnica? That is a potent herb, used for mending bones and staunching heavy bleeding. May I ask what you need it for?" Marlon replied.

"You may, but it is none of your concern," Adriel said curtly.

"I see," Marlon said although it was clear he did not. "Well, might I interest you in any of our other wares?"

"No, just the arnica," Adriel insisted.

"As you wish." Marlon shrugged with an air of intrigue.

I felt Marlon's eyes studying me as he rang up our purchase. "And what about you, my dear? Are you as friendly as your boyfriend?"

"We are not..." I began

"She is not..." Adriel continued. We turned to each other, both unsure of what to say.

"I'm surprised, the way you two seemed to... be in sync. My apologies for assuming," he continued politely though the laughter in his voice could not be contained.

My face warmed and I turned away. There was a sharp intake of breath. "Your eyes," Marlon began. "They are quite unique. Have you always been an unseer?"

Adriel stepped in front, shielding me from Marlon's line of sight. "Why do you ask?"

"I lost my sight at eight years old," I answered quickly, hoping to end this interaction.

"Eight years old? How fascinating," Marlon mused. "Have you ever tried to cure it?"

"I . . . there is no reason to cure it. It just is."

"Hmm," Marlon pondered. "You may be right, but have you ever tried?"

"This conversation is over," Adriel interrupted. "Do you have the arnica or not? If not, we can be on our way."

"Very well, sir," Marlon acquiesced, ringing up the jar and providing us with instructions for use. "You will need a stove to heat it properly. Do not attempt to use a fire, as it may not heat the arnica consistently. It's best to add lemon water for binding, but it will sting. And remember, you won't be able to move the affected bone for twelve hours after setting it."

Twelve hours. We would have to stay overnight, and it would slow our progress. As we prepared to leave, the obeah unexpectedly tapped my shoulder. "If you change your mind and wish to discuss your vision further, I am here."

Adriel quickly stepped between us. "We should get going," he said brusquely.

As we exited the apothecary, Adriel exhaled sharply. "I thought I was going to have to deck him."

"But we have what we need," I said. I ducked as raindrops coated my forehead.

"Yes, it appears we will need to stay in town tonight. I saw an inn not too far back. They should have a couple of rooms."

I nodded. "Let's go."

At the inn, we were greeted by the gentle sound of waves lapping against the shore and the creak of palm trees swaying in the wind.

Adriel took the lead, approaching the owner to negotiate our accommodation for the night. I listened as he engaged in conversation with an easy charm. It was not lost on me that he had never displayed this side of himself in the short weeks that I'd known him. Still, throughout the day, I noted a lighter, less gloomy mood emanating from him.

Moments later, he returned.

"Well, it seems we have a bit of a problem," he began. "The Festival of Lights is this weekend. The northern lights will be on display, and every inn and tavern, including this one, is fully booked for miles."

My heart sank. "What should we do? Try our luck with a campfire?"

"It will be difficult to maintain the consistent heat we need," he said. "However, the owner's wife took pity on us and offered the lighthouse. They warned us it has not been occupied in quite some time, but it is dry and the stove works."

"Lighthouse?" I asked.

"We cannot be too choosy, I'm afraid."

I marveled at how the novelty of sharing a room with Adriel had worn off. At this point, it would feel abnormal not to share a space with him.

The streets would be crowded tonight. That would allow me to blend into the night unseen. I just needed to put together a distraction long enough to get away.

When we arrived at the lighthouse, we had to climb several stories of the winding staircase until we made it into the apartment at the top. The musty smell of time hung in the air, blending with the salty scent of the sea coming from the windows. Adriel gripped my hand to steady me on the uneven steps. I fought back the urge to respond to his touch, feeling the warmth of his fingers against mine.

With a protesting creak, the door swung open, its hinges struggling against years of disuse. The neglect was evident in the thick layer of dust that filled the air and the cobwebs that clung to my hair. I couldn't help but cough as it tickled my nose and clung to my throat.

Adriel began clearing a path for us. He blew forcefully at something and let out an explosive sneeze as he brushed away the remaining dust from a cold metal surface.

"That's the stove," Adriel said. "It will work if we don't set the whole room on fire. Be cautious with this window. There is a box in front of it, but no screen. It is a straight drop to the sea below," he said as he walked me through the room.

I took a deep breath, inhaling the scents of the ocean and the nearby beach. "The sand reminds me of home."

"Do you miss it?" he asked.

My voice wavered as I spoke, "There's very little for me to go back to. My mother's maid, Kaliyah, was my closest confidante. I miss her greatly." Memories of home flooded in, causing a bittersweet ache in my chest. "And Kwasi, although who knows if he will be able to go back home. I hope he is okay."

"From where I stand, he has always been a man of self-preservation," he said with an air of judgment.

Anger speared through me.

"Just because you entered my memories uninvited, doesn't mean you get to judge him."

He rapidly tapped his hand on the wall. "Who is the crueler one?" he asked. "The one who scarred you, or the one who stood by and watched?"

My fists clenched at my sides. "You know nothing," I said, feeling the heat rise in my cheeks.

He stepped closer, placing his hands on my shoulders. "I know more than you think."

I turned angrily away from him, seeking solace in the mundane task of preparing the arnica. I heard Adriel come beside me to light the stove with dracite and steel.

"How can I help with this?" he asked.

"We need lemon water."

"I will track some down," he replied, setting down his pack and swiftly disappearing out the door.

I rolled my eyes, realizing he'd left the pack because he assumed I could not make it out of the lighthouse without him. How wrong he was. He could not have played more easily into my hands. I would make it out, but first, I needed to make sure he could not follow for some time.

In his absence, I couldn't resist the urge to rummage through his belongings. My hands quickly found what I had been searching for—his water jug. I pulled out the nightshade I'd hidden away from my evening with Nayeli. The question was how much to use. Too little, and it may not work; too much, and it could kill him.

The temperature dipped, indicating that the sun was setting. I busied myself with measuring the arnica and setting up the stove. Adriel returned from his errand, panting slightly as he climbed the steps with a basket overflowing with lemons.

"It was not easy to find these, but I managed," he said breathlessly.

Together, we brewed the concoction over low heat, the sweet scent of citrus filling the air. Adriel leaned against the wall, keeping an eye on the festivities below as we waited for the mixture to simmer. He took a swig of water before he spoke.

"I'm sorry," he said with a hint of regret in his voice.

Surprised, I turned toward him. "Sorry for what?"

"For judging Kwasi so harshly. I know firsthand how complicated family can be."

I wasn't sure what to say, so I simply replied, "Thank you."

We sat in comfortable silence as Adriel checked on the arnica while I anxiously tended to the eggs. There was no doubt that the eggs had doubled in size. Soon, they would be too heavy for me to carry alone. When the arnica was ready, we cautiously poured it onto the fractured portions of the egg. Adriel described that a yellow-tinged layer formed on the top, seeming to seal it, at least for a time.

I breathed a sigh of relief, carefully touching the ridged shell. "Come on, baby girl. Show me that you are okay," I pleaded.

I checked on the others, hearing their hums clearly, but Mwana's was absent. With no activity, I feared the worst.

"Anything?" Adriel asked.

I picked up her egg and cradled it in my arms. I shook my head.

"I don't think it worked," I said mournfully.

Adriel put his hand over mine. "I am sorry."

Tears formed in my eyes. "It was foolish to think I could ride Drakkar. If I hadn't fallen . . ."

"Don't go down that road. This isn't your fault," Adriel assured.

I held the egg to my cheek and began to hum like I used to for Kwasi, like our mother did for us, all the while rocking Mwana. My aura called out to the dragon I'd never met, but already felt a kinship to. I was lost in the sorrow of what would never be when I heard a low whistle. My head shot up.

"Did you hear that?" I asked, looking around the room.

"I don't hear anything," he said.

I stilled my body, wondering if I was losing my mind, until I heard it again. My heart stilled as I looked down at Mwana. Her aura was present, a soft purple in color, and she was whistling the tune I had just been humming. I hummed louder and waited. I sighed with relief when she whistled it back.

"What is happening?" Adriel asked anxiously.

"She's singing to me," I said tearfully. "I think she is going to be okay."

"Really?"

I placed her back next to the others and marveled as her tone mingled with the others, combining to make a beautiful harmony.

"Yes," I confirmed.

Adriel released a breathless laugh, his arms reaching out to pull me into a hug. Overwhelmed by the rush of emotions, I didn't think twice before leaning into him.

"You did it!" he exclaimed, his voice filled with awe. "You saved her."

The embrace lasted longer than it should have, but neither of us seemed to care. His scent—warm and earthy, like sandalwood—wrapped around me, heady and intoxicating. It was dizzying, the way it made my thoughts scatter, and for a moment, I forgot everything else.

"Are the northern lights on display tonight?" I asked, pulling away. "I hear people gathering below."

Adriel nodded, taking my cue and putting distance between us. "Yes, they are. But honestly, I've never seen the appeal. Just a bunch of colors in the sky."

I needed him to keep talking, so I could shake off the feelings threatening to overwhelm me. "Describe it to me," I said.

He hesitated. "I already did."

"No," I clarified. "Describe it as if it's your first time seeing them. Like you're seeing it through a child's eyes."

After a moment and a swig from his canteen, he finally gave in and tried to put it into words for me. "I see streaks of blue and green intertwining with soft pinks against the stars."

"It's more than colors and stars," I interjected. "It's the stillness of the night, broken by the gentle rustle of the wind through the palms. It is the soft crunch of sand beneath feet and people's excitement peeling off in waves below."

Catching on, he whispered, "Imagine the sky as a vast, shimmering canvas filled with the most magnificent colors you've ever seen. It is like a magic show, with lights flickering like eternal flames."

"I can see it," I mused.

"Think of ribbons of green, the color of fresh grass in the spring-time, dancing across the dark sky. Then imagine streaks of pink, reminiscent of a sunset, swirling and twirling as if they're being painted by the wind itself. And every now and then, hints of purple and dashes of blue add to the ever-changing landscape."

A smile spread across my face. "I knew you had it in you."

He murmured something under his breath, but I couldn't quite make out what it was.

"What did you say?" I asked curiously.

"You have a way of getting inside my head. Not just last night, but even now as we sit here talking. You were sent to live in a pit, forgotten in that place, yet you see the world more vividly than anyone I know. It makes me want to experience it in the same way that you do." He took a sip of water before continuing. "I wonder if you'd be open to trying something . . . with your back?"

"What do you have in mind?" I asked cautiously, curious and hesitant at the same time.

"The scars on my body are from the fire that took Odina's life. The fire I continue to have nightmares about," he admitted. "I haven't been able to fully use my battlemage since then—except for the tattoos I've put on my body."

His words sent flutters through my chest. To tell me that his battlemage was damaged was no small thing. The admission was reckless, intimate. It was a truth that could destroy him if spoken to the wrong person. That he entrusted me with it made my breath catch. All I could do was nod, too stunned to form a coherent response. The sound of fabric rustling and buttons being undone filled the room. My heart raced.

"What are you doing?" I asked, my voice betraying my alarm.

"May I approach?"

His words set off flutters within my chest as I felt the heat rising in my cheeks. His footsteps grew louder until he stood right in front of me. He took my hand in his and gently intertwined our fingers. Then, to my surprise, he pressed our joined hands against his bare chest. The roughness of his callused skin against mine made me shiver.

He started at the top and slowly moved my fingers across his chest, revealing more and more of his toned abs and defined ribcage. With each passing moment, I became increasingly aware of a pattern within the roughness of his skin.

"What is this?" I finally gathered the courage to ask.

"I could have these burn marks removed, but I never have because they remind me of what I lost, what I took for granted." He paused before continuing, his voice heavy with emotion. "I decided to make something new with them. You asked about my battlemage before. Mine is blue fire, cool to the touch when I want it to be. And with it, I tattooed a dragon over my burns."

He moved my hand lower to his hips, where the tail curved.

"They were Odina's favorite. She always wanted to see a dragon in her lifetime. I promised her so many times that I'd take her to Ujuima, but something always kept us away."

Suddenly, he dropped my hand and stepped back.

Without thinking, I reached out and took both of his hands in mine, my own voice now trembling with emotion. "Thank you for showing me."

He sucked in a sharp breath. "I could do it for you, too, if you want," he said, his voice just above a whisper.

I turned around and pulled my hair back from my neck, unsure of this game we were playing. "What would you suggest?"

He took his time tracing my upper back, tenderly touching each scar. A fire burned between my thighs, and my heart thundered against my ribcage as his warm hands traced soothing circles on my back.

"You could pick anything, and it would be beautiful," he said, pressing his lips to one of the scars marring my skin.

A soft moan escaped my lips. He flipped me around to face him and pushed me back against a wall.

"I want to kiss you," he said almost mournfully.

"Why don't you?" I asked breathlessly.

He gripped my chin, pulling our lips so close our breath intermingled. As he pulled me closer, we both panted furiously.

"I'm afraid if I kiss you, I will be forever undone," he breathed. "I'd want to erase anyone else who has kissed you before."

I knew we were teetering on the edge of something, something I could not easily come back from. As we stood facing each other, his chest heaved as his lips perched dangerously above mine. But just as quickly as he had taken control, he pulled away. I stumbled back slightly, my hands brushing against his thigh . . . and something else.

He turned around and quickly walked toward the window.

"Something is not right." He took another swig of water before spitting out a mouthful. "What have you done, princess? What did you give me?"

He retched as he tossed it to the floor.

"I . . . it was nightshade. It should not affect you like that!"

Still hunched over, he gasped, "This is not nightshade. And why are you giving me nightshade? Are you trying to kill me?"

My mind raced as I tried to figure out what had gone wrong. I pulled the remainder of the herb from my pocket and held it to my nostrils.

"It may be tribulterres," I said, embarrassed.

"You gave me a stamina potion!"

My face heated, and I could not blend into the cobweb-filled walls enough. "It was supposed to be nightshade!"

"And that is better? You could have killed me," he grunted. "You might have already."

I stood, moving toward him. "I can fix it," I said, forgetting that my dress was unbuttoned. It began to fall away from my neck.

"Get back," he growled. "Stay where you are. I do not need your help."

"If you just allow me to—"

"Stand back!" he said, halting my steps. "Please!"

There was a hint of desperation in his voice, enough that I went back to my seat and regarded him carefully, buttoning up my dress.

"Maybe if you described the symptoms," I began hesitantly, "perhaps I can help you through it."

"I do not think you understand what is happening," he rasped. "I will spare you the details."

I had an inkling. The other pit masters had never been shy about boasting of their exploits, as if my blindness meant I couldn't hear their crude stories. I hadn't taken the potion, so what excuse did I have for my own behavior? I'd wanted him to kiss me, to touch me. That much was undeniable. But now I felt ashamed that I'd manipulated the situation, unintentionally pushing him toward something he clearly did not want.

We sat in silence for some time until he said, "Look in the right pocket. I packed a few of the journals from the library. Would you please read one to me?"

I walked over, trying not to act too familiar. It did not seem like a good time to mention I'd snooped through his things earlier. There were exactly three journals, but I already knew that. I picked up the first one and used the soft pads of my fingers to read the Elliarb.

Journal of Melo Wiyotak

Date: 7th Sunturn, Year of the Gathering Stars

Today marks the beginning of a new chapter for our people. As I stand atop the ancient cliffs overlooking the valley below, I feel the weight of responsibility upon my shoulders. It is up to me to lead my people to a new home, a place where we can thrive and prosper once more.

For generations, we have wandered the wilderness, searching for a land to call our own. Now, fate has led us here, to this hidden valley nestled between towering mountains. Here, I have decided to find our new settlement, a place that I have named Wiyotak, in honor of our ancestors who came before us.

Date: 10th Sunturn, Year of the Gathering Stars

Already, the land reveals its secrets to me. The soil is rich and fertile, promising bountiful harvests for years to come. The river that winds its way through the valley teems with fish, providing sustenance for our people. And high above, the cliffs are home to caves that reveal ancient mysteries waiting to be uncovered. As I explore our new home, I cannot help but feel a sense of wonder. Everywhere I look, there are signs of life—

"Can you read that in a more monotone voice?" he interrupted. His voice sounded strained.

I couldn't contain my laughter, and instead of following his request, I decided to do the opposite. My voice deepened, taking on a sultry tone as I continued speaking. I watched his aura, imagining his face being caught between confusion and panic. I found it funny that my voice could unravel his control. But the more I teased, the more his carefully constructed composure cracked, and I couldn't help but find it absurdly entertaining. There was something satisfying about watching him flounder, even for just a moment.

If I were being honest, it felt good to have the upper hand for once.

Date: 18th *Sunturn, Year of the Gathering Stars*

I've met the native inhabitants of this land, but no more. We must push them and their dragons out. But they always come back in droves of force. We need to figure out how to cut off their source of power. Their eggs.

My heart stopped. *The eggs?* I kept reading breathlessly.

It's called dracite. The dragons detest it, but once it's in their diet and water, it lowers the production of eggs, which has proven useful. However, they've learned to hatch the eggs in the Saelerian Mountains, where there is a spring rumored to be filled with Phoenix Tears. We must find a way to end their reign.

The book fell from my hands. "Saelerian Mountains. That must be where Drakkar is taking us—to the spring of Phoenix Tears!" I said excitedly.

But when I turned in Adriel's direction, I heard a loud splash echo from below, and fear pulsed through me.

Without hesitation, I scrambled to the open window and hoisted myself over the barrier, desperately calling out for him. "Adriel! Where are you?"

My heart leaped out of my chest as I continued to call for him. Now I'd done it. I'd pushed him too far. With a sense of urgency, I tied my hair up in a messy bun and rolled up my sleeves, ready to jump in after him.

I listened to the waves below. If I dove in, there was no guarantee I'd hit the water, but guilt burned through me. I had to do something.

I called for him again, hoping he'd respond, so I could at least know in what direction I needed to jump. There was no response and no sign of his aura. Panic surged through me as I called for him again until my voice was hoarse.

I took a deep breath as I pulled myself up. There was a very slim chance I would survive. I turned back to where we'd placed the dragon eggs. If I died, who would care for them? I turned back to the window, resolved in what I had to do. Time was running out.

Before I could make a move, the wooden door behind me creaked open and water dripped onto the floor.

"Adriel?" I called out, my voice trembling with worry.

He walked over to me, his body dripping seawater into puddles on the floor. In one swift motion, he grabbed my waist and bent down, his rough hands skimming against my thighs. Despite my efforts to remain composed, I couldn't deny the tingling sensation his touch sent through me. His fingers paused when they reached a hidden pouch strapped to my left upper thigh.

He grasped the bundle and flung across the room. Startled, I staggered back until the cold stone wall pressed against my spine. Before I could recover, he closed the space between us, seizing my wrists and pinning them high above my head in an unyielding grip.

"Poison me again," he growled in warning, "and I will end you."

CHAPTER THIRTY-FIVE

Adriel

My anger seethed and boiled like hot coals, threatening to overwhelm me as I glared at Asha. Her calm demeanor only fueled the intensity of my emotions. I'd let my guard down, and now I was paying for it. The memory of my hands gripping her wrists and the straps of her dress lingered, the warmth still ghosting my fingertips. My own sweat mixed with the water dripping down my face and forearms onto the wooden floors below.

"Poison me again, and I will end you," was all I could manage before turning away.

Shaking my head to dispel the memory, I reached for the discarded journal Asha had been reading from. Of course, it would be found in Atim's brother's journals, the one place I hadn't thought to look. It seemed we now knew our destination: the Saelerian Mountains.

Asha continued to fuss over the eggs, cradling them in her arms as she lay on the bed.

I ought to tie her to it, after what she tried to pull. What was her plan? To kill me so she could have them for herself?

I quickly dismissed the thought as it was replaced with others of how turned on I'd be at the sight.

What was wrong with me? I should be furious, not fantasizing about a woman who was, well, who *had been* engaged. But Enapay had seen to that, hadn't he? And though I knew I should feel some shred of guilt, I couldn't find it in me to regret the way things had turned out.

I sat by the window, keeping a watchful eye on her. When her breathing finally evened out and I was sure she was asleep, I reached into my pack and pulled out the carefully wrapped scarf. Unfolding it just enough, I breathed in the faint scent of argan and jasmine before folding it back up and letting sleep take over me as well.

I awoke only because the sun was fully shining into the window of the lighthouse. Asha watched me from the bed. She'd retrieved Mwana, whom I'd cradled in my lap overnight.

"How long was I out?" I asked.

"It's nearly mid-morning," she said.

"Mid-morning! How could you let me sleep for so long?"

"Your aura is different," she noted. "It's still tightly coiled, but it has loosened around the edges."

I wasn't entirely sure what she meant but I did feel refreshed, invigorated even.

"Did you poison me while I slept?" I grumbled.

I watched her play with her hands, looking guilty as sin. "It was wrong of me. I won't do it again."

I snorted in response. "You said that last time. Why are you so intent on killing me?"

"I'm not! That's not what I intended."

I crossed my arms. "And what exactly did you intend? To seduce me, so that you can run off with the eggs?"

Her face flamed. I knew I needed to stop, but I was enjoying watching her squirm.

"Where do you think you were going in the middle of the night, in a town you do not know?"

"I don't know!" she said. "I don't know that we can trust you."

I cocked my head. "We?"

She closed her eyes. "Drakkar and I worry you will take the eggs from us."

I leaned my head back, looking at the planks above me. "And what use would I have with a bunch of eggs I cannot hatch? Tell me."

"I'm sorry. I don't know how many times you want me to say it."

The memory of how badly I'd wanted her burned in my mind. It had taken every ounce of willpower to stop myself from kissing her senseless—and more. I knew it was the potion's influence, but that didn't make it any easier. Even the sound of her voice had been enough to undo me. In the end, the only thing that had helped was throwing myself into the cold sea below.

"How is Mwana?" I asked, desperate to steer my thoughts away.

She smiled. "She's stronger today. I think she's going to be fine," she said. "They will want to hatch soon, I think. We must find this river of Phoenix Tears Melo spoke of."

"We?" I said, eyebrow raised. "Every time I turn around, you are trying to kill me."

She smiled. "Kill you, never. Temporarily debilitate you, maybe." When I did not laugh, she sighed. "It is going to be very difficult to make it up north without you. I understand that now. But I am committed to getting these eggs to their homeland. You may join us, but I have no desire to bring these dragons back to Wiyotak. But if you assist me, I will talk to Drakkar. Perhaps you can come to some kind of arrangement."

"Joint custody?"

That earned me another smile, and I realized just how much I craved them, like a I was starved of air. "That might be pushing your luck," she teased. "But maybe he'll share more about where they came from... and how more might be brought into this world."

I ran a hand through my unruly hair. "I can live with that."

She nodded, and we began packing up the few belongings we had and set off to find Drakkar. As we entered the busy streets, I noted the increase in the number of soldiers. It made sense with so many visitors for the festival to have extra security to keep order and prevent public drunkenness. Still, they made me uneasy.

The old cloaks we found provided some semblance of disguise, but I knew they wouldn't be enough to conceal Asha's blindness. It was quite possible that word had reached Tideport about the runaway princess. My heart raced with dread as we made our way through the bustling city streets, each step feeling heavier. The town was teeming with people, and we were mere specks in a sea of chaos. Every corner seemed to hold a new threat, with more guards patrolling, more eyes watching our every move.

I tightened my grip on Asha's hand as I led her through the maze of bodies, trying to blend into the crowd while also keeping a watchful eye out for any lurking danger. And then it happened—a momentary stumble from Asha that revealed her distinct indigo hair. My heart skipped a beat as the guard turned around, his eyes lingering on Asha for a moment too long. Suspicion flickered in his gaze, and my blood ran cold.

I knew him. He had been one of the trainees at the Guardian Academy, but his arrogance and lack of discipline had caused him to fail the trials. I had made sure he never made it further than that. Would he recognize me now? Would he expose us? It was not that he wasn't tough or brave enough. It was just that only the elite joined the Guardians, the best of the best. Everyone else served in the infantry or as a lowly palace guard. I pulled Asha closer, hiding our faces even more as the guard approached.

"Don't I know you from somewhere?" he asked, his voice laced with suspicion.

I shook my head, my pulse racing as I searched for an escape route. But before I could move, whispers around us turned into loud exclamations.

"Princess," and "Ujuima," they said, their voices filled with excitement. "And there's a reward to be had."

"Run!" I called.

My heart pounded in my chest as we broke into a desperate sprint through the crowd. We had to get out of here.

"Hey, you! Stop!" the guard yelled as we raced through the crowd.

I had trained for moments like this, but Asha hadn't. We could not travel as fast as we needed to, and I needed to get us out of the streets. We had no time to waste. With fear driving us forward, we tore through the crowd, our pursuers hot on our trail.

The voices of our pursuers grew louder, and people in the crowd began to look in our direction.

"Over here!" I heard in the distance.

Like an answered prayer, Marlon, the obeah, appeared from behind his shop and motioned for us to follow him. It was risky to trust him, but we had few options. Dragging Asha away from the crowd, we followed him.

"Come, come! Before they see you."

He directed us to enter through the back door, which led to a small room lined with shelves stacked with herbs and spices. Marlon stopped in front of a coffin-like structure and wound up a device at its base. With a creak, the door opened to reveal a dark concrete room inside.

"No!" I said firmly. "How are we supposed to breathe in there?"

"With this," he said, shoving a fistful of moist herbs into our hands. "It is lungworm. You don't have any other choice. You can chew that and be still, or you can try your luck with the city guard mounting the steps as we speak."

In that moment, banging sounded at the back door. We were out of options, out of time.

I turned to Marlon. "You know who I am, don't you?"

Marlon looked at the back door. "We don't have time for this," he said.

"Before we trust you, I need to know," I demanded.

He nodded. "Yes, war chief. I know."

The two of us locked eyes. "If you try anything, I will kill you," I said before pulling Asha into the cramped space of the coffin-like structure, and watched as the door closed behind us.

I glanced up as the sharp clang of a nail being driven into wood sounded through the space. He was sealing us in. I pushed against the entrance, but it didn't budge. I might have just sealed our fate. The air was thin in the room. We would run out of oxygen soon. I quickly chewed on the lungworm. It tasted how I imagined common worms might taste. I gagged on them, but the few I managed to keep down began to work, my lungs expanding with a little more ease. I glanced at Asha, who was also breathing better, her panicked gasps easing slightly.

Outside, we could hear faint voices and what sounded like breaking glass. They were tearing apart the shop in search of us. I unsheathed my blade, prepared to defend ourselves if they found us. Sweat beaded on my brow as we waited, listening for any clues from outside.

Asha slid onto the floor patting the concrete beside her.

"I can hear them," she whispered. "I can see their auras. There are at least ten. It is going to be a while. Come sit."

"How can you be so calm?" I asked.

"I am not afraid of the dark," she whispered.

At first, I ignored her, too agitated to remain still. But after some time, I sat cross-legged beside her, our knees touching in the cramped space.

"How do you stand it?" I whispered.

"Stand what?"

"The darkness. I am going out of my mind. I'm not even sure if my eyes are open. It makes me feel . . ."

"Vulnerable," she offered.

"Weak."

She placed a hand on my arm, and I silently prayed I hadn't sent us to our deaths.

"I was weak before I lost my sight," she continued. "I don't think being blind has made me any weaker. I believe it has helped me see what others don't see."

"What do you see when you look at me?" I asked curiously.

She did not answer right away, seeming to mull over my question.

"Your aura—it has writhing blue strands. I have not seen anything like it before," she said carefully. "It looks . . . pained, wrapped in a blue flame."

The words echoed in my mind, though I wasn't sure what to make of them.

"I've held my battlemage in for so long. I can do parlor tricks, like I did in the tunnel, but I fear fully using it again," I admitted. "I've tried many times, but I just come up empty. Others fear me because they've heard tales of it. They have seen the destruction I can do. No one knows that I—" My voice cracked. "No one knows how weak I really am."

I could feel her hands on the edges of my mind, what she called my aura. Although I had grown accustomed to her touch, it still made me uncomfortable, like I was exposing my soul for all to see. She pulled away, her voice barely above a whisper.

"It's in there," she whispered. "Your fire. I can feel it. You haven't lost it."

That was comforting to hear. I would have said more, but the wood door began to splinter as nails were being removed. I stood, sword in hand.

"Get ready," I warned her through gritted teeth. "Someone is opening the box."

I grasped my sword, thinking of any scenario where we could make it out alive if the person outside that door were an enemy and coming up empty.

The door creaked open, and without hesitation, I pushed my way out, knocking Marlon onto the ground in the process. He scrambled to shield himself behind his hands as he cried out frantically, "It's me! It's me! They are gone."

I assessed the chaos around us before helping Marlon get back to his feet. The apothecary was in shambles, with every surface turned upside down and broken. If this were where Marlon earned his livelihood, he would surely be ruined. Satisfied that the shop was clear, I helped him stand on his feet.

"Thank you for your assistance. We'd better get going."

"You cannot," he said gravely. "Look out of that curtain there." He pointed to the window that faced the front of the shop.

I cautiously peeked through and saw a line of city guards stationed outside. We were trapped.

"I have taken the liberty of calling for reinforcements," Marlon explained in a somber tone. "They will be here soon. We should be ready."

"Who are these reinforcements?" I asked suspiciously.

His eyes narrowed. "Old friends. Very loyal. There is no reason to be alarmed."

"We don't even know you," I shot back, my hand instinctively tightening around the hilt of my blade.

"And yet," he interjected. "I am your only way out of here."

"He is right," Asha said. "We are grateful for your assistance, obeah."

We waited in uneasy silence, every creak of the walls making my muscles tighten. My gaze never left the doors, rehearsing in my mind what I might do if the guards returned to finish what they had started. The stillness stretched until it felt unbearable, like the day would never end.

Just as the sun began to set, a shrill screech cut through the air, followed by a sudden burst of light that bled through the cracks in the blinds. Bursts of bright light flashed against the windows followed by crackling pops and loud explosions. My ears rang from the sound.

"What is that?" I asked, ducking as light filled the sky.

A devilish grin filled his face. "Our diversion. Let's go."

I took Asha's hand in mine as we stepped out into the dark of night. The sound of screams filled the air as sparkling orbs of fire shot through the streets, leaving a trail of destruction in their wake.

"What are they?" Asha asked, her eyes wide with wonder and fear.

"We call them starbursts," Marlon replied proudly. "Beautiful, but fairly harmless. They are quite handy in a pinch. Now come on!"

Leading us through a maze of narrow alleys and behind buildings, Marlon brought us to a desolate stretch of beach. With a flick of his wrist, a group of men on horseback charged toward us. They were all dressed similarly, in simple tan robes, and most of them carried weapons at their sides.

A man held out the reins of a sturdy horse to me. "We must leave now! We will guide you to safety."

I took the reins, thankful to see a double saddle so that Asha and I could comfortably ride together. I lifted her up and asked pointedly, "Are we captives? Or are we free to leave?"

The young leader ran a hand through his thick, unruly beard before responding.

"You are not our captives. We can lead you out of this city. Once we are clear, you may leave as you wish."

I studied him for a moment, thinking through our options. I did not think for long as I heard shouts in the distance. There was no time to come up with a new plan. I nodded before mounting behind Asha.

"Drakkar?" she whispered.

"He found us before," I said. "He will find us again."

CHAPTER THIRTY-SIX

Asha

We rode for what felt like endless miles outside of town. The wind whipped through my hair, stinging my cheeks. My body was still full of adrenaline by the time we came to a stop at a small outpost. I worried we were straying too far from Drakkar.

Marlon and his group welcomed us in, and we were introduced to their leader, Zariah. Something in Adriel's demeanor had changed when we met with the group. The way his body tensed against mine made me wonder if he was waiting for something.

Inside the outpost, the warmth from the hearth enveloped me, and the savory scent of stew made my stomach grumble. I inhaled the warmth of the lodge, soaking into my bones. The scrape of blades being sharpened, the heavy thud of dozens of boots trudging through sand, and the unmistakable scent of roasting meat told me everything I needed to know. This wasn't just an outpost; it was a military camp.

"You are not just an obeah, are you?" I asked Marlon.

He chuckled. "Indeed. I am an obeah, an inventor, a scholar, and a Lightwarden. We are the Lightwardens of this region."

I furrowed my brow in confusion. "What exactly is a Lightwarden?"

Adriel spoke up. "Religious zealots who believe in some sort of savior destined to save the world."

Zariah spoke then. "You know nothing of what you speak."

Adriel's hand moved to his sword as he stood beside me, and others around us followed suit. Marlon quickly defused the situation with a soothing voice as I reached out my hand to Adriel in a calming gesture, silently urging him to put away his weapon and take a seat once more.

"Let's calm down, gentlemen," Marlon warned.

"Tell me more about the Lightwardens," I said, turning to Marlon.

"Did you know there was a time when dragons ruled this land?" he asked. "We worshipped them because they were fierce, not the tamed beasts we see today. The dragons were powerful, able to fly great distances and build nests for their offspring."

"It is hard to imagine," I admitted.

"That is because men discovered dracite and its power to tame dragons. Once that happened, everything changed. Dragons were no longer revered; they were hunted. Wiyotak led the charge in their eradication, while kingdoms like Ujuima and Firepeak saw dracite as a weapon, a tool to seize power. And so, the five kingdoms rose, with Ujuima at the forefront. But the dragons . . ." He paused, his gaze distant. "They became shadows of what they once were. Broken. Diminished."

"Where do the Lightwardens come in?" I asked.

"Not everyone agreed with the practice of eradicating dragons. In fact, some fought alongside the dragons. They were called the Lightwardens. But the dragons, who were prone to prophecy, told the men they fought beside that they were destined to lose. They said that for centuries they would lie and wait until the 'Anointed One' arrived to deliver them from their captivity."

"Anointed One?" I asked. All the men in the room shifted, listening intently to the story.

"The dragons foretold of an Anointed One who would bring about their salvation. A woman with hair as dark as midnight's veil, skin as brown as earth, and eyes that shone like honey under a moonlit sky. She would emerge when dragons were in their most desperate hour, armed not with sight nor weapons but with words of immense power and a heart full of courage. She would be their guiding light, their savior." As the old man finished his tale, I felt the attention of everyone in the room focused solely on his words and the hope they brought.

My jaw dropped. "What are you saying? You think the Anointed One is me?"

Marlon rose from his chair and knelt before me on the floor. His words were filled with conviction. "I knew it the moment you walked into my shop. We have been waiting for your arrival, princess."

My throat tightened. "No, you are mistaken. I am not this anointed person. I am just a dragon pit master trying to escape an arranged marriage. I can't be a savior to anyone. I am blind."

He gently touched my feet in reverence. "Exactly. You are our hope. You are indeed our savior."

"No!" I protested, standing up abruptly. I turned to Adriel. "I would like to leave now."

"I told you this was a bad idea," Zariah's voice chimed in. "We should have done it my way."

Adriel's voice dropped, sharp as steel. "And what way is that?"

Marlon raised his hand, silencing them both. His voice carried an eerie calm. "Bring her out."

The room seemed to hold its breath as a long creak of a door opening sounded nearby. Soft footsteps approached as my skin prickled with unease as I braced myself for a trap.

Then a voice, warm and achingly familiar, broke the silence. "Princess! It is really you."

My breath caught, the world seeming to split on its axis. That voice—I hadn't heard it in so long, yet it wrapped around me like a piece of home. "Kaliyah?" I gasped.

"Yes, child. It is I."

Tears welled in my eyes as I reached out, pulling her into a tight embrace.

"Kaliyah, I thought I'd never see you again. I've missed you so much."

"As have I, child. As have I," she murmured, patting my back gently. When we finally pulled away, she held me at arm's length. "Now, tell me everything. I want to hear it all."

CHAPTER THIRTY-SEVEN

Asha

Kaliyah led me to a secluded back room where we could talk in private. I wrapped my arms around her once more, still in shock.

"What are you doing here?" I asked, my mind racing with questions.

"Zariah is my son," she said softly, her voice holding a tinge of sadness.

"How did I not know you had a son?" I exclaimed, unable to comprehend how such a significant detail could have been kept from me.

She let out a heavy sigh and explained, "I had him when I was very young. Your mother arranged for him to be sent away to school and given an education. I wanted him to have a better life than I could provide." She patted my hand gently. "Without you in Ujuima, there was no one left for me to stay for. So I came here."

My grip on her hand tightened as her words sank in. "And here you are, just when I need you more than ever."

In a hushed tone, Kaliyah asked, "What about the eggs, Your Highness?"

I reassured her, "They are safe with me." I tapped the satchel at my side, where they were securely stored.

"What do you plan to do with them?"

"I intend to take them to their home in the mountains," I replied. "They will have the best chance of survival there."

She pursed her lips as she often did when I chose a path she did not particularly care for. "Have you thought about keeping them here? Having three dragons could provide a great deal of security for the Lightwardens."

I shook my head, a tinge of panic creeping in. "No one must know about them. I promised their mother I would keep them safe."

"Don't worry. I won't say a word, child. An oath to a mother is sacred."

"Could you tell me what this prophecy is about?" I asked. "It cannot refer to me."

Her voice grew solemn. "My son has talked about it for some time. All the people here fully believe it. They even worship the old gods. It is a bit . . . disturbing."

"Why stay then?"

"He's my son. I have missed most of his life. He wants to do good, truly. But he is a warrior through and through. He will not support an emperor. Something will have to replace the system, I suppose." She shifted closer to me. "I do not know if this prophecy refers to you, child, but they want me to convince you to stay. They believe you are the key to dismantling the five kingdoms and dethroning the emperor."

I shook my head. "Adriel said there were twenty men. How are they going to take down Ujuima?"

"They did not want to alarm your friend, so much of the army is camped elsewhere. There are nearly twenty thousand men and women ready to fight."

I sat with her words for a moment, taking them all in. "Why do they hate Ujuima and the other kingdoms? I know taxes have been high, but that isn't enough to topple the five kingdoms."

She patted my hand patiently. "I'm afraid you have been shielded from the harsh realities of life for far too long. Even during your exile, you were protected from the poverty and desperation that plagued most of the kingdom. The emperor forbade your coming into contact with impoverished people so that dragon pit masters would be filled with noble sons and daughters. It was wildly unpopular."

I remembered the entitled, arrogant young pit masters. Many of them weren't worth anything, which was why I'd been relied on for so much. Now I understood why they loathed me.

"Ujuimans are fortunate," she continued, "living in the wealthiest kingdom thanks to high taxes and resource consolidation. But other cities . . . they have not been so lucky. The people have suffered greatly for a long time."

"Why did my father not do something?" Even as the words left my lips, I knew the answer.

My father did not care. He cared about power. Power was currency. It was his life's purpose.

"Will they let me leave?" I asked.

"I do not know, princess."

I leaned on her shoulder. "Could you get us out?"

"I will try. My son may not heed my counsel, but if there is a way, I will find it for you," she promised.

Resting my head against Kaliyah's shoulder, we stayed like that until she asked, "Adriel? What is your relationship with him?"

I hesitated, my stomach twisting in knots. The truth was, I was not entirely sure myself.

"What do you mean?" I asked indifferently, or what I hoped passed as such. "He is helping me get to the Northern Mountains."

"You two seem . . . close. The way he looks at you, the way he touches you—like you're his. I noticed it the night you met, too. You should have seen how he sprinted across the dance floor to keep you from getting tangled up with the other dancers." My head lifted so quickly, I heard an audible crack. "Really?"

"Yes. Elan certainly took notice, and so did the emperor."

I chewed my lip, taking it in. "Well, we aren't anything but a means to an end for each other."

She patted my hair. "I have to say that is a relief to me. I hope you don't mind my saying so, but . . . I don't think you should trust him. He is dangerous."

I sat up feeling unsettled. What did she mean? What did she know about Adriel that I didn't? Before I could ask for more, we were interrupted by Zariah and his men.

Clearing his throat, he addressed me gravely. "Your attendance is required in the strategy room. Please follow me."

I was led through a series of corridors until I finally heard Marlon greet us.

"Welcome, Princess Asha," the voice echoed through the grand hall, its source a mystery to me.

As I stepped forward, my eyes widened in wonder as I saw colorful orbs of light flow from a source on the wall. The light danced in a mesmerizing display, cascading up to the ceiling and mingling with other hues: purple, green, red, and blue. It reminded me of the aura crystals that Kitchi had shown me in the garden, the ones that Adriel had personally put in just for me.

"What is this?" I breathed in amazement.

"This room is a remnant of the Lightbearers," Zariah explained. "They were powerful beings who could control light and channel it into fire."

My eyes widened. "I'm confused. Is that the same as Lightwardens?"

"Lightwardens are protectors of the dragons and their realm," he clarified, "while Lightbearers rode them and wielded their fire as a weapon."

"You said remnant. What happened to them?" I asked, unable to contain my curiosity.

"Nobody knows," Zariah added. "They have not been seen for centuries, but they all had one thing in common."

I cleared my throat, eager to know more. "And what is that?"

"They were unseers," he whispered in my ear.

My body went rigid, not just from his proximity but from the weight of his words.

"So what? You think I am a Lightbearer because I am blind?" I retorted, my voice trembling with frustration. "I was born with sight."

But Marlon's gentle voice interrupted. "You mentioned you were eight when you lost your sight. That is about the age a Lightbearer begins to harness their abilities. Tell me, princess, what were you doing when you lost it?"

Fury ignited within me, threatening to consume any sense of control I had as the memory flooded back to me like a tidal wave. "I was sparring."

"Emperor Idris was a brutal man. I imagine he was quite hard on his children as well. Tell me, princess, did you fear for your life that day?"

I hesitated before responding, unsure of how much to reveal. "We are taught never to assume we will leave the sparring mat whole," I finally replied, keeping my tone neutral.

A hint of amusement crept into his voice. "You were afraid. Fear is a necessary ingredient for Lightbearer abilities to manifest. I mentioned that I could help you regain your sight. Lightbearers are blind until they bond with a dragon. Once that bond is solidified, it is possible for their sight to return."

My mind raced at this revelation. Was that why I could see when flying on Drakkar's back? Had I truly regained my sight, even if only for a moment?

"Tell me more," I said.

"There have been very few Lightbearers in existence, but they were incredibly powerful, formidable weapons."

A weapon? His words were not lost on me.

"You still have no proof that I am one."

"You confirmed it when you walked in here and saw the lights."

I must have looked confused because he took a moment to explain, like I was a toddler, trying to understand what was happening.

"You see, we cannot see the light ourselves," Marlon explained. "Only a Lightbearer can perceive it. It emits the same frequencies as an aura. It seems that part of your abilities has already unlocked itself. You are quite powerful indeed."

"Am I being held captive here?" The question burned on my tongue.

There was a pause before Marlon spoke again.

"It depends," he began cautiously.

"On what?" I demanded.

"On whether you will help us bring down the five kingdoms."

I scoffed, incredulous at the request. "And how could I possibly accomplish that?"

Marlon replied in a grave tone, "I think you underestimate yourself. We will find you a dragon and see what you can do. In the meantime, you will be our guest."

"Where is Adriel?" I demanded.

"He was less cooperative than we had hoped." A couple of the men grunted in the background.

"May I speak to him?" I asked.

"You may see him soon. Now, if you could kindly hand over your pack so we can check for weapons, we can get you settled."

Burn it. I held onto it tightly and laughed. "You all are afraid I have an assassin's blade in here. Even if I did, how would a blind girl use it?"

A hand reached for it. I slapped it back. "Don't touch me. Is this how you treat your guests?" I snarled.

Marlon took on a placating tone. "Alright. You may keep it... for now." He sounded very much like an annoyed parent. "Take her to her quarters."

I was settled in my room, feeling foolish for once again getting myself ensnared in a man's game. The idea of my being a Lightbearer was absurd. I shook my head, unwilling to entertain these claims now. I needed to find my way back to Drakkar—and fast. But the idea of escaping seemed impossible, with me not knowing the layout of this outpost. Counting my steps upon entering had proved useless, as there were constant twists and turns through different rooms.

I had to think.

Sliding down against the wall, desperation took hold as I buried my face in my shaking hands. *Drakkar, where are you?*

"I am awaiting your return."

I jolted in surprise, my heart racing as I recognized his familiar voice. *"Drakkar? Is that you?"*

"I'd like to know who else it would be."

I scrambled to my feet, knocking over a nearby table in my haste. *"I need your help. A group of men have taken me to their outpost. Can you find me?"*

"Tell me which direction. Did you go through the forest or along the beach?"

"There was sand, so it must be the beach."

"I am on my way. See if you can find your way outside."

I cursed in exasperation. *"How am I supposed to do that?"*

"You have a unique perspective of the world. It makes you powerful, not powerless, so use it. I will see you soon."

His words struck something within me that had remained dormant for too long. No one had ever seen my lack of sight as something powerful. I'd accepted it because I had to, but had I really? It was always something that was undesirable, not something to be honed or wielded.

"I'll find a way."

I centered myself and focused inward, letting my heightened senses guide me through the unfamiliar surroundings. With each inhale and exhale, I listened intently to the sounds around me. The distant footsteps of men pacing, the faint rustling of a metal cart being pushed down a hallway, followed by hushed voices discussing plans for dinner. I strained my ears, listening intently for any other clues. Amid the many sounds, I detected the gentle rustle of the wind outside, its whisper carrying hints of the world beyond these walls.

I rose from my seat and moved. Step by step, I navigated the room, hands outstretched until they touched the cool, paned surface and a doorknob. Could it really be this easy?

Heart pounding with anticipation, I turned the knob and felt the door swing open beneath my touch. Without hesitation, I pushed through and stepped onto a balcony overlooking the sea. The salty breeze kissed my skin, and for a moment, I allowed myself to bask in it.

A blast of frigid air smacked me in the face, carrying with it the overpowering scent of saltwater and brine. The icy wind sliced through my clothes, raising goosebumps along my flesh as I stepped out onto the balcony. As my fingers grazed the railing, a smile tugged at the corners of my lips. That smile quickly faded as I stumbled on uneven ground and reached out blindly for something to steady myself.

My hands found a rough stone at my feet, which I promptly threw forward, listening intently as it tumbled below me. These were stairs, and they were steep. This was why the door was unguarded. It was treacherous even for someone with sight. The balcony would be too narrow for Drakkar to land.

I steeled myself, determined to make the descent. The wind howled relentlessly, whipping around me as I stood at the top of the stone staircase. With every step, my heart pounded so loudly I could barely hear anything else.

Gripping the rough surface of the stone wall, I hesitated, unsure if the ancient railing would hold my weight. With a deep breath, I took the first tentative steps, my foot finding purchase on the worn stone beneath me.

The descent was treacherous, with uneven steps and moisture-slick surfaces. I stumbled. My chest clenched as I fought to regain my balance. Panic clawed at the edges of my mind, threatening to overwhelm me with its suffocating grip.

I tripped again, my foot catching on a protruding stone. For a moment, I teetered on the edge of the staircase, my arms windmilling wildly as I fought to stay upright. Desperation flooded my body, urging me to keep moving, to find my footing.

With a surge of adrenaline, I lunged forward, my fingers scraping against the rough surface of the stone wall as I frantically pulled myself back from falling. The problem was I had no idea how high up I was. It could be several feet or a few inches to the bottom, but I dared not test out that theory by falling.

Breathless and trembling, I continued my way down. Finally, after what felt like an endless descent, my feet met solid ground. My knees were scraped and bruised, trembling with exhaustion, but I had made it. Tears streamed down my face as I collapsed onto the safety of the earth. Exhaustion washed over me, but so did overwhelming relief. I'd made it.

The sky cracked with a deafening roar, unleashing a deluge of rain that pounded against my skin like a barrage of debris. Urgency fueled my every move. I trudged through the storm, calling out for Drakkar. Each droplet felt like a sharp sting as I pressed forward, my heart racing with desperate urgency to find Drakkar. Water seeped into every crevice of my body, weighing me down and making each step a struggle. But I was free.

With each step, I shed the layers of clothing that bound me. My fingers fumbled with the buttons, urgency lending strength to my movements as I stripped away the last bit of restraint, leaving only my white dress behind.

In the midst of the storm, I stood alone, the fabric of my dress clinging to my skin, and I laughed. The sound echoed into the night, a joyful release born of my newfound freedom. Above, the unmistakable sound of Drakkar's wings cut through the tumult. With a graceful descent, he landed before me.

I mounted his back without hesitation, feeling the familiar warmth of his scales beneath my fingertips. With a powerful beat of his wings, we rose into the storm-laden sky, leaving behind the constraints of the world below. Nothing else existed except for us and the freedom we shared in flight.

The air was electric. A metallic taste coated my tongue as my body tingled from the crackling of thunder in the air. As Drakkar carried me into the night, something came over me. I clung to his scales.

"Drakkar," I whispered. "What is happening?"

"What is meant to. Don't be afraid."

Lightning speared through me, and I screamed. My eyes illuminated, and suddenly, I could not only feel the rain but also see it falling from the sky in large sheets. I gasped as I saw the lightning flash through the sky, illuminating the buildings below.

"I can see," I said, shivering along his back.

"What do you see?"

Raindrops fell onto Drakkar's thick scales, each one catching the light of the moon and refracting into a rainbow of colors that made up his unique hide. My breath hitched as I reached out to touch them, only for the drops to roll off like rivers onto the forest floor. "I can see the rain. I can see my hands," I said, feeling how my fingertips wrinkled into deep canyons. I looked down at the sea of green and gasped at the thousands of leaves that trembled from the gusts of the storm. "I can see the trees. Drakkar, I can see the stars in the sky!" I laughed, captivated by the smear of constellations blurred from my tear-filled eyes. "I can see everything!" I yelled into the night.

"As long as you ride me, you will have sight. You will see what I see," he said. "We should get you out of the rain."

I sighed, guilt weighing heavily on my body. We could not leave, not yet. "Wait! We have to get Adriel."

Drakkar rumbled in disapproval. "This is a bad idea."

Probably. Still, I urged Drakkar to fly us back toward the outpost. "We can't do this without him," I insisted. "I won't make it to Saeleria alone."

"I'll never understand why you doubt yourself so much," he grumbled.

I ignored his comment, my focus shifting to the chaotic scene below. I took it all in, trying not to pass out from the onslaught of images I was seeing. My vision blurred as my brain tried to make sense of it all. Where would Adriel be?

With each beat of Drakkar's wings, I strained to catch a glimpse of the telltale glow that would lead me to him.

And then, like a beacon in the darkness, I saw it—a shimmering blue light that radiated with familiarity. It emanated from the farthest reaches of the outpost. Drakkar's powerful wings sliced through the air as we closed the distance between us.

I called out to Drakkar, asking if he could land on the roof where Adriel's aura shone brightest. With a groan of assent, Drakkar angled his wings, banking sharply as he descended toward the rooftop below.

The sudden appearance of a dragon atop the outpost drew the attention of everyone below, and I could hear the shouts and cries of alarm as the men rushed out to see what was happening. But amid the chaos, I kept my eyes fixed on Adriel, spotting him among the throng of figures below.

With urgency, I leaned forward, calling out to him with all the strength I could muster.

"Adriel!" I yelled, my voice carrying over the tumult of the storm. "Adriel!"

I could see him standing amid a throng of figures, his sandy brown skin glistening in the rain. For a moment, it seemed as if time had stopped, the world around us fading into insignificance as our eyes met across the distance. Adriel stood amid the chaos, staring up at me with intense umber eyes. All else faded away as our gazes locked and held across the distance. The look he gave me took my breath away.

I took in every detail of his appearance for the first time: the sharp angles of his jawline, his shoulder-length hair blowing loosely from its braid, and his intense eyes that seemed to pierce through me. With a determined stride, Adriel broke free from the crowd, his gaze locked on me and never wavering as he strode my way.

"What took you so long?" he called.

Chapter Thirty-Eight

Adriel

A deafening roar shook the building, causing everyone to scramble for cover. The sound rang through my bones, and I could feel the ground tremble beneath me. The ceiling groaned, and chunks of stone rained down as something massive landed on the rooftop with a thud.

Amid the chaos and panicked shouts, one voice stood out, shouting to take cover. But I couldn't look away from the shattered window where I saw her, standing tall and confident amid the destruction.

A large black dragon leaped down from the rooftop, its wings spread wide, and its razor-sharp claws clicked against the cobblestones. I recognized Drakkar right away, but it was not his imposing presence that stopped me in my tracks. It was her, Asha.

She was wearing a white dress that now clung to her body. The rain soaked through the thin fabric, accentuating every seductive line and curve. Her eyes, once a warm honey brown, now crackled like golden bolts of light.

But what truly captivated me was not her change in appearance, but the way she seemed to look right through me. Our eyes locked in a magnetic pull, rendering me helpless to do anything other than walk toward her.

"Adriel, it's me," she called.

I broke free from the crowd running from the dragon, though my gaze remained on her. Realizing we had little time to make our escape, I mounted Drakkar, sitting behind Asha.

I wanted to say so much to her, but all I could manage was, "Ash and bone, what took you so long?"

She glanced back at me, and that was when I saw it: her eyes, sharp and focused, met mine with a clarity that hadn't been there before. A satisfied grin spread across her face, and in that moment, I was certain. She could see. Her sight had returned. The realization hit me like a large wave crashing down on me, and for a heartbeat, I was too stunned to speak. But there was no time for questions as Drakkar surged forward, carrying us away from the chaos. Drakkar flew through the night toward the coastal city of Oceana. We would take a ship northwest to avoid having to travel through Ujuima and Firepeak, where a dragon would surely be noticed.

Drakkar panted as we landed. I descended and held out my hands to help Asha, but she ignored them and dismounted with expert grace. As she left Drakkar's side, however, her eyes shifted back to their usual honey brown.

"Can you see me?" I asked.

She shook her head. "Not anymore. I can only see when I am in contact with him."

I looked to Drakkar. "What does he have to say about that?"

She sighed in frustration. "Not much. He's being cryptic. Have you heard the word Lightbearer?"

My eyes shot up in surprise. "I have read about them, sure. Those fanatics we just left call themselves the Lightwardens, but it is a self-imposed title. Lightbearers are written about, but none have been seen since . . ."

"Since dragons could fly," she finished.

I looked between her and Drakkar. Things were finally clicking into place. "Burn it to hell! Are you saying . . . do you know what this means? What you could do for the five kingdoms? The Lightbearers were the rulers of the land before Ujuima became the center. If there are more like you, it could turn the power dynamic on its head."

She bit her lip with concern. "In every history book I have ever read, a power shift means war. War means many people die."

"People are already dying, princess!"

She flinched at the way I'd said her title. Asha had been shielded from the atrocities Ujuima had inflicted on the world. Thanks to the emperor, every man and woman was expected to serve in their armies in some way, which bred never-ending conflict. I took a softer tone, hoping to convince her.

"What the Lightwardens are planning will throw the five kingdoms into an all-out war against each other. You could offer them an alternative."

She shook her head. "Marlon seemed to want to use me more than ask for my help. I do not think what they have planned for me is good."

"That may well be." I was silent for a moment. "Perhaps there is another way. There has to be."

We decided to let Drakkar rest. We left him behind to sail along the Aragon Sea to the Saelerian Mountains. He would meet us in a few days.

As Asha and I boarded the ship, relief washed over me in waves. The private quarters we'd managed to secure provided a brief reprieve from the chaos that had consumed our lives in recent days. With loft beds tucked away in the corner, it was a small sanctuary amid the bustling activity of the ship.

We'd disguised ourselves as merchants. I'd assisted Asha in tucking her hair under a wide-brimmed hat and a borrowed traveler's cloak. We were a married couple looking to sell our wares to the northern markets. It was a lie flimsy enough to pass casual scrutiny but convincing enough to grant us passage.

We wasted no time in settling into our new lodgings. I was fortunate to be able to snag a few changes of clothes for us both. It was a much cooler climate up north, and both of us would need blanket wraps and moccasins to keep ourselves warm.

After filling our bellies with hot food, exhaustion weighed heavily on me. Asha was already breathing softly in her bed, curled up around the dragon eggs. Her body swayed gently along with the lulling ship. I grabbed the bed above and nestled beneath the warm blankets, letting the rhythmic sound of the waves rock me to sleep. For the first time in what felt like an eternity, I allowed myself to relax, knowing that we were finally on our way north.

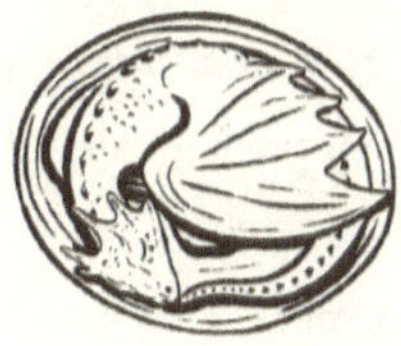

As the ship sailed across the calm waters, I spent most of my time on deck, enjoying the fresh air and salty sea breeze brushing against my cheeks. Asha, on the other hand, remained in the cabin with the dragon eggs, constantly worrying over them.

Even when I offered to take a turn, she would refuse and insist on staying by their side.

One evening, I managed to coax her out onto the deck with a flask of mead and a deck of cards. She claimed to have never played Enchanted Empires before, but when she expertly laid down her spell card, I knew better.

"Who taught you this game? More importantly, who taught you to cheat at this game?"

She laughed deeply. "I'm the blind one here. Who is cheating whom?"

"I can tell you know the difference in texture and thickness of the cards, so don't act all innocent. Who was it?" I held my breath, hoping it wasn't Ekon or some other man she'd met in the dragon pits.

A rueful smile tugged at her lips, but it didn't reach her eyes.

"It was Kaliyah, actually. The woman you saw with the Lightwardens. She practically raised me after Mother died." She looked off into the distance, seeming to suppress a memory. "It is what we played to distract me after one of Elan's torture sessions."

I kept my face neutral, but I was silently raging inside, fantasizing about all the ways I wanted to make him hurt, for her.

"How did you stand it?" I said, throwing my cards down. "How could you stay there when your own family turned their back on you?"

Her eyes widened in surprise at my question, as if no one had ever asked her before. She stared at her cards as if committing them to memory. She laid them down, three spell cards to my one. She'd beaten me again.

"I suppose I could not imagine any other way," she said. "Where would I go? Who would provide for me?" She pointed at herself. "How could I ask anyone to shoulder my burdens? It would be cruel."

"Is that all you think you are? A burden?" I asked softly.

She chewed on her lip, deep in thought. "That's all I've ever been."

I shook my head incredulously. "You are Princess Asha Osei, born into the most powerful house of the five kingdoms. You've endured your family's cruelty with a strength most people could never fathom. You're brave, fearless even. The first time I saw you, you'd climbed into a dragon's cage without a second thought. I've seen battle-hardened warriors tremble in the presence of dragons, yet you handle them with ease. And through it all, you've managed to keep your heart kind and beautiful." I reached for her hand, holding it gently between mine. "Being blind is the least interesting thing about you."

I stopped myself, realizing I'd probably said too much. A small grin tugged at my lips as I noticed her cheeks flush.

"It sounds like I have finally grown on you," she whispered.

I laughed, trying to play off the breathlessness that I felt. "I wouldn't go that far, princess, but your presence is tolerable."

She looked at me like she wanted to ask me a question, but did not know where to start.

"Then will you allow me to do something?"

I swallowed hard, struck by the realization that if she asked me to walk the plank, I would. She could ask me anything, and I would agree to it.

"Will you allow me to peer into your aura again?"

Anything but that.

"It's just," she continued. "You are sleeping so much better now, and I believe that with a little more work, you could access your battlemage again."

"What if I lose control? What if I set the ship on fire?"

She shook her head. "I trust you to keep it contained." She motioned around us. "And it's not like we're in the middle of the ocean or anything. We can open a window and you can jump in, but I don't think it will come to that."

"How do you know?" I asked, panicked.

"Because your battlemage is the least interesting thing about you," she said. Her lips turned upward at how she was able to use my words against me.

"And," she added, "I believe in you."

I turned it over in my mind, weighing all the repercussions. I believed Asha could help me, but I'd die before losing that control with anyone else.

"Okay, but we stop when I say stop," I said firmly.

"Of course."

"And you let me finish off this mead before we try."

She frowned at that but nodded, and I proceeded to get good and drunk.

We were in our quarters. She sat next to me on her bed, holding out her hands. I placed mine atop hers, and immediately I felt a tug on my aura. She tried again and again, but each time, she pulled her hands back as if burned.

"What's happening?"

"You are fighting me," she said with exasperation.

"Sorry," I said.

She stared at me for a moment before she stood and began to loosen the ties of her tunic.

"What are you doing?" I asked as she began to lower it beyond her shoulders.

My jaw dropped and my breath hitched at the sight of her collarbone, wondering what she looked like behind the loosened fabric over her chest.

"You offered to tattoo my back," she said, lowering the tunic further for better access. She turned around, and her back was bare in front of me. I cleared my throat.

"Not tonight. This should be something we take our time with."

"It is my back. I get to decide when the time is right, and the time is now. Let's go."

I studied her face, searching for hesitation, but her chin lifted with that stubborn resolve I'd come to know too well. Realizing her mind was made up, I exhaled and carefully gathered her hair over one shoulder, exposing the expanse of her back. My chest ached. I lifted my hands and gently traced the marks. I felt her inhale sharply.

"I told you," I murmured, reluctant to add to her pain, "we don't have to do this tonight."

"Tonight," she insisted, voice steady even though I could hear the flicker of nerves beneath it. "Hurry, before I change my mind."

"Relax," I said. "It won't hurt."

I felt her muscles soften under my palms, surrendering. Gathering my focus, I let my battlemage flare. Heat prickled across my skin as beads of sweat gathered on my brow. Carefully, deliberately, I began. My energy outlined the scars, reshaping them into something new, something hers. With each stroke of light and power, I pressed harder against my own restraint, terrified of misstepping.

Time seemed to stretch, every breath of hers syncing with mine. I added shading, texture, life. Only when I was sure it was worthy of her did I finally pull back, heart pounding in my chest.

"What is it?" she asked.

"It's a mategwes rabbit," I explained. "They look a lot like jack-alopes, but their horns are larger and made of ivory. The mategwes are fierce, known for taking down creatures much larger than themselves, like the king cobra. It's not finished, of course, but it's a start."

"A mategwes," she whispered, tracing it with her fingertips. "I love it."

"It will itch some as it continues to heal. We should wrap it," I suggested.

"Maybe later," she said. Her hand interlaced with mine, something she had done many times, and yet, this felt different somehow, intimate. "Thank you," she said with tears in her eyes.

I used my other hand to wipe them away, but stopped when I noticed her skin had a faint glow. I gasped, feeling a strange warmth spread through me.

"What are you—" I began, but I was lost.

The acrid scent of smoke filled my lungs as I stood in the armory, hurling bursts of blue fire at targets. Each shot painted streaks of light across the dimly lit room as I adjusted the size and intensity with each blast. I was mid-throw when Odina strolled into view. My hand jerked to the side just in time, narrowly avoiding sending a blast straight toward her.

"What are you doing out so late at night, Odina?" I asked with agitation. "I could have hit you."

She didn't flinch at my tone, but instead met my glare with a calm expression that only served to irritate me further. She brushed her curls from her face, a movement she always did when she was about to admit to doing something reckless.

"Mesof is in labor," she admitted. "I could use your help. Father forbade me from going, but he might change his mind if you come with me."

"This again?" I asked, rolling my eyes. My tone was clipped as I threw another burst of fire, smaller this time, watching it collide perfectly with the bullseye. "I've told you so many times, Odina, let others worry about those in the village. You are just learning the craft. You aren't expected to make house calls."

She threw her hands up in exasperation. "Haven't you ever heard of doing good just because?"

I smirked. "Nothing is just because, sister." I leaned back, tossing a flicker of flame absently between my hands as I spoke. "Everything is a transaction, whether you want to admit it or not. Mesof gets help delivering her baby, and you get the self-satisfaction of proving us all wrong about you belonging in the Healer's House."

Her face puckered in anger, her lips pressing into a tight line. I'd struck a nerve.

"How can you be so cold?"

"We both know Mesof can't deliver her baby because of her joint instability. She shouldn't be pregnant in the first place. What if she passes that on to her child? It seems cruel to me," I continued casually, throwing an orb of flame high into the air and watching it dissolve into rings of smoke above our heads, "and for what it is worth, Father will never approve of you working there, anyway. He only allows you now to give you something to do until you are married."

Her expression darkened. "For someone so full of promise, you are so blind. I don't know how to make you see," she said, meeting my gaze. "But I pray that you do, and that I'm around to see it."

I rolled my eyes at her dramatics, though guilt tugged faintly at my conscience. "I love you, too," I said dryly, turning back toward the targets. Another blaze erupted from my hand and hit dead center once again, flames licking hungrily at the edges before dying down. "But no—I'm not going with you."

"Fine," she said, turning defiantly. "I'll go alone."

I looked away, throwing another blast of fire at the target. It hit the center and set the target ablaze.

"Do what you want," I sighed. "You always do."

With a look of sadness, Odina squared her shoulders and walked out the door, ignoring my calls for her to return. Yes, I disagreed with her, but she was still my sister, my blood. I had a few more rounds of practice, though my aim suffered slightly. I pulled away, having lost my concentration anyway.

Restlessness gnawed at me as I wandered through the palace halls, guilt settling like a weight in my chest. I couldn't shake the feeling that I'd been too harsh. After what felt like hours of pacing, I finally decided it wouldn't hurt to check on her. I saddled my horse and rode into the village.

"No!" I cried, pulling myself out of the memory. "I don't want to go there."

"This is the part I need to see," Asha said, rubbing a thumb in a soothing motion along my palm. "We can stop if you want, but we are so close."

I took a deep breath. Everything in me told me to run, to look away, but as I looked into Asha's eyes, I was reminded of the memory she'd shared with me. If she could be that brave, I owed her the same. Even if it meant she might see me differently afterward.

"Okay," I whispered, my voice barely audible. I closed my eyes, steeling myself, and let the memory pull me back in.

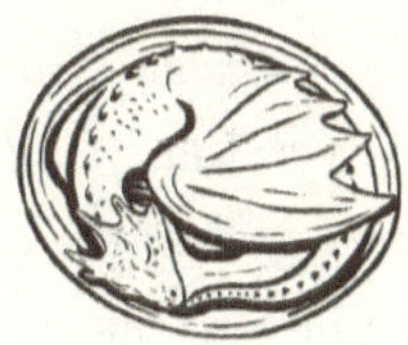

I stopped my progress as I watched fellow Guardians chase after a man they were trying to detain. His figure darted through the narrow streets like a shadow slipping between cracks. My gaze followed him, taking in his bony frame—his ribs nearly visible even beneath his tattered tunic. I noted how thin he was, like food had been hard to come by. Yet despite his frailty, he moved with an agility that spoke of desperation and survival.

I leaned over my pommel with amusement as the Guardians stumbled over barrels and cursed under their breath as he evaded their capture.

"Do you need assistance?" I asked.

"No, Your Highness," they said, glancing back at me. "He tried to subscribe to the Guardians, but he has something wrong with him," one continued between labored breaths. "He did not pass his auditory measures. We plan to take him to the mines."

I nodded in approval as they hurried after him.

As they resumed their chase, I straightened up in my saddle and urged my horse forward at a leisurely pace. The thin man—no, the boy—had caught my attention more than I cared to admit. What could have driven someone with such an affliction to risk everything by attempting to join our ranks? The Guardians were not known for their leniency or compassion; rules were rules, and failure meant exile or forced labor in the mines.

He was quick, outmaneuvering us at every turn. Unlucky for him, I was faster. I scaled a cabin and climbed into a nearby tree, lying in wait for him to come out of his hiding spot.

Perched high above like a predator lying in wait, I scanned the area until I spotted him pressed against a tree trunk. To anyone else, he would have been invisible, his form shimmering faintly as it blended seamlessly with the bark, but I recognized the telltale signs immediately. A camouflage battlemage? Interesting.

Once the other Guardians ran by, the boy's figure shifted as he was no longer camouflaged with the tree trunk.

Interesting. He had a chameleon battlemage. I would not have expected that.

I descended from the tree, and he whirled himself around. I hurled my battlemage in his direction, forcing him into a corner where he could be easily apprehended. He cowered, his back pressed against the ground, and I approached with another fist of fire glowing in my hand. But as I drew closer, my arm faltered, the flames flickering and dying out.

He was younger than I'd initially thought, still a child. His face was not one of fear, but of unwavering determination.

"Please, Sire. I want to join the army, to be a Guardian like you. I will be a good fighter; let me prove it to you."

I studied him carefully. "Who are you, boy?"

He kneeled on the ground, bowing his head at my feet. "I am the son of Shawano Sonbi. Your Highness, allow me to serve you, and I swear you will not regret it."

My breath caught at the name. Shawano had been one of the fiercest Guardians in our regiment. His age forced him into retirement, but his missions were infamous. He was still regarded fondly, enough to overlook that his son had a hearing defect. His family must have hidden his condition.

"My father is ashamed of me. He doesn't say so, but he hides me away. I am not even allowed to refer to him as my father. This is my chance, my one shot to make him proud. Do not send me back. It would dishonor him."

The law was clear: if you couldn't fight, you were exiled or brought to the mines to work the land. He shouldn't be here; he shouldn't have even tried.

I did not have time to think for long because smoke filled my nostrils. I turned to see flames dancing on rooftops, spreading across the village uncontrollably.

"Odina!" I called. I looked back at the boy once more. "Run," I said sharply, grabbing his arm and shoving him away. "Run and don't come back."

"But—" he began, his voice rising in protest.

"Go!" I barked, leaving no room for argument.

Without waiting to see if he obeyed, I pivoted on my heel and sprinted toward Mesof's house.

"Odina!" I called again until I had no more breath in my lungs.

My heart stalled as I passed row after row of houses that were all ablaze. I had done this. I had put Odina in danger.

By the time I made it to Mesof's flat, it was already on fire. A young girl holding a newborn wrapped haphazardly in sheets stood outside.

"Odina?" I called. The girl turned around, and my face fell as I realized it was not her. Tears streamed down the young girl's face. I leaned down to grasp her shoulders.

"Where is she?" I demanded. The girl was unable to speak as shock set in. "Tell me! Is she in there?"

"She went back in to get Mesof," she cried, her body beginning to shake. "They have not come back out."

I spared no more time and ran into the burning building.

"Stop! Your Highness," the young boy called.

"Odina!" I yelled. As soon as I entered, burning wood planks from the roof fell on top of me. Small hands circled my legs and began pulling me away.

"No!" I choked out between coughs. "No! Odina!"

The hands didn't relent; they dragged me back through the doorway and into open air just as another section of the roof caved in behind us with a deafening roar.

"You didn't start the fire," a familiar voice called. "Come back, Adriel."

Asha's words pulled me out of my thoughts. I blinked furiously, but I couldn't bring myself to look at her. My mind was a chaotic swirl of emotions as tears streamed down my face, each one filled with both grief and guilt. I wept, not just for Odina—for Mesof, and for the young boy who'd been sent to the mines because of the way he had been born.

"You didn't start the fire," Asha repeated, breaking through my thoughts. Confused, I looked up at her.

"What?"

"The fire was a pale yellow, like the blaze of a dragon. Your flames are blue. You didn't set this fire. Someone else did. You didn't kill Odina."

"I never said my flames killed her. I said that I am responsible for getting her killed," I said quietly.

"How could you have known there would be a fire? Odina was strong-willed and would have gone to help regardless of anyone's permission. And you went after her."

"I should have!" I shouted. "My father was warring with yours over the conditions of our people." I shook my head. "We should have known any type of defiance would be met with the fire of his dragons."

Asha pulled away slightly, holding a hand to her chest. She looked like I'd just struck her.

"My father, he did this?"

"Why do you think I am so hellbent on securing dragons for Wiyotak—so we are never that vulnerable again?" I placed my face in my hands. "If I'd just gone with her, maybe I could have saved her. Maybe she'd still be alive."

She leaned in once more, taking my face in her hands. "Maybe," Asha agreed gently. "But even if you were with her, the house collapsed. She wouldn't have survived, no matter what you did. You are lucky that you survived. Your battlemage saved you. And so did Ashkii."

She'd been there, watching as Ashkii dragged me from the flames. How could I send him to the mines after that? I couldn't. In fact, I'd made sure no one would ever be sent to the mines against their will again.

The weight of it all pressed down on me as I whispered, "I failed her."

I felt a steady grip around my heart. It was soothing, coaxing more tears forward. I breathed in deeply, opening myself up to her.

"Odina was honorable," she began, her words deliberate and measured, "and compassionate." Her golden eyes met mine, unwavering in their intensity. "She'd have forgiven all that you hold on to." Her touch was warm, grounding me as though pulling me back from the edge of some unseen abyss. "Why can't you give yourself what she gave to everyone else? It is her legacy; one you can carry on as long as you live and breathe."

Her words struck a chord within me. My breath hitched as I stared at her, unable to look away from the fierce sincerity etched into every line of her face.

Then a sudden heat coursed through me, racing down my arms toward my palms. My eyes widened as two flames erupted from my hands. I looked at them in shock, utterly rocked by their appearance. I relished the feeling of the blue fire coursing through me once more. I had not seen that level of magic since Odina's death. She'd done it. Asha had found a way to bring it back. A rush of emotions flooded through me—disbelief, anger, compassion, forgiveness . . . love? My gaze fell upon Asha's golden eyes and heart-shaped face. Did she realize how stunning she was, how utterly amazing?

Acting on instinct alone, I pulled her onto my lap, craving an even deeper connection. My eyes were drawn to her slightly parted lips as she breathed heavily against me. As I traced trails of fire along her back, she let out a sigh of pleasure. I touched my fingers to her chin, bringing her closer. Holding my breath, I waited, hoping she would give some sign that she wanted me to close the distance between us.

"Adriel?" she breathed. "We shouldn't. I know you feel this way now, but it is just our auras. It will pass."

Our noses were nearly touching, our lips mere inches away.

"Is it?" I mused. "Then why have I been dreaming about your lips all day?"

"I did not poison you this time, I swear."

Her lips turned upward and I was lost. I made to close the distance between us, when we were interrupted by loud knocks at the door.

"War chief, are you in there? Marlon wants to speak to you."

I cursed under my breath. Not now. This could not be happening right now. I brushed the wetness from my eyes as Asha stood quickly, disentangling herself.

"What is Chato doing here?" she asked, eyes wide.

The knock sounded again.

"How does he know Marlon?" she whispered.

I ducked my head. "Let me explain."

CHAPTER THIRTY-NINE

Asha

I scrambled to compose myself, hastily fastening my tunic and smoothing out any wrinkles in my clothes. My skin still burned from his touch. Confused and flustered, I pressed a hand to my forehead as I tried to make sense of what had just happened between us and why Chato was suddenly behind that door. Adriel, too, attempted to fix his disheveled appearance before opening the door.

"I am sorry, war chief," he began, clearing his throat. "I did not know you two were sharing a room."

"Chato, how did you find us?" I asked, trying to make sense of the situation.

Chato said nothing for a moment, but his feet shifted nervously. He was clearly having a silent conversation with Adriel. I spun around angrily.

"How does Marlon know where we are? Adriel, why are you not as concerned as I am?" My heart raced trying to put the pieces together.

Adriel sighed heavily before saying, "I did not want you to find out this way. I have to go. Chato will walk you off the boat. I will explain everything. Just give me a few minutes."

Before I could protest, he was out the door. My jaw fell open. What did he not want me to find out? I gathered the satchel and walked with Chato.

"Are you really not going to tell me anything?"

"Asha, I . . . can't." His voice cracked on the last word. "Please hear Adriel out. It is not what you think."

I scoffed. "What I think is that Adriel and Marlon are working together. I think he has made a deal with the Lightwardens. Tell me it is not true."

I kept waiting for Chato to deny it, but he did not. My heart sank. "Was I just a means to an end to you all? Did you even care about me?"

"Asha, it is not like that. Please believe me."

I shook my head in frustration. "How can I believe anything when you won't tell me the truth?"

"You are right. We haven't been honest with you, and I am sorry," he said, his words filled with regret.

I could not muster the empathy to pay them any regard. He silently led me off the ship and into the town of Dawn's Peak through a group of men.

"Princess. Over here!" Ashkii called jovially. Chato waved him off, and the voices began to quiet as I walked by. He brought me to a room and explained that Adriel would be back as soon as he could. It was a sitting room with food laid out, but I had no intention of eating.

Once Kitchi left the room, a sob escaped my throat. I had been so foolish. For a moment, I had gone against my better judgment and let my guard down with Adriel. I felt like I was finally seeing him for the first time, and what I had unraveled was so captivating, so beautiful,

I gave in to my feelings without considering the consequences. His touch was like magic, and I longed to be back there, except now I knew he wasn't being honest with me. Now I knew he thought of me as a stupid girl whom he could seduce into whatever plans he had in mind from the start.

I sat in that self-pity for a long while before pulling myself together and thinking through a way out.

The sound of the door opening caught my attention, and I watched as Adriel's aura entered, no longer the color of midnight, but a deep blue, like the center of the deepest pool in my father's palace. It was familiar, but changed. It seemed calmer and more controlled.

He spoke first. "Would you like to sit down?"

I leaned my hands on the wooden table before me. "I want answers, Adriel."

"Well, I'm going to sit," he said, scraping a chair across the floor as he pulled it from the table. "Where do you want me to start?"

"Start from the beginning," I demanded.

His fingernails dug into the wooden table before him. The only other sound was the roaring of my heart in my ears.

"I first came into contact with the Lightwardens when searching for dragon eggs three years ago. I found their beliefs to be . . . eccentric, but they held oral histories of the time when dragons roamed the earth. Of course, there was mention of Lightbearers, but I never believed their prophecy to be true. I had never met Marlon until we happened into his shop a few days ago, but I had met Zariah."

He paused.

"Zariah and I came to an agreement this year about what to do with Ujuima when the emperor died. I thought we had more time," he whispered. He sucked in a breath. "I know he was your father, but you of all people know how cruel he could be. This is why the other kingdoms want to rise up against . . ."

"Did you kill him? Did you kill my father?" I asked pointedly.

"No!" he said indignantly. "He had desert lung, a bad case of it."

My chest tightened. Desert lung was caused by inhaling too much silica over a long period of time. It was a painful, slow death.

"But I would have known," I said.

"Would you? You hadn't seen him for years. Few have. He thought he could hide it, but word spread quickly. Probably Elan's doing."

"Then, the Lightwardens did," I said, rejecting his explanation. "You said he died suddenly. Desert lung takes years." It wasn't a question, and he did not deny it.

"I don't know. Truly, I do not. I did not kill your father, princess," he paused before admitting, "but I wish I had, for Odina."

A tear escaped the corner of my eye. "So, that is your answer? A life for a life."

"I wanted him to die by my hand, yes, but not so soon. The Lightwardens wanted to move the timeline up for invading Ujuima, and I would not agree to it."

"What did you think would happen?" I spat.

He sighed heavily. "I should have known. I should have anticipated, but the emperor had cheated death so many times, I just didn't think they would go that far."

"You all are murderers! Is that your plan then?" I asked. "To invade my homeland? Kill all the people I grew up with, wipe Ujuima off the map?"

"We hope Elan will be reasonable and surrender."

I shook my head in disbelief. "You are a fool if you think he will surrender. You don't know him. He'd willingly sacrifice every single person rather than give up his power. Is Enapay a part of this?"

Shame laced Adriel's next words. "He has wanted to invade Ujuima for a long time. It appeared that he had betrayed us. I would not be surprised if he discovered our plans and communicated them to Elan. That was what I was discussing with Zariah and Marlon. Every Wiyotakin Guardian loyal to me has moved north to evade capture or death. That is why Chato, Kitchi, and the others are here."

"I see," I said despondently. "So Wiyotak is no longer a player for the Lightwardens."

"Nearly all the Guardians are loyal to me. Wiyotak is practically defenseless at this point because the army is here. However, Winnow has gathered whom he can and has joined with Ujuima. They are marching north as we speak. They will be here in a day or so."

"I cannot believe this."

"This conflict began sooner than I would have liked. I'd hoped to get Entioch on board before now, but they are staying neutral and will support whoever comes out on top."

"And Firepeak will fight for Ujuima, I assume," I said.

"Our progress has been slow, but we have made some headway there. The recent deal between Elan and Enapay for dracite has caused tension among the other kingdoms, but I doubt it will be enough to persuade them to join our cause. However, it may be enough to prevent them from fighting against us with their full force."

He stood from the table and approached. He reached for my hand, and I stepped back as if he had burned me.

"Don't touch me."

"Asha, you know as well as I that Elan cannot ascend to the throne. He will destroy the five kingdoms. He must be stopped. We must make a better life for all."

I weighed his words. Of course he was right. Elan was a monster and would get worse as emperor. "If this was your plan all along, Adriel, why bring me into it? Why would you need me at all?"

Adriel poked at the fire, stirring the loose logs. The flames flickered. "The hope was that a union between Enapay and yourself would help the people of the kingdoms to accept Enapay as emperor. And . . . you were a condition for the Lightwardens' cooperation. They have been watching you for some time as the answer to their prophecy."

"And what is this damned prophecy? What do I have to do with it?"

"There is only one part of the prophecy they have shared with me: 'Her soul burns with the fire of dragons' might. She was born of shadow and light. She walks a path unseen, harnessing the power of her dragon's flame to forge a path toward unity and peace.'"

I laughed. "And you all think that is me. That could be anybody!"

"Marlon seems certain, and honestly, after I saw you with Drakkar, I am beginning to believe." He reached for me again, and I pushed him away.

"Things for me have changed. I thought maybe they had for you too, after—well, we've grown close, haven't we?" There was a slight tremble in his voice, like he was hurting. Good. I wanted him to bleed.

"So, your plan was to lie with me and convince me to go along with your plans."

Now his voice held anger. "It was not like that, and you know it. You cannot possibly think this was all a game to me. After all that we have been through? You are the only person I have shared that part of me with."

I crossed my arms. "You've lied to me before. How do I know what you say is true now?"

"Because things could be different now. We have the eggs," he whispered. "Drakkar is willing to take us up the mountain. With the help of dragons, this war would be over before it began. Don't you see, everything is different now?"

Tears threatened to spill, but I held them back, not wanting him to see that he had broken me. It was worse than Elan or my father, because neither had ever shown a shred of kindness toward me. But Adriel had weaseled himself in somehow. It was too much.

"I need you to leave."

"Princess. . ."

"Now." My voice was thick with venom. "I need you to leave now."

He quieted before saying, "Okay. I will give you an hour to think it over. There are no open windows in here, and all exits are guarded by my men. Do not attempt to escape, please."

The last word hung in the air, heavy with desperation, as if he were clinging to some fragile hope that I might change my mind.

I nodded, and he turned away to leave.

I did not need an hour to make a decision. I had already decided. The days of men making decisions for me were over. I'd forge my own path moving forward, for me, and only me. I needed to find a way out of here. I paced the room, exploring every nook and corner. He was right. It was sealed up tight.

"Drakkar?" I called.

"I am nearby, Little One," he roared. "I sensed your distress and turned back. How do you want to proceed? Shall I burn everyone to ash?"

"Not yet. I don't think I can have that on my conscience. Give me a moment to think of another way."

A knock sounded on my door. "Go away, Adriel!" I called.

"It's me, child," Kaliyah said as she entered.

"Please, Kaliyah. I have endured enough betrayal for one day. I cannot take any more."

"I did not know the details of what they have planned for you, Asha, I swear, and I still do not. They have not shared them with me. But I made your momma a promise to look after you, and I intend to keep it," she said.

I cocked my head. "What are you planning?" I asked.

Amusement coated her voice as she said, "These men think they have this place locked up tight. I was born in the north, and I happen to know that all northern buildings have basements for when the weather gets bad. Many of them are hidden behind fireplaces," she said, pouring water on the fiery logs. They began to simmer as she doused the flames. "This will be tricky. I brought a cloak, so you don't burn yourself."

I heard her tap lightly, and then a hinge snapped.

"Here it is," she said. There was a groan of stones rubbing against each other as Kaliyah pulled open the stone door. "It is still quite hot. Best move quickly. I have some gloves for you, too. Do not let your skin touch the stone. I wish there were another way."

I embraced Kaliyah, tears trailing my cheeks. "Thank you, Kaliyah. You've always been a friend to me."

"And I always will, child. Now go!"

I tightened the satchel around my shoulder and placed the fireproof cloak and gloves on. The stairs were narrow and winding, and I gripped my walking staff tightly as I descended into the darkness below. I resisted the urge to reach out and touch the stone walls, knowing they would be hot to the touch. Sweat trickled down my back as I made my way deeper into the unknown depths below.

After what felt like an eternity, a cool breeze greeted me as I reached the basement level. Kaliyah had estimated it would take about forty paces to get there, but now I needed to find a way out. As I paused to catch my breath, I could hear voices echoing from overhead.

"Are we going to talk about this, Adriel?" Kitchi said angrily.

Adriel's response was muffled, but I could tell he was annoyed.

"Not tonight, Kitchi, I have enough on my mind," he snapped back.

"This cannot wait, Adriel." She took in a deep breath. "Are you going to make me say it?"

I heard chairs shift overhead as one of them began to sit. "What do you want from me, Kitchi?" he conceded.

"I want you to admit that your plans have gone to hell because of your attachment to her. Tell me I'm wrong."

There was a moment of tense silence before Adriel spoke again. "What is your point?"

"I see the way you look at her. You have to tell her. Tell her now!" Kitchi's voice was urgent, insistent even.

My blood boiled with curiosity and frustration as their voices faded into the distance. As they moved further away, I could not hear anything. Deciding not to linger further, I continued down the hallway, relying on my sense of touch to guide me through the maze of rooms.

Soon, I could hear more voices above, this time belonging to two men. "She will never trust us now. It's best we move on without the Guardians," one of them said.

"Patience, Zariah," the other, Marlon, replied calmly. "We have plenty of strings to pull. We just need to wait and see which ones will be most effective."

"Did you see the way Adriel looks at her?" Zariah's voice was filled with malice.

Marlon chuckled. "The way we hope all men will look at her soon enough."

"He will never allow us to go through with the plan."

"Perhaps not," Marlon agreed in a quiet tone. "But soon we won't need his permission for anything."

My heart raced at their words. What were they planning? Would they hurt Adriel? I had to get out of here before it was too late. My fingers moved frantically until I found a latch that wasn't bolted shut.

Elation filled me as I turned it open and walked freely into the night.

CHAPTER FORTY

Asha

With a heavy breath, I pushed deeper into the night air, pausing only when I heard a distant rustling, then a faint voice. My heart skipped a beat as I froze in place, straining to identify the source of the sound.

"Asha," a voice called out, startling me. It was Kitchi.

I hesitated, torn between the urge to flee and the dread of being caught and dragged back. Before I could make a move, Kitchi was beside me.

"If you are trying to escape into the trees, you are going in the wrong direction," she said, her tone strangely gentle.

I swallowed hard, realizing that she was right. The voices were coming from ahead, not behind. Kitchi grabbed my shoulders and pointed me in the right direction. As we hurriedly made our way through the trees, I couldn't help but ask the question that was now burning on my mind.

"Why are you letting me go?" I whispered.

"I'm not," she replied. "He is." I didn't need to ask who she meant. "We saw you were not in your room. He's there now, having a conversation with the wall so that you can get away. Hurry," Kitchi urged, her grip tightening on my shoulders.

"Kitchi?" I asked.

"Yes?"

I shuffled my foot where I stood. "Do not trust them, the Lightwardens. Do not trust Marlon."

"I never have. Our alliance is like an arranged marriage. Each of us wants something, and things will only remain civil until one of us gets it." She reached out and embraced me. "Whenever the two of you meet again, be gentle with his heart okay?" If I did not know any better, I would have thought she was tearing up.

"Don't worry. We are unlikely to cross paths again," I pushed away my own emotions that were rising to the surface.

"You will, he will make it so," she said before walking away.

I did not have time to analyze the complicated relationship I had with Kitchi, and definitely not the one I had with Adriel.

I walked deeper into the darkness of the trees, my heart racing with each step. I didn't have time to worry about the branches that tore my skin to ribbons or dwell on why Kitchi was choosing to help me now or what Adriel's actions meant. All that mattered was getting as far away from this place as possible.

"Drakkar," I called.

"I'm coming, Little One."

The cold wind stung my cheeks and prickled my skin as I stood shivering, my eyes searching the dark sky for any sign of him.

And then, a glimmer of a familiar shadow dotted across the sky. Tears sprang to my eyes as I watched him approach. His massive wings beat against the wind as he landed gracefully. Without a moment's hesitation, I ran to him, throwing myself onto his neck.

"Drakkar," I choked out, my voice thick with emotion as I buried my face in his scales. "I am so lost."

He rumbled softly in response, his warm breath washing over me like a comforting blanket. I clung to him desperately, my whole body trembling with relief and gratitude. For a long moment, we stayed like that, neither of us speaking as I let the tears flow freely at last. Drakkar allowed me this moment of respite, his presence a steady anchor amid everything.

Eventually, he nudged me gently with his snout. It was a silent request for me to pull away and meet his gaze. And as I looked into his deep, intelligent eyes, I knew what he was asking of me. We couldn't stay here, not with danger lurking around every corner. We had to leave, to escape to safety before it was too late.

With a trembling hand, I reached out and grasped his neck, hoisting myself up onto his back. Drakkar lowered himself to the ground, allowing me to climb astride him before spreading his wings wide.

And then, with a powerful leap, we were airborne, leaving the ground behind as we soared into the night sky. The world fell away beneath us as we climbed higher and higher, the wind whipping through my hair as we flew north toward the mountains.

My sight returned, and I drank in every detail of the landscape passing beneath us—the snow-capped peaks, the wintry trees, and the frozen rivers winding through the land. It was a breathtaking sight, like a painting come to life, and for a moment, I forgot all my worries as I simply savored the beauty of the world around us.

The wind rushed past us as Drakkar soared through the crisp mountain air. I gazed in awe at the towering peaks surrounding us, their jagged edges cutting through the sky like the teeth of some ancient beast.

The Saelerian Mountains surpassed my wildest dreams. Instead of the barren and desolate slopes of Ujuima, these were covered in a thick blanket of snow that glistened like a million diamonds in the bright sunlight. But it was the glimmering golden flecks scattered throughout the snow that truly took my breath away.

As we flew higher, Drakkar's strained voice cut through the rush of wind. "Are you ready for me to take you to Saeleria?" he asked.

"I am," I replied confidently, though my heart raced with uncertainty.

"We do not have to. I could take my brood and come back for you."

"No, I made Seraphina a promise. I will see to their safety into Saeleria myself."

"Very well," Drakkar said with a tired huff, his powerful wings straining as we flew closer to the gorge's entrance.

As Drakkar carried me onward, I couldn't help but feel a sense of anticipation building within me.

Drakkar descended with a powerful jolt, his landing far from graceful. I clung to his scales, my heart pounding in my chest as I struggled to maintain my balance. With a soft huff, he folded his wings, the great arcs of them settling against his sides. The ground beneath us was rough, jagged with rocks, and he shifted slightly as his weight settled.

I glanced around, taking in our surroundings. We had reached the Shadow Basin, one of two entrances into Saeleria. Its dark depths stretched out like a gaping hole, eager to swallow us whole. Even with the sunlight beginning to peek out from behind the mountains, there was little illumination in the rocky expanse.

I squinted into the shadows, trying to discern the shapes hidden within. The space was tight, filled with large boulders and towering mountain walls that narrowed as they ascended. I strained my ears, listening for any sign of movement or life within the basin. I heard the faint rush of water nearby, echoing off the rocky walls, but I couldn't see its source. It was as though the mountain held its secrets close, refusing to reveal them to anyone who dared to travel within.

With a deep breath, I tightened my grip on Drakkar's scales as we ventured forward into the basin. Fear turned my stomach, creating a whirlwind of emotions that threatened to overwhelm me. The journey through the basin was far from easy. Drakkar navigated the winding paths like a champion, his large wings brushing against the rocky walls as we ventured deeper.

We came across a trickling waterfall, a hidden cave beyond. We were at a dead end. I looked closer at the vines trailing along the cave's entrance. Drakkar's movements became hesitant, his powerful form faltering. He let out a low groan, his eyes fixed on the cascading water ahead.

"You must enter Saeleria alone. The dragons must find you worthy of entrance. This is where I have to leave you," Drakkar said, his voice grave and solemn.

I felt a pang of apprehension.

"Listen to me when I say this," he continued, his gaze intense as he locked eyes with me. "This path will lead you to Saeleria. Whatever you do, whatever happens, stay on the path. Do not leave it. I will meet you on the other side."

I nodded, my heart heavy with the gravity of his words.

"Promise me," he insisted, his voice tinged with urgency.

I reached out and gently nuzzled his snout, feeling the rough texture of his scales beneath my fingertips.

"I promise," I whispered, my voice barely audible over the cascading water.

Drakkar regarded me with a worried expression, his eyes filled with concern. "Do not leave me, Little One," he said. "Take care of my brood."

As I looked up at him, a small smile tugged at the corners of my lips.

"I will," I assured him, my voice steady despite the uncertainty that lay ahead. I patted the satchel against my waist, noting that the dragon eggs were much heavier than they once had been.

With a final nod, Drakkar spread his wings and took to the air once more, disappearing into the darkness with a graceful sweep of his massive form. And as I watched him vanish, my sight dimmed to black as I walked into the entrance.

CHAPTER FORTY-ONE

Asha

I cautiously made my way through the entrance of the cave, my senses on high alert despite the tranquility of the surroundings. The air was thick with the scent of earth and foliage, and the gentle rustle of leaves. I tapped my stick along the stone path, trying to keep one foot in front of the other.

The deeper I went, the colder it grew. My skin prickled as though unseen eyes were watching me. "Hello!" I called. My voice reverberated throughout the cavern, but there was no response. The silence reminded me too much of my first days in the dragon pits. I'd been just a girl at that time, battered and broken. I'd been cast out like I was nothing. *You are powerful, not powerless.* Drakkar's words echoed in my head. I did not believe this but my dragon believed it for me, and I could hold on to that.

Then, a voice broke through the silence, smooth and seductive. The entire cavern seemed to be wrapped with a malevolent presence.

"Welcome to my home, dear. You have traveled far to come here, as so many others have before you. Why do you think you deserve to come to Saeleria?"

"I was invited," I answered. "By Drakkar and his mate Seraphina."

A slithering sound sent a shiver through me as something inched up my ankles. I shook it off and moved forward more quickly.

I whipped around, trying to locate the source of the voice, but it swirled around me like a storm. "Who are you?"

"There is a price for entering Saeleria."

I shuddered out of the way at the feel of phantom arms reaching for me. "What is it?"

"It is small, inconsequential really. Perhaps you'd like to turn back."

"No!" I said quickly. "Tell me."

"To enter Saeleria, all you have to do is look at me." Then the voice changed from seductive to a deep voice intertwined with a chorus of others. "Come, dear. Let me see your eyes."

I stared straight ahead and felt a force swirl around me.

"Look at me!" the voice screamed.

My heart leaped out of my chest, and I decided to keep moving forward.

"Why won't you look at me, my dear?" it purred, sending a shiver down my spine. Now I could hear the unmistakable sound of a snake's tail rattling.

"Look into my eyes," the voice commanded again.

The creature didn't seem to realize my blindness as her words dripped with frustration. Then the rattling stopped. Was it getting ready to strike? I gripped my satchel and clenched my hand tighter to my walking stick, remembering what Drakkar had said. *Whatever you do, whatever happens, stay on the path. Do not leave it.*

I clung to those words as if they were air.

Then I heard the voice taking in a deeper tone.

I tensed, my instincts warning me of the danger lurking beneath the honeyed words. But just as I was about to turn away, another voice shattered the illusion, cutting through the air like a blade.

"Asha!" it called out behind me. The voice was familiar, filled with desperation and regret.

"There you are," he gasped.

"Adriel?" I asked, turning around.

"Asha, it's me. I'm sorry. I'm so sorry I lied to you." Strong arms embraced me, nuzzling my hair and neck as his hair fell around me like a curtain.

My heart clenched at his words.

"You were right. I've been an ass." He caressed my face so softly, brushing his thumb slowly across my lips. "I should have kissed you when I had the chance," he whispered. "I wanted to in the lighthouse, on the ship. Burn it, I want to now."

My breath caught in my throat. I began to speak, but he silenced me with a finger.

"I am so stupid for not having realized sooner. Please tell me you feel the same way."

I searched deep within myself. This was what I'd wanted for some time. I just never thought I could have it, and yet here we were.

"I do," I whispered.

"Then kiss me. I've dreamed about your lips since the moment we met. Kiss me, Asha."

He leaned in a breath before meeting my lips. All I had to do was lean forward. But as he drew near, his aura filled my vision. Instead of the blue hue to which I was accustomed, the aura was sickly green. There was something wrong. This did not feel right.

"You are not him," I said weakly.

Adriel paused, but his grip tightened. "Hmm? What did you say, my love?"

"You're not him," I repeated, firmer this time, wrenching myself free from his hold.

I turned and began walking down the path again, my fingers still tingling from his touch.

He reached for me once more, his fingers icy and damp as they brushed against my skin, pulling me back into his embrace.

"Please, Asha," he begged, his voice trembling with desperation. "Just one kiss."

I recoiled, every instinct screaming at me to escape. "Adriel doesn't call me Asha," I said sharply, my voice cutting through the air like a blade.

Before he could react, I shoved him away with all my strength and broke into a sprint. His pleas and honeyed words chased after me, but I didn't look back. My feet carried me before my mind caught up, pounding against the stone as I sprinted forward. His voice clawed after me, sticky and cloying.

"Why won't you look at me?" he called out after me, his voice fading into the distance. "No one wants you. No one will ever want you." I pressed forward determined to keep going.

"Asha! Look at me!" the creature screamed, only it was my father's voice, sharp with disdain. "You are a stain on our family name. You are no Osei!"

I stopped then, just for a second. "You are right. I'm not. I am Asha, and you are nothing but a bad memory of a terrible father."

The whole cave shook with the sound as I raced forward. I knew that this was not my father, not the man I had come to care for.

I stumbled out of the dark, suffocating confines of the cave, blinking in the bright sunlight as I collapsed onto the soft grass below.

As I lay there, panting and disoriented, I realized with a shock that I could see the moss beneath me, its vibrant green hues dancing before my eyes. Slowly, hesitantly, I lifted my gaze, and what I saw took my breath away.

Before me stretched a beautiful, lush meadow, bathed in the golden light of the sun. Full trees swayed gently in the breeze, their leaves whispering secrets to the wind, while mounds of colorful flowers dotted the landscape like jewels. It was like a scene from a painting, so vivid and surreal that I couldn't help but wonder if I had died. But as I looked down at the precious eggs cradled in my satchel, their warmth and weight were a tangible reminder that I was here and that the scene before me was real.

"Why can I see?" I whispered to myself, my voice barely audible over the rustle of the wind through the trees. But there were no answers, only the soft chirping of birds and the distant murmur of a stream.

With a trembling hand, I pushed myself upright, my eyes scanning the tranquil grove below. And that was when I saw them—two dark blue dragons, their scales shimmering in the sunlight as they drank from a crystal-clear stream.

One was larger, a male, and a female nestled close beside him. They looked up at me with curious eyes but turned away, recognizing that I posed no threat.

I watched them for a moment, my heart swelling with awe and wonder at the sight before me. I moved forward, giddy with all the sights. More dragons roamed in shades of green, red, and blue. None compared to the size of Drakkar. This had to be Saeleria, but where was Drakkar? He'd said he'd meet me on the other side. I journeyed forward, unsure of where I was going.

A large dragon approached with a smaller, angled head. It was copper in color. Once it was close, it bowed before me. It was an unnerving sight.

"Good morning, Princess Asha. I congratulate you on making it through the Shadow Basin. Very few do."

I wasn't sure how to respond, so I said, "Thank you."

"The Great Dragon requests your presence. If you care to follow me, I will take you to him."

"The Great Dragon?" I asked.

"Ah, yes," he said in realization. "You wouldn't know. The Great Dragon is like your emperor or king. Great Dragon Mattias would like to receive you now."

"I am waiting for my friend—"

"Drakkar," he interjected. "Yes. He is with Great Dragon Mattias. Come, they are waiting for you."

The dragon, whose name I'd come to learn was Zephyr, led me through fields and caverns. I marveled at the majestic dragons we passed along the way. Most of them regarded me casually, as if only mildly curious about my presence among them.

We arrived at a set of steep stone stairs flanked by large stone dragons. Fire roared from a series of torches that lit the way. I began my ascent, refusing to pause because if I did, I might collapse and not make it all the way up. With a heavy breath, I leaned on a column at the top of the stairs. A pair of towering stone doors stood before us. With a powerful push from Zephyr, the doors swung open, revealing a grand chamber beyond.

I stepped inside and looked around in wonder. The lair was unlike anything I had ever seen. It was meticulously crafted from stone and gold with expert precision. Intricately carved dragon sculptures lined the room in various poses, each one more menacing than the last.

But it was the center of the room that truly caught my eye, a circular space with a carving of fire being wielded, its flames dancing with an otherworldly light. There were no thrones, as one might expect in a throne room, but the atmosphere was no less imposing.

As I gazed around in wonder, a hush fell over the chamber, and I felt a presence approaching from the depths of the caverns. With a low rumble, a massive silver dragon emerged, his teeth bared in a silent snarl as he slinked forward with a predatory grace.

The sweat that beaded on my forehead ran cool as I met the dragon's gaze, his eyes flashing with intelligence and power. This had to be Great Dragon Mattias, and he looked furious. He roared, a sound that came deep from his belly.

"She can understand the old tongue, Great Dragon," a familiar voice called from the balcony. I looked up to see Drakkar bowing in submission. It was odd to see him this way, bowing to anyone. Still, he watched me with a glint in his eye, or was that pride?

Mattias gazed at me. "I am told you are blind, princess. You do not look blind to me."

I began to speak, but he interrupted. "If you can see, how did you get past Oxu? You should be stone right now." I started to speak again, but he continued. "I hear you were the last to see my beloved daughter Seraphina alive. Tell me why I should not roast you on a spit right now?"

Drakkar growled above me. Mattias regarded him with a warning, as if letting him know he would not back down from a challenge. "Or maybe I should kill you, Drakkar. You were supposed to keep her alive!"

Several dragons began to growl in unison. Were they agreeing with the Great Dragon?

I removed the satchel from my arm and lifted the flap. "If I may, Great Dragon. She entrusted me with these before she passed. I have journeyed for weeks to bring them back home."

Everyone was silent. No one made a sound as Mattias stared at the eggs. He moved closer, and it took everything in me not to cower as he towered over me. He brought his head closer, inspecting them.

Then he said, "Sweet ash. They are real. We have not seen dragon eggs in a millennium. Seraphina bore these, truly?"

"She did," Drakkar said.

Mattias regarded Drakkar. "And you let *her* carry them in here? She could have died! You put their lives at risk."

Drakkar opened his jaws slightly as if in warning. "I knew she would survive. Seraphina chose her to bring them home."

Mattias cocked his large dragon head before turning his golden eyes to me. "You have dragon eggs, and Drakkar can fly. You can see, but only here in Saeleria, and when you fly with him," he said as if putting the pieces together.

"She is true," Drakkar said. "The first Lightbearer in centuries."

I turned to Drakkar in shock. Had he heard Marlon's theories, or had he come to the conclusion himself? I tried but failed to understand how he could possibly know that.

Mattias nodded. "What Drakkar says is true. The first of your kind that we have seen in many years. I am honored to have you in our house."

Then he did something that took me off guard. He bowed to me.

"Thank you for bringing the blood of my blood home to me. I am forever in your debt. Anything you ask of me, it shall be yours."

I was shocked by his words. "Right now, all I can think to want is a warm bath and a bed, if you have one."

"It is yours."

I squeezed the clutch of eggs one more time, lovingly, before placing them in his jaws. He took them and flew off.

Zephyr came to my side. "This way, princess."

CHAPTER FORTY-TWO

Asha

Zephyr walked me to a private chamber. I wouldn't say it was fit for a mortal, exactly. There was no bed, just a mound of poppies growing beneath a tree.

"What is that?" I asked.

"We do not have beds anymore. Some find lying on a bed of flowers to be comfortable."

My eyes twitched.

"I suppose," he continued, "we could get a bed commissioned for you if you decide to stay with us."

Stay? I had not thought about it. My goal for so long had been to get the eggs to Saeleria. Now that I'd accomplished that, I wasn't sure what was next or where I would go. Unable to think that far ahead, I asked about the large crack in the wall, which was filled with moving water and divided the room.

"Your bath," Zephyr explained.

He blew a flame into the water, and I watched the water boil beneath. Once he was gone, I immediately stripped down and floated on the water, letting the heat soothe my aching muscles. I relished the smooth stones massaging my feet, and never had I missed soap so much.

But relaxation soon gave way to reflection, and with reflection came the flood of complicated emotions tied to Adriel. He had killed my father—or at least played a part in his death. And now, he was plotting to invade and destroy what was left of my home.

Home. The word echoed in my mind. Had it truly felt like home since my mother died? And yet, despite everything, I still felt a deep, unshakable connection to it. It struck me that I didn't feel the same tangled emotions when I thought of Kitchi, even though she had lied to me, just like the others.

I pulled myself out of the water, which had long since cooled, and dressed myself in the robes that were provided. Apparently, this was what the Lightbearers wore when they lived among the dragons. A knock came on my door, and I smiled when Drakkar entered.

"How is the brood?"

"Well. We think all three will be viable."

I sighed with relief. "I'm so glad. They have been all over the world, it feels like."

"Thank you, Asha."

I looked up in surprise at the emotion in his voice. We locked eyes as unspoken words moved between us. I nodded before turning away to hide my tears.

"This is Seraphina's room, isn't it?" I asked.

"Yes," he said sadly. "Poppies were her favorite. I requested this room for you. She would want you to have it."

"I am very sorry, Drakkar. Being back here must be hard for you."

"Not as hard as losing her. At least she led me to you. I am thankful for that."

I smiled at him weakly. "You don't have to stay if you don't want to."

"I want to stay. It makes me feel close to her," he growled softly.

"I'm glad I can share it with you."

Drakkar twisted his head in a way that would be unnatural for humans. "What is that on your back? Did he mark you?"

Heat rose to my cheeks, and I shifted uncomfortably under his gaze.

"It sounds crass when you say it like that. He was trying to help. It is just a mategwes rabbit tattoo."

Drakkar shook his head disapprovingly. "That is not just a mategwes. It is a portrait of you."

My eyes widened. "Show me!"

Drakkar's eyes flashed like golden embers. My head snapped back as my own eyes blurred until I could see myself through Drakkar. I skimmed my body until it landed on my back. The mategwes was there. He had done a good job strategically placing it over my scars. But in the background was a portrait of a woman. It was a portrait of me, or at least how Adriel saw me. My hair blended with the night sky, making it nearly undetectable, but Drakkar's sharp vision, of course, missed nothing. I wore the white gown that his grandmother had given me. I gasped at the way he'd captured my soft features and the exact color of my eyes. In my hands, I held the eggs, looking at them almost in reverence. It was the most beautiful drawing I had ever seen. I almost forgot to be upset that he had snuck the image in without my permission. I shook my head and blinked furiously, disentangling from Drakkar's sight.

"Of course he did," I said. "I will find a way to have it removed."

"What happened between the two of you on that ship?"

"I don't want to talk about it, Drakkar." I groaned.

"But a man who would draw you like that . . ."

I cut him off, motioning to the poppies. "What am I supposed to do with this?"

He watched me carefully, concern and curiosity warring within his expression.

"That is why I am here. Dragon riders sleep within the tails of their dragons, at least they used to. I hear it is quite comfortable, at least for the night," he said carefully. "Would you want to try it?" He held his breath expectantly, and I sensed that this was something very important to him, sacred even.

I threw my hands up. "It can't be any worse than sleeping directly on flowers."

He let go of the breath he was holding before lying on top of the flowers, crushing them beneath his weight. He curled his tail in a circle, leaving an opening for me. Exhausted, I lay my head down on his tail and closed my eyes. He was right; it was comfortable. He curled his tail tightly around me, and I fell asleep in seconds.

Drakkar stirred beside me as an urgent Zephyr pulled me from my slumber.

"Come to the dormitory," he called out, his tone tense with worry. "Something has happened."

My bones ached from the days of travel, but I rose wearily, wishing I could curl back into Drakkar's tail. We followed Zephyr through a maze of passageways, the dim light of torches casting flickering shadows on the stone walls. I clung to Drakkar's back, urging him onward as we ascended higher and higher, the air growing thinner with each step.

Finally, we reached the top of the tower, and I gasped as we stepped into the dormitory. The room was like nothing I had ever seen before, its walls dotted with glowing stars that shimmered in the darkness. At the center of the room stood a pulsing orb of light, its glow casting a warm and comforting radiance over the gathered dragons.

Several of them clustered around the orb, their eyes fixed on its mesmerizing glow with a mixture of curiosity and concern. Among them stood Mattias, his regal form towering above the others. As our eyes met, he motioned for me to approach, his expression grave.

Heart pounding, I stepped forward, my gaze drawn to the swirling images projected by the orb. And then I saw him, Adriel, standing in the Shadow Basin, his figure surrounded by flames that danced and flickered.

A gasp escaped my lips at the sight of him surrounded by the one thing he had been running from since his sister died.

"What is he doing?" I asked.

"It appears that he is trying to enter Saeleria."

"But why?" I stammered as all the dragon heads turned toward me. Silence enveloped the room as rows of dragon eyes narrowed.

Drakkar cleared his throat. "You would probably be able to answer that best, Little One."

Was he coming after me? Was it to marry me off again? Use me in whatever plan he and Marlon had for me? Or did he plan to sell me another pack of lies?

My heart stuttered as I watched Adriel pace back and forth, his gaze fixed on the stones laid out above the molten lava below. The fiery river flowed like a deadly serpent, its surface shimmering with an unnatural heat that seemed to sear the very air around him.

"Why does the basin look different?" I asked.

"The basin can morph into any place Oxu decides," Mattias replied. "She finds what scares you and forces you to face it."

His movements were cautious as he tested the stability of the stones beneath his feet. There were pockets of fire that shot up sporadically, spitting fiery embers onto Adriel's clothing. He grimaced as they burned holes through his clothes.

Adriel took a tentative step forward, his movements cautious as he tested the stability of the stones beneath his feet. My breath caught in my throat as he placed all of his weight on the stone, and I felt a surge of relief wash over me as it held firm beneath him.

With a steady hand, Adriel reached into his pocket and pulled out a handful of coins. My heart raced as he dropped the first coin onto the stone in front of him, holding my breath as it immediately sank into the fiery abyss below. This was the challenge he faced. He needed to determine which stones would carry him forward.

He flipped a coin onto the next stone, and I watched with bated breath as it landed with a soft clink, holding firm against the infernal heat. Taking a deep breath, Adriel steeled himself for what lay ahead, his determination unwavering as he prepared to leap across the chasm of fire and stone.

With each leap, he drew closer to an opening that would bring him to Saeleria. Sweat dripped down his back, making his tunic cling to his torso, emphasizing the muscles underneath. He was undeniably attractive and undeniably stupid for taking such risks. He leaped again, and this time he nearly lost his balance. The coins in his hands scattered, but he regained his balance. There were three stones left. He bent down and studied them. I imagined that he was looking for any clue that the stones were solid. He unlaced his left boot and threw it forward. It landed and quickly sank.

I held my breath as he threw the other boot, hoping that it would hold. It did not. That meant he would have to jump three stones' lengths. There was no way he could make it. Drakkar flinched as I gripped his scales too tightly.

"We have to stop this," I said. I looked to Drakkar, then to Mattias. "Stop this! I will get him myself!"

"I'm afraid he has already begun. Once they begin, we cannot interfere," Mattias said.

"I'm telling you to interfere. You owe me!"

Mattias regarded me carefully. He struck me as someone who was not used to being yelled at, much less by a mortal, even if I was supposedly a Lightbearer.

"I can do nothing," he said with an air of finality.

As tears flowed freely down my cheeks, I turned back to the orb and watched as Adriel weighed his options. If he leaped and missed, he could lose a foot or sink to the bottom to his death. He closed his eyes and cupped his hands. A blue flame flickered to life. It grew steadily, and I gasped, realizing what he was doing. The flame expanded until it stood as tall as he was, and without hesitation, he stepped inside.

The dragons around me murmured their appreciation. Once he was fully engulfed in the flame, he took a tentative step forward, then another. It was working! He had done it.

Whispers of approval filled the room from the dragons around me, their eyes fixed on Adriel's display. As he moved further into the flames, taking hesitant steps forward, I couldn't help but feel pride.

But he stopped in his tracks and looked around as if searching for something. A figure darted past him. Oxu? "Princess!"he called eyes wide with panic.

Adriel turned as if to follow her and step off the path. I couldn't let that happen.

"Stop!" I cried out in desperation.

To my surprise, he froze and looked up. Could he hear me?

"Stay on the path," I urged him.

"Princess?" he called out uncertainly.

I gasped when I saw Oxu's form. She moved effortlessly toward Adriel, her body swaying hypnotically as the serpents in her hair twisted and turned restlessly. Her long fingernails resembled sharp claws that could easily tear through flesh and bone.

"Close your eyes, Adriel," I warned him urgently. *"Whatever she shows you is not real."*

"How do I know you're real?" he challenged me.

My mind raced as I desperately searched for any small detail that only we would know. And then it came to me.

"There was a scarf," I began, my voice trembling slightly with emotion. *"I never saw it with my own eyes, but I felt it in my hands. It's made of Wiyotakin silk and has a blue dragon design on it. You saw me admiring it on my first day in Wiyotak."*

He faltered for a moment, a smile tugging at his lips. He reached into his pocket and a white and blue silk scarf, the one I'd just described, unfurled from his hand. He tied it around his face and began to move forward. It gleamed in the darkness and bore the image of a majestic dragon that resembled Seraphina. I gasped, realizing that he had indeed bought it that day and had kept it all this time. Adriel tied it around his head, shielding his eyes.

As I looked back at Drakkar, I could feel his gaze on me. He growled warningly, clearly not approving of my interference.

"Tread carefully, Little One," he said, using our connection instead of the dragon common tongue. I could see in his eyes that he understood me, even if he did not agree.

"Stay on the path, Adriel," I repeated firmly, hoping to convey my message without making it too obvious. He walked the rest of the way to the rocky shore and collapsed, covered in sweat. It must have been hard to conjure that much battlemage after so many years. I swallowed as he entered the cave, which was shrouded in darkness.

"Drakkar!" I called.

"I am ready," he said.

I climbed onto his back, and we flew out of an open window. The dragons behind us shouted in delight as they watched the only flying dragon they had seen in many decades.

We flew to the same opening I had come from. I leaped from Drakkar and started running.

"Adriel!" I called. "Where are you?"

I saw his aura before I saw his face. He looked up, the scarf still tied loosely over his eyes. His tunic was gone, discarded somewhere, leaving his chiseled stomach, broad chest, and muscular arms bare to the evening air. His hair, freed from its usual braid, cascaded around his face and shoulders, catching the breeze.

"Princess!" he called, his voice carrying across the meadow as he moved toward me, his steps awkward but determined.

I didn't hesitate. I ran to him, the grass brushing against my legs, my heart pounding in time with my footsteps. I stopped just inches from him, both of us breathless, the space between us charged with something electric.

"Princess," he began, his voice breaking, "I was a fool. If you can forgive me, I . . ."

I didn't let him finish. I climbed into his arms, allowing my legs to wrap around his waist.

"My name is Asha," I whispered, my voice soft but firm, before I closed the distance between us, my lips meeting his.

The kiss was slow at first, tentative, but as I leaned into him, I felt the scarf slip from his eyes, and I reveled in the surprise that flickered across his face. His lips were soft, like velvet, and I sank into them, tasting him, savoring him, as if I could pour everything I felt into that single moment.

"Asha," he murmured, his voice low and rough, as if testing the sound of my name on his tongue. "Asha," he said again, pulling me closer, his arms tightening around me.

My body melted into his, every curve and line fitting together as if we were made for this.

"I'm here," I breathed between kisses, my hands tangling in his hair. "Why did you come after me?"

"I was lost without you," he admitted, his lips brushing against mine with each word. "I realized I want you . . . I need you."

In one fluid motion, he shifted, his body guiding me gently onto my back in the soft grass. He hovered over me, his kisses trailing down my neck. Each touch sent shivers through me, igniting a fire that had been waiting to burn. The world around us faded, leaving only the two of us tangled together in the meadow as the stars began to peek through the twilight sky.

"You needed me? Why?" I gasped, my breath catching as he suddenly stilled. He lifted his head, his eyes locking onto mine, intense and unwavering.

"You took my hand," he said, his voice low and earnest, "and pulled me out of my darkness. I didn't understand it at first, but you . . . you make me want to be better. For you. All I want is to be with you, to make up for every hurt you've ever endured, especially the ones I caused. Wherever you are is where I want to be."

His words hung in the air, raw and unguarded, and for a moment, the world seemed to fade away, leaving only the two of us.

Sensing my hesitation, he spoke again. "Asha, please say something," he pleaded.

Without thinking, I hit him on the chest. His eyes widened, stunned, but he didn't pull away. I hit him again, and again, until tears started streaming down my face. He had lied to me. He'd had a hand in my father's death, then lied again. In that moment, all of my pent-up emotions came pouring out, and he let me release them, allowing me to pound against his firm chest. He took every strike like it was nothing and everything, which only fueled my anger.

His hand reached out and took mine, bringing it to his lips in a gentle kiss. A wave of emotion washed over me the moment his lips grazed my skin.

"I deserve every bit of your anger, Asha. I am sorry."

I watched him through blurry eyes and saw nothing but sincerity in his gaze. Without another word spoken, we simply lay there with our bodies pressed together, finding comfort in each other as we both tried to catch our breath.

But then I remembered that we weren't alone.

"We have an audience," I whispered, nodding my head toward Drakkar, who was glaring at us disapprovingly. Adriel followed my gaze, spotting the dragon, and we both burst into laughter at the absurdity of the scene.

"He does not like me, does he?" he said with a grin.

"Don't take it personally. He only likes me." I grinned back.

"Your eyes are gorgeous," he whispered. "Are you going to tell me how you can see?"

Drakkar interrupted our revelry. "I do not want to break up this . . . reunion, but the dragons are calling us back. Something is wrong."

Adriel rolled away from me and helped me stand. I quickly mounted Drakkar and coaxed him to allow Adriel on, too. When we'd returned, the dragons clamored around Mattias, their voices rising to a pitch until the Great Dragon roared and fire blazed above.

"What is happening?" Drakkar asked.

All eyes turned to us. Mattias studied Adriel for a long moment before saying, "Shadowcasters."

"Shadowcasters?" Drakkar repeated. "You're sure?"

The Great Dragon nodded. "They are headed toward the mortal armies."

"What is a Shadowcaster?" I asked.

Mattias answered, "Where Lightbearers bring light, Shadowcasters exist to extinguish it. They are the reason there are no other Lightbearers left. Long ago, the two factions went to war, with the intent of bringing down all the kingdoms, including Saeleria. Hundreds of thousands of innocents died at their hands. The Lightbearers managed to trap the Shadowcasters beneath stone, but the cost was their own destruction. Now, somehow, the Shadowcasters have escaped. They've been sighted near the mountains of Wiyotak."

I translated this for Adriel. His whole body went rigid.

"Adriel?" I asked.

"We've been mining in those mountains. We have to warn the Guardians."

"We have to warn everyone," I said. "Even Elan's army." Adriel glanced sharply at me but did not argue.

Mattias growled violently. "*You* have brought them back," he said, pointing to Adriel. "They will destroy everything. We only have one lone Lightbearer to combat them with, and she is untrained."

"There must be others. If I am here, there have to be more."

"You don't understand. The Shadowcasters will not wait until the Lightbearers are trained and ready."

I stood taller. "Then, we must be ready."

He regarded me carefully.

"Where can we find them?"

"If there are even any in the five kingdoms, they should be easy to find. They will have a distinct aura, and they will be unseeing outside of Saeleria."

"Blind and distinct. Got it."

"There's more, I'm afraid," Mattias continued. "Emperor Elan is marching on this man's little army." He pointed in Adriel's general direction. Adriel clearly recognized that we were talking about him.

"He knows," I said, wondering again why he had left the Guardians.

"What he doesn't know is that the Shadowcasters are also headed that way."

My blood chilled. "Well, come with us. You must help us save our people."

Drakkar and Mattias shared a look. Finally, Drakkar said, "They cannot be involved. Dragons only get involved in the affairs of men when they are bonded with a Lightbearer."

"What? So, you are just going to abandon us?"

Smoke curled out of Mattias's nostrils. "Find the Lightbearers. Bring them to us, and we will fight beside you. We cannot until that happens."

"Burn it to hell! What use are you dragons if you won't fight!" I shouted.

Mattias said nothing.

I looked around the room at the dragons, daring them to meet my gaze, and they looked to the floor, even Zephyr. "Fine! We will save our people ourselves."

Mattias looked grave. "You should not leave until we have permanently restored your sight."

My jaw dropped at the words. "What do you mean?"

"I mean, as soon as you leave here, you will lose your sight once more. There is a simple ceremony you can undertake to prevent that from happening."

I thought about his words, turned them over and over again in my head. That was all I had ever wanted for so long. With sight, I could have earned back favor with my father, trained to be a proper warrior. I would have been able to elude the many who tried to prevent me from returning the eggs to Saeleria, and could have fought all the men who tried to force me to bend to their will. And yet, my blindness was a part of me. It had been my strength, my only companion during those isolating years, and the one thing that had bonded me to Drakkar.

"No," I said.

Mattias cocked his head in disbelief. "No? You don't want your sight to be permanent?"

"Asha," Adriel said behind me. "Maybe you should . . ."

I turned to Adriel, and the look on my face made him not finish his sentence. "I am done taking orders. I will live by the rules of my own making." I turned back to Mattias. "I appreciate the gesture, but no. I now understand that I am not blind. I can see what others cannot."

Mattias nodded. "If you are sure."

"I am," I said, climbing onto Drakkar once more.

"Then be well and bring back the Lightbearers."

Adriel climbed on behind me, and we took off into the sky.

"You did well, Little One," Drakkar called. "You have proven your-self worthy."

Chapter Forty-Three

Asha

Drakkar's endurance had increased with multiple flights. We flew over the two camps, the Guardians and Lightwardens and Ujuima with a mix of other kingdoms. They were stationed across from each other, with a hill the only thing separating them. The tension filled the air as Adriel and I descended, the clash of armies poised on the brink of conflict. I could feel everyone's eyes upon us as we landed with dramatic flourish, Drakkar's wings clapping against the wind with a thunderous roar.

"Adriel, what is the meaning of this?" Marlon demanded, his voice filled with confusion and concern.

Adriel wasted no time in taking command, his gaze sweeping over the assembled Guardians with a sense of urgency.

"I cannot explain now," he said, his voice tight. "But we need to leave this place immediately."

Zariah, ever defiant, stepped forward, his eyes flashing with anger. "And why should we listen to you?" he challenged, his voice dripping with skepticism. "Elan's army is nearby. We have an advantage here. Why would we retreat?"

"We don't have time for this," Adriel insisted, his tone growing increasingly urgent. But even as he spoke, the Lightwardens continued to argue among themselves, their voices rising in discord.

Amid all the discourse, I noticed that a calming presence was missing.

"Where is Marlon?" I asked, looking around the camp.

The Lightwardens quieted, and a sense of foreboding washed over me.

"Where is he, Zariah?" Adriel growled.

"We don't know," he said finally. "He was not in his room this morning. All of his belongings are undisturbed."

"Something is wrong?" I whispered.

"A messenger!" a Guardian yelled in the distance.

Adriel motioned for me to stay back, but I shook my head. I was not going to sit on my hands like a good little princess. Instead, I approached Drakkar with the wind whipping around us. His powerful form moved through the grass with ease, parting the army like a sea of warriors.

A small army of figures approached our lines from the opposite direction. Behind them, the banner of the Ujuima army fluttered in the wind, its vibrant colors a stark contrast to the grim, battle-ready atmosphere. At the forefront was a man who carried himself with undeniable authority. He was strikingly handsome, his rich, deep brown skin glowing under the sunlight, and his short-cropped hair framed a face etched with resolve.

"State your business, Ekon," Adriel called.

Ekon, of course. I had not seen him with my eyes in ten years. Once he spoke, I recognized him all too well.

He stopped a few paces away, his eyes flickering to Drakkar until they settled on me. "I have been instructed to deliver a message from the future emperor."

I glanced at Adriel, who stood nearby, his expression unreadable. With a nod, he motioned, "You may deliver your message."

Ekon reached into his satchel and pulled out a sealed letter. His movements were deliberate, showing no signs of aggression, yet the tension was undeniable. He handed the letter to Ashkii, and Adriel broke the seal, my heart pounding as I read the words within.

Ekon did not wait for Adriel to read it. He recited it from memory, likely for the Lightwarden's benefit. "Elan's demand is clear: surrender, and he will spare your lives. All he asks is the return of his beloved sister—Princess Asha."

I looked up, meeting Ekon's gaze. His eyes were steady, betraying no emotion, but I could sense the weight of them. This was no simple task for him either.

"Tell Elan," Adriel said, his voice firm, "that this army will not be cowed by threats. We will not surrender, and Princess Asha will not be handed over like some bargaining chip."

Ekon's expression didn't change, but he nodded once. "I will relay your message. I have one more Elan wished me to deliver to the princess."

He looked toward me. "Princess, Elan wishes you to know that he is aware of Prince Kwasi's betrayal. If you do not surrender yourself to him by dawn, Kwasi will face execution."

My jaw dropped. "Ekon, please, you have to help him."

"You did this, Asha," he said. "Only you can make it right."

Adriel quickly moved between us. "You have your message, Ekon. Now leave."

Ekon's expression tightened. "Very well." He looked back at me. "Asha, you have until dawn. The dragon is not welcome."

He turned his horse sharply, snapping the reins in his hands. Without another word, he spurred his mount into a gallop. I watched the back of his head until he disappeared behind the hill.

Adriel turned his worried expression to me. "Asha, I know what you are thinking. Elan will kill you both or worse if you go to him. Please let our army do its job."

I slid off Drakkar and lowered my head into his chest. "I know you are right. What about the Shadowcasters? We don't have much time."

"We will have to strike fast," he said, kissing my hair. "We attack now when they least expect it. Perhaps this mystery army could serve as a distraction. We will get Kwasi back, Asha."

I was uncertain whether his words were for my benefit or his. He squeezed my hand.

"Every time I turn my back, you leave. Please stay this time. Stay with Drakkar. Do not leave our camp." He gently lifted my chin with his finger. "I cannot do my job if I am worried about you. Promise me you will stay put. I will lose my mind if you are in harm's way."

I nodded.

He shook his head. "I need you to say it. That you'll stay, or I swear I will tie you up like I did when we first met."

"You wouldn't dare."

His eyebrows rose, but his face fell as he leaned his forehead against mine. "No, I wouldn't. It was worth a try."

"I'll stay," I whispered, standing on my toes to nestle my head in the crook of his neck.

"Thank you," he said, holding me close.

As soon as he departed to begin giving his men orders, I wasted no time.

"Drakkar," I whispered, reaching out to touch his rough scales, "I need a diversion."

Drakkar's voice rumbled in my mind with a mix of concern. "Asha, you just promised you would not leave. I don't like the man, but he is wise in this. It's clear that Ekon's message was meant for you, to get you to do this very thing."

I took a deep breath, steeling myself. "I don't know if I'm being foolish, or if Adriel will forgive my lie, but it's my decision to make. Kwasi is my brother, and I cannot leave him behind."

For a moment, there was only the sound of Drakkar's breathing and the distant clamor of the camp. Then, with a low growl of acceptance, he agreed. "Very well, Asha. Do not die."

I felt the rush of wind as Drakkar launched into the sky, his massive wings beating powerfully. Moments later, the sound of startled shouts and clashing weapons filled the air as he swooped down on the far side of the camp, creating chaos among the Guardians. I was blind without Drakkar, but I could see the cluster of auras and turned to walk in the opposite direction toward the Ujuima camp. I moved swiftly, my steps silent and deliberate as I slipped through the underbrush, guided by the sounds and scents around me. The edge of the camp drew closer, and I could feel the adrenaline coursing through my veins.

I estimated I had made it halfway when a familiar presence made itself known.

"Asha," Ashkii said in a soft whisper, filled with concern. "What are you doing?"

I turned toward the sound of his voice, frustration mingling with relief. "Ashkii, you need to head back."

"You are trying to get your brother alone, aren't you? Why can't you just wait for Adriel?"

"I don't have time for this. Are you going to rat me out or not?"

"I won't rat you out," he replied firmly. "I'm coming with you."

I inhaled sharply. "Why? You should stay here. It will be dangerous; you could be killed."

He tapped my shoulder. "You of all people should understand what it is like to be counted out just because you are deemed weak. Plus, you'll have a better chance with me here. I am a master of getting into places without being seen. Let me help."

He was right, of course. Still, I hesitated for a moment, weighing the risks of bringing him on my foolish mission. But deep down, I knew we would have a better chance together. With a reluctant nod, I agreed to let him join me.

"Fine. But if anything goes wrong, you run. Understood?"

"Not a chance, Your Highness." I rolled my eyes, but I did not know how to persuade him otherwise.

Together, we moved swiftly and silently through the maze of tents and patrols in the enemy Ujuima camp. The night cloaked us in shadows as we navigated through the hive of activity. Ashkii's hand occasionally brushed my arm, signaling me to stop or move on when needed. My heightened senses guided us past the few guards that remained on duty.

As we approached the entrance to the main tent where the leaders of the Ujuima army were gathered, I paused and listened intently. Inside, voices argued in hushed tones about their plans for attack.

We continued to move cautiously through the camp, our movements nearly imperceptible.

"Stay close," I whispered to Ashkii, my hand tightly gripping his arm for reassurance. He nodded in understanding as we weaved through the maze of tents and soldiers. My heart pounded with anticipation; the air suddenly shifted—Kwasi's aura. He was close.

"This way," I urged Ashkii, trying to sense the auras within as I searched for my brother.

"There!" I said, pointing. "He's there."

As we drew closer to an empty tent, Ashkii signaled that there were no guards nearby. We slipped inside undetected. The interior of the tent was hot and stifling. I could see Kwasi's aura and hear his strained breaths. We made our way toward him, but before I could reach out to untie him, he winced and mumbled through the gag in his mouth.

"Kwasi," I whispered urgently, gently touching his shoulder. "We are here to rescue you."

"Ash," he murmured weakly. "You shouldn't have come. It's a trap." His words sent a shiver down my spine. We needed to move quickly.

"It's alright, Kwasi. We will get you out of here," I reassured him while trying to loosen the restraints around his hands. But he suddenly tensed up and spoke again before I could finish untying him.

"He knows," he rasped. "He knows about the eggs." Before I could react, a muffled sound came from behind us.

"Ashkii?"

But before we could do anything else, a heavy blow struck me from behind, causing searing pain to explode in my skull as I slowly lost consciousness.

CHAPTER FORTY-FOUR

Adriel

The time had come for the battle to begin. I mounted Candy and rallied the Guardians with my war cry. Drakkar was making some commotion in the background, but I could not heed it.

"Kitchi!" I yelled. "Take care of that, and do not leave Asha's side," I said, pointing to the Drakkar. She nodded before hurrying off.

The Guardians finished strapping on their armor and readying their swords and bows as they mounted their steeds.

"Guardians of the Realm! Lightwardens of the mountains!" I cried. "Today is a good day to die—for our Ujuima brethren."

"Hu hah!" they chanted.

My hair flew behind me as I used my battlemage to amplify my voice. "We are the Guardians, protectors of the realm, defenders of the innocent, and warriors of unmatched courage. Look around you. See your brothers and sisters in arms, each one of us forged in the crucible of countless battles. We have faced darkness before, and each time, we have emerged victorious. Today will be no different."

"Hu hah!" they chanted. In my peripheral vision, I saw Kitchi waving her hands in the distance. I nodded, turning back quickly to the men and women before me.

"The warriors of Ujuima believe their dragons make them invincible, but we know the truth. They wield their dragons with cruelty, but we fight with honor and bravery. Their strength lies in fear and domination of others; ours lies in unity and resilience. Raise your swords, steady your bows, and prepare your battlemage. Guardians, to battle!"

"Guardians, to battle!" they cheered.

"Victory or death!"

I charged forward, wielding my sword with deadly precision as the Guardians followed close behind. The night was alive with the sounds of war: steel clashed against steel, screams and battle cries pierced the air, and the stench of blood and death hung thick in the darkness. My heart raced with adrenaline as I led the charge, channeling every ounce of fierce magic within me through my sword. With each swing of my fiery blade, I felt a sense of satisfaction as enemy soldiers fell to the ground in agony. Their cries echoed in my ears, but I paid them no mind. There was no time for mercy or pity. Every second was precious, a fleeting chance to save Kwasi.

Amid the chaos, a hand suddenly grabbed at my shoulder, and I instinctively whirled around, nearly impaling Kitchi with my blade.

"Adriel, Asha's in the Ujuima camp!" she screamed, her voice barely audible over the sounds of battle. "She's here. We have to find her!"

My world stopped as terror gripped my chest, unable to let go. She couldn't be. She promised. I closed my eyes.

Of course she would go. It was Kwasi.

Every obstacle on the battlefield suddenly became a barrier preventing me from reaching Asha. The thought of her in Elan's hands ignited an all-consuming rage within me.

CHAPTER FORTY-FIVE

Asha

I awoke lying on the sand. I noted its familiar texture. My head throbbed, and my limbs felt heavy as I tried to move. The sound of voices reached my ears, distant but growing clearer.

"She cannot be killed, Elan," said an insistent voice. It was Marlon.

"I am emperor, and I will decide who lives or dies," Elan's voice replied coldly. Then the voices stopped. "Sister, we know you are awake."

I struggled to sit up, every movement sending waves of pain through my body. The realization of where I was hit me with a blow: the sand, the echoes, the muffled djembes. This was a sparring ring. I was back in the place of my childhood, a place both familiar and fraught with memories.

"Marlon," I croaked, my voice weak but determined. "What is the meaning of this?"

There was a brief silence, and then Marlon spoke again, his voice closer now. "Asha, I'm afraid I have made another deal, one that I believe will ensure your safety."

"What of your precious Lightwardens?" I spat out.

"The Lightwardens have proved useful until now. I'm afraid my allegiance lies elsewhere."

I laughed. "With Elan? You will be sorry. He will betray you."

Marlon said nothing. Elan's presence loomed, his aura dark and oppressive. "Now, now, sister. No need for that."

"Where is Kwasi?" I demanded.

"Kwasi?" he called. "Why don't you say hello to our sister?"

Kwasi was silent. Elan walked over and bore down on him.

"Kwasi, you are being rude. I said, 'Say hi to dear Ash.'"

Kwasi groaned. "Fuck you, Elan."

Elan laughed before giving him several swift kicks to his body. I heard ribs breaking.

"Stop!" I called.

"Oh, I plan to keep him alive for a time. But first, I need to know where my dragon eggs have gone."

I schooled my expression to give away nothing. "Dragon eggs? I don't know anything about dragon eggs. They no longer exist."

Elan cracked his knuckles. "I was so hoping you would play dumb with me, sister. It makes this next part so much fun."

Dread filled my heart, and the scars on my back tingled from the memory of his cruelty.

"I am going to enjoy beating it out of you, but I admit it will be much more enjoyable for me if you fight back. Do you recognize this place?" he asked, circling me. He laughed. "Truthfully, I did not know Kwasi had it in him to beat you so badly. He has always been so weak. I was just sad I never got to spar with you myself, dear sister. But we will soon rectify that."

My brows furrowed in disgust. "I do not know what you are talking about, Elan, and I will not fight you."

Elan only chuckled darkly, his voice filled with malice.

"Oh, but I know that to be untrue, sister. You told Ekon about the dragon eggs, did you not? And yet, you kept Kwasi in the dark. Interesting. That leaves you to be my sole source of information."

A wave of betrayal crashed over me. "Ekon must have been mistaken," I said tersely.

"Perhaps," Elan taunted, "but I highly doubt it. He knows the punishment for deceiving his emperor. Flying dragons in the hands of my enemies is bad enough but dragon eggs is something I cannot have."

I gritted my teeth, feeling anger surge through my veins. "You already have dragons at your disposal. Why do you need eggs as well?"

Elan's smirk widened. "Ah, but you see, these eggs inspire hope among others that they, too, could one day wield dragons against us. It poses quite a threat, wouldn't you say? Only Ujuima warriors are chosen to control the dragons, and only under my rule."

As he spoke, I heard the distinct clang of a sword hitting the ground at my feet. Stooping down to pick it up, I felt it was made of solid steel, no longer just a practice weapon for training purposes. So much for his not intending to kill me.

"Ah, here lies my dilemma. I have made certain agreements with Marlon here. And he is very invested in you living in exchange for the keys to my enemy. I may not kill you, but nothing in my deal says that I cannot kill our dear brother."

My heart clenched. I'd already lost our mother; I couldn't lose Kwasi.

"It is up to you, Asha."

"Forget about me, Ash," he groaned. "Don't give the asshole the satisfaction."

I grasped the blade in my hand, rage coursing through my bones, and for the first time, I was not afraid. I stood tall, the sword steady in my hand as I channeled Moki's words: Anticipate where he will be. Stay alert.

"Let's go," I said.

Elan let out a menacing laugh. "Finally, our sister shows some backbone. Initiate!" he called out, and suddenly the djembe drums began to pound loudly behind us. The rhythm pulsed through my body as I focused all my senses on Elan's movements, trying to anticipate his next strike.

"I must say," he remarked with a smirk, circling me slowly like a predator stalking its prey, "I was disappointed to hear that you had run off with War Chief Foxtrail. You are many things, Asha, but I never would have pegged you for a whore."

His blade fell and caught my ribcage. I grunted as I pulled away, ignoring the warmth of my blood seeping into my tunic. Enraged by his cruel words, I bit down hard on my tongue until it bled, determined not to fall into his trap again and lose control. The makeshift arena beneath my feet felt cold and unforgiving as we circled each other, the murmurs of the onlookers fading into a dull roar. I had to play this right, or I was dead. I tried to remember everything I'd learned sparring with Chato, Moki, and Adriel.

"Come on, Asha. Where are my eggs?" Elan's voice dripped with malice, cutting through the tension.

I didn't reply, my breath steady and controlled. The air shifted as he moved, and then the first strike came—a powerful blow that sent me sprawling to the ground. Pain radiated through my body as the taste of blood filled my mouth.

"Pathetic," he taunted, his laughter echoing cruelly. "How do you expect to win when you can't even see?"

I pushed myself up, wiping the blood from my lips, determination hardening my resolve. "I don't need to see you to know who you are, Elan."

Elan was no fool, and he toyed with me, his laughter echoing in the air. I gritted my teeth, my muscles tensing as I waited for the perfect moment to strike. Elan lunged forward, his knee digging into my stomach with a force that stole my breath away. Kwasi's distant shouts echoed in the background, urging me to fight back. I quickly rolled away and rose to my feet. We circled each other again, the sand shifting beneath our feet.

This time, I focused on the subtle cues: the sound of his breath, the rustle of his clothes, the shift in the air.

"It's sad, really, that you would open your legs for the first person to show you attention. Did you know that Marlon here has a prophecy that you must die for the Shadowcasters to return?"

Focus, I thought. *Don't let him distract you.*

"It is nonsense, honestly, but your precious war chief believed it." I felt a tightness in my chest as I vacillated between disbelief, hurt, and rage. Elan continued. "Did you know he'd planned on giving you to him?"

My body grew hot as pain lodged in my throat. Instead of reveling in the sting of his words, I lunged. I was ready. Anticipating his block, I sidestepped and struck back, landing a solid hit to his side. He snarled, retaliating with a fury that sent sharp pain slashing across my skin. I cried out, collapsing to the ground, feeling his battlemage scratching and tearing at me. Blood dripped from my wounds.

"Where are the eggs?" he demanded, his voice a roar above the chaos. Marlon and Kwasi's screams punctuated the air.

As I writhed in pain, he dropped his sword in favor of his battlemage. Memories flooded my mind. I saw my childhood: the cruelty of my father and Elan, the constant feeling of isolation, the death of my mother. I remembered the endless nights of feeling not good enough because I wasn't what everyone wanted me to be. But these memories, these emotions, were not weaknesses—to feel them made me stronger; they were my power. I gathered all those feelings—the anger, the sorrow, the loneliness—and used them.

Reaching out with my mind, I found Elan's aura—dark, twisted, and vile. He recoiled, screaming as I connected with him.

For the first time, I could see him—not with my eyes but with my mind. I saw all his evil deeds, the blackness surrounding him, and the pleasure he took in others' suffering. It was overwhelming, but it fueled my resolve.

"Elan," I said, my voice steady despite the pain, "you are the one who is weak."

I pushed deeper into his mind, forcing him to confront his own darkness. His screams grew louder and more frantic as the blackness he reveled in turned on him and consumed him. A figure yelled and ran to his side—Ekon, I realized. He threw himself between us, taking the brunt of my battlemage.

As Ekon thrashed beneath me, an explosion sounded around us, pushing me onto my back. Shell-shocked, I lay there, assessing for injuries.

I was mostly uninjured, but what was that? I rolled over, feeling the rough ground beneath me. My first instinct was to call out for Kwasi, but instead, I found myself in the grasp of strong, unfamiliar hands. They pulled at my shirt collar with a force that seemed almost inhuman.

"Marlon," I croaked, trying to make sense of what was happening. "What are you doing?"

He laughed, a wild and manic sound. "They're here, Asha! Our Shadowcaster brethren have finally come!"

Confusion clouded my mind as I struggled against him. "Who? What are you talking about?"

"The Shadowcasters, our true family. Haven't you been listening?"

"I thought you were a Lightwarden."

Marlon snorted dismissively. "The so-called Lightwardens are nothing compared to us. But with your power, what we could do would be unlimitless."

"What do you want with me?" I asked, attempting but failing to escape his grip.

"I want you to join us," he hissed eagerly. "Become one of us, and together we will be unstoppable."

"But . . . I am a Lightbearer," I protested weakly. "That is what you said."

"Lightbearers and Shadowcasters are two sides of the same coin," Marlon insisted. "With just a flip, you could easily become one of us."

Panic surged through me as I realized the danger I was in. I tried to use my battlemage, but it was drained.

A sudden commotion erupted as a figure lunged onto Marlon from behind, the sound of scuffling feet and grunts filling the air. My heart raced as I strained to make sense of it.

Then, cutting through the noise, Ashkii's voice rang out, urgent and commanding.

"Asha, run! Get out of here!" His words were a lifeline, and I knew I had to move—now.

Another explosion knocked me back. Warm hands grabbed me and pulled me away from the fray. It was Adriel, his voice filled with desperation as he asked if I was okay.

"We have to go!" he urged.

I was reluctant to leave, but I knew I was more likely to find Ashkii with Adriel and Drakkar. I allowed him to carry me out of the melee. Men and women screamed around us, flying with blades and battlemages. Adriel lifted me onto a horse, shielding me as he fended off attackers with practiced ease. The sounds of screams and clashing weapons filled the air as we raced away from the battlefield.

I drifted in and out of consciousness, my body exhausted, and my battlemage depleted. But I felt safe in Adriel's strong embrace.

CHAPTER FORTY-SIX

Adriel

"Asha!" I bellowed as I charged forward with even more determination. I cut through tents and bodies without hesitation.

My sword blazed a trail of destruction as I ran toward a bright silver light that pierced through the darkness. It had to be her. But as I drew closer to the source of the light, an explosion rocked the ground beneath me and sent me flying backward. The impact knocked the air from my lungs, and pain seared through my side. Ignoring my injuries, I forced myself back up and looked around frantically.

"Asha!" I called out, my voice hoarse with desperation. But she was nowhere to be found.

Panic surged through me as I searched the chaos around me, fear and guilt clawing at my heart. I couldn't lose her, not after I'd just found her.

Figures began to emerge from the trees, their eyes glowing like pools of liquid amber, burning with an otherworldly fire. Their tattered garments were blackened and ripped, as if consumed by some dark force. They moved with a chilling grace, draining the battlemage powers from both Ujuiman and Guardian warriors alike. We stood no chance against them.

No fucking chance.

In the midst of chaos, I caught a glimpse of blue hair in the sea of violence. Asha. She was being dragged by Marlon straight toward those fiendish creatures. I didn't think—I just moved, darting after her. Marlon screamed as I approached, but before I could raise my blade against him, something I'd longed to do since I met him, a flash of battlemage struck me.

The tiniest tendrils of it touched my body, and all the breath left me in an instant. It was like thousands of tiny needles piercing my skin, sucking away my battlemage powers like a thirsty beast draining water from its prey. This was their tactic. They stripped their victims of their magic first to make them easier to kill.

One of them, his face obscured behind a skeletal mask, grabbed hold of my armor and began crushing it in his iron grip. As he looked into my eyes, a glint of recognition crossed his features. He grinned at me with sickening pleasure.

"You are not ready yet, but don't worry. You will be soon enough," he said, like it was a dark promise.

With one swift motion, he opened his mouth, and a thick cloud of black smoke poured out. I shut my eyes tightly and clenched my teeth together, but the smoke found its way into my nostrils and throat, causing me to gag and choke. Everything went black as I fell to the ground, my body paralyzed and helpless.

When I finally regained consciousness, the battle still raged on around me. But my focus was singular—Asha. She lay sprawled on the ground, motionless. I crawled over to her, every muscle in my body protesting with pain. I wrapped my arms tightly around her, a fierce protectiveness overwhelming me.

I could make no sense of what had just happened or who these Shadowcasters were, but I knew one thing for certain—I had to get Asha out of here.

"We have to go!" I urged.

"No . . . not without Ashkii and Kwasi," she protested.

"Asha, the Shadowcasters have Ashkii. We need to leave now if we want to survive. Kwasi is already with us." The last was a lie, but I hoped it was true. She could hate me for it later, as long as she survived this.

Summoning the last remnants of my strength, I staggered to my feet, Asha's weight heavy against me. The battlefield blurred around us, but I set my sights on the forest's edge, on the chance for escape. With every step, I fought the darkness creeping into my vision, determined to save her, no matter the cost.

CHAPTER FORTY-SEVEN

Asha

My eyes fluttered open to the warm rays of daylight filtering through the makeshift canopy above. I rolled over, feeling a heavy weight on my body, and realized I was cocooned in Drakkar's tail. Beside us, Adriel lay sleeping, his face twisted in a restless expression.

As if sensing my wakefulness, Drakkar spoke. "You worried me, Little One. Don't do it again."

A small smile tugged at my lips. "I'll try to remember that."

Adriel stirred awake with a groan, his stubble-covered chin scruffy and his clothes rumpled and stained. My heart clenched with worry, hoping the stains were not blood.

"You're awake," he said.

"How long has it been?" I asked.

"Six hours," he replied, rubbing at his stubbled chin absently.

My eyes widened. "Kwasi?"

"He's fine, just a bit bruised," Adriel reassured me.

"Ashkii?"

"The Shadowcasters have him," Adriel confirmed my fears. "Moki and Chato are scouting for any sign of their whereabouts."

My heart clenched with guilt. I shouldn't have involved him.

"And Elan?" I asked hesitantly.

"We have not heard from him. I suspect he is alive. Otherwise, the Ujuima would be positioning themselves differently. He must be compromised somehow because Wyrmwood and Entioch have opened their negotiation channels with us, which they've never done before." A small smirk played at the corners of his mouth. "Was Elan your doing, then?"

I shrugged nonchalantly. "I only wish I were there to see it."

I tapped Drakkar's tail. "And you, Drakkar, how are you faring?"

He lowered his gaze to me. "Better than you, Little One. I thought I told you not to die."

I smirked. "I kept my promise."

Drakkar growled in response as if that was not what he meant by "don't die."

"Could you give Adriel and me a moment?"

Drakkar groaned in protest, but he stood to leave, grumbling under his breath about having perfect hearing from miles away. My sight left me as soon as he stormed out of the tent.

Once Drakkar's footfalls softened in the distance, Adriel reached out to grab my waist in a familiar gesture, but I pulled back instinctively.

"I suppose Marlon told you some things," he said quietly.

"About the prophecy, and how you planned to sacrifice me."

"When I made the deal, I did not know you. I did not even know you were the one they were looking for until Tideport. By then, everything had changed for me. I had changed." His voice was thick with emotion.

"You have been dishonest with me to the point that I do not know what to believe or if I can ever trust you again."

"I deserve that," he said, his voice solemn. "I know I don't deserve you, and that I may never regain your trust. I just want you to know that whatever you wish of me, I will do."

He stepped closer.

"I love you, Asha Osei. From the moment you fell into my arms that day at the Fire Festival, I haven't been able to get you out of my head. It's maddening and wonderful all at the same time. You've inspired me to do things I never thought possible. You make me want to abandon all the plans I so carefully crafted over the years. None of it matters to me anymore. Nothing matters but you. "

My heart ached at his words, the raw honesty in his voice cutting through the walls I'd built around myself.

"Even if you don't feel the same way," he continued, lowering himself to his knees before me, "I am your most humble servant. I serve you and only you. If you tell me to send the Guardians after Elan, I will. If you tell me to defeat the Shadowcasters, I will find a way. I would burn down the world for you if you asked, with no question and no regret." His breathing was shallow and rapid, as if he couldn't get enough air.

"And if I tell you to leave, that I never want to see you again?" I snapped.

His body quaked as if he'd been stricken. "Is that your wish, then, princess? Do you wish never to see me again?"

I lowered myself onto the ground, my knees sinking into the soft grass. Gently, I cupped his face in my hands and pulled him toward me.

"Truly, I could live without seeing you again." His body seemed to sag at my words as if I had just confirmed his worst fears. "But to never hear your voice, or feel your touch, or taste your lips—well, I won't stand for it."

My lips collided with his, and he met them with a fervor that stole my breath. His hands tangled in my hair, pulling me closer as we lost ourselves in each other. My hand rested on his chest, feeling the warmth of his skin through the thin fabric of his shirt. Breathless, he broke away from our embrace but kept close enough that our noses brushed against each other.

"I've been wanting to do that for so long," he admitted, his voice husky with emotion. "Drakkar, the bastard, would not let me near you."

He scooped me into his arms and gently laid me on the bed. He pulled away, and my body cried out for his touch.

"What are you doing?" I asked.

His hand roamed freely along my body, starting at my stomach, then slowly inching up to the laces of my tunic.

"Just admiring," he murmured.

Impatient, I helped him release the laces, opening the garment until my breasts came free. My nipples hardened not from the morning air, but in anticipation of what would come next. I heard a sharp inhalation of breath as his hands paused.

"We should stop. You are still recovering—"

I boldly took his hand and placed it on top of my right breast. My body arched at the sensation as I craved more. I laid my hand over his and squeezed.

"Don't you dare," I breathed.

That was all the encouragement he needed. Adriel moved his fingers under my tunic. My body was on fire as his other hand reached to pull up my skirt.

"You are so beautiful," he said between kisses.

I was overcome with desire, eager for him to relieve the ache between my legs. His fingers teased the edges of my underwear before brushing past them.

"You are so wet already," he rasped, running his fingers along the contours of my aching core.

I wanted him so badly, but when he lowered my underwear, I flinched slightly with fear. It was so slight, I was surprised when he immediately released me. The bed creaked as he sat on the edge.

"Did I hurt you?" he asked with concern.

"No!" I said, reaching for him. "I'm fine, keep going."

Instead of allowing us to resume, he took my hands in his and kissed them gently.

"Asha, have you ever, that is, I always assumed that you and Ekon were . . ."

"No," I said firmly. "Other than a kiss here and there, I have not—" I paused, feeling a bit embarrassed. "I have never been with anyone."

Deciding this conversation was too much, I pulled away, attempting to retie the laces of my tunic.

"If you don't want to anymore, I understand."

"I do," he said, and my head whipped to his in shock. He leaned closer until his lips were inches away from my collarbone. "You don't know how much—how I'd hoped for this moment. Asha, I don't want this to be your first time. Your body is healing still, and there is so much happening."

I shivered as he placed a kiss at the top of my breast.

"I want this," I moaned.

"Me too. Believe me, every part of me is screaming for me not to be a gentleman right now, but," he said, moving to my ear, "I want to take my time with you. When I make you mine, I want the only worries in your head to be how many ways I'll make you scream my name."

My lips parted at his words. Before I could protest further, he said, "Let's take it slow."

I sighed heavily, taking his face in my hands. "If we must," I relented. "Shall we call for Drakkar then?"

His lips claimed mine, and I could feel his smile against them before he pulled back.

"I'm a gentleman, not a saint. I had something else in mind," he paused. "It is going to require me to discard your undergarments." It was meant to be a statement, but I heard the question in his voice.

I swallowed. "That would be fine."

He gave me one more lingering kiss before I felt the bed dip with his weight. He sat by my feet, slowly moving the skirt up my legs. Adriel leaned forward, kissing my inner thigh with tenderness, stopping only when he reached my undergarments. He waited patiently, allowing me time to pull away or change my mind. I had no intention of stopping this. I wanted him more than I cared to admit. He tugged on the pretty snaps, and I could not help but whimper in anticipation. I gasped as his hands splayed on my stomach, gently touching the bandage on my side.

"You'll tell me if anything hurts." It was a command. All I could do was nod.

"Say it," he demanded. "Promise me."

"I will," I breathed, writhing under his touch.

Seeming satisfied, he raised me onto his lap. I gasped at the feel of him underneath his trousers. His hands closed beneath me and lifted until I felt the warm air of his breath at my entrance. I inhaled sharply.

"What are you—" I didn't get to finish as I felt his tongue. He licked once, then paused as I began to pull away. He held me steady before his tongue claimed me once more.

"How is that?" he asked.

"I'm not sure." I lifted myself onto my elbows so that he could hear me. "Do it again."

He lifted me higher, draping my legs against his shoulders, and this time he dipped his tongue inside me. I moaned and fell back to the bed like my bones were jelly. My thighs trembled as his tongue curled inside me, stroking me until I saw stars.

I clutched the bedsheets.

"Adriel," I moaned.

"Yes, princess?"

"Please. More, faster," I said, barely able to string words together.

I felt a smirk on his lips. "I am at your command," he said before sinking his mouth in again.

Searing pleasure ripped through me as I arched my back. I placed a hand over my mouth to keep the sounds of pleasure in check. Adriel released me momentarily to rip my hand away.

"I want to hear you. I want to hear what I do to you. If you don't hold back, neither will I."

He moved back to my entrance and pushed in with his tongue in earnest. I was writhing against him now, chasing something. The pleasure of it sliced through me. My mind went blank as wave after wave of pleasure consumed me, as his tongue danced expertly within my core. He held nothing back, each stroke unraveling me further.

"That's it," he murmured against me. "Let go, Asha," he said as he placed a finger inside me.

"Adriel!" I gasped as my body shattered around him.

I arched again and again as the power of my bliss rocked through me. Adriel finally pulled away to lie on top of me. His elbows on the bed kept him from crushing me beneath, as he swallowed my final whimpers in a kiss that felt like devotion. My fingers gripped his shoulders, desperate and pleading, as the last tremors of pleasure coursed through my body, leaving me trembling and boneless.

Adriel kissed the top of my head and held me close. Once my mind had cleared a little, my hands moved against the hardness of his body. He caught my wrists, gently pulling them away.

"Don't misunderstand. I want you, Asha, but I can wait."

"But you just gave me *everything*," I protested.

"Not everything, not yet." He crushed me tightly against him, and I felt his heart thundering against me.

"How can I not—"

"Hearing you undone is enough," he said. "When the time comes, I'll savor every second. But tonight? Let me worship you like this. Let me hold you."

We lingered, his hands threading through my hair as mine traced the shimmering edges of his aura. With every stroke, his body tensed; blue flames flickered to life along my spine, searing yet sweet. I arched into him, claiming his mouth in a kiss that tasted of recklessness—until Drakkar's growl shattered the stillness.

"Mortal mating rituals are repulsive," he lamented.

Adriel and I broke off the kiss, laughing at Drakkar's disapproval.

Feeling slightly breathless, I patted my stomach and joked, "I may need actual sustenance. Perhaps we should eat."

Adriel chuckled, teeth grazing my earlobe. "I already have." I giggled under his teasing, but he rolled over, and the bed lifted as he stood. "I will see what we have."

Before he could move away, I couldn't resist pulling him back, allowing him one more lingering kiss. I clung to his body, reveling in the feeling of him on top of me. I poured everything I had into it, not wanting him to question for a moment how I felt when I was with him. His weight anchored me, and I poured every hope, every promise, into the press of our lips.

"You sure you're hungry for food?" he murmured against me.

My traitorous stomach gurgled in response. He laughed before promising to return, pausing at the tent flaps.

"If you keep looking at me like that," he warned, voice fraying, "I'll forget every oath I've sworn just now. I can deny you nothing, Asha. When I come back, *you* decide how far we go, and I will follow."

Then he was gone, his aura dissolving into the night. I felt a pang in my heart as he went. My legs wobbled slightly as I stood.

"Drakkar?"

"We must hurry if we are going to be gone before he gets back." I raised an eyebrow at him. "You think I don't know a goodbye kiss when I hear one? Where to, Little One? Saeleria?"

I climbed up his back and patted his neck. "No. Mattias said there are other Lightbearers. Let's go find them."

"As you wish."

With a powerful flap of his wings, we soared into the open sky, leaving behind the Guardians, the Lightwardens, and if I was being honest, the piece of my heart that belonged to Adriel.

CHAPTER
FORTY-EIGHT

Adriel

I clinched my fists as I watched Drakkar rise in the night with Asha on his back. *Look back,* I begged silently, nails biting into my palms. *Turn around.* But her gaze remained fixed on the horizon. I stepped forward, as if sheer will might call her back, but no sound left my lips. Only when she vanished into the dark did I close my eyes, slowly kneeling to the ground. I'd buried my worry into that last kiss, clinging to her lips as if mine could convince her to stay.

Now I turned back to the tent, where the sheets carried the ghost of her scent. I'd felt alive with her in my arms and now all I felt was a mocking breeze that seemed to slice through my heart. In that moment, I almost envied her blindness. Some goodbyes were just too brutal to watch.

EPILOGUE

Three eggs rested amid delicate poppies, their shells glimmering with fiery hues. The ground began to rumble as the dragons inside fought to break free from their hard calcium prisons. With a burst of fire and a booming roar, Mwana emerged, her sharp talons tearing through the fragile shell. She extended her body until the egg casing fell away and let out a triumphant growl upon seeing her siblings, Igbo and Ala, stumbling toward her, their shells long discarded. Together, they roared into the dark night sky.

About The Author

Dr. Iman Christians has been in love with love ever since she picked up her first Babysitter's Club romance. Since then her fascination has blossomed into a lifelong passion for stories with battling kingdoms, moody dragons, and the kind of magic that only comes from love. Today, she writes sweeping romantasy novels that center characters who rarely get the spotlight—heroes and heroines whose voices deserve to be heard and celebrated. When she's not weaving worlds filled with epic adventures and forbidden love, Iman is living out her own love story with her husband, chasing after their two adorable children, and sharing her home with a cat she's wildly allergic to, but far too attached to ever give up.

Check for updates of Book 2: Dragon Bride by signing up for the newsletter or visiting imanchristians.com

www.ingramcontent.com/pod-product-compliance
Lightning Source LLC
Chambersburg PA
CBHW030043130726
47901CB00007BA/1773